"You've missed your train."

Though my brain was fuzzy with laudanum and I wanted nothing more than to lie down in the middle of the street and sleep, I understood the import of the train leaving without me. I was free of Rosemond and could return to Kindle. I managed to smile. "So I have."

My happiness was short-lived.

"Laura!"

Rosemond in her ridiculous blue dress stalked toward us holding a flour sack, her powdered, pox-scarred face a mask of fury. The ugly woman turned around and stood shoulder to shoulder with me. "Who's that?"

"My kidnapper."

Praise for Melissa Lenhardt and

SAWBONES

"Packs a big punch with grit and raw passion. There is mystery, murder, Indians, bounty hunters and intrigue. The women are brave, intelligent and don't take crap from anyone. Lenhardt is a talented, creative writer; she has a grand slam out of the park with *Sawbones*."   —*RT Book Reviews* (Top Pick!) 4.5 stars

"Raw, gritty, and sometimes graphic, Melissa Lenhardt has crafted a page-turner. In *Sawbones*, the women are smart, brave, and at times 'incorrigible.' The plot twists, unique characters and intriguing story of passion and betrayal make this a book well worth discovering."

—Jane Kirkpatrick, *New York Times*
bestselling author of *A Light in the Wilderness*

"Absolutely loved it! I couldn't tear myself away from *Sawbones*. An epic story of love and courage that sweeps from east to west, *Sawbones* will rip right through you."

—Marci Jefferson, author of *Girl on the Golden Coin*

"A beautiful, heartrending story of courage, survival, [and] loyalty, [that] depicts the depths to which a human can sink and the highs to which we can rise above it all when hope is strong.... *Sawbones* is on my list of 2016 favourite reads."

—*Scandalicious*

"You will fall in love with Catherine, as I did, as she struggles to assert herself in a violent and treacherous world, fighting not only prejudice but evil."

—Sandra Dallas, *New York Times* bestselling author

"*Sawbones* is a thoroughly original, smart and satisfying hybrid, perhaps a new subgenre: the feminist Western."

—*Lone Star Literary Life*

"Melissa Lenhardt has given us an amazing heroine and sent her on a thrilling journey from the teeming streets of New York City to the vast wilderness of the Texas frontier. Dr. Catherine Bennett's adventure will keep you turning pages long into the night!"

—Victoria Thompson, bestselling author of
Murder on St. Nicholas Avenue

"It was damn brilliant and I absolutely loved it!...It was [the] mix of loveliness with the book's vicious, ruthless side that made *Sawbones* so compelling....I was ecstatic to find out that there will be a follow-up called *Blood Oath* coming out later this year. You can be sure I'll be devouring it as soon as I can get my hands on it."

—*Bibliosanctum* (4.5 stars)

"If you are looking for a book that is well-written, has a gripping story-line seasoned with mystery, suspense, [and] a little romance, then you have come to the right place, my friend!...From the first to the last page, *Sawbones* is a raw, gritty tale that takes us back to a time when rules didn't apply, when heartbreak was a way of life and tomorrow was a gift. Weaving facts and fiction Melissa Lenhardt gives us a story so rich in detail and horrific truths, you finish the book with so many questions, so many emotions and ready for more."

—*Margie's Must Reads* (4 stars)

"The adventure was nonstop, never giving way to a slow moment....My heart was repeatedly ripped to shreds and mended...a thrilling, unpredictable roller coaster that held my heart from the start."

—*My Book Fix*

BADLANDS

By Melissa Lenhardt

BADLANDS

BOOK 3 OF THE
SAWBONES SERIES

MELISSA LENHARDT

www.redhookbooks.com

Redhook Books/Orbit
Hachette Book Group
1290 Avenue of the Americas
New York, NY 10104
hachettebookgroup.com

First Edition: June 2017

Redhook is an imprint of Orbit, a division of Hachette Book Group.
The Redhook name and logo are trademarks of Hachette Book Group, Inc.

The publisher is not responsible for websites (or their content) that are not owned by the publisher.

The Hachette Speakers Bureau provides a wide range of authors for speaking events. To find out more, go to www.hachettespeakersbureau.com or call (866) 376-6591.

Library of Congress Cataloging-in-Publication Data
Names: Lenhardt, Melissa, author.
Title: Badlands / by Melissa Lenhardt.
Description: First edition. | New York, NY : Redhook Books/Orbit, 2017. |
Series: Sawbones ; book 3
Identifiers: LCCN 2017011479| ISBN 9780316505376 (paperback) | ISBN
    9780316386784 (ebook) | ISBN 9781478950004 (audio book cd)
Subjects: | BISAC: FICTION / Historical. | FICTION / Romance / Western. |
    FICTION / Mystery & Detective / Historical. | FICTION / Action &
    Adventure. | FICTION / Westerns. | FICTION / War & Military. | GSAFD:
    Adventure fiction. | Western stories.
Classification: LCC PS3612.E529 B33 2017 | DDC 813/.6—dc23
LC record available at https://lccn.loc.gov/2017011479

ISBNs: 978-0-316-50537-6 (trade paperback), 978-0-316-38678-4 (ebook)

Printed in the United States of America

LSC-C

10 9 8 7 6 5 4 3 2 1

For Ryan and Jack,
for giving my life purpose, and a fair amount of drama

PART ONE

GRAND ISLAND

CHAPTER
1

The train lurched to a stop and let out a long sigh, exhausted from its trek across the featureless plains of Nebraska. The shouts of the railroad men and the clang of metal against metal pierced the thick air, heavy with the threat of rain.

"She still asleep?"

Fabric rustled as someone in the compartment stood. "Not what I'd call it, but yes."

With my eyes closed against the sight of Rosemond Barclay's fine dress and my mother's necklace around her throat, I heard the sarcasm dripping from the whore's honeyed Southern accent.

"Want me to stay with her while you stretch your legs?"

"If you don't mind," Rosemond said.

"How long it gonna last?"

"Her pain? I'm not sure. I've never seen the like. I'll get us something to eat. I'll be quick." The air around me changed and I smelled lavender, Rosemond's scent. I felt Rosemond's presence and imagined her leaning down to stare out the window, or at me. "Though with that line, I'll be lucky if I don't miss the train."

"Better hurry, then."

The compartment door slid open and closed and I was alone with the man who Rosemond called Dunk, a Negro who did everything she bid without question. Standing well over six feet, he was an imposing specimen of a man, but when I was doubled over in pain, or numb from the opiate, he picked me up with soft, gentle hands and carried me.

I opened my heavy eyelids but couldn't manage more than halfway. My head rested against an open window warmed by the sun and grimy with coal dust inside and out. I rubbed my fist against the glass and gazed through the small, partially clean circle at the activity outside. Passengers and railroad men scurried across the narrow platform and around Rosemond Barclay as if there were a protective cushion around her, though their heads turned and more than one gawped in appreciation. She made a show of putting on a pair of gloves, reveling in the attention no doubt, before continuing on down the steps and across the wide, busy street. She queued up at the end of the line of customers waiting to enter a narrow building. The whore didn't need to draw attention to herself; her plaid periwinkle-and-white dress stood out against the sober mourning attire still worn by the majority of women, even seven years after the war.

"You awake?" Dunk said.

"Is that what you call this?" With a tongue thick and dry from laudanum, enunciation was difficult.

"Miss Rose went to get us something to eat."

I nodded. "You have anything to drink?"

He leaned down and pulled a flask from his boot. He uncorked it and handed it to me. I took a long pull and coughed, spitting a good portion across the car. I covered my mouth with my hand and tried to regain my composure while

Dunk laughed, but not impolitely. "That's corn mash," I said, my voice hoarse.

"You've had it before?"

"Once," I said. I cleared my throat and drank again, ready for the taste and keeping it down. "Thank you." I returned the flask to Dunk and noticed the knife secreted in his boot when he returned the flask to its home.

"You're welcome."

My gaze drifted to the black-and-white painted sign nailed to the depot. GRAND ISLAND STATION. From my vantage point, with dry plains stretching out behind the wide-spaced buildings—one thing the West had plenty of was space—and not a river in sight, let alone an island, the name seemed a disingenuous designation. But Grand Island, Nebraska, wasn't the first Western town built on an ostentatious idea and duplicity, and it wouldn't be the last.

My eyelids drooped closed and in my mind's eye I saw a nattily dressed man standing on a barrel, with a young girl on the ground beside him, handing out leaflets.

Timberline is, by far, the most picturesque spot for a town in all of the Colorado Territory. The Rockies, that's where the future is!

What of the Indian threat?

We will be traveling under the protection of the Army. The Indians will be no threat.

"It's all built on lies," I murmured.

"What?"

Dunk's expression was open and honest. There was no guile in this man. He would be an easy mark. No wonder Rosemond employed him.

"The West," I said. *My life.* "Where are we going, Dunk? That's your name, isn't it?"

The man smiled. "Yes, ma'am. We're going to Cheyenne, then on to Boulder." His smile turned into a grin. "Then on to the mines."

"The mines? Rosemond is leaving Saint Louis for a mining town?"

Dunk laughed. "No, ma'am. She staying in Boulder. With you."

"With me?"

"Got a lot there. House on the way. Starting over, she say. I been wanting to try my luck in the mines for years, but Miss Rose always talked me out of it. I knew she been softening to the idea a' goin' west for a few months now. Then she came home with you and we were gone next day. I owe you a debt of thanks."

"Happy to be of service," I said.

There was a knock on the door. Dunk stood and slid it open. The dark-skinned conductor glanced at me and lowered his voice. "You lookin' for a game?"

Dunk tried to shield the conductor from my view. "May be."

"Last car."

Dunk returned to his seat and rubbed his hands up and down his thighs.

"Don't stay on my account," I said.

"I told Miss Rose I'd look after you."

"You're guarding me, you mean?"

Dunk's expression turned sheepish. "No, ma'am."

"Where would I go?" I nodded toward the town plopped down in the middle of the plains. "Besides, I'm too exhausted to move. Go on. Rosemond will be back soon."

Dunk rubbed his hands together and stood. "You sure?"

I closed my eyes and nodded. I heard Dunk pull a bag down

from the overhead shelf, rifle through, and return it. The door opened and closed, and I was alone.

I sat up straight, took a few deep breaths to steady my queasy stomach and spinning head. I wasn't sure what Dunk meant about me staying with Rosemond, but I didn't want to wait to find out.

Holding on to the open window, I stood on wobbly legs and retrieved the bag on the shelf. Inside were a few men's clothes, a razor and soap, and an old copy of Shakespeare's *Othello*. I flipped through the well-worn pages and stopped at the front. *To Dunk, Elizabeth Jennings March, June 20, 1857.* I dropped the book back into the bag and exhaled. No money. Of course Dunk took his money with him. I returned the bag to its place and looked around the compartment.

A bulging leather notebook tied securely with a leather string lay on the bench across from me. I untied the notebook and a pencil, the cause of the bulge, fell from the marked page. Expecting a journal and hoping for a secreted sawbuck, I stared dumbfounded at a sketch of a woman sitting on a bench, her head leaned against the window, asleep.

Me.

I flipped back through the notebook, finding much of the same. Women and men, in various poses and states of dress, an occasional landscape. Doodles, half-finished character studies, two birds sitting on a windowsill. A dark-skinned man from behind, his head turned as if looking over his shoulder, his back crisscrossed with long scars. A naked woman, looking down and away from the artist, dark curly hair exploding from her head and down to her shoulders. It was the most complete and detailed sketch and when I flipped forward I saw why: pages and pages of starts and stops, of small sketches focused in on different angles, different parts of the body, trying to achieve the artist's vision.

I glanced out the window, searching for Rosemond. She'd advanced to the shebang doorway and would be inside soon. The urge to escape from Rosemond and whatever future she'd kidnapped me for was overwhelming, but even in my drug-addled state I knew escape would do me little good without money.

A woman in a dark dress clutching a blue-and-orange paisley carpetbag stepped into my line of sight, obscuring Rosemond. Her head turned on a swivel, searching for someone. She stood approximately where Rosemond had, but with strikingly different results. Where Rosemond had been met with admiring looks from the men on the platform (and, like most of the West, it was nearly all men), men caught sight of this woman and their expressions turned from a willingness to admire to a quick aversion of their eyes, and maybe a tip of their hats to disguise their rudeness. The woman stood as if a rod were strapped to her back, her shoulders and long neck straight in what could only be a defiant mien.

The woman's head stilled and, after a brief pause, she stepped forward and stopped. I followed her gaze to see what caught her eye. A man—a farmer by the looks of his plain dress, sun-burned face, and slicked-down hair—stood twenty feet away, holding his hat in his hands in much the same way as the woman held her bag. Unlike most of the men, he stared at her for a long moment. Disappointment morphed to disgust and he turned on his heel, shoved his hat on his head, and walked away. The woman's body leaned toward the departing man, as if readying to follow, before straightening. She turned toward the train. I saw her face for the first time, and I understood the revulsion.

Her nose was too small, her face too long, her jaw too strong, her skin too freckled. Full lips struggled to contain her protruding teeth. A fringe of wiry orange hair escaped the edge of her sugar-scoop bonnet. Her green eyes, though, were beautiful, and stared straight at me, full of pride and challenge, and I knew being rejected or stared at wasn't the worst that had ever happened to her.

A tall man with a hat pulled low walked behind the woman, jostling her and breaking our gaze. A small strip of his white collar showed between his longish dark hair and the navy-blue coat he wore. Buff-colored pants were tucked into the top of his cavalry boots, well worn and dusty from the trail. He held a Remington rifle loosely in his right hand and favored his left leg. A stream of smoke trailed behind his head and I knew he held a thin cigar between his teeth.

I dropped the notebook. It was Kindle, come to find me. Rosemond hadn't been lying about helping me on Kindle's behalf. I grasped the open window and yelled, "Kindle!"

My voice was barely a whisper, and the man continued on without stopping, down the steps of the platform and into town. I stumbled across the compartment and opened the door on the third try. Ricocheting down the hall on legs I could scarcely feel, I tripped down the stairs and fell onto the platform on my hands and knees. The redheaded woman was next to me, helping me up with strong, thin hands. I stripped my arm from her grasp and tried to run in the direction the man had gone, but stumbled again. Why wouldn't my legs work?

"Let me help you." The woman lifted me up, put an arm around my waist, and walked me in Kindle's direction while I craned my neck searching for him. The steel-gray sky was thick with the earthy smell of impending rain.

"There." I pointed at a saloon down the street and the woman dutifully carried me along. We navigated through horses, wagons, and pedestrians, drawing our own peculiar interest: an ugly woman holding a carpetbag in one hand and her other arm around a pale, ill woman. I reached for the porch column and pulled myself up the step. I rested my cheek against the coarse wood, hoping for a wellspring of strength to propel me inside the saloon and into Kindle's arms.

"You can't go into a saloon," the woman said.

I stumbled through the open door and stood for a moment, letting my eyes adjust to the dark. A card game at a table to the right of the door. A bartender polishing a glass behind planks of wood resting on two cracker barrels. A cracked mirror behind him. The jagged reflection of a thin woman with disheveled hair and bruises beneath her eyes. My mouth watered as the oaky scent of whisky drifted around me. I followed the sound of a woman's laughter coming from the back.

"Hey!"

Finding my legs, I made it to the hallway in the back and stripped open the canvas curtain door of the first room. Empty. I moved to the room across the hall, startling two women in various states of undress. I went to the next room and ripped open the curtain. Kindle had his back to me, facing the naked woman on the bed, her hand between her splayed legs. My stomach lurched with nausea. "Kindle?" My voice was barely a whisper.

"She your wife?" the whore said.

The man turned and appraised me. A thin mustache hung limply from his upper lip, framing a cruel mouth and taking no attention away from his pockmarked olive complexion.

"That dope fiend? Hell no." The man grabbed my arm and threw me out the door and straight into the bartender, who lifted me up and tossed me over his shoulder like I was a bag of leaves. He stalked through the saloon and dropped me on the ground outside in the middle of the only puddle in the street. With shaking arms, I pushed myself into a sitting position, horse piss dripping from my jaw, and looked up into the ugly woman's face. The sun was behind her head, masking her expression.

"I told you not to go in there." I took her offered hand. She pulled me up and released me quickly. She flicked the excess urine from her hand, bent down, and wiped it on the bottom of her skirt. "Was it him?"

I shook my head.

She sighed. "I'm sorry."

The train whistle screamed and the train labored forward toward California.

"You've missed your train."

Though my brain was fuzzy with laudanum and I wanted nothing more than to lie down in the middle of the street and sleep, I understood the import of the train leaving without me. I was free of Rosemond and could return to Kindle. I managed to smile. "So I have."

My happiness was short-lived.

"Laura!"

Rosemond in her ridiculous blue dress stalked toward us holding a flour sack, her powdered, pox-scarred face a mask of fury. The ugly woman turned around and stood shoulder to shoulder with me. "Who's that?"

"My kidnapper."

CHAPTER

2

Laura, dear, what are you doing wandering around in your condition?"

My eyes were inexorably drawn to the necklace adorning the whore's throat. My mother's sapphire-and-pearl pendant had traveled from New York City to Galveston, across Texas and Indian Territory to the Mississippi River. It was my protection from destitution, the seed money Kindle and I would use to start a new life. Rosemond touched the necklace and smirked. I imagined reaching out and ripping it from her long, vulnerable neck.

Rosemond's demeanor changed as soon as she caught sight of the redheaded woman. She reached for me, smelled the sour aroma of urine, and drew back. Her lip curled, but her voice was solicitous, as if speaking to a child or an infirm elder. "What happened?"

"She was thrown out of that saloon," the redheaded woman said. I followed her outstretched arm and saw the man I'd followed earlier leaning against the post, smoking a cigar and watching us.

Rosemond smiled at the woman. "And who are you?"

"Cora Bayle."

Rosemond's smile turned into a wide, wolfish grin. "That certainly clears up my confusion."

"I thought I saw Kindle." Despite the shot of moonshine Dunk had given me, my tongue refused to work properly. My words came out in one long slur.

Rosemond's grin didn't waver, but I saw a small muscle pulse in her jaw. "And now we've missed our train."

"What's wrong with her?" Cora asked.

"Her monthly courses. Excruciating pain." Rosemond switched the flour sack into the hand holding her purse and grasped my elbow with the other. "Thank you for your help. Come along, Laura."

Cora stepped between us. "She said you kidnapped her."

Rosemond raised one eyebrow and took a long moment to look Cora Bayle up and down, her gaze settling on Cora's heavily freckled hands white-knuckling her carpetbag. When Rosemond finally looked at Cora's face again, her expression cleared. "Nora."

"My name is Cora. Who are you?"

"Rosemond Barclay. Her sister." Rosemond stepped slightly away from me, and Cora followed. "You look like an intelligent woman; surely you can see my sister isn't in her right mind." I tried to stand steady on shaky legs.

"I see she has a days'-old black eye and a lump on her forehead above it. I also see she's high, most likely on laudanum."

"You have experience with it?" When Cora didn't respond, Rosemond continued. "It is the only thing that gives her relief. Unfortunately, it makes her unsure on her feet. She falls regularly. I try to keep her in bed, to monitor the amount she takes, but you know how sneaky dopers can be. I left her alone for mere minutes and she snuck away, probably trying to find more opiates."

13

"She was looking for a man."

Rosemond laughed gaily. "Aren't we all?"

Cora couldn't keep the flush of embarrassment from over-taking her pale complexion. Rosemond's sly expression told me she noticed. "Laura was abandoned by her husband. He was quite the rake. A gambler, drunk, and womanizer. I tried to warn her."

"No." I shook my head but couldn't dislodge the words I wanted to say from the brick wall in my mind. I hit my fore-head with my fist, and the dull throbbing returned. I rubbed my eyes against my threatening tears. "That's not true."

"She defends him still." Rosemond shook her head. "I've tried to make her understand it's a fool's errand to rely on a man to make her happy or provide."

"A fool's errand?"

"Men can and do leave, and where does that leave the woman? Destitute, at the mercy of family, if she has any, with few options of making a living." Cora's chin rose higher. Rose-mond looked at me. Her smile was caring, but her eyes were flinty and cold. "Laura is destitute. Completely reliant on my goodwill. As well as my bank account."

The threat was clear. I glanced toward the end of the street. The prairie yawned into the bleak, featureless distance. Storm clouds hung above the ground like a curtain of smoke after a battle. I had nowhere to go and no money to get there. I searched the main street for the sheriff's office, my only option. As if read-ing my mind, Rosemond threaded her arm through mine and turned her attention to Cora. Thunder growled in the distance.

"Well. I suppose that's our cue to procure lodgings for the night. Thank you for your help."

We moved off. I looked back at the saloon. The man I'd fol-lowed was gone.

I allowed Rosemond to pull me along, hoping her bottle of laudanum had missed the train as well.

Five minutes later we were in a surprisingly lavish room on the second floor of the hotel. A canopied bed anchored the room. A white ceramic chamber pot was visible beneath the bed, and its matching pitcher and bowl sat on the chest of drawers. A straight-back chair and table were tucked into the corner on one side of the bed; on the other side a three-paneled partition blocked off a large copper tub. I went to the window, pulled back the dusty-smelling red drapes, and stared through the wavy leaded glass at the street below. A man wearing a tin star stood on the porch of the building across the street talking to the man I'd followed into the saloon, the Wanted posters nailed to the wall flapping in the breeze next to them. The sheriff lit the other man's cigar, then his own cigarette. They smoked and stared in the direction of the coming storm. They tipped their hats to Cora Bayle, and the sheriff spoke to her while motioning to the storm and to the hotel. Cora replied, and he nodded, touched his hat again, and the two men meandered down the street in the direction of the saloon. Cora Bayle glanced up and down the street, a lost and aimless expression on her face. Thunder broke, louder this time, and a gust of wind blew a poster from the wall.

Rosemond turned me away from the window and slapped me across the face so hard I almost fell to the ground. She grabbed my upper arm and pulled me close enough I could see the flecks of gold in her brown eyes. She put her finger in my face. "Don't you ever do that again." Her smallpox scars, normally well camouflaged with paint, stood out white against her red, angry complexion. "Where's Dunk?"

"In the last car of the train, I suspect. Gambling."

"Godammit," she said under her breath. "You better pray

to God Dunk gets off at the right station and remembers our trunk. Everything we need to start over is in that trunk. Money, the deed to a lot, the receipt for a prebuilt house. If Duncan…" Her fingers dug into my upper arm before releasing me, and she walked away in frustration and anger.

"Duncan told me you're starting a brothel in Boulder."

She wheeled around. "He what?"

"He told me everything. I don't know what you expect from me…but I'm with you only until Kindle is freed and comes to find me."

"Kindle is in the brig in Saint Louis. He won't be coming after you anytime soon, if ever."

"They won't execute him."

"We can only hope." She stared at me with disgust. "I thought you were different."

"Than what?"

"Women like Cora Bayle who can't function without a man taking care of them."

"I'm not like her."

"Chasing after a stranger because you think he's your husband? You better hope she didn't understand what you said."

"What do you mean?"

"You said his name."

"I did?"

She shook her head and sighed. "We're traveling across a country buzzing with the story of Kindle's arrest, and speculation you're alive." She motioned toward the window. "There's nothing else to do but gossip in towns like this. You wandering around calling out for Kindle doesn't help. I'm trying to help you."

"By kidnapping me?"

"I told you on the boat: Kindle asked me to help you, to save you from Lyman, and the hangman's noose."

"You can say it as often as you like, but I will never believe Kindle asked you to help me. He knows how I—" *Loathe you.* I caught myself, Rosemond's threat of my destitution fresh in my mind. She crossed her arms and waited, eyebrows raised as if she knew what I'd wanted to say. "If Kindle is executed, I hardly care about my own neck."

She uncrossed her arms and rolled her eyes. "Kindle is a good man, I'll grant you, but *really*, Laura. I didn't think you would buy into the myth of love and marriage hook, line, and sinker."

"A woman like you couldn't possibly understand."

"A whore, you mean?"

"Yes."

"You're right. I've never met a man whom I wanted to be beholden to." She caressed the cheek she'd slapped as if asking forgiveness, and cradled my face with her hands. "Laura, how many years did you live without a man?"

I didn't answer.

Rosemond smiled wryly. "Come now. We can be honest with each other. Thirty? Thirty-one?"

I shrugged one shoulder. Rosemond laughed. "So vain. I like that about you. Did you need a man to accomplish your goals? Become a doctor to the women of Washington Square?"

I shook my head.

"No. You did it on your own. William was a good man, as far as men go, but do you honestly think he would stand by and let you have a profession? He would expect children, a wife to cook and clean. Within a year you would have precisely the kind of life you rejected when you went to medical school."

I turned my head away, but Rosemond moved it back. I

looked down, remembering my argument with William on this subject. "You know I'm right," she said.

"No. We agreed."

"Laura. Men will say anything to get what they want. Even Kindle. You would have given in to his wishes in the end, you and I know it. Close your eyes." Her voice was soft and consoling. I furrowed my brows, my stinging cheek reminding me not to trust Rosemond Barclay. She smiled, as if reading my mind. "I'm not going to hurt you. Go ahead. Close your eyes." She closed hers, and I followed suit. "Imagine you're free. No one is chasing you. You can have whatever life you want. What is it?"

I saw myself walking down the wooden sidewalk of a burgeoning town, holding my medical bag in my hand, people greeting me with a smile and calling me Doctor.

"Where's Kindle?" I opened my eyes to Rosemond's knowing gaze. "Was he there? You don't have to answer. You've survived for thirty years without him, you can survive the next thirty without him, too. Of course you want to be with him, you're in love. But you have to come to terms with the idea you might not get the chance." Rosemond rubbed her thumb along my lower lip. "If it's about sex, I can help you." Her gaze settled on my lips and her mouth opened slightly. I pushed her hands away and stumbled back.

Rosemond laughed. "Don't be such a prude, Laura. William told me enough for me to know you're an energetic lover." I lunged toward her, but she moved away quickly. I fell to the floor, her laughter ringing in my ear. "If he lives, there's no doubt he'll chase your snatch across the world, if necessary."

I looked up at her. "You're disgusting."

"I'm not the one on the floor, covered in horse piss and dope sweat."

"No, you're the one forcing laudanum down my throat."

"I'm hardly having to force it on you. You've been in pain."

"You're trying to keep me under control."

She shook her head. "You're determined to see everything I do through a negative lens. I wish Kindle had given me some token to prove to you I'm doing this on his bidding. Lord knows you're more trouble than you're worth." She walked to the bed and pulled the bottle of laudanum from her purse. She uncorked the bottle and waved it underneath her nose. "If we're judicious with it, it should last until we arrive in Boulder." She held it out to me. "Do you need it? Or are you feeling better?"

Though my mind was clearing, my hands shook, the outward evidence of the bone-deep trembling in every part of my body. One sip would alleviate it. I turned away and sat heavily in the chair, exhaustion seeping from every pore. "I need to get back to William."

"Why? To save him?"

"Yes."

"Maybe you aren't aware, but the yarn Henry Pope spun about you two dying in Indian Territory has been proved a lie. When you walk into Jefferson Barracks claiming to be Kindle's wife, you will be taken into custody immediately."

"Mary! I'll go to Mary, work through her." As soon as I said it, I knew it for a ridiculous idea. But, once uttered, I was committed to the argument, if only to keep from admitting Rosemond was right.

"Kindle's sister? I'm sure the Pinkertons have already visited her, are probably watching everyone who goes in and out of the orphanage."

I balled my hands into fists against the tremors. "I'll cable Harriet Mackenzie. She helped us escape Jacksboro. She will help William, testify on his behalf."

"And risk her own reputation? How many times do you expect other people to save you?"

"I don't. It's not like that."

"Laura, Kindle knew the consequences of his actions, and he knows how to save himself, if it can be done. He has a better chance of acquittal if you aren't there, confusing the issue."

"I'm his wife. I should be there."

Rosemond inhaled dramatically and spoke at the ceiling. "Why do I ever try to reason with emotional women?" She leveled her gaze at me. "Even if they would listen to you—which they wouldn't; you'd be sent to New York immediately— anything you say will be dismissed as biased because you're his wife. Now, I'm done talking about this. You cannot go back. There's nothing you can do."

I bristled at being told what I could and could not do, what was and was not possible. How many times had I flouted the rules and gotten what I wanted, sometimes by sheer force of will? This situation was different. If I failed, it might cost Kindle his life. I'd already put Kindle's life at risk more times than I wanted to count. I wouldn't do it again. But moving west, away from Kindle, was unbearable. My heart was being stretched thin, like a rubber tube, and would eventually snap.

"I want to be there, near him." I swallowed the pride lodged in my throat and forced myself to beg. "Please. Let me have that at least."

"No."

"I doubt William wanted me to help you open a brothel."

Rosemond laughed. "I'm not opening a brothel, Laura. If I were, you'd be the last woman I'd ask for help. Kindle wanted me to take you to safety, which I am. Though I'm starting to regret my decision. He has no idea where we are. It's the safest way." There was a knock at the door. "The farther away from

New York you get, the better." Rosemond opened the door, and the hotelier's wife and another man walked in carrying four buckets of steaming water. They dumped it into the copper tub.

The woman stared at me, my fists balled, my chest heaving. "Gets cold fast."

Rosemond peeked into the tub. "One more trip with water."

"Four buckets are plenty for a bath."

"Your husband assured me my every need would be met."

The woman glared at Rosemond, taking in her fine dress and the expensive necklace around her neck. "I'm sure he did."

"Four more buckets. Soap and towels."

The woman left, rattling her buckets in disapproval.

Rosemond set the laudanum on the chest of drawers, bent down to see her reflection in the dappled mirror, and adjusted her hair. She removed my mother's necklace and dropped it in her purse. "No need to tempt the locals. I'll go to the shebang and get you a dress. Or would you prefer men's clothes?"

"We aren't finished with our conversation."

"Yes, we are." She walked out of the room, leaving the bottle of laudanum on the dresser to mock me.

I'd barely settled into the bath before the hotelier's wife bustled back into the room without knocking and picked up my clothes. "Miss High and Mighty wants me to wash these. Acts like I'm a common laundress."

"It's how she treats everyone. She didn't say thank you, did she?"

The woman harrumphed. "No."

"I thought not. Well, thank you, for the bath and washing my clothes."

The stout woman nodded, somewhat consoled.

"What's your name?"

"Martha Mason."

"I'm Laura, nice to meet you."

Martha nodded curtly, as if unused to a friendly word or female camaraderie. She was built like a bulldog: short and thick with drooping jowls and large, slightly protruding eyes. Her hands were thick, strong, and chafed. Deep red gashes split her skin on the tips of her thumbs, the result of hard work in the cold, dry winter air of the plains. She waddled slightly when she walked, not from obesity but most likely from constant pain in her legs from standing and moving all day. I suspected her thick legs would be a map of popped veins. Painful and incurable. I ran my hands over my smooth, unblemished legs, realizing for the first time they were the one area of my body that had seemed to come through my yearlong ordeal unscathed.

"Poor woman."

"What?" I asked. Martha stood by the window. Fat raindrops spattered on the glass. The sky outside had darkened until it almost looked like nighttime.

"The hatchet-faced redhead. She's about to get doused. I should probably go get her inside. Bet she doesn't have the money for a room."

"Why do you think that?"

She looked over her shoulder at me. "If they had money, they wouldn't be mail-order brides, now, would they?"

"I suppose not."

"Gabe Bullock, the scoundrel, left her high and dry. Heard him talking weeks ago like he'd be the one to get a pretty one. Gabe always has been a big talker, especially for a plow chaser. Though in his defense, she's one of the homelier ones I've seen."

"You see a lot?"

Martha nodded. "Men realize pretty quick they need a woman out here, and there sure ain't many single ones to be had. The single ones are snatched up like that." She snapped her fingers.

"You think if Cora stayed she would find a husband?"

"That her name?"

"Yes. I saw the scene on the platform. How did you hear about it?"

"Gabe went shooting his mouth off down at the Jug. Don't take long for news to travel in Grand Island. To answer your first question, I don't know. You'd think so, but she is ugly as a mud fence. 'Course, not many a man around here'll want to take her, being as Gabe rejected her." She gazed off in the middle distance, and her mouth turned down. "Those who will would give her a hard life." She shook her thoughts away, smiled thinly, and said, "Well." She bundled my clothes beneath one arm and went to the door. "These'll be ready in the morning."

"Thank you. Would you do me a favor?" Martha's eyes narrowed, as if afraid I was about to take advantage of her. "Would you take the laudanum away?" I nodded at the laudanum sitting on the dresser.

"Don't you need it?"

I want it, desperately. I inhaled sharply and ignored the throbbing in my head, the thrumming beneath my skin, the alternating hot and cold sweats. But the pain in my abdomen was thankfully gone. "No. I'm feeling much better."

"Suit yourself." She picked up the bottle and closed the door behind her.

I leaned my head back against the edge of the tub, closed my eyes, and thought of my father, Matthew Bennett. My dear sweet father whose last months had been spent in an opiate haze, trying and failing to rid himself of the chronic pain that was a result of his injury in the war. How my patience had run thin with his addiction until, with the hubris of youth and inexperience, I finally told him precisely what I thought of his weakness. He'd died not long after, without my ever having the opportunity to apologize, to tell him how much I admired him, how I wanted to become a doctor to be like him, that my anger and shame was born of the loss of my dream of working in a practice together. I'd refused to give him any quarter and now here I was, seven years later, beset by the cravings that tortured him and finally killed him.

"Forgive me, Papa." I took a shaky breath. "Help me."

The quiet room taunted me. There was no one to help me. I was alone.

As best as I could figure it had been three days, at most, since Kindle had been arrested on the steamboat and Rosemond "saved" me from John Lyman. Between the concussion the boatman had given me on the Mississippi and the pain-fueled opiate haze, the ensuing days were a blur of impressions instead of memories.

I held out my hand and stared at the thin silver ring on my left hand. My wedding ring, the only thing Kindle had left of his beloved mother. I closed my eyes against the memory of my recent conversation with Rosemond. It was only natural my dream would go to my profession first. I'd spent many more years becoming a doctor and practicing as a doctor than I'd known Kindle. Of course he was part of my ideal future. Who was to say I couldn't have a family and a profession? I opened my eyes. Society, for one. Most assuredly, the Wanted poster that followed me. Possibly Kindle.

Where was he? What was he doing? Had he been tried and convicted or found not guilty and released? I had no idea how slow the gears of military justice worked. Kindle could be forgotten in a damp cell for months for all I knew. Or he could be on his way to find me this moment, and find me he would.

He could have been convicted, shot, and buried by now as well.

No. I couldn't think it. Wouldn't think it. He must have friends in the Army who could help him, testify for him. He was well respected by his superiors, his peers, and his men. He would not be executed.

I shook the thoughts from my mind, sat up, and lathered the thin rag Martha had given me. It would feel good to be clean again, though how clean I would get was difficult to determine. The water in the tub was dingy with dirt and blood from my unwashed body. Disgusted with the idea of sitting in my own filth, I stood and accidentally caught sight of myself in the mirror across the room. The soap and rag slipped from my hand. The benefits of a healthy diet and exercise from six months at the orphanage had evaporated. My hair was lank and dirty, my skin pallid, a yellowing bruise on my forehead and purple half-moons beneath my sunken eyes. I looked like a corpse. I felt like one, too.

Martha Mason walked in. "These is fro—" She stopped when she saw me. I didn't move, too entranced by the vision of the living corpse standing in front of me. Martha closed the door softly behind her, placed the clothes she held on the dresser, and came over to me. "Sit."

I obeyed. I pulled my knees to my chest and hugged them. Martha got the pitcher from the dresser, thankfully filled with fresh water, and poured a portion over my head. She lathered my hair and gently massaged my scalp. I pressed my eyes into my knees and tried to keep from crying. Since the fateful night James Kline found me on the snowy streets of New York City and told me I was accused of murdering one of my patients, my life had been out of my control. Whenever I'd tried to wrest control back from fate, something befell me. The snatches of happiness with Kindle were always short-lived, and followed with worse challenges, physically and mentally. Was this what my life was going to be? Lurching from tragedy to tragedy, the moments of happiness being subsumed by heartbreak and misfortune? What happiness would I find if Kindle wasn't with me?

"This isn't me."

Martha poured water over my head and didn't reply. She toweled my hair somewhat roughly and draped it over my shoulders. She lifted my left arm, studied the burn scars. Her eyes drifted to my right hand, slightly deformed despite having almost full range of motion back. "The West ain't for the faint of heart, and that's a fact. You faint of heart?"

"I never thought so."

"You look it." She stood and went to the chest where my new clothes lay. "Miss High and Mighty says she's your sister. That true?"

I thought of Rosemond's threat of abandonment and destitution. What would Martha do if I told the truth? Would she give me money to return to Saint Louis? What would Rosemond do if confronted about kidnapping me? Would she reveal who I was? Have me sent back to New York City?

Martha narrowed her eyes. Was this a test? I wouldn't put it past Rosemond to pay Martha to test my loyalty. Somehow I knew if I was found wanting, being sent back to New York City would be the best option, and therefore the one Rosemond would be least likely to choose.

"Yes, she's my sister. How did you come to be in Grand Island, Nebraska, Martha?" I asked, eager to divert her attention.

"I was a catalog woman myself. Thought I was getting a grand hotelier. Came out in sixty-seven and discovered it was a dirty tent, but we made it work. 'Course, I did the work and Ed takes the credit and the money. Built this in sixty-eight when the traffic got steady."

"You've been here five years?"

"Feels like ten." Martha sighed.

"You don't like it?"

"Would you like living in this godforsaken place?"

"Probably not."

"There you go. Here're your clothes. Come on down for dinner."

"Thank you. For everything."

Martha nodded, shrugged, and left.

I dressed in the scratchy, cheap mourning attire—Rosemond's idea of a joke, no doubt—and ran my fingers through my hair as best I could. I opened the drawer to see if there was a forgotten comb or brush and saw something more useful.

For the first time since being separated from Kindle, I smiled.

CHAPTER
3

I stood at the top of the stairs and surveyed the Grand Island Hotel, remembering almost a year earlier when I'd stood at the top of similar stairs and caught sight of Kindle in full dress uniform, handsome and dashing. The admiration in Kindle's eyes when he took in my blue silk gown.

You look ravishing.

I shook my head to clear the memory. I patted my hair and looked down at my current dress, which hung on me like a forgotten coat on a hall tree. No one would call me ravishing now. Rosemond would be put together exquisitely, like high-priced whores are wont to do, and I would look the dependent relative I pretended to be. I straightened my shoulders, trying to stop my body from trembling from opiate withdrawals. I pressed my hand into my stomach against the nausea. After my bath I tried to eat one of the sandwiches Rosemond had purchased, but my stomach rebelled and I vomited it up. It would take enormous willpower to not do the same at the dinner table. The paper stuffed inside my sleeve crinkled. I pushed it farther up my arm and held the edge of the sleeve closed in my palm. The last thing I needed was for Rosemond to find my letter.

Cora walked through the hotel front door and looked

around. I waved and caught her eye, and motioned for her to come up the stairs. I went back down the hall, out of sight of the entryway, and waited.

Cora's shoulders and hat were wet from rain, and she smelled of mildew. "Laura?" She untied the ribbon holding her bonnet on and removed it, splattering water onto the floor.

I peeked down into the entryway. "Did you see Rosemond in the dining room?"

"I didn't look." She smoothed her red wiry hair, without success in taming it.

I pulled the letter from my sleeve and held it out to Cora. "Will you mail this for me?"

Cora's brows furrowed. "Why not ask your *sister*?" Her emphasis on the last word made me know she wasn't buying our story for a second. Still, I continued with the lie.

"It's to my husband's family. Rosemond would refuse."

"Why?"

"Does it matter? Just know she won't do it for me. She likes having me completely under her thumb. Please?" I hated her a little for making me beg.

Cora reluctantly took the letter and put it in her bag.

"Thank you." I glanced down the stairs and saw Rosemond come around the corner. I leaned into Cora. "Hold me up."

Rosemond's expression was one of concern. She called up to us. "Laura, are you all right?"

Pretending to be feeble wasn't difficult. "Just weak is all. Cora saw me and came to help."

"She's always there when you need her," Rosemond said. Cora tensed. I squeezed her arm in warning.

At the bottom of the stairs Rosemond took my other arm. I pulled away from both her and Cora. "Thank you, but I will walk on my own power."

Rosemond shrugged, and let her gaze travel to Cora. "Whatever do you have in that carpetbag?"

"What do you mean?"

"I mean, why didn't you leave it in your room?"

Cora's face reddened. "I like to keep it with me."

"Indeed." Rosemond took in Cora's sodden appearance like a wolf sizing up its next meal. "Martha found you. Invited you to dinner with us?"

"Yes, thank you for the invitation. It was . . . unexpected."

"It's the least I could do after you came to my sister's aid. I hope you're hungry. I've ordered us a feast. There is no way we will be able to finish it all. Come." Rosemond slipped her arm into Cora's and led her into the dining room, leaving me to make good on walking on my own. I did an admirable job of it, though my eyes darted around the front desk and the office behind, wondering where Martha would have put the bottle of laudanum.

The dining room was half full, with the majority of the hotel's guests in the saloon across the lobby. Lively piano music and men's laughter floated through the hotel, though it did little to give the staid dining room an air of celebration. I stopped dead at the sight of the man from the brothel sitting alone at the back table, smoking a cigar, his chair tilted up on its hind legs. A thin tendril of smoke curved into the air in front of the man's unblinking eyes.

"Laura?"

Rosemond touched my arm, her questioning moving from the stranger to me. I shook my head slightly and turned away from his unwavering gaze only to meet Cora's comprehending one.

Rosemond sat Cora across the table from her, forcing me to sit between the two, though thankfully with my back to the stranger. Rosemond had said I mentioned Kindle's name to Cora. Did I say it to that man as well? I rubbed my sweaty palms on my skirt and tried to put the man out of my mind.

"Wine?" Rosemond lifted the bottle in the middle of the table and tried to pour a glass for Cora. The redheaded woman placed her hand over the top. "I don't drink."

"In general, or wine in particular?"

"I do not partake of alcohol."

"More for us."

I nodded. Cheap wine gave me headaches and I was fairly confident whatever wine was to be found in Grand Island, Nebraska, would qualify as cheap. But I couldn't be discerning. Cut-rate or not, wine might help ease my shakes. I reached out to grasp the glass but paused. I squeezed my hand into a fist, inhaled, and concentrated. I picked up the glass and brought it to my mouth, ashamed at the quiver in my hand. I gulped the wine, determined that it was indeed some of the worst wine I'd ever tasted, and set the goblet on the table. I looked up and realized Cora and Rosemond had been watching me. One with an expression of concern, one with amusement.

"So, Cora." Rosemond lifted her glass like a queen gesturing to her ladies-in-waiting and said, "Tell us your life story." Rosemond drank the wine without grimacing and placed the glass on the table.

"Oh, it's not interesting."

"Don't sell yourself short. I'm sure it's scintillating."

Cora narrowed her eyes. Rosemond looked as if she was struggling not to laugh. Cora clasped her hands together and rested them on the edge of the table. "I grew up in Maine with an alcoholic father and consumptive mother." Cora's eyes flicked to me and away. "When she died the care of the children and my father fell to me, being the oldest. When they grew up, I took care of my father. He died recently, leaving me nothing more than the clothes on my back, the furnishings of the house to sell for what I could, most of which went to pay his tab at the saloons in town, and this ugly carpetbag."

"Well, that explains your aversion to alcohol and your attachment to the bag." Rosemond drank deeply from her wineglass. "And how did you come to be on a train to California?"

"I answered an ad in the paper."

"For?"

The muscles in Cora's jaw pulsed. "A teacher."

"Of course. In Grand Island?"

She lifted her chin. "No, Denver."

"And my sister made you miss the train?"

"Not at all."

"But I thought..."

"I decided to get off at Grand Island. I've been on a train for a thousand miles. I wanted a day or two on solid land."

"And Grand Island was such a better choice than Omaha." Cora reddened, realizing too late her lie was thin. To Rosemond's credit, she moved on quickly. "Do you have a room in the hotel?"

Cora paused. "No, not yet. I've been walking around the town."

Rosemond pursed her lips and nodded as if this were one of the most reasonable answers she'd ever heard. "Strolling in the rain is refreshing." Martha Mason came to the table carrying three plates loaded with food.

"Martha dear, this looks wonderful," Rosemond said.

It did, and it smelled wonderful as well. A chunk of pork roast doused with a brown gravy, lima beans in a thick white roux, collard greens, and a large slab of corn bread covered the plate completely. My mouth watered as my shaking hands picked up the utensils. Rosemond and I were digging into our food when we realized Cora had dropped her head in prayer. I glanced at Rosemond and for once our thoughts were in harmony. Neither of us had much use for God. He hadn't done anything to help me this past year; I doubted he cared enough to grace what I was about to eat.

The dinner was an obstacle course. The beans fell off my trembling fork and my hands were too weak to cut the roast, which was tougher than it looked. The greens were long and unwieldy and dripping with grease. I settled for picking a corner off my corn bread. It was greasy and gummy but delicious all the same. A few moments after I swallowed, my stomach cramped from the shock.

"I have a friend," Rosemond said, picking up the previous thread of conversation, "who answered an ad in Colorado for a schoolteacher."

"Do you?"

"She was married within three months."

"And is she happy?" Cora asked.

"From what I gather from the one letter she sent, he isn't completely reprehensible. She had her pick, you see, being the only single woman in a new town. She wasn't very pragmatic. She chose the poor, principled man instead of waiting for a rich one."

"She married for love."

Rosemond laughed. "I doubt it. You seem like a pragmatic woman."

Cora's mouth twisted into a wry smile. "With a face like mine, I've had to be."

"Do not say that," I said.

Cora furrowed her brows. "Why? It's the truth."

"Your only armor against other people's insults is a belief in yourself. Agreeing with them gives away your power," I said.

"What power?" Cora laughed. "I am alone in the world, nearly destitute, and a woman."

"It didn't stop me fr—" Rosemond kicked me under the table.

"Cora," Rosemond said, "are you sure you wouldn't like some wine. A sip? To celebrate. It's quite good."

Cora's gaze traveled between the two of us. I picked a bit of corn bread and ate it, chastising myself for almost giving away my identity. "What are we celebrating?"

"Making new friends." Rosemond raised the wine bottle in question. Cora nodded and Rosemond splashed wine into the goblet.

Cora drank and her face twisted in disgust. "That's good wine?"

"It's not the worst I've ever had." Rosemond laughed.

Cora tilted the glass back and held it out to Rosemond, who filled it up. Cora drank again, licked her lips, and placed the glass on the table. "Laura, you look familiar. Have we met before?"

"Not that I recall. I've never been to Maine," I said.

We all knew Cora Bayle had a memorable face. The only way she would have known me, however, was from the Wanted poster that had been dogging my feet since February last.

Cora speared a few beans on her fork and took a dainty bite. "I suppose you have one of those faces."

"Laura would have thousands of friends if she knew everyone who said she looked familiar," Rosemond said.

Cora studied me. "No, I'm certain I've seen your face before. I'm sure it will come to me. I've always been good with faces."

Disappointment clouded Rosemond's expression. With something like resignation, she motioned to Martha, who disappeared into the kitchen. Rosemond refilled her own wineglass.

"I suspect you either have the money for a room or train fare, but not both."

"Why would you think that?" Cora asked.

"You said you were practically destitute. Obviously, you'll save it for train fare. You can't stay here with everyone knowing your potential husband rejected you." Rosemond cut her roast, placed a few pieces on my plate, speared my uncut portion, and put it on her plate.

Cora placed her fork and knife on the table. "How did you—" Cora's breath caught. She wore her mortification like a second skin.

Rosemond cut my meat up and returned it to my plate. "He was talking about it in the shebang, I'm sorry to tell you. Bullock was his name, I think. It was reprehensible, and I told him as much. What kind of man promises a woman a home and marriage and reneges on the deal?"

Cora gripped the edge of the table and breathed deeply, trying to regain her composure.

Rosemond smiled at me and nodded toward the food on my plate. She treated me like an invalid, and who could blame her? I'd been acting like one. Trembling and shaking like an addict. Unsure of what she wanted of me. Destitute. Completely under her thumb.

"I understand how terrifying it is to be alone, with nothing but your own wits and body to survive," Rosemond said.

"My body?"

"When everything else is gone, it's the one thing of value women have. Even you would make a fair living. You wouldn't starve, at least. I don't want it to come to that. For you. I'll be happy to pay for your room tonight, as well as give you extra money for your journey. We don't have much. Most of our belongings are still on the train, but we can spare five dollars."

I watched Cora throughout Rosemond's speech, noting the flush crawling up her neck until it covered her face and reached her ears.

"Why?" Her voice was tight.

"I hope I never ignore another woman in need. We have so few advantages, as it is. Helping each other when we can seems the least we can do."

Cora narrowed her eyes at Rosemond, as if trying to judge her sincerity. Her gaze traveled to me and her face softened before she averted her eyes.

"I appreciate your offer, but five dollars will do little to help."

Rosemond's jaw muscle pulsed and her eyes turned flinty, but her voice retained its compassion. "I do wish we could help more, but we will have to buy new tickets, pay for dinner, the room. Your room."

Cora reached down into her carpetbag, pulled out a piece of folded paper, and placed it in the center of the table. For a moment, I thought it was the letter I gave her, until Rosemond snatched the paper, folded it over again, and put it in her lap.

"The Wanted poster?" I asked Rosemond, who nodded once but didn't take her eyes from Cora.

"Calling the man 'Kindle' helped, as well as using the name Laura. You look nothing like that photo now," Cora said, her voice soft.

I stared at my plate, jaw clenched. I didn't want to be reminded by this woman what I'd lost.

"You want five hundred dollars," Rosemond said, voice flat.

Eyes downcast, Cora shook her head. "They've updated it."

Still keeping her gaze glued to Cora, Rosemond unfolded the paper. My head turned back and forth, watching them. Cora, mortified that she'd been reduced to extortion, and Rosemond livid and defiant at being bested by a pathetic, lonely woman. After an extended glare, Rosemond dropped her eyes to the poster. One eyebrow crooked up and she handed it to me.

I covered my mouth. "A thousand dollars, *dead or alive*?" I inhaled a long, shuddering breath. Before there'd been the remote chance I would be able to mount a defense in a court of law. The necessity of bringing me in alive no doubt reduced the number of bounty hunters willing to chase me; why bother with the long trip back East for five hundred dollars? A dead body for one thousand dollars would bring every trigger-happy desperado and destitute farmer out of the woodwork, searching for Dr. Catherine Bennett, the Murderess. Or a rejected spinster with no options or future.

I jumped at the sound of a loud thump behind me. I looked over my shoulder and saw the stranger rise from his table. He walked past our table, touching his hat to us, and out of the dining room and into the saloon.

I took a shuddering breath and let my gaze travel from the stranger to Cora to Rosemond, one threat to another. This was what my future held, being constantly under danger of exposure, arrest, or manipulation by everyone I met, and now death. The only person I could trust completely was in the brig in Saint Louis. Even if he was alive, he would be no help to me now.

"I want your necklace," Cora said to Rosemond.

The last indignity. I swept my plate off the table. It shattered on the floor. Everyone in the dining room stopped eating and stared at me. Cora and Rosemond didn't take their eyes from each other. The game was between them. I was merely a pawn.

Martha Mason came running from the kitchen. "Well, I'll declare! Look at the mess you've made."

"Please bring me another plate, Martha," I said, glaring at Rosemond.

"It'll cost extra."

"My sister will pay."

Rosemond wiped the corners of her mouth with a napkin and said, "Sorry for the mess, Martha. It was an accident. Bring my sister another plate."

Martha left, grumbling as a young boy came through the door, holding what looked like a letter.

"'Ere a Cora Bayle here?"

Cora's head jerked toward the boy. She raised her hand slightly. "Here."

The boy walked to Cora and held out his empty hand. Cora hesitated. Rosemond came to her rescue. "Here," she said, pulling a coin from her reticule. The boy took the coin and bit it. Satisfied, he handed the note to Rosemond and left. With an arched eyebrow, Rosemond held it up between her thumb and forefinger, taunting Cora, whose present coloring reminded me of the bright red dirt of Palo Duro Canyon.

"Please hand me my note."

"Technically it is mine, since I paid for it."

Cora inhaled and exhaled slowly, gathering herself.

Rosemond pursed her lips. "Who could possibly know, or care, you're here? Hmm." She studied the handwriting on the outside of the note. "Looks masculine." She looked over the top of the note at Cora. "And uneducated. This must be from your former future husband, Mr. Bullock. Has he had a change of heart? Is your future secure?"

"Give me the letter."

"You can do much better, Cora. Even with that face."

I snatched the note from Rosemond and held it out to Cora. When Cora grabbed the note I didn't let go. I made her meet my eyes.

"Are you going to turn me in or kill me?"

"Kill you?" Cora had the grace to seem scandalized at the idea. Most like she was. She hadn't lived in the West long enough to be hardened by the struggle to survive. Martha Mason watched us from the edge of the room.

"Most of the people who have threatened me in the last year are dead." I let the note go and Cora fell back, her eyes full of fear. She pushed away from the table, picked up her carpetbag, and left.

Martha set my new plate in front of me. I picked up my utensils and, with steady hands, cut a chunk of roast and lifted the fork to my mouth. I continued to eat, letting the food nourish me, the strength seep back into my bones. I drank deeply and was halfway finished with my meal before I glanced at Rosemond. She was sitting back in her chair, holding her wineglass near her head, an expression of deep admiration on her face.

She lifted her glass in toast and said, "There she is."

CHAPTER 4

The rain had settled into a soft mist more akin to fog than rain. I opened the window, hoping a chill breeze would cool the anger that heated my skin. A trickle of sweat ran down the small of my back.

Rosemond placed the bottles of whisky and laudanum on the dresser with a clunk.

"Martha took that away."

"And gave it back to me."

"I don't want it."

"And I don't want you to have it. But you won't be able to sleep tonight without it."

"Of course I will. I'm exhausted." Having gone through opiate addiction with my father after the war, I knew Rosemond was right about the insomnia, but I didn't want to give her one ounce of power over me.

"No need to play the tough with me, Laura. Though superb job with that sniveling wench, Cora."

"It wasn't an act."

Rosemond grinned. "I know." She portioned out a shot of whisky, put a few drops of laudanum in it, and held it out to me. "See, barely any to speak of. It will merely help you sleep."

I stared at the glass, torn between the craving I was struggling to resist and the need to keep my wits about me. Cora might be easily vanquished, but Rosemond was another case altogether. I didn't believe for one second she was helping me because of some sort of respect or long-held affection for Kindle. More than that, I couldn't believe Kindle would ask her to.

Rosemond sighed, put the glass down, and undressed. "You can either take it and sleep in the bed with me or sleep on the floor. I won't be kept up all night with a doper going through withdrawals."

I turned from my temptation and back to the window. The mist dampened the lamplight shining through the sheriff's office window. A shadow of a person walked down the deserted street. I leaned forward and watched Cora Bayle walk up the train platform steps and disappear behind the depot. I thought of the letter in her carpetbag, most likely read and a confirmation of my identity.

"Why hasn't she turned me in?"

"Cora?"

I nodded.

"She's not the type." Rosemond spoke from close behind me. I looked at her over my shoulder. She was stripped down to her bodice and petticoat.

Since escaping New York City a year earlier, money—earning it, managing it, retaining it—had been almost as consuming an idea as survival. Going back to my father's death, medical school, and the thin times before my practice blossomed, money had been a constant worry. I had at least had a profession to fall back on. Cora Bayle had nothing at all. "I'd turn me in for a thousand dollars."

"She put on a good show, but Cora Bayle is decent, deep down."

"I'm a decent person."

Rosemond stroked my hair and smiled wistfully. "I have no doubt you were. You're a survivor now."

I turned my head away. I wanted to argue with her, but I knew her words were true. I saw the faces of the men killed by me or in my name since coming west, and knew if confronted with the choice of survival and their lives, I would choose survival.

"Is her future husband a decent person?"

After a pause, Rosemond said, "I wouldn't worry too much about that."

"Why?"

"The note was from me. By the time she figures it out, we'll be gone."

"You knew she recognized me all along."

"I suspected. You didn't?"

"No." I rubbed my forehead and pinched the bridge of my nose. The laudanum not only took my pain away, it took away my discernment. "I shouldn't have threatened her."

"Nonsense. I don't think you fully appreciate the reputation you have, Laura. Come to think of it, I'm impressed Cora had the courage to confront you at all. She understands now that she's no match for you. Her fear of you will keep her waiting for Bullock all night. Who was the cowboy in the dining room?"

"The man I followed into the brothel."

"Did you call him Kindle?"

"I don't know."

Rosemond nodded and pursed her lips. "You need a new name. How about—"

"Helen. Helen Graham."

"That's rather specific."

"It's from a book I read once."

Rosemond raised her eyebrows and with a wry grin said, "You don't look much like a Helen, but if that's what you want."

I stared out the window at the glowing sheriff's office window. Now that the reward was "dead or alive" I couldn't even find safety there from those who would use me for their own ends. If I turned myself in, what were the chances I would survive the night?

Rosemond moved into my line of sight. "I know what you're thinking."

I crossed my arms. "That I have little chance of surviving without you?"

Rosemond's mouth quirked up. "Oh. I *didn't* know what you were thinking, but I'm glad you realize it. I'm not your enemy."

"You aren't my friend, either."

"Maybe not now. But I will be."

I laughed. "It's highly unlikely I'll be friends with my husband's whore."

"That was before your time."

"Was it?" I thought of Kindle's refusal to answer my question about his night with Rosemond on the riverboat.

Did you fuck Rosemond? It's a simple yes-or-no answer.

My gaze lingered on the glass of laudanum-laced whisky on the chest of drawers. I drew nearer to it, like a moth to a flame. It would be so easy...

I turned abruptly. "Are you so unappealing to women you have to kidnap me and coerce me to be your friend?"

Rosemond's smile slipped and her face tightened. I'd hit a nerve. "Since you have so conveniently forgotten, I'll remind you: Kindle asked me to help you. If I hadn't, you would be in a damp New York City jail cell being measured for a noose right now. Or, considering the latest Wanted poster, you'd be dead. I think a little fucking gratitude is in order."

"Why did you agree to help me?"

"You won't believe me."

I crossed my arms and waited.

"I like you."

I scoffed.

"Are you so repulsive to women you can't believe one wants to be your friend?" Rosemond said.

She turned my insult around and aimed it perfectly. Female friends had always been thin on the ground with me. With the exception of Harriet Mackenzie, I couldn't remember one who had sought my friendship. I'd misjudged Harriet terribly, and wasted the little time we had together. Was I doing the same with Rosemond?

"I need your help to start a new life. A woman alone is a target. Men would assume I'm searching for a husband, or a huckleberry to take care of me on the side."

"In a mining town?"

Rosemond's head jerked back. "Why would you think that?"

"Dunk told me."

Rosemond shook her head. "Duncan has big dreams about striking it rich in the silver mines, and he's welcome to tilt at that particular windmill. I, on the other hand, am not delusional. I have no intention of setting up shop in a mining town. I'll be near enough so he can come back when he fails."

"What if he succeeds?"

"I'll be the first to congratulate him. He deserves good fortune. As do you, Laura. Helen."

My good fortune was sitting in a jail cell in Saint Louis, not standing in front of me. "Who will believe we're sisters?" We were roughly the same height, but Rosemond was all soft, voluptuous curves, with dark hair, red lips, and porcelain skin marred slightly by smallpox scars. I was poorly endowed and slim, with dark blond hair that lightened to the color of honey when exposed to the sun for any length of time.

"If you saw some of the whores I worked with, you'd know I can do wonders with very little. With you, though, most of my work will be accomplished by getting you off the dope, feeding you, and keeping you out of the sun."

"And then what? We open a brothel together?"

Rosemond looked away. "I'm done with that life."

I crossed my arms over my chest. "You're afraid the life isn't done with you."

She met my gaze. "Nearly every miner, sodbuster, gambler, and businessman heading west went through Saint Louis."

"And you fucked your share."

Rosemond's mouth twitched into a smile. "Yes."

"Won't you be recognized, with your scars?"

"Most like. But if you tell a lie with enough confidence, people will doubt themselves, and that's all I need."

I chuckled, thinking of the dozens of lies I'd told in the last year. "If you need a liar, you've enlisted a master."

If I couldn't return to Kindle, I needed to hide somewhere. Pretending to be Rosemond's sister temporarily was a better idea than anything I could come up with. Settling down in the West had been my original plan when I left New York City, and I was curious what life in one of the new, rough-and-tumble towns would be like. "What's our story?"

"We're sisters from back East starting a new life. You're a nurse, I'm a painter."

"A painter?" I remembered the sketchbook and the obvious skill exhibited by the artist.

"I wasn't always a whore, Laura."

"Of course not." I was struck with a sudden curiosity about Rosemond's prior life. What events led to her becoming a whore? How did Dunk fit into the story? The questions didn't have time to fully form before Rosemond continued, her eyes sparkling with grand plans and impossible dreams.

"I leave whoring behind and you get a safe place to wait for Kindle. A fresh start with a new name."

My laughter died off into a long sigh. "I've tried that, three times now." I went to the window and pressed my nose against it. The sheriff's office was dark. "It never works."

"It will this time."

I glanced over my shoulder again. Rosemond was climbing into bed. "Why?"

"Because, Helen, I always get what I want."

CHAPTER
5

The toe of a boot nudged me awake.

I opened my eyes and saw a carpetbag lying deep beneath the bed, a clean strip of floor amid a thin layer of dust leading to it. My head was thick and heavy, memories hard to recover, but the telltale feel of opiates flowed through my body. Slowly, I remembered tossing and turning, and finding solace in the glass of whisky on the dresser. There, memories ended. Why I didn't get back in bed, I couldn't know.

Someone nudged me again. "Wake up."

I lifted my head and a string of saliva dripped from the corner of my lax, numb mouth. I wiped it, roughly, having trouble controlling my arms, and sat up. The blanket covering me fell from my shoulders, revealing the fact that I had slept in my clothes. A man wearing an open-necked blue striped shirt with a tin star pinned on his leather vest looked down on me with a disgusted expression. His boots were muddy but his black hat was pristine, as was his gray handlebar mustache.

"You Laura Barclay?"

"Who?"

"It's her, but you're wasting your time, Sheriff," Martha Mason said. "Look at her. She can't hardly lift her hand, let alone a knife."

"Where's your sister?"

"I..." I glanced around the empty room, lifted myself up higher, and checked the bed. Disheveled and vacant. I slumped down. "I don't know. Why?" Using the footboard, I pulled myself to my feet and leaned heavily against the canopy pole.

"You two had dinner with Cora Bayle last night," the sheriff said.

"We did."

"Things get a little heated?"

"Heated?"

"She's no use to you, Sheriff Toomer," Martha said.

"Why are you asking about Cora?" I asked.

"Someone killed that hatchet-faced redhead," Martha said.

My brain felt like it was covered with heavy brocade drapes. "I've never killed anyone with a hatchet." My brows furrowed. *A bounty hunter was killed with a hatchet, but I didn't wield it. Did I?*

Bile rose in my throat. I swallowed and spoke with a thick voice. "You think I killed Cora with a hatchet?"

"See, Sheriff? She don't know what the hell she's talking about. Come on downstairs and we'll find the sister."

The sheriff held up his hand to silence Martha. "Cora was murdered on the train platform sometime last night."

"How horrible. Poor thing."

"Heard you threatened to kill her last night," the sheriff said.

My mind sharpened and cleared in an instant. "I did no such thing. I would never threaten someone like that. Besides, do I look capable of killing anyone?" I hoped I looked as poorly as I felt. If Sheriff Toomer's evaluation of me was any indication, I did. Relief surged through me like a drink of cold water. "How did she die?"

"Stabbed," Toomer said. "In the throat."

"A messy business." I held out my arms. My hands and sleeves were clean.

"How do you know?" Toomer said.

"I am..." *A doctor.* I smiled thinly. "I was a nurse in the war. I know how neck wounds bleed."

"What side?" Toomer's ice-blue eyes bored into me. He was still fighting the war.

"Confederacy."

He nodded slowly, suspecting my lie, no doubt, but not able to prove it. Rosemond breezed through the door. I sat on the bed, exhausted from trying to be strong.

Rosemond wore my laundered dress, her bosom straining against the bodice.

"Laura? What's going on?" She noted the tin star pinned on the man's vest. "Sheriff?"

"You Rosemond Barclay?"

"Yes."

"She your sister?"

"Yes. What's the meaning of this?"

"You two were the last people to talk to Cora Bayle last night. After she left you she was murdered on the train platform. Stabbed in the neck."

"I suppose we weren't the last to talk to her." Sheriff Toomer furrowed his brows. "Her murderer would have been," Rosemond clarified. "What kind of town is this? I heard a whore was killed last week as well, correct?"

Toomer's eyes narrowed. "How did you hear that?"

"The town is talking of little else. Frankly, I'm glad to be leaving. Grand Island, Nebraska, doesn't seem safe for a woman, does it?" A train whistle sounded in the distance. "Is that the east train or the west?"

"East. The westbound train is readying to leave."

"We should hurry, sister." Rosemond held out her hand to me.

"Martha said Miss Bayle received a note during dinner?" the sheriff said.

"She did. Looked like a masculine hand. From her killer, no doubt. I don't suppose you found the note on her person?"

Toomer's ice-blue eyes fell on me. There was more than one note on Cora's person. He knew who I was from the letter I'd given Cora.

I closed my eyes, tilted my head back, and inhaled, at peace. It was over. No more running. No more being manipulated by people like Rosemond, or used as a pawn by men like Cotter Black. No more looking over my shoulder and worrying if the man walking behind me was a Pinkerton, finally come to track me down. I was going home. Back to New York, to face whatever might come. I thought of Kindle. Maybe if I cooperated, I could convince the sheriff to take me to him, to say good-bye.

"We found nothing on her at all," Toomer said. I opened my eyes, which went automatically to the bed, underneath which sat a carpetbag. Cora Bayle's.

"I told you you were wasting your time here," Martha said. "You oughta be talking to Bullock. He gave me the note."

"You didn't tell me that," Sheriff Toomer said.

"Didn't I?"

"You must excuse us, Sheriff, or we'll miss our train," Rosemond said.

"Thank you, ladies," the sheriff said, touching his hat.

Martha shut the door behind him. Rosemond dropped to

her knees and pulled the carpetbag from beneath the bed. She pulled my mother's necklace from it and held it out to Martha, whose eyes lit up.

"What are you doing?" I demanded, standing.

Rosemond glared at me but didn't answer. She kept hold of the necklace. "What did you do with the dress?"

"Burned it in the stove."

"You sure it's gone?"

"It's ashes. I made sure."

"This is worth the reward for my sister, at least. You get out of town. East, far away from us and Grand Island." Rosemond released the necklace.

"With pleasure." Martha left, but instead of heading to the main stairs, she turned toward the back stairs and was gone.

Rosemond picked up Cora's carpetbag. "Let's go."

"You killed Cora," I whispered. "Why?"

"She was a threat to us." She shoved her free hand into my chest. I looked down and saw the letter I gave Cora twisted in Rosemond's fist and streaked with dried blood. "What were you thinking, giving her this letter? Did it not occur to you she would read it?"

"Of course not. I didn't know she recognized me when I gave it to her. Anyway, you said she wasn't the type to turn me in."

"I lied. Everyone's the type to fucking turn you in. Don't you get that yet?" She shoved me away and went to the dresser. She lit the oil lamp and set the letter on fire. It curled and smoked, destroying my grand idea to contact Mary Kindle. A grand idea that had left an innocent woman dead.

Rosemond dropped the letter into the ceramic water basin and said, "I went to meet Cora last night to give her the necklace and buy her silence. Imagine my surprise when she waved the letter in my face and refused. Without the letter, we could have argued you're not the same person because you do look like hell, Laura. But, thanks to you, that option was gone."

"I thought you'd kidnapped me. You hadn't bothered to tell me where we were going or anything at all."

"You've been high as a kite. Hell, you could barely talk a day ago, let alone lift a fork to your mouth." Rosemond stuck her finger in my face. "No more dope. If you hadn't called out for Kindle on the street, Cora would be alive and we'd have your mother's necklace, and don't you forget it. You're going to get yourself killed."

"You don't care if I die. You just want to use me for your own means."

"You're goddamn right I do. Don't you ever go behind my back again or I guarantee you will never see William Kindle again."

CHAPTER
6

Rosemond's mood worsened as we traveled west.

The journey alone would have been enough to put a traveler in a bad mood. The landscape outside the window was barren and flat, a featureless plain that I thought I'd grown accustomed to traveling across Texas and Indian Territory. However, seeing it slide past hour after hour was a tax on the mind. This was what the US government wanted to steal from the Indians? Let them have it, I said. Living here would drive the sanest person to madness.

Having to leave Grand Island in a rush, we paid the fare and boarded the early-morning train, the emigrant train— overcrowded, sweltering, and slow; I suspected it was what pushed Rosemond's mood into the terrifying territory in which it currently resided. Though, to give her the benefit of the doubt, the weight of murdering an innocent woman might have started to weigh down her conscience. The constant reminder of Cora Bayle's carpetbag sitting on the bench between us didn't help.

I turned my head slightly and watched Rosemond. She stared straight ahead, her mouth set in a thin line, her eyes narrowed, her shoulders rigid. She looked less like a well-paid whore and more like a woman on the edge: tense and unsure of the future.

The train slowed and stopped next to a platform backed by a few buildings. It was a nameless whistle stop with little to offer or recommend. Fellow passengers stood to stretch their legs but didn't wander far from their seats out of fear of losing them.

Rosemond looked at the platform with anticipation. It was empty, save the depot master and a man selling nuts and coffee from the back of a handcart. Or trying to. The passengers looked through the window at his wares, and down at their own meager provisions. Rosemond settled back into her seat, anger pulsing off her in waves of heat.

"Dunk isn't here?"

She glared at me. "No, he isn't fucking here. He's in Cheyenne, waiting for us."

The woman sitting in front of us turned slightly in her seat but knew better than to comment. She'd tried to admonish Rosemond earlier but had gotten a salty earful for eavesdropping.

I lowered my voice so we couldn't be heard over the din of conversation in our overcrowded carriage. "So why do you keep looking for him at every stop?"

Rosemond dropped her voice as well. "Because he's not used to me not being around to tell him what to do. There's no telling what he might get up to."

"He's not a child, you know."

Rosemond glared at me. She opened her mouth to respond but closed it with a click. She pushed her shoulder nearest me forward, and shifted slightly on her seat to block the sight of me. She stared across the car and out the opposite window in silence, her jaw tense from the effort to keep her thoughts to herself. It was too much in the end. She faced me again.

"He'll be wiped out by the time we get there."

"He's a poor gambler?"

She closed her eyes. "He's my responsibility." She rubbed her forehead, made a fist, and pressed it to her lips.

"How long have you known him?"

"Since childhood."

I waited for her to elaborate, but she did not. With Rosemond's lilting accent and her comportment, I suspected she'd grown up in a well-to-do Southern household. From there, it was easy enough to fill in the blanks. I knew she wouldn't be inclined at the moment to tell me her life story, and part of me didn't blame her.

"Was he the man in your sketchbook?"

"What?"

"The man with scars on his back."

"Were you snooping?"

"Yes. I was searching for money. You left it on the seat. You're very good."

Rosemond inhaled deeply, covered her mouth, and coughed, at the stench of body odor surrounding us, most like. I'd taken to breathing shallowly, and through my mouth, but it did little to help. I was afraid a fair amount of the tang was coming from me. Rosemond's hands couldn't remain still, clutching and unclutching each other. "Thank you," she finally said.

"You're welcome."

I stared out the window longingly at the tea cart on the platform. I was hungry and I needed something to soothe my parched throat and to rid my mouth of the lingering taste of laudanum. We'd left the room so quickly we'd forgotten the bag of sandwiches on the dresser. "Would you like for me to buy us some coffee?" I offered. I sniffed and wiped my watering eyes.

Rosemond dug into her purse and handed me a small handkerchief with *RM* monogrammed in royal blue in one corner. "With what?"

"You mean—" I dabbed at my eyes.

Rosemond's voice was low. "I used the last of our coin on train passage."

"And you gave away my mother's necklace to Martha Mason." I couldn't keep the anger and bitterness from my voice. I knew Rosemond had little choice, but I hated that the necklace had traveled so far to end up in the grubby hands of a pioneer woman eager to escape her life.

"Which I wouldn't have had to do if not for your mistakes."

I looked down and clasped my trembling hands together. I rubbed them in an effort to wipe off the layers upon layers of blood that had covered them for months. I leaned near Rosemond and spoke low enough that it couldn't be overheard by our nosy neighbors. "You didn't have to kill her."

"Didn't I? She was a threat to you."

I scoffed. "Do not act like you did it solely for me, for my safety. Without me, you can't start a new life."

She looked down her nose at me. "Can't I?"

Of course she could, and my actions were perilously close to losing me the only ally I had. The thought of being on my own was suddenly terrifying.

My blood turned cold at the realization. What had happened to me? Where had my independent, self-assured spirit gone? Was I no better than Cora Bayle, desperate for someone to take care of me?

I thought of the months Kindle and I had spent at his sister's orphanage outside Saint Louis. We had settled into a routine, which had been both satisfying and stifling. For the first time in my life, I'd felt like part of something bigger, a family, and a cause: teaching young women about medicine. I'd started to entertain the idea that teaching might be where my future lay: encouraging others' success while subsuming my own. Now, traveling west, I felt an underlying excitement and freedom I couldn't deny. It was the same excitement I felt when Maureen and I left Austin a year earlier. The thrill of the unknown, of possibilities. I realized it wasn't being alone that frightened me, it was not having someone to share the adventure with. Until Kindle was free, why not Rosemond?

"I did her a favor," Rosemond said, not looking at me. "She would have had a hard, miserable life, married to a farmer or miner, and that was if she was lucky."

It was a moment or two before I shook off my own musings to realize who she was speaking of: Cora Bayle. "Rosemond," I chastised. "What a horrible thing to say."

She glared at me from the side of her eye. "Don't be a hypocrite, Laura. You know I'm right."

"Maybe so, but the difference is, I would never say it aloud."

Rosemond rolled her eyes and angled herself away from me again. "God, you can be insufferable," she said over her shoulder.

The train jerked forward and we were on our way again.

I placed Cora Bayle's bag on my lap and opened it.

Rosemond grabbed the handles to keep it closed. "What are you doing?"

"Seeing if she had any money."

Rosemond removed her hand and looked away, the corners of her eyes tightening, her hands twisting, fidgeting, and rubbing in a familiar way. I placed my hand over hers to quiet them. Her fidgeting stopped. I leaned close. "You've never killed anyone."

Her neck spasmed, as if swallowing something caught in her

throat. "Of course not," she said in a hoarse whisper. "Why would I?"

I wanted to tell her it would get easier, that she would forget, but I wasn't sure she would. Cora Bayle was as close to an innocent as I'd met in this whole debacle of my life since I left New York City. There was a difference in killing a woman like her and killing an evil man like Cotter Black. The memory of putting a bullet in Black's head assaulted me at the strangest moments, all these months later. I doubted I would ever be totally free of it, though I felt no guilt for his death. Cora Bayle was another matter.

I took Rosemond's hand and held it firmly. She stilled, and only her eyes moved to gaze at our joined hands. I placed my lips next to her ear and whispered, "I apologize. For getting off the train. For Cora." Rosemond shuddered. I squeezed her hand and continued. "I'll be more careful going forward."

She pulled her hand from mine, turned her head away, and wiped her eyes. I left well enough alone and turned my attention to the carpetbag.

"A Bible, of course," I murmured.

The Bible was old and worn at the edges. Dates of births, deaths, and marriages were written in a scratchy hand on the inside cover; Cora's name was the only one without a death date. I closed the book and put it on the seat between me and the wall of the train. A hairbrush and mirror, two pair of bloomers, a washcloth and soap, a jar of salve whose label promised relief from achy joints. I opened the jar and sniffed, and was assaulted by the scent of camphor. I dug out a teaspoon and rubbed it into my hands. I held them out in front of me and pulled them back quickly when I couldn't control the trembling. Goose bumps popped up on my arms and I shivered. Rosemond watched me rub my arms from the corner of her eyes but didn't comment.

I closed the jar of salve and dropped it back in the bag. A small rectangular wooden box turned out to be a sewing kit with well-used pewter instruments: a thimble, bodkin, stiletto, needles of various sizes, and a spool of white and blue thread. My hands stilled at the sight of neatly folded lace-edged cloth at the bottom of the bag. I lifted it and stared at the top of a woman's gown. Cora Bayle's wedding trousseau. The material was soft, the lace fine, and I knew Cora had splurged on this, had poured all of her hopes and dreams of her future into this one item. With a sick stomach, I shoved the gown into the bottom of the bag. I felt around, found a small coin purse, pulled it out, and twisted the clasp open.

Rosemond took it from me and we looked into the open purse at two coins.

Fifty cents.

Rosemond clicked the purse shut and sighed. "Dunk will be waiting at Cheyenne, with our trunk." Her voice was confident, but her expression was not.

We rode in silence for an hour or more, each lost in our own thoughts. Rosemond spent her time worrying with the coin purse, clicking the clasp open and closed until I finally snapped at her to stop. With a smirk, she stared at me and continued on as before.

I kept my laudanum cravings at bay by thinking of Kindle and the blood-covered letter Rosemond had shoved in my chest. I had to get word to Kindle's sister, Mary, so he would know where to find me when he was released, or if he... No. I wouldn't consider any other possibility. Kindle would prevail.

I yawned and glanced around the passenger car. A narrow

aisle separated the hard wooden benches lining the outside walls. Men, women, and children were crammed on every available surface, their suitcases and knapsacks shoved beneath the seats and overflowing into the aisles. Women held babies and toddlers, some shushing the babies and their hungry cries with soft cooing, others with a brash word or a slap. The older children ran up and down the aisle, thinking it a great adventure, no doubt. The teeming train was no different from the tenements they had recently left, but whereas the cities offered no hope of bettering themselves, the swaying train would lay them off at a new beginning in the West where, with hard work, everything and anything was possible. As the newspapers promised.

Mixed in among the families were way travelers—cowboys, hunters, miners, and businessmen—traveling between towns on business. They were loud and rough, and a couple let their eyes linger over the women in the carriage longer than politeness allowed. One particular businessman, with a head as round as his protruding belly, was turned almost completely around in his seat, staring with narrowed eyes at me and Rosemond for the better part of fifteen minutes. Finally, I turned my head to Rosemond and said in an undertone, "I think the man in the checked pants recognizes me."

Rosemond didn't look at the man. "It's not you he recognizes."

"You know him?"

The tip of Rosemond's nose was stark white, in contrast to the blush of anger overtaking her face. The *click-clack* of the train helped camouflage our conversation. "He recognizes a whore when he sees one."

"Don't be absurd," I snapped. "You look no different than any other tired, foul-tempered passenger wearing an ill-fitting dress."

Rosemond's expression darkened further, as if insulted by being seen as anything other than desirable.

"You can't have it both ways, Rosie."

She glared at me. "There's only one person in this world allowed to call me *Rosie*."

"Who?"

"Not you."

"Ma, look!" A young boy in the seat behind us yelled and banged on the window. "Eagles!"

In the distance, dozens of birds sat atop misshapen mounds dotting the plain, flapping their wings in protest when new birds would land close by. A few birds alighted on the ground and poked at the mounds from the side.

I inhaled sharply as the vision from the Cheyenne cleansing ceremony returned vividly to my mind. Once cleansed in the river, I hadn't thought much about the vision, so thrilled with regaining my strength and emotional connection to Kindle. When I did think of it, I'd assumed the vision was merely knowledge buried deep within me coming to the fore to set me on the right path. But I'd never seen rotting carcasses of buffalo scattered across the plains. Had the vision been a premonition of things to come? I thought of Camille King, a madam in New York City and the friend who helped me escape. She had appeared to me and her words had woken me from the vision:

Men are pathetically easy to manipulate, to control. It's the women you need to worry about.

I stared at Rosemond as a cold knot of dread settled in my stomach.

"What's wrong?" Rosemond asked.

"Nothing."

My eyes drifted to the window, where mounds of dead buffalo continued to slide by.

"What are they doing?" the boy asked.

"Those aren't eagles, young man, they're buzzards."

The businessman in the checked pants was standing in the aisle, leaning across Rosemond and me to look out the window.

"And those are buffalo carcasses they're eating," he said.

"Buffalo!" the boy said, awed.

"Yep. Shot from a train. Skinners go behind. See?" He pointed ahead, and sure enough there were five wagons loaded with buffalo skins next to five carcasses. The skinners were close enough that we could see they were covered in blood, gore, and sweat.

I leaned back into the seat, chilled to the bone at the sight of the men Cotter Black had threatened to sell me to if I didn't do as he wanted all those months ago. The businessman grinned down on me, his bright eyes lingering on my bosom as if fantasizing about what was beneath the scratchy dark material. "Turn your stomach?"

I glared up at him. "No."

He straightened and looked between me and Rosemond, the same bright leer lighting up his eyes. He held out his hand. "Sean Isaac."

After a pause, Rosemond held out her hand. "Eliza. My sister Helen."

Isaac's face fell. "Eliza. A beautiful dark-haired woman with a face of scars. I was sure your name was Rosemond."

"You've mistaken me for someone else," Rosemond said.

Standing as he was, Isaac held on to the bench in front of us to steady himself against the swaying motion of the train. "That's too bad. I couldn't help but overhear a little of your conversation."

Rosemond tensed but remained silent. I pressed my leg against hers. "A gentleman would hardly admit to eavesdropping on ladies' conversation."

Isaac leaned forward and whispered, "I ain't no gentleman."

"That's quite obvious," I said.

"I can help you with your money problem." Isaac leaned forward and whispered in Rosemond's ear, but loud enough for me to hear. "I have three dollars burning a hole in my pocket."

She stood and moved into the aisle. She stared at the man and without a word turned and made her way out of the back of the carriage. Isaac waited a beat and followed.

I turned and watched her go in stunned silence. Was she accepting his offer so I could drink a cup of coffee?

I laid my head against the window. The sun was high in the sky, but the spring air was brisk. I wrapped my arms around me to control my shaking, as much for laudanum withdrawal as the chill, and closed my eyes. So much for Rosemond's desire to start a new life. I meant it when I told her she looked no different from anyone else on this train. I thought of her as a whore, but my judgment was clouded by the certain knowledge of the fact and my uncertainty about what had passed between Kindle and Rosemond a week before on the riverboat. I didn't want to believe my husband would lie with her, but he was a man, she was a manipulative whore, and to protect my identity he had been selling the idea that I meant no more to him than a paid companion.

Though it pained me to admit it, I had to be fair to the version of Rosemond who'd sat next to me on the train: there was nothing in her demeanor, speech, or comportment to mark her as a lady of the night, and, except for her scars, I doubt Isaac would have recognized her as such. More like he stared at us with wishful thinking, and his hopes were granted by a woman who was broke and knew of no other way to earn money.

I sighed. I couldn't let Rosemond degrade herself because I was thirsty.

I rose, picked up Cora Bayle's carpetbag, and followed. Passengers who'd been practically sitting on top of one another immediately took our bench. I walked across the open-air platform joining the cars into another carriage exactly like ours. A canvas curtain separated the latrine from the seating area. I could easily peek through the edge but did not. Instead, I knocked on the wall to the ladies' side. "Wait yer turn!" said a broad Irish brogue. Not Rosemond. I knocked on the men's wall as someone exited, adjusting his gun belt. The man stared at me with dark brown eyes. A wispy black mustache hung down past his chin. I stepped away and backed through the curtain into the women's latrine. I lost my footing and fell on my bottom, right on the feet of the woman sitting on the shitter.

"What did I tell ya?" she screamed. "Get out."

I scrambled to my feet, apologizing the whole time, grabbed my carpetbag, and went back into the small space between the latrines. The man I'd mistaken for Kindle leaned against the wall, chewing a matchstick. "You have a way of barging in on people, don't ya? Who are you looking for this time?"

I stepped back into the aisle and away from the man. His deliberate insouciance awoke the impression of danger I'd felt the first time in his presence. Halfway down the aisle, I turned and walked away. When I was through to the other train I knocked on the wall next to the women's latrine; when no one answered, I entered. I pressed my free hand to my stomach, swallowed the urge to vomit, and waited for my breathing to return to normal. Panic flooded my chest as memories from months earlier exploded in my head. Cotter Black's face illuminated from below by firelight, his blood oozing onto the red dirt of Palo Duro Canyon, the sound of his voice in my ear. I grabbed my head and squeezed my eyes shut, trying to banish the images. I forced myself to think of Kindle, his smile, the feel of his fingertips like feathers on my skin, the way his eyes darkened with desire in the most inopportune times.

I'll never let anything happen to you.

I opened my eyes and took a few deep breaths. Straightened my shoulders. Kindle wasn't here to protect me, and the last thing I needed to do was turn into a blubbering mess at the hint of a threat. Had the dark-haired man threatened me? No. But he was dangerous, I had no doubt. I needed to find Rosemond, and I needed a weapon.

Not necessarily in that order.

I stared in thought at the ground speeding by beneath the hole that served as the latrine. A knife would be the best weapon, easiest to conceal, but difficult to steal. I had nothing to trade except my medical knowledge. My luck wasn't running hot, so the chances of a woman suddenly going into labor were slim. The train was full of men, which meant gambling and the possibility of violence. Unfortunately, my medical bag was in the trunk in Dunk's possession, or so I hoped. I hadn't seen it since I climbed on the Mississippi River flatboat to escape.

I shook my head in disgust. How far I'd fallen to wish ill on others for my own benefit.

The train slowed and leaned to the right. No doubt being shunted off to a side track to make way for the express train. I exited the latrine and went to find Rosemond, part of me hoping my little fit hadn't made me too late to stop her from a mistake, another part wondering if she'd earned enough for two cups of Arbuckle's.

Sean Isaac found me waiting at the top of the stairs to exit the train, blousing my dress in an attempt to cool down from the hot sweats that had overtaken me.

He leaned against the opposite wall and watched me. "You sick like your sister?"

I glared at him. "Excuse me?"

"The French pox. You got it?"

"No."

He licked his lips and looked me up and down. He jerked his head toward the lavatories and said, "Won't take but a minute. Two dollars, easy money."

I took in Sean Isaac from head to toe, as if considering. He wore a sweat-stained brown felt derby and pants that had once been a bright yellow-and-orange check but were faded and dingy from wear. His waistcoat and jacket were brown, and his collarless shirt was open at the neck, revealing a triangle of chest hair. His teeth were crooked but surprisingly clean. He had a weak chin and thin lips, a combination that my father had always judged harshly. *You can have a weak chin or thin lips, Katie, but both together are the hallmarks of a devious character.*

The brakes squealed as the train shuddered to a stop. I unlatched the chain that served as meager protection from falling down the stairs while the train was moving. I leaned in close to Isaac and let the chain fall. "Two dollars?" I said, and backed away from the stairs.

Isaac stepped forward, his back to the exit. "I'll do three if you start by suc—"

My fist met his nose before he finished his disgusting proposition. He tumbled out of the train and onto the ground. I walked down the stairs, shaking the pain from my hand, and stood next to him. He rolled around, clutching his nose and screaming as blood oozed between his fingers.

"Oh, settle down," I said, crouching next to him.

He pulled his hands away and stared at the blood in shock. "You cunt! You broke my nose!"

"Yes, well, maybe next time you'll keep a civil tongue in your head."

"A civil tongue?"

"You propositioned me and called me a cunt." A crowd had gathered. The women gasped.

"After you punched me in the nose!" I tried to move his hands away. "Don't touch me!"

"I can fix it, if you'll stop acting like a child."

"A child!"

"Wot, didja get beaten up by this little woman?" a man in the crowd said. The men laughed.

"She didn't beat me up." Isaac's voice was nasally.

"Unless you want to sound like that for the rest of your life, you'll let me fix your nose."

"Let her fix it," someone in the crowd said. "Can't make you look much worse."

"But *she* punched me in the nose!"

"You said she didn't," several voices from the crowd argued.

"Yeah, which is it?"

Isaac knew he was caught. I held my hand out to help him sit up. He took it, grudgingly. I felt the sides of his nose and found the break. I positioned my thumbs on either side of his nose and paused. "Have you had this done before?" I asked.

"No, I—ahhh! Bitch!"

I stood quickly and backed away. The men in the crowd moved forward. "None of that. This little lady helped you."

Isaac glared at me, wiping the blood from his mouth with the back of his hand. One man helped him stand and dusted his backside off. He slapped the man's hand away.

"That'll be three dollars."

"What for?"

"Fixing your nose, of course."

Isaac opened his mouth and stepped forward. Cotter Black's doppelgänger stepped between us. "Pay the woman. She provided a service, she deserves remuneration." When Isaac

paused, the dark-haired man seemed to grow in stature, though he didn't move an inch.

Isaac reached into the pocket of his waistcoat, pulled out three silver coins, and slapped them into my outstretched hand. He turned away with ill grace and the onlookers moved off to find amusement somewhere else.

The stranger turned to me and held out Cora Bayle's paisley brocade carpetbag. His thick, square-nailed fingers were embedded with the brown leather dust of a man who spent his life in the saddle. The thick hair covering the back of his hand couldn't camouflage the map of rope burns and scars. "This yours?"

"Yes." I lifted my gaze to his face and forced my voice to be steady. "Thank you, Mr...."

"Salter." He dipped his head, touched his hat, and walked across the muddy wagon track to a tent with the word SALOON painted on a broken board hanging over the opening.

The entire town consisted of a saloon, a café, and the depot, all housed in dirty, drooping canvas tents, and a corral containing three horses. Down the track a piece was the rotting and rusting remains of one of the notorious hell-on-wheels temporary towns set up to support the building of the transcontinental railroad. On a slight rise behind the town graveyard stood a burial ground with five visible wooden crosses, leaning southward from the relentless northern winds that rushed across the flat land. It was the most depressing town I'd yet come across in my travels. I supposed there was little money to be made from the emigrant train, and the more ambitious businessmen had long left for more prosperous railroad towns.

I stared at the three dollars in my hand. It wasn't enough to buy a horse and tack to return to Kindle, not that I would want to travel across Nebraska without a gun or a partner. I

dismissed the idea of approaching Salter as soon as it entered. My misjudged trust of Cora Bayle was too fresh. I'd much rather take my chance with the volatile woman I knew than the madman I didn't. Rosemond was clever, and dangerous, but so was I. When I had my wits about me, we were evenly matched.

Returning to Kindle would have to wait a while longer.

CHAPTER

7

I found Rosemond throwing dice with five men in the back of the baggage car.

All six faced the back wall, allowing me to observe without being noticed. Rosemond was in the center, of course, her dark hair coming down from her bun in soft tendrils. She threw the dice against the wall and raised her hands in victory when they settled. The men groaned good-naturedly while Rosemond raked in the small pile of coins. A large Negro noticed me and nodded in my direction. "Wanna join, miss?"

Rosemond turned and saw me. Her face was flushed with happiness and pleasure, making her look almost innocent and giving me a glimpse of who she might have been before life set her on the path of being a whore.

Of the woman she wanted to be now.

"Hello, Sissy." She raised an eyebrow and smirked. "What do you have there?"

I looked down at the bottle I held in one hand. "Milk." I held up the hand holding the carpetbag and a folded handkerchief. "A chunk of cheddar cheese and two thick slices of apple cake."

Rosemond gathered her money and put it in her purse. "You're quitting?" the Negro asked. "Aren't gonna give us a chance to win it back?"

"I need it worse than you, Jethro."

"Oh, I doubt that," the man laughed.

"If I stayed, I would clean you out, and you know it."

The man shook his head. "I do. You're the luckiest woman I ever met."

"Skill, Jethro. Skill."

The men closed in the spot in the semicircle Rosemond vacated and forgot about us almost immediately. Jethro nodded, smiled, and touched his flat hat.

"How much did you win?" I asked.

"Ten dollars."

"You turned two bits into ten dollars?"

"The better question is, where did you get money for that?" She looked at my loot.

"I fixed a man's broken nose."

Rosemond opened the handkerchief, picked off a corner of cake, and ate it. She closed her eyes and groaned. "That's good."

"You told Isaac you had syphilis?"

She shrugged. "It was either that or make a scene. I'm lucky he's one of the few smart enough to care." She took the milk and drank. She wiped the cream from her upper lip and said, "Milk? You aren't going temperance on me, are you, Sissy?"

"Don't call me Sissy."

"Don't call me Rosie."

"Deal."

Rosemond drank from the bottle again.

"I couldn't remember the last time I drank milk, and it looked delicious," I said by way of explanation.

Rosemond gave the bottle back to me and said, grudgingly, "It is."

"You're flush. You buy the whisky."

"Do you think we have time?"

I shrugged. "I heard we have thirty minutes."

She agilely hopped down and watched me stumble on the last step, but I found my balance before I fell.

Rosemond laughed.

"I have my hands full. You could've offered to help."

"And miss seeing that bit of gracefulness? Not on your life." She put her arm through mine. "You don't like being teased, do you?"

"It depends on who's doing the teasing."

"Hmm. Kindle was a great one for teasing."

I inhaled sharply.

"Oh, stop bristling every time I mention him," Rosemond said. "I fucked him, but he married you. You win." She studied the handmade sign above the tent saloon door. "Atrocious lettering." She released my arm and turned to face me. "When we meet up with Dunk at Cheyenne, I'll cable a friend in Saint Louis and get news of Kindle for you. Put your mind at ease." She ducked into the tent, and I followed.

Lanterns hung on the two poles down the center of the tent, illuminating the fact that we were the only women among a group of about ten men sitting at five tables and standing at the makeshift bar. Salter sat alone at a table in the back, a bottle of whisky before him, watching everything through hooded eyes. Rosemond went directly for the one empty table and sat down, seemingly oblivious to our obtrusiveness. She lifted her hand to the bartender, who stared at us for a long moment before coming around the bar and over to our table.

"Women ain't allowed."

"Our money spends as well as theirs. A bottle, two glasses." Rosemond put a dollar on the table and looked up at the man.

His thick mustache twitched with indecision and irritation. A man trying to scrape a living in a dying town couldn't be choosy about where his coin came from, but the man in him bristled at the idea of a female invading the sanctity of a man's saloon. The man opened his mouth but Rosemond pulled out another dollar and said in a loud voice, "The next round's on me."

The men murmured their assent and the bartender picked up the coins.

I held my hand out to Rosemond. "Give me some of your winnings," I said.

"So you can make your escape? I don't think so."

I leaned across the table. "Don't you think I already considered that with my own money?"

She narrowed her eyes. "Why didn't you go?"

"Three dollars won't buy a horse and I'm not stupid enough to travel across the plains alone." I motioned to her to give me the money.

"Why?"

"I spent a dollar and got this. You spent two dollars on whisky. You need me to make sure you don't go broke before we get to Cheyenne."

"It won't matter. Dunk will be there with our trunk and money."

"You weren't so sure an hour ago."

"Every station we come to and he's not there increases the chances he's in Cheyenne. We were always getting off at Cheyenne. Taking the train south to Boulder from there. He'll be there, lost as a lamb, most like."

"Why Boulder?"

"I have a friend there."

"A man?"

She didn't answer.

"Why 'Eliza'?"

She studied me for a moment before replying. "It's part of my full name."

"Rosemond Elizabeth Barclay?"

"Close enough."

The bartender pulled a bottle from the shelves behind the bar and brought it with two glasses to our table. "Women buying men drinks," a man at the bar said. "Don't that beat all? Guess that's a change for a couple a' whores like you."

The murmuring crowd went quiet and Sean Isaac turned to face us. Even in the low light I could see the bruises around his eyes. Dried blood rimmed his nostrils.

"Better keep a civil tongue, mister," Salter said, "or the little lady will break your nose again."

The bartender put the whisky and glasses on the table and addressed Rosemond. "You broke his nose?"

"No," she said, perplexed.

I arranged the cheese and cake on the table between us and asked the bartender, "Can I get a larger glass? For my milk. And a knife for the cheese?"

He grasped the extra shot glass, dragged it along the table as if it were a great effort to pick it up, and returned to the bar.

"You broke his nose?" Rosemond said. "Why?"

"He propositioned me."

She leaned forward. "I can't protect you if you insist on making a spectacle of yourself every time we get off the train."

"I didn't make a spectacle."

A man called from across the bar, "How's your hand, Blondie? Looks a mite swollen."

"My hand is fine, thank you."

Rosemond raised her eyebrows and twisted her mouth into

74

an expression easy enough to decipher: *Didn't make a spectacle, did you?*

"There's two kinds of women in the West: whores and wives," Isaac said.

"There's also whores who want to be wives."

"And mail-order brides."

"And spinsters looking to be wives."

Rosemond and I stared at each other across the table. Her expression was fixed with good humor, but I could see the irritation and anger beneath. I almost pitied her as I saw her realize that what would hold her back wasn't that she was a whore, but that she was a woman.

The bartender stabbed my cheese with the knife, shocking Rosemond and me back into our chairs. We looked up at the man. His displeasure with serving us was clear. Rosemond poured a shot of whisky and drank it, her eyes never leaving the bartender's dirty face. "Thank you," I said, pouring milk into my glass. I cut a chunk from the cheese and served Rosemond. The bartender moved away.

Rosemond drank three more shots in quick succession.

"You sure drink like a whore," Isaac said to Rosemond. "Does that make her your wife?" Isaac said, motioning to me. The men laughed.

I leaned forward and placed my hand over Rosemond's to stop her from taking another shot. "You're right. I made a mistake. Let's go."

"No." She removed her hand and drank again.

I leaned back and shook my head. "I thought you were smarter than this."

She set the shot glass down with a click. "Than what?"

"As I said earlier, you cannot have it both ways. If you want respectability, you've got to give up the freedoms of a whore."

"Freedoms?" She laughed.

"Playing dice in the back of a train. Drinking in a saloon." Whisky sloshed onto the table as she poured another drink. "Stumbling drunk out of the saloon." She threw the whisky back and poured again.

I couldn't drag her out of the saloon, and I couldn't leave her alone. Resigned to seeing through whatever point Rosemond was trying to make, I peeled the waxy red rind from the bright yellow cheese, carved a chunk from the block, and ate it slowly, savoring the tanginess on my tongue. I drank my milk and ate half of my cake in silence as Rosemond brooded and drank her bottle. I portioned out more of the cheese and half of her cake and placed it in front of her, folding the remainder in the handkerchief for the rest of the journey. I pulled her bottle to me and corked it. I sat back in my chair and watched Rosemond twist her empty shot glass around on the whisky-dampened table. It was somewhat comforting to see Rosemond brought low. I could let her drink herself into a stupor, steal her money, and head back to Kindle. If her eyes were any indication, she wasn't used to drinking whisky. Surprising, considering her profession.

Despite my antipathy for Rosemond, I couldn't forget she'd saved me on the Mississippi, and killed Cora to protect me. I couldn't help but admire her drive to start over, nor could I deny the part of me that felt a camaraderie with any woman who pushed against society's expectations.

"Do you know how I started my practice in New York?" I asked.

"Treating whores," she said. When I jerked my head back in surprise, she said, "Your story's been pretty well canvassed across the papers. I wasn't sure that tidbit was true, but apparently so."

I nodded. "I'd graduated from Syracuse Medical College, at the top of my class, and was scraping the bottom of my savings account at the end. I moved back to the city to start my practice but couldn't find a patient. Every doctor in town shunned me, told lies about me so no one trusted me to take their temperature, let alone deliver their children or remove a tumor."

"Even the other women docs? There aren't many, but you aren't the only one."

I tensed and felt my face flush with chagrin. Rosemond had stopped twirling her glass. I pulled it toward me, uncorked the bottle, poured a shot, hated that my hand shook. "I wanted to prove myself equal to the men. I wasn't interested in help from the Blackwells, though they offered. Once. I burned that bridge well and good."

"I'll be frank, La—Helen. It's a wonder you got as far as you have, what with your arrogance."

"Thank you for telling me what I already know. I suffered for my hubris at the time." I paused. And later. Would I have fled New York City if I'd had female allies in the medical profession? Would the support of the Blackwells and others have helped me at all? I would never know the answer to those questions. I cleared my throat and continued my story. "I treated families in the slums, but they couldn't pay. Oh, they tried, God love them. Their meager payments fed Maureen—she was my maid—and me more than once. But it wasn't enough. And I wanted *more*, you see. I hadn't endured the ridicule and resentment of medical school, of the medical establishment in the city, to become a poor man's doctor. I would only prove my point if I was the doctor of choice for the upper class." I poured another shot.

"Problem was, we were starving. Me and Maureen." I chuckled, stared at the amber-colored liquid, and threw it back. "I'd delivered a baby for an Italian woman and was walking home with a half a loaf of bread and a small bottle of olive oil for my trouble. That night, we wouldn't starve. But it was the end of October and we didn't have the money for coal."

"Why didn't you sell your mother's necklace?" Rosemond interrupted.

I smiled and nodded. "Excellent question. Selling my mother's jewelry would have meant I'd failed, that I couldn't do it on my own. Luckily, a man tumbled down the front steps of Joe Fisher's boardinghouse at the right moment." I poured more whisky for me and Rosemond and drank my shot. "We didn't freeze or starve that winter. The following spring, I got my toehold in Washington Square and my practice flourished."

Rosemond clapped slowly. "Bravo, and look at you now."

"I'm right back where I started, taking care of a whore to survive." I leaned forward. "What's your story, *Eliza*? How did you end up as a high-priced whore on the Mississippi?"

A low rumble vibrated the ground and in the distance a train whistle sounded. The men finished off their whisky, tossed coins on the table, and rose to leave.

"The express," I said.

Rosemond slapped the table with her hand. "Thank God I won't have to listen to you blabber on anymore."

"You're a mean drunk, aren't you?"

Rosemond rose shakily to her feet. "I'm worse when I'm sober."

I gathered our meager provisions and stood as well. I placed the leftover food in the carpetbag, pulled out a notebook, and held it out to Rosemond.

She narrowed her eyes. "What's this?"

"A sketchbook. It's on the small side, but the shebang's selection was limited. There's a pencil inside." Rosemond stared at it as if it were a snake, and a bright blush rushed up her neck and across her face. I shook it at her. "It's more for me than you, so you'll stop clicking that damn coin purse open and closed."

She took the notebook with a sly smile, more comfortable with impertinence than vulnerability.

Salter stopped at our table. A short cigar had replaced the matchstick in the corner of his mouth. Rosemond appraised him from head to toe, but Salter kept his eyes on me. "You need to stay on the train till your destination."

"Why?"

"Two women traveling alone. It's safer to stay with the families." He touched his hat, turned, and left.

Rosemond's gaze followed him out the door, and I palmed the knife off the table and slid it up the sleeve of my dress.

CHAPTER 8

Eighteen hours and twenty-three stops later, we pulled into Cheyenne, Wyoming, an exhausted, short-tempered, putrid-smelling mass of humanity. A good portion of the passengers tumbled out of the train. The relief of those remaining was short-lived when they saw the platform teeming with a new group waiting to board, set on California. The tall station clock in the middle of the platform chimed six a.m.

Rosemond stopped on the bottom train step, scanning the crowd for Dunk. I stood behind her and looked, but didn't remember Dunk clearly enough to be a good spotter.

"He'll be sitting by the depot, our trunk at his feet, waiting. Mark my words."

Rosemond had said it so many times I got the feeling she was trying to convince herself of its truth rather than believing it herself. "There!" I said, pointing down the platform to a man in a bowler hat sitting on a bench.

Someone pushed us from behind. "Come on, lady. Get a move on!"

I nudged Rosemond and she stepped down. I took her hand. "This way."

When we got within sight of the man, he stood and went

forward to meet someone else at the same moment we saw he was white. Rosemond dropped my hand and turned around, searching. She walked to the end of the platform and was lost in the crowd. I started to follow but stopped. I looked in the opposite direction. The crowd was thinning quickly. If I was going to slip away from Rosemond, this was my opportunity.

I caught sight of Rosemond searching the platform and pushed aside all thoughts of escape. Her eyes were wide with a frantic worry, and I knew she expected the worst, which meant destitution for her, and God only knew what for Dunk.

I waited at the edge of the platform. "Do you see him?" she asked.

"No. There's a hotel." I pointed to a long two-story building built almost on top of the railroad tracks. "He's probably waiting for us there."

Rosemond grabbed my hand and pulled me toward the hotel.

The inside of the Union Pacific Hotel was caught between its rough-hewn origin and its quest to be first class. A polished mahogany front desk sat on a plank floor, a ceramic spittoon on the floor at one end, a dented tin one at the other end. Workers were replacing metal candle sconces with gaslights. Off to the side of the lobby, the dining room was half full of cowboys, miners, and businessmen eating breakfast. The smell of bacon, eggs, and biscuits made my stomach rumble. An emigrant family from the train had wandered into the hotel: the man loaded down with bags, the woman holding an exhausted child in her arms, and two other children who had been some of the more energetic at Grand Island but were now listless and vacant-eyed. The parents looked around the hotel with longing but spoke together briefly and went out the front door.

As I took the scene in I realized Rosemond and I were the only women in the room.

Rosemond moved to the front desk. The clerk looked at us and smiled. "May I help you?"

"Yes, I'm looking for my employee. His name is Duncan. Large Negro." Rosemond lifted her hand a foot above her head.

The clerk's pleasant expression darkened. "Yes, Duncan. He was here but he isn't any longer."

"Can you tell me where he went?"

"The jail down the street."

"Jail? What happened?"

I watched Rosemond closely as the man answered. "He pulled a knife at a craps game last night. He took issue with losing his money."

Rosemond's pockmarked face paled, but she kept her smile fixed. "Dunk never was good at throwing the bones."

"Was anyone hurt?" I asked.

"I'd say so. Killed a white man."

Rosemond shifted and I put my arm around her waist to hold her up. "Was Duncan staying here?" I asked.

"No. We don't serve niggers."

Rosemond opened her mouth, but I squeezed her waist and spoke first. "My sister and I need a room for the night. Do you have one available?"

"One, though it's little more than a closet. We're full up."

"Fine. How much?"

"Five dollars."

"For a closet?" Rosemond said.

The clerk shrugged and looked behind us. "I imagine one of those cowboys behind you'll take it."

"We'll take it," I said.

"No, we won't," Rosemond said. "Come on, Helen."

I smiled at the clerk, raised a finger, and said, "We want the room. Excuse us, for one minute." I pulled Rosemond aside. I lowered my voice but didn't curb my anger. "Enough. We're here, and almost destitute. We need to talk about what we're going to do." Rosemond opened her mouth again, but I raised my finger. "You want my help going legitimate, I have a say in what we do." I felt the knife hidden up my sleeve. "We have been traveling for two days and I'm dirty and exhausted." I'd lied to myself that the body odor I smelled on the train was a miasma from the mass of people. In truth, I knew from the experience with my father that it was I who smelled, my body secreting the remnants of the opiate.

"Dunk needs to know I'm here, and I need to figure out what I can do to help him." She paused. "If anything."

"I am not going anywhere until I clean up. Do what you want, but I'm taking the room."

"Your two bits won't cover it."

"Good thing I lifted your winnings while you were passed out between Buda and Kearney Junction." I walked to the counter and smiled at the clerk. "We'll take the room."

The man narrowed his eyes at us but pushed the hotel log toward me. "Sign in."

Rosemond watched me sign "Mrs. Helen Graham and Miss Eliza Ryan" in a sloppy script and push it back to the clerk, who handed me a brass key. "Top floor, end of the hall. Facilities at the end of each hall."

"Thank you."

"If you want to see that nigger you better hurry. There was talk of hanging him at dawn."

"Tomorrow?" Rosemond asked.

The clerk glanced at the clock above the door. "No, twenty minutes ago."

Rosemond's face paled, and she turned and ran out of the hotel. I followed.

The sheriff's office was one of the few stone buildings in town, asserting the town leaders' commitment to law and order as well as the protection of their investments. Two deputies holding rifles stood in front of the door. Men milled around nearby, waiting restively. The sound of hammering punctuated the early-morning quiet.

Rosemond stopped at the sight of the armed guards. She closed her eyes and inhaled deeply a few times. She rotated her head in small circles, opened her eyes, and smiled. Her expression transformed from terror to provocative, though I could still see the fear on the edges. She walked forward and stopped in front of the guards.

"We're here to see the prisoner," she said.

The guards made no secret of assessing us from head to toe. My vanity was slightly wounded when their gazes traveled quickly, and uninterestedly, over me but lingered on Rosemond.

"What for?"

"We're friends of his."

"Are you?"

"I've known the prisoner since we were children," Rosemond said. She placed her small, soft hand on the guard's arm. "Please let me see him one last time." Her voice trembled slightly.

The guard spit tobacco juice on the ground and surveyed the crowd with narrowed eyes. "Best be quick. Not sure how long this crowd will be quiet." He opened the door.

"Gentry!" A fat, red-faced man sitting at a desk stood as we walked in. "I told you no more visitors."

"They're friends of the prisoner," he said, and closed the door.

"Are you the sheriff?" Rosemond asked.

"Yep. Enoch Hall. Gentry shouldn't have let you in. It's not safe for ladies to be here right now."

"Sheriff Hall." Rosemond held out her hand. "I'm Eliza Ryan, and this is my sister, Helen. We're here to see your prisoner, Duncan March."

I perused the bulletin board of Wanted posters. There mine was, front and center. I flushed and turned away, keeping my face averted from the sheriff.

"What business do you have with that big buck?"

I glanced at Rosemond, whose smile never wavered, but her voice cooled. "He works for me."

"Does he?"

"He was a slave of my father's and after the war he came to work with me. He helped me run a boardinghouse in Saint Louis."

"Did he?" Hall looked Rosemond up and down. "We have a couple of those in town ourselves. You come out here to start your own?"

"No. Passing through. We got separated from Dunk in Grand Island. My sister and I missed the train. We've been checking for him at every stop. Imagine our surprise when we find him in jail in Cheyenne."

"Well, he killed a white man."

"So we heard. When is his trial?"

Hall laughed. "Twenty men witnessed it. He'd already be strung up if there was a big enough tree within fifty miles." He jerked his thumb. "They're reinforcing the gallows right now. He's uncommon big."

Rosemond placed her fingertips lightly on Hall's desk. "Surely there's something that can be done, Sheriff. Jail time? A fine? A promise to leave town and never return? As you probably noticed, Dunk is a simple-minded man. I've known him his entire life and he's never hurt a soul."

"Oh, I find that hard to believe. A big buck like that working for a beautiful woman like you? I'm sure he's had cause now and then to hurt a man."

Rosemond's shoulders straightened as she inhaled. I stepped forward and intertwined my arm with Rosemond's. "May we see him?" I said.

Hall studied us, his eyes lingering on me. I thanked God for the first time that my hair had lightened so much as to make the photo taken of me four years earlier almost unrecognizable. Age, weather, and want had transformed my smooth, round face into one with sharp cheekbones and fine lines around my eyes and mouth. The dark circles under my eyes and the paleness of my complexion from my body adjusting to life without laudanum no doubt disguised me further. I was horrified at the visage I presented, but I held his gaze steadily.

"You sick?"

"Recovering, thank you." I cursed my body for the hot flash that was coming on, which Enoch Hall would probably mistake for embarrassment. Why couldn't it have been the chills, instead?

Hall lost interest in me. He turned his head and yelled, "Webster!"

A middle-aged man shuffled into the front room. He wore a gray slouch hat and a double holster. "Yep."

"These ladies want to visit the nigger."

Webster worked his mouth, turned his head, and spit a stream of tobacco juice perfectly into the spittoon next to the wall with a solid *ding*. "Yep." He turned and walked back into the room he'd emerged from. Rosemond and I followed.

The back of the sheriff's office was twice as large as the

front. Four cells with small, barred open windows set high in the stone walls were divided down the middle by a narrow walkway. The sound of the crowd outside was more prominent back here. A heavy fog of fear hung in the air.

At the far end, a man sat on a chair outside the cell, head bowed, his pale hands gripping large black ones. Beneath the man's murmured prayer, I heard Dunk sobbing, softly. A woman stood next to the preacher, head bowed. Rosemond made a strange, strangled sound.

"What's wrong?" I whispered.

She stared at the tableau with a pale, stricken expression on her face, her chest heaving with small, sharp breaths. "Rosemond." I put my hand on her arm and shook her. She looked at me, her eyes unfocused. "Are you ill?"

As she stared at me, her eyes cleared and her color returned. "No. I'm fine."

The preacher said, "Amen," but kept his head close to the cell. He murmured to Dunk as the woman lifted her head and saw us for the first time. Her dark hair was pulled back into a tight bun, but tendrils of curls managed to escape, giving her head a bristly look.

"Who is that?" Rosemond said to the deputy, her eyes fixed on the couple.

Webster spoke up. "Preacher and his wife. Reverend Bright. Nice fella. Not your typical Methodist."

The Reverend stood and released Dunk's hands. He stepped back and let his wife move forward, picked up his chair, and followed. Reverend Bright's wife walked past us with a brief nod.

"Portia," Reverend Bright said, a little sharply. The woman stopped at the door and turned. The Reverend motioned for her, and she came forward. He held out his hand to Rosemond. "I'm Reverend Bright, and this is my wife, Portia."

Rosemond took his hand briefly. "I'm Eliza Ryan. This is my sister, Helen Graham."

Portia Bright's eyebrows lifted and her gaze shifted from Rosemond to me, revealing a pair of clear blue eyes, with a brilliant orange ring around the irises. Mesmerized by her eyes, I barely heard the conversation between Rosemond and the Reverend.

"You must be the woman Dunk mentioned," Reverend Bright said.

"Yes. We got separated at Grand Island. Surely there's something we can do to help him," Rosemond said.

"I'm afraid not," Reverend Bright said. "The town leaders think it's a clear case, despite the fact that the other man pulled a gun on him. If Mr. Duncan were a white man, it would have been termed self-defense and that would be the end of it. Since he's a Negro, they're going to hang him."

Webster spit into a nearby spittoon. "You let one nigger get away with killing a white man, they'll all think they can do it. You got five minutes to say your piece to him." Webster nodded toward the cell. Rosemond moved down the hall.

Reverend Bright smiled at me and ran his hand over his balding head. "You haven't visited before?"

"We've only arrived in town. Dunk stayed on the train while Eliza and I got out for food and drink. One thing led to another, and we missed the train," I said.

"Where are you heading?"

"Boulder."

"Indeed? That's where I met Portia," the Reverend said, gazing with affection at his wife.

"Don't you want to say your good-byes?" Portia Bright cut in. Her singular eyes flamed with animosity.

I jerked my head back in surprise and felt my face redden.

As Portia glared at me, I realized my mistake. Of course she was offended by the way I'd gaped at her earlier. "Of course. Excuse me."

When I arrived at the cell, Rosemond and Dunk went silent. Dunk's eyes were red and tears streaked down his cheeks. "I didn't mean to do it. You gotta help me."

"What were you doing gambling, anyway?"

Dunk looked down at the floor. "I was waiting for you on the platform, and I heard this man talking about a game. I was bored, and thought one game wouldn't hurt. Help pass the time."

"How much of my money did you lose?"

Dunk wouldn't lift his eyes.

"Did you lose my lot in Boulder?"

Dunk nodded. The men outside started whooping and hollering. "You gotta help me, Miss Rose."

"Of course I will. Where's the trunk?"

"I checked it at the depot. The sheriff took the ticket."

Rosemond glanced down at the end of the hall. The Reverend and his wife were gone. Webster leaned back in the chair, reading a newspaper. There was a banging outside, like wood on wood.

"BRING HIM OUT, SHERIFF!"

Webster folded his paper and unhurriedly went into the main room.

Rosemond patted Dunk's hand. "Don't you worry. I'll get you out of here."

"How?"

"You let me worry about that."

"Rosemond," I said, but she'd turned and walked away.

I heard Dunk say, "I'm sorry," as I followed.

"Tell those men to go away," Rosemond said to the sheriff.

The Reverend was at the front window with his wife, who looked terrified. Holding a rifle in his hand, Webster stepped out of the office and closed the door behind him.

"Settle down, settle down," Webster said.

"Bring that nigger out here!" a man yelled.

"And why would I do that? He ain't had his trial." The sheriff and Deputy Webster laughed.

Ignoring the crowd outside, Rosemond sat on the edge of the sheriff's desk and smiled as if they had all the time in the world. She touched Sheriff Hall's arm lightly and said, "What can I do to set my friend free?"

The sheriff's eyes raked over Rosemond with a leer of understanding. "There's only so much I can do."

"You can at least ensure he has a fair trial. I do believe the law requires it." She squeezed his arm. "My gratitude would know no bounds."

Portia shot forward, surprising the sheriff, who reluctantly took his eyes off Rosemond. "Sheriff, this has gone far enough. Do your duty and send this crowd away this instant. Duncan deserves a trial as much as the next man." Her face was flushed and her eyes blazed with indignation.

Reverend Bright, astonished at his wife, recovered himself and stepped forward. "Portia is correct, Enoch. Send the crowd away. Do you want Cheyenne known for mob justice or law and order?"

Rosemond studied the preacher's wife, who kept her eyes steadily on the sheriff, as if her undivided attention would will him to do as she bid.

The door burst open and pandemonium broke loose. Men carrying rifles and yelling obscenities flooded the small office and made their way to the cell. The deputies and sheriff did their best but couldn't stem the tide of the mob's bloody enthusiasm. Reverend Bright pulled Portia and me away from Hall's desk and into the far corner before diving into the crowd, entreating them to stop.

"Where is she?" Portia said, panicked.

Rosemond was nowhere to be found. I moved forward and pushed through the crowd to the edge of the desk. Relief swept over me when I didn't see her prone form on the floor. Above the cacophony, I heard a female voice. "No, please! Don't take him!"

Two men dragged Dunk between them, his mouth bloody, his eyes unfocused. Rosemond held on to the arm of one of the men. He tried to shake her off but she held fast. "Don't! Please stop!" Another man lifted his rifle and hit Rosemond on the temple. She went limp and collapsed in a heap. I lunged forward, but Portia beat me to her, throwing her body over Rosemond's. The men continued on around us, like a herd of cows being driven around an obstacle.

The Reverend followed the crowd, his entreaties falling on deaf ears. Soon the office was empty, save us. Portia held an unconscious Rosemond in her arms. I dabbed the handkerchief Rosemond gave me on the train against the cut on her head. Through the open door we heard clearly the loud cheer from the chair. Portia sobbed. "It's best she's unconscious."

"Yes."

I stood and went to the door. Whoops and hollers of all sorts of vile comments assaulted my ears. I glanced back at Portia and Rosemond. Yes, it was better that Rosemond would not witness the death of her friend. I moved toward the spectacle.

"Where are you—" Portia's voice was soon lost amid the clamor of the crowd. Dozens more than had stormed the office gathered around the gallows, with more and more people arriving by the minute. Women, children, men. Old and young. I walked into the crowd, being jostled forward from one person to another, until I was near the front. I looked up at Dunk, hands tied behind his back, a noose being tightened around his neck. Mostly unconscious from the blows to his head, he leaned into the man holding him steady while another tightened the noose around his neck. The man holding him slapped Dunk's face, waking him. He looked around, confused, then realized what was happening. His terror-filled eyes searched the crowd for Rosemond before falling on me. I held his gaze, fully aware that his fate rested squarely on my shoulders. He knew as well as I did that I could do nothing to save him. His face hardened into a mask of hatred.

The hangman released the trapdoor and Dunk fell to his death.

The show was over, but not the celebration of it. The crowd faced away from the gallows and toward the photographer who had set up on a rooftop opposite. I watched from the front of the sheriff's office, disgusted with the spectacle and the urge to chronicle every event, no matter how abhorrent or evil. I cursed Matthew Brady and his battlefield photography, and knew that photographs such as this would only become more common as photographers like William Soule traveled the West.

I rubbed my queasy stomach and glanced over my shoulder in the direction of the office where I'd left Portia and Rosemond. I couldn't avoid facing Rosemond and the accusation and blame I knew would be in her expression. And anger. She couldn't be angrier than I was at myself. One more death attributed to my hubris. Would Death ever stop following me?

I propelled myself forward, determined to meet Rosemond's anger and do whatever I could to atone for Dunk's death. I was making a mental list of what I needed to do—attend to Rosemond's wound, inquire about Dunk's funeral, convince the sheriff to release the trunk to us, get Rosemond back to the hotel to rest—when I entered the office and saw Rosemond leaning against the sheriff's desk, pale-faced and shaky. Portia stood near, reaching out toward Rosemond to dab the handkerchief against her wound. They looked startled, as if I had caught them in the middle of a secret conversation.

Rosemond straightened, hope in her eyes and expression. I shook my head slightly and she slumped again. Portia reached out as if to catch her, but Rosemond moved away, toward me. She opened her arms and pulled me into a strong embrace. Brief astonishment at this unexpected reaction—I'd expected anger and a good slap across the face—was softened to compassion when I realized she was crying. I tentatively wrapped my arms around her. I'd offered condolences to family in my time as a doctor, but I couldn't remember the last person I'd embraced in grief. It was foreign, and awkward. Portia watched us closely, still holding the bloody handkerchief. Rosemond, feeling my lack of response, squeezed me and said in my ear, "Sister," to remind me of the role I needed to play. I held Rosemond tighter, wondering how much longer the embrace needed to last, when the Reverend and Sheriff Enoch Hall walked through the door. It was a convenient excuse to release Rosemond.

When I looked at her closely, I was alarmed. Her vacant eyes wavered and I feared she would swoon, and soon. I knew she wouldn't want to faint in front of these strangers. "We need to get you to the hotel," I said. I gently took her elbow, but she pulled away.

"You took a ticket from the prisoner, Sheriff?" she said.

"What happened to your head?" Sheriff Hall asked.

"It's nothing. The ticket?"

"Anything in the condemned man's possession becomes public property."

Rosemond sidled up to the fat man and touched his shoulder. "It's the claim ticket for my trunk, you see, which I left in Dunk's safekeeping."

"Can't trust a nigger with something like that," the sheriff said.

"I don't think—" the Reverend started.

"Obviously," Rosemond said. She leaned against Hall's desk. "Dunk gambled my money away last night. So, you see, all my sister and I have is what's in my trunk. It's worth nothing to you, but to us it's invaluable." Her soft and vulnerable voice worked its charms on the sheriff, but Portia grunted in disgust. I suspected Rosemond's tone was due more to a concussion than an attempt at charm.

"Well, you've got a point. Opened it up, o' course. Didn't rightly know what some of it was."

Rosemond smiled beautifully at Hall. "I'm a painter, Sheriff."

"Are you? Portraits and the like?"

"Yes, though I will need to make my living painting signs. For the new businesses, you see."

"A beautiful woman like you doesn't need to be standing on a ladder painting words on a building."

"I need to feed myself and my sister."

"I imagine there's plenty of people hereabouts would like to have their picture painted."

"You think so?"

Hall patted her hand. "You leave it to me."

"Do you know people in Boulder?" Portia Bright said to the sheriff. Hall and Rosemond turned to look at her. "Your *sister* said you were headed to Boulder."

Rosemond's brown eyes cleared enough to critically study

Portia Bright, any appreciation for Portia's aid in her time of need apparently forgotten. "Yes, that was the original plan." She turned her attention back to the sheriff. "But one new town is as good as another. Isn't that right, Helen?"

"They all seem shockingly similar to me," I said.

"There you have it." Rosemond straightened. "Would you have the trunk sent to the Union Pacific Hotel?"

"Of course. Right away."

"We need to make arrangements for Duncan's funeral. Please take him down from the gallows so his body can be prepared."

"Oh, I think he needs to be up there a little longer. Remind people of the consequences of killing a man."

"Remind Negroes of their place, you mean," Portia said.

Sheriff Hall shrugged.

I stepped forward, readying for an argument. Rosemond placed her hand on my arm and moved in front of me. "Thank you, Sheriff. Please send word when we can take Duncan's body. Reverend, will you perform the ceremony?"

"Of course."

Rosemond nodded her thanks and turned her attention back to Sheriff Hall. "I would like to paint your portrait, as a token of my thanks for returning my trunk, and your attention to releasing Duncan's body as soon as possible."

"Oh, well," the sheriff blustered. "Never sat for a portrait before."

"It will give us the chance to get to know each other better."

The sheriff's face reddened further. "I'd like that."

"Then it's settled." Rosemond turned and, with a nod to the Reverend and another survey of Portia Bright, left the office.

She waited for me outside the door. Despite the warm morning sun, a chill raced across my body. I hugged myself against it. She looked across me in the direction of the gallows, which was thankfully out of sight. Her expression hardened, but she wouldn't look at me.

"Let me see." I reached out to inspect the bleeding wound on her temple.

She held up her hand. "Don't," she said, and walked away.

CHAPTER
9

An hour later, I returned to our closet-sized room, rubbing my wet hair with a thin towel. Rosemond lay curled in a ball on the bed, where I'd left her. I tiptoed into the room and closed the door quietly. The wardrobe door creaked when I opened it, the noise deafening in the quiet room. I placed my soiled dress in the bottom of the wardrobe until I could figure out how to wash it and hang it dry and closed the door quickly.

The entire room was full of loud obstacles: the uneven floorboards; the lid to Rosemond's trunk that had been delivered, as the sheriff promised, by a hulking man moments after we arrived in our room; the bed when I sat down.

"I'm not asleep," Rosemond said, her voice muffled.

"I was trying to be quiet."

She didn't reply.

My medical bag sat on the single chair in the room. When I opened Rosemond's trunk I hadn't been sure the soft leather case would be within. I removed a small bottle of carbolic and sprinkled a few drops into the water basin before dropping my instruments and thread in to sterilize them. I wet a cloth in the basin and squeezed out the excess. I maneuvered myself between the trunk and the end of the bed and around to Rosemond's side. I knelt down. "Will you let me see your wound now?"

Rosemond turned onto her back. Blood was smeared on the pillow where her head had rested. Soft scabs had formed over the one-inch gash in the center of a tender purple bruise on her left temple. I touched the wet cloth lightly against it, and Rosemond winced. "That stings."

"It's supposed to. I need to stitch it up."

"Will it hurt?"

"I can go downstairs and buy a fifth of whisky—"

"No. We don't have the money." Rosemond sat up and swung her legs over the side of the bed. She gripped the mattress.

"Dizzy?"

She nodded and swallowed. "Hand me my purse."

I retrieved the small purse from the dresser and handed it across the bed. Rosemond removed the bottle of laudanum and drank. I watched her, my mouth watering and longing for the pleasant numbing that she would soon know. She grimaced. "God, this is horrid."

I picked up the basin and walked around the bed. "It grows on you."

I placed the basin and a folded towel on the bed. I removed the instruments and laid them on the towel to dry while I finished cleaning the wound with the carbolic-soaked cloth. Rosemond watched me thread a needle with a slightly trembling hand.

"Should I be worried?"

I met her dark eyes. Now wasn't the time to tell her I hadn't sutured a wound since before my hand had been ruined by the Comanche. "I can manage a few stitches."

"Will it leave a scar?"

"A small one."

"What's one more, I suppose."

I tied off the thread. "Ready?"

Rosemond inhaled and nodded. I hesitated, hoping the months of needlepoint and massage had worked. I pushed the needle through her skin, taut from the bruise. She flinched and cursed, and I paused, watching the color leach from her already pallid face. Her jaw pulsed. I placed a hand on her shoulder. "It will be over soon."

She nodded very slightly, and I continued. "Tell me about Duncan," I said.

"Why?" Her voice was harsh. I met her steely gaze briefly before returning to my task.

"When Maureen died in Texas, I didn't have anyone to reminisce with."

"What about Kindle?"

"He was unconscious for most of our early acquaintance. It was incredibly lonely, not having anyone to share my memories with." Rosemond didn't respond, and I tried a different tack. "We are pretending to be sisters, after all, and I might be asked about Duncan. I think it's best I know something of his story. He was your slave?"

She exhaled as if resigned. "Yes. The son of my mother's maid. We were roughly the same age, and grew up together."

"You were close?"

Rosemond chuckled. "Of course not. He was a slave. My mother was sure that line was never crossed. But he was a house slave, so we were around each other quite a lot, and he had to do whatever I asked." She stared into the middle distance. "When I was fourteen I had great dreams of becoming an artist. I'd mastered still lifes and landscapes, and I decided it was time I mastered the human form and not the fully clothed forms of the slaves, family, and visitors who indulgently sat for me. I stood for hours in front of my mirror, drawing nudes of myself in a separate notebook I hid beneath my mattress. There was only one thing left for me to learn."

Her eyes met mine. "Duncan didn't want to. He knew the consequences if we were ever found out. As did I. But I can be persuasive."

"You seduced him?"

She rolled her eyes. "I promised to teach him to read. It was illegal, you know. I convinced him the risk to both of us was equal. A blatant lie, that. But Duncan was conditioned to obey and it didn't take much convincing.

"We started with him removing his shirt. Innocent enough. That wasn't enough for me. I was an artist!" She closed her eyes and laughed at herself. "We never touched each other, but what man can stand nude in front of a woman without a physical reaction? It was fascinating, watching it take shape. Duncan was mortified and tried to cover up, turn away. I wouldn't let him.

"You can imagine my mother's scream when she walked in and saw us. Duncan was sold the following day to the next farm over. As a field hand. The overseer was known to be a brute, which is why my mother sold him there. Duncan was given ten lashes as his welcome. The field hands treated him almost as bad. They thought house slaves were uppity and took every chance they had at making Duncan pay."

"What was your punishment?"

"Watching Duncan receive his, and being kept apprised of every subsequent beating at the hands of that horrid man. My father stepped in after a few months. Bought Duncan back and sold him to a Nashville hotel."

I tied off the last stitch and snipped the thread with scissors, elated at my hand's performance. "Why would he do that?"

"I have my suspicions," she said, wryly. "I lost track of Duncan for years, until I saw him in Nashville during the war. When I moved to Saint Louis, I took him with me."

"He forgave you?"

She nodded. "I promised to finish teaching him to read, and paid him more handsomely than he was being paid in Nashville. Money that he used to gamble." I dropped my instruments back into the sterile solution. "You're finished?"

I smiled. "Talking always distracts my patients."

Rosemond rose and went to the mirror. She leaned forward to inspect my work.

"Will you forgive me?" I asked.

She straightened but didn't turn; instead she held my gaze in the mirror. I'd seen the same expression on her face over dinner with Cora Bayle and I knew she was calculating her next move, trying to determine how she could manipulate me into getting what she wanted. What *did* Rosemond want? A new life was too simple an answer for a woman as complex as Rosemond Barclay. Was she Rosemond, high-priced madam, or was she Rosemond, artist? I doubted she knew the answer to that. Both sides of her personality would be warring with each other, fighting for supremacy. I understood the conflict in her expression all too well.

"Why should I forgive you?" she asked.

I picked up the basin and towel and met her at the dresser. "Because I have an idea about how to earn money."

She raised her eyebrows. "Are you going to go around breaking men's noses and fixing them?"

"No. My hand couldn't handle it. I'm going to find a game."

"A game? A poker game?" She laughed.

"I was thinking faro," I said, bristling at being laughed at.

"Are you any good?"

"Of course I am." It was a slight stretch of the truth. While in England I'd only ever played other women, but I'd been told by a man with enough experience to know that, with a little practice, and instruction, I would be able to hold my own against tougher opponents.

"You wouldn't be playing against bored women, you know."

I turned my attention to cleaning my instruments, bewildered at Rosemond's insight. I ignored the comment. "There's more to the plan."

"Do tell."

"I find a game and you come later, indignant at my vice. It establishes you in town as a morally upstanding character."

"Yet it ruins your reputation."

I shrugged. "I don't plan on staying any longer than it takes to help you put down roots, or Kindle to be freed."

Rosemond was quiet while I finished attending my instruments and returned them to my medical bag. "I'll take your silence as acquiescence. How much do we need to get established?"

"One thousand dollars."

"Don't be absurd. You said Duncan lost two hundred fifty dollars."

"In cash. The lot was worth a thousand. Plus, the loss of your necklace. I should make you earn two thousand."

"The necklace was mine. I should take its worth out of whatever I earn."

"You forget two things. One, you getting off the train led to the loss of your necklace. Two, I could turn you in to the sheriff and get a thousand dollars."

"You know I can't earn one thousand dollars in one night, starting with a five-dollar stake. I'll have to earn it over time.

How much do you need to bury Dunk and get a lot to put your house on?"

She lifted her gaze to the ceiling as if calculating. "Two hundred."

"That I can do."

"And if you lose everything?"

I flexed my right hand. "I suppose I'll have to start breaking noses."

"Let's hope it doesn't come to that." She reached into her trunk and removed a small porkpie hat festooned with a long pheasant feather sticking out of a thick navy band. She popped out a dent in the crown and set it on her head at a jaunty angle.

"Where are you going? You really should stay and rest."

Rosemond secured her hat with a gold, pearl-tipped hat pin. "I promised to telegraph about Kindle."

"Oh. Of course."

I turned away, ashamed that Kindle and his fate had completely slipped my mind. The memory of Dunk alone in his cell, receiving counsel from an unknown minister, was replaced by the image of Kindle receiving last rites from his cousin, Father Patrick Ryan. Kindle's sister, Mary Margaret Kindle, held his hand with bowed head, the plain gray headscarf of her order concealing her expression. Kindle stared into the middle distance, hatred and betrayal at my absence clear on his face.

Once I made restitution for Dunk, I had to return. It didn't matter that I couldn't help Kindle, and my arrival might lead to my arrest and deliverance into the hands of my enemies in New York City. My place was with my husband, not in a frontier town helping a whore start a new life, no matter how admirable I thought her endeavor.

"Are you coming?" Rosemond asked, her hand on the doorknob.

"What?"

"To the telegraph office?"

I opened my mouth to tell Rosemond I had to leave but closed it before uttering a sound. I knew instinctively Rosemond wouldn't let me go easily. She was single-minded in her goals, and now, without Dunk, she would be alone.

She watched me, a picture of guileless patience, waiting on my answer.

"I'll speak to the clerk downstairs about a game."

"Excellent idea," she replied, and walked out the door.

CHAPTER
10

Rosemond looked up from the telegram she was writing, smiled, and handed it to me to read.

Hannah Pryor, Bond St. St. Louis. Send word of Capt. WKs trial ASAP. RB

"We don't have the money to be verbose," Rosemond said.

I handed it back with a nod. While Rosemond took the paper to the man behind the counter and paid, I scanned the bulletin board for my Wanted poster. Advertisements for goods and services, some handwritten, some professionally printed, ranging from blacksmithing to hotels to restaurants to tent sales to freight hauling to the Sweetwater gold mines.

"Anything interesting?" Rosemond said.

I yawned. "No painter."

"A good sign."

We stepped out of the telegraph office.

A line of five wagons loaded with supplies and men drove slowly past us. A man sitting on top of one of the wagons raised his hat and called, "Good-bye, beautiful! Next time you see me, I'll be a rich man!"

"Not fookin' likely with your claim," an older man said, amid laughter from the others.

Undaunted, the young man said, "Wait for me!"

We watched as the supply train pulled out of town and onto the plains. "Which of us do you think he was talking to?" I said.

"Whichever one of us would take him."

For as much as the towns in the West were a dirty mess and full of shysters and crooks, there was an underlying energy and optimism that appealed to me. The push west was based entirely on hope: for a new life, the opportunity to shake off the chains of the East, to take control of one's own destiny without interference from the government. Everyone west of the Mississippi had bought into the idea that energy, hard work, and tenacity was the recipe for success, and a single-minded selfishness had grown up around it. When a Western settler looked at you, they didn't see a customer, but another rung on the ladder to their own success. The successful men masked this selfishness with obsequiousness; the failures believed them.

And Rosemond fit right in.

Despite myself, I admired her desire to start a new life. I'd known enough whores to have long since lost my moral superiority on the subject; women had no rights and few options. I would never judge a woman who used the one advantage she owned outright, her body, to feed herself and her family. But whoring couldn't last forever. There was a physical toll on the body that caught up with everyone eventually, and add to that the opiate addiction afflicting so many and the diseases they were inevitably riddled with, and there came a time in every prostitute's life when her means of survival would be taken from her. Rosemond was smart enough to quit before her profession ravaged her. Knowing her even for a short time, I had no doubt she would be successful. With or without my help.

Rosemond walked away from the telegraph office and in the opposite direction of the hotel.

"Where are you going?" I asked.

"To see Dunk."

I put my hand out to stop her. "Oh, Rosemond, don't."

She stared at my hand on her arm until I removed it, then lifted her steely eyes to mine. "What kind of coward would I be if I didn't look upon what I wrought?"

"You didn't bring that on Duncan, I did, and the knowledge of it will haunt me all of my days." I swallowed the sob that threatened to escape me as his final expression filled my mind. "I don't think it wise for you to see him like that, but I cannot stop you, nor will I go with you. I refuse to let you guilt me into seeing him hanging on the gallows, again. I will make restitution by finding a game and earning enough to bury him properly."

I hurried away, my stomach twisting at her words. *What kind of coward would I be if I didn't look upon what I wrought?* I thought I'd become hardened to death after my flight across Indian Territory, but now I knew I was not. A small part of me was relieved I'd retained my humanity, but the rest of me grieved for the wanton loss of life caused by my decision to leave New York City. Kindle had convinced me the deaths in Indian country were no loss to the world, and I'd comforted myself with the thought. The deaths of Cora Bayle and Duncan March offered no such solace.

I stopped on the wooden sidewalk in front of the Union Pacific Hotel and looked back down the street the way I came. Cheyenne's business day was in full swing. Teamsters drove wagons in and around one another on the wide main street, with only few arguments and shouts breaking through the din of jingling tack, snorting horses, and general indistinct cacophony common to all busy towns. Stray dogs skulked around on the edge of the streets and in the alleys, searching for scraps. A young boy sold newspapers on the corner. Two other boys hid in an alley and peeked around the corner. When the newspaper boy turned toward them, they stepped out into the street and threw a chunk of horse manure at him, hitting him squarely in the eye. The two urchins ran off, laughing. The newspaper boy wiped the manure from his face and continued on with his job.

I looked to see if Rosemond had taken my advice. Of all the activity in my sight, there were only two women walking down the street. Neither was Rosemond.

I slid into the line for the front desk behind a hirsute man with the look and smell of a miner long used to being alone. Or was the smell coming from me? A discreet sniff near my shoulder confirmed that the opiate withdrawal was overcoming my recent bath. A glance in the mirror on the wall opposite the front desk told me I would need to use Rosemond's paint tonight to protect against my wildly fluctuating complexion.

The clerk finished his business with the miner in front of me and smiled as I stepped to the counter. I looked around, leaned forward, and lowered my voice. "I was wondering...?"

"Charlie."

"Charlie." I smiled again, hoping I didn't look like a dope fiend searching for a fix. "Would you happen to know of a game where a woman would be welcome?"

The desk clerk studied me with a knowing air. "I might." Charlie placed his hand palm up on the counter.

I smiled. "Charlie, if I had money enough to bribe you, I wouldn't need a game, now, would I?"

The clerk shrugged. "I'm sorry. I can't help you."

"We know how this works. You get a kickback from the dealer for sending people their way."

"The last time I sent a woman she broke the bank."

"I have no intention of breaking the bank."

Charlie scoffed.

"I'm not a gambler. I need to earn a specific amount, and I'll stop."

"How much?"

"Enough to get me back East, and eat along the way."

"Just you? Not your sister?"

I smiled conspiratorially. "She doesn't approve of gaming. Moving west was her idea, not mine." When Charlie looked unmoved, I begged. "Please?"

He sighed. "Rollins House Hotel tonight, eight o'clock. Ask for Lily Diamond."

"You're a peach."

I walked across the crowded lobby, the bed upstairs beckoning my exhausted body and mind. I needed to rest to be mentally agile enough to win at faro, a game I hadn't played in some years.

"A thousand dollars is a lot of money for a dead body," a man with a showy set of neck whiskers said.

I stopped at the bottom of the stairs, my hand on the newel post. Perspiration popped out on my upper lip and I swallowed the lump of fear lodged in my throat.

"The Langtons can afford it," his companion replied. The man puffed on his pipe and continued, "Can you blame them? She's proved a difficult piece of calico to take alive. I wonder what man she's seduced to save her this time."

"I understand she's lost her looks, after being taken by the Comanche. Who would want to poke her, after those savages had their way?"

"There's more than one way to fuck a whore."

The men laughed heartily and I walked up the stairs on unsteady legs. I rushed down the hall to the communal bathroom and just made it to the commode before vomiting bile from my empty stomach. I wiped saliva from my mouth with the back of my hand, ignoring the tears rolling down my cheeks.

Why was I surprised, or upset? I knew how men talked, what they thought of me. But it had been a long time since I'd heard it firsthand. The armor I'd built up over years of fighting against the misogyny had weakened during my time with Kindle. He provided me with protection, and I had gotten soft as a result. I splashed water on my face and stared at myself in the mirror. I didn't need to worry about people recognizing me from the Wanted poster. I was too different. I suppose I should thank the Comanche for the broken nose and the hardening of my countenance. The only thing that could give me away was myself, my actions.

And Rosemond.

Would she turn me in after I won her money as retribution for Dunk's death? Would I do the same to her if she'd been responsible for Kindle's?

Yes.

I went into the bedroom and checked the contents of my medical bag before latching it. I glanced around the room, thinking. Planning. How observant was Rosemond? If I took the bag downstairs and checked it at the desk, would Rosemond notice the bag was gone? Everything else in the trunk was Rosemond's, and off-limits. Besides, I didn't want her things. My medical bag and enough money to buy a train ticket back to Saint Louis and to eat along the way. I would have plenty of time on the train to decide what to do next. Cable Sophia, the young woman I mentored at the orphanage, in the code I used in correspondence with my cousin? If the Pinkertons were watching the orphanage for me, they would be focused on correspondence to Kindle's sister, not a sixteen-year-old mulatto orphan. I had no doubt she would do whatever she could to help me, but was it fair to ask? No. She had her life in front of her. I didn't need to risk her bright future for my own skin.

I would worry about my destination later. I needed to earn money for Dunk's funeral, a small stake for Rosemond, and enough to get me away from a woman I couldn't fully trust to keep my identity secret. Once again, I needed to go where I was unknown to anyone, friend or foe alike. This time, I would go alone.

❧

I was lying on the bed in my shift fighting off a hot flash when Rosemond returned.

"Did you find a game?"

"Yes. And you are the disapproving sister who must be kept in the dark."

"Good. Resting up for tonight?"

"Yes. This bed is atrocious. I adjusted the slats so if we balance just right, we shouldn't fall beneath the bed."

Rosemond removed her hat. "We should have the answer from my friend in the morning."

"Okay."

Rosemond paused, the long gold hat pin primed to puncture her head. "Okay? I thought you'd want to know as soon as possible."

I closed my eyes. "Whether we go this afternoon or in the morning won't change what the answer is. I need to focus on winning two hundred dollars."

"Huh." The bed creaked as Rosemond lay down next to me. "I told the agent to only give the answer to me."

"Why?"

"I don't want you sneaking away without fulfilling your promises."

"Why do you think I'd do that?"

"Because it's precisely what I would do. Be quiet. I'm starving and the only way to not think about food is to sleep."

"My eyes are closed. You're the one who keeps talking."

The small, windowless space felt like a jail cell. I hadn't slept since Grand Island, and my sleep there had been laudanum-induced. Any rest it had provided was negated by the shivering craving for more of the opiate the following day, and exacerbated by the uncomfortable train ride. My legs and arms suddenly felt like they weighed a hundred pounds, my brain like a boll of cotton. I crossed my arms over my chest and let the sound of Rosemond's steady breathing lull me into an uneasy sleep.

CHAPTER
11

I expected Lily Diamond to be flashy, possibly a madam earning extra money by dealing faro, presiding over a smoke-filled room full of men. Instead, the woman I found in the tea room at the Rollins House Hotel was a diminutive, plain-looking woman in full mourning, sitting on a cushion to give her enough lift to sit square to the table.

She spotted me and her round face broke into a jolly grin. "You must be the fill-in Charlie mentioned. Welcome!"

"Thank you."

"I'm Lily Diamond."

"Helen Graham."

The room was small and feminine, with pale pink wallpaper patterned with rosebuds and intertwined with greenery. Lily Diamond and two women sat at a bare table in the middle of the room. The other two cloth-covered tables were shunted off against the wall out of the way. Lily shuffled cards with a deft hand and dealt. There was no shoe, no abacus for counting cards, and room for only four players. My suspicion that this wasn't a faro game was confirmed when the woman with her back to me turned around, and her open, friendly expression morphed into one of irritation.

"Hello, Mrs. Bright. Good to see you again," I said.

Portia Bright nodded, but didn't speak.

"Oh, you've met Portia?"

"Yes, today at the jail."

"Did you and the Reverend go visit the condemned man?" Lily asked.

"Yes."

"I suppose he repented," the third woman said with derision.

"Now, Amalia, the Lord forgives those who ask," Lily said.

Amalia harrumphed and held her hand out to me. "Amalia Post."

"Helen Graham. Nice to meet you."

Lily motioned to the open chair. "Have a seat."

I sat and adjusted the neckline of my dress, hoping against hope it would cover my cleavage. I'd dressed in one of Rosemond's more revealing gowns, hoping to distract my male playing partners with what little cleavage I had on offer. Now I sat conspicuously with three fully covered, prim women. Portia pointedly ignored me. She truly didn't like me, though I couldn't figure why.

"What are we playing?" I picked up my cards.

"Bridge."

"You do know how to play," Portia said.

"Of course. Are we betting?"

All movement stopped and the women gaped at me. "No, dear," Lily said. "Just for fun."

I paused. *Damn you, Charlie.* It would be rude to leave, but every minute here meant one less minute earning money to leave. I hoped Rosemond would make her entrance soon.

"What a relief," I lied. "I'm terrible at gambling."

We went around and bid. Lily declared the trumps and I laid down my dummy hand.

"Why were you visiting the prisoner?" Amalia asked.

I gathered my thoughts. I'd expected to be quizzed but not so soon. I'd decided the less detail the better, as all good liars know. "He worked for my sister, Eliza. We'd hoped to be able to help him."

"It is untenable that there wasn't a trial," Portia said, taking the first trick.

"True, but he would have been convicted," Amalia said. "It was only delaying the inevitable."

"It doesn't make it right, Mrs. Post," Portia said.

"What brings you to Cheyenne, Helen?" Lily asked, trying to turn the conversation from death.

"I came with my sister."

"Why?" Portia asked.

"Why?"

"Why did your sister come west?"

"I suppose she was looking for adventure. Something new. She had a friend who came out here and I think it motivated her to do the same."

"Who?" Portia asked.

"My, aren't you curious tonight, Portia," Amalia said.

"We get so few women who move to Cheyenne," Portia said. "Especially single women."

I chuckled. "I assure you, Eliza isn't here for a husband."

"And you?" Portia asked.

"Nor am I." I lifted my hand and showed my thin wedding ring. "Enough about me," I said, hoping they wouldn't quiz me about my husband, where he was, and why I wasn't with him. "Tell me how you ended up in Cheyenne."

"My husband owns one of the general stores in town," Amalia said.

"Mrs. Post is being modest," Portia said. "She's as good at business as her husband."

"Indeed?"

"I own some property," Amalia said.

"Women can own property?" I said.

"You didn't hear of it?" Portia asked, narrowing her eyes at me. "It was all over the papers last year."

Not only did Portia not like me, she was suspicious. I sighed and decided the only way to deflect her curiosity was to dust off the flibbertigibbet personality that had been a somewhat successful disguise in Indian country.

I waved my hand in dismissal. "Oh, well. Who reads the papers? Such frightening stories. It brings me low, always has. And what man wants a serious wife? None that I've ever known."

"You've had a lot of husbands?" Portia asked.

"No, dear, just the one."

"Where is your husband?" Portia asked.

"In Europe on business. Which is why I have plenty of time to help my sister settle into her new home. The West is thrilling, don't you think?" I pursed my lips at Portia. "Or are you not the excitable type? You strike me as very practical. Levelheaded. Today was the perfect example." I included Amalia and Lily in the conversation with a glance. "She threw herself over my sister to protect her from the mob."

Lily gasped. "You were there when the mob came in?"

"We *were*. My sister got a horrible gash on her head. Good thing I was a nurse in the war. Stitched it right up."

"You," Portia said.

"Yes, dear. I'm quite good at needlepoint. You have the most extraordinary eyes," I said. "I was incredibly rude, staring at you as I did when we first met. I do hope you'll forgive me?" I grasped her hand and gave her my best vacuous, pleading expression.

"Of course she will," Lily said. "Portia is one of the sweetest women I know."

"Indeed?" I said, not believing it for a second. "Now, Amalia. You were talking about women and property rights?"

"Yes, and we have the right to vote. I served on a jury last year, was the foreman," Amalia said. "It was a murder case. Two murders, in fact."

"Goodness! What happened?" I asked.

"Found guilty and hanged. So, you see, I have experience with capital trials. If a white man is hanged for murder, what else should a Negro who killed a white man expect?"

"I suppose he expected a fair trial, as the white man received," I said.

Amalia ignored my comment. "There is no fun sitting on a jury where there is a murder case to be tried, but it's a civic duty. If women want to be seen as equals, we cannot shirk our responsibility."

"Or give the men any reason to take the right away," I said.

"Oh, they've tried," Lily said.

"Mrs. Post put a stop to it," Portia replied. "Went straight to the governor."

Amalia focused on her cards, but she did not blush or preen at the compliments. She took it like it was her due and nothing more. No need to simper away her accomplishments. I liked her immensely.

"My husband sells building supplies. Canvas tents, mostly," Lily said.

"I always thought that would be a going concern in the West," I said.

"It is," Lily said. "He sells them the tent when they arrive, then the prefabricated building, then the tools to make repairs."

The last round of cards was played and the tricks tallied.

Amalia pulled the cards to her and shuffled. A waiter walked in and placed a tray of coffee, mugs, and small cakes on a table. "Thank you, Don." Lily rose. "Who wants coffee?"

We all accepted. "Let me help," I said.

While Lily poured, she asked, "How will you and your sister make a living?"

"Eliza is a painter," I said. "Does either of your husbands have a sign painter he recommends to his customers?"

"There's one in town, but he isn't good and charges a fortune. Does she paint signs?" Amalia asked.

"She does."

"That's hardly an appropriate job for a woman," Lily said. "Standing on ladders like they do."

"I'm sure she would prefer to make a living painting portraits, but in a booming town like Cheyenne, signs are more practical."

"Have her come talk to me at our store on Fifteenth Street," Amalia said.

"I will."

"She shouldn't dismiss portraiture," Portia said. "Cheyenne is the state capital. It is overrun with self-important men who want to leave their mark on the world."

"Portia, that is ungenerous," Lily said.

"But the truth. What about you, Helen?" Portia said. "What do you do?"

"I'm a midwife."

The women laughed softly. "Not much call for a midwife in Cheyenne," Amalia said.

At my perplexed expression, Lily clarified. "Men outnumber women by—what was it at the last census, Amalia?"

"Six to one."

"Better hope your sister is a good painter," Amalia said, pragmatically.

"Portia might be a patient soon enough," Lily said with a sweet smile.

Portia's face flushed.

"What is going on here!"

Rosemond stood in the door of the room, anger morphing to confusion. Her chest heaved in false indignation beneath the tasteful neckline of my dress. "Hello, Sissy," I said, brightly. "We're playing bridge, of course."

"Oh, is this your sister?" Lily asked.

"Yes. Come in, Eliza. Pull up a chair and watch," I said.

Rosemond came in hesitantly, her plan to cement her reputation as an upstanding citizen to a room full of men thwarted. I made the introductions. "Eliza Ryan, this is Lily Diamond and Amalia Post. And of course you met Portia Bright today."

"Yes." Rosemond's voice was strained. "Good to see you again. And nice to meet you," she said, taking in the other two.

"Don't hover, Sissy. Pull up a chair." Rosemond glared at me but pulled a chair over and set it between me and Portia.

"Did you have a nice rest?" I asked, voice sweet.

"Yes, I did. Thank you for not waking me."

"It's the least I could do. How do you feel?" I looked into Rosemond's eyes and was happy to see they were steadier than earlier in the day.

"Is that your handiwork, Helen?" Amalia said, nodding toward Rosemond's temple.

"It is."

Amalia scrutinized my stitches. "Fine job."

"Thank you."

"Helen tells us you're a painter, Eliza," Amalia said. The

conversation went over the same ground I'd just trod, allowing me to sit back, watch, and listen. Lily and Amalia drove the conversation, with Rosemond answering questions as if she were on the witness stand. For the first time since I'd known her, Rosemond was stiff and ill at ease. Maybe respectability was going to be more difficult for her to pull off than I thought.

When they got back around to my inability to contribute to our livelihood, I said, "I merely came to help my sister settle in. I don't plan to stay." Rosemond lifted her chin and studied me. I realized my mistake and kicked myself.

"Too bad, Portia. I suppose Doc Hankins will have to do for you," Amalia said.

"A doctor? Are you ill?" Rosemond asked, pulling her gaze from me to the minister's wife.

Portia shook her head, but wouldn't look up. "No."

"For the baby," Lily said.

"You're *pregnant*?" Rosemond asked.

The woman blushed again and shook her head. "No."

"But soon," Lily said, patting Portia's hand.

Rosemond relaxed, sensing weakness and eager to pounce. "How long have you been married, Portia? May I call you Portia?"

Portia met Rosemond's gaze. "Of course. I've been married six months."

"A newlywed," Rosemond said. "And not pregnant yet."

"God will bless us in due time."

"Indeed." Rosemond turned to me. "You look peaked. I'm happy to take your place if you'd like to go rest."

"Oh, thank you, Sissy." We rose together and I took Rosemond in my arms and whispered, "Don't alienate these women. You'll need friends when I'm gone."

Rosemond placed a lingering kiss on my cheek and held me

at arm's length. "I'll be quiet when I return so as to not wake you." She stroked my cheek in a very unsisterly way.

"Thank you." I pulled away. "And thank you, ladies, for being so welcoming. I hope to see you again before I leave."

"We're here every Tuesday night," Lily said.

"Are you?" Rosemond said, sitting in my place. "How fun."

I left the room and with a pang of trepidation. Rosemond was coming into her own, and I wondered which of the women she would insult first. Amalia and Lily seemed oblivious to sarcasm, but I suspect Portia saw straight through me and Rosemond. If Rosemond felt threatened, the minister's wife didn't stand much of a chance. I almost felt sorry for her.

CHAPTER
12

The Union Pacific Hotel lobby was quiet, and a different man was behind the front desk. Asking for help finding a female-friendly game would be pointless, I suspected. It couldn't be that difficult to find a game in a town such as this. But I was a woman, alone, with nothing more than a stolen knife secreted in my boot to protect me. I couldn't carouse around town searching for a tiger sign pasted to a window indicating a faro game. The tall grandfather clock chimed nine thirty. When it stopped, I heard the sound of faint laughter came from the back of the hotel.

Of course.

I walked down a hall past the dining room and found what I was looking for.

The long, rectangular room spanned the entire east wall of the hotel. A polished bar with a mirror hanging behind it sat at one end of the room. Thick drapes and heavy carpet muted the noise of the roulette table. Brass gas lamps on the wall and a large chandelier hanging from the center of the ceiling lit the room with a warm yellow glow. Acrid-smelling cigar smoke hovered over ten playing tables being presided over by white-shirted dealers. I stepped through the door and was immediately stopped by the same burly man who'd delivered Rosemond's trunk.

"No women allowed."

I leaned to the left and pointed at a redheaded prostitute with a mole on her left cheek so prominent, I assumed it was fake. "There's a woman right there."

The man crossed his arms. "Ruby's a sporting woman. Are you?"

I smiled. "Not the kind you mean, I fear. I'm here to play."

A man materialized next to me. "She's with me." Salter. I recoiled instinctively, and my stomach lurched. Salter stared at the doorman and didn't seem to notice my reaction.

The burly man licked his lips and wouldn't meet Salter's eyes. He stepped aside and said, "Good luck."

Salter held out his arm to me. "Ready, dear?"

I took his arm and shuddered. "Thank you."

"You're welcome."

We walked across the room to the cashier. "What's your game...?" He looked down at me expectantly. "I never caught your name."

"Helen Graham."

His gaze roved over my face, as if searching for familiarity, or a lie. He nodded. "Mrs. Graham, what is your game?"

"Faro."

I exchanged my five dollars for a single chip. Salter watched with an amused expression but didn't comment.

I sat down at a faro table and almost laughed when I saw the two men from the lobby sitting across from me. They nodded an acknowledgment at me, and I returned the greeting. I closed my eyes and inhaled deeply, reminding myself that I was the only one who could give my ruse away. When I opened my eyes, I saw the entire table watching me. I smiled and looked around for a waiter. I lifted my finger and said, "Whisky," and turned back to the table. The men glanced at one another with raised eyebrows and amused expressions, with Mr. Neck Whiskers letting his gaze linger on my décolletage. I tried not to blanch; distraction was the reason I wore the dress, after all.

My drink arrived and play started. I focused on the game instead of the players, determined to build my stake to give myself some breathing room. It didn't occur to me that the whisky was bottomless until I swayed in my chair during a dealer shuffle.

There was no clock on the wall, and the curtains were drawn over the windows. Salter was filling my glass. I put my hand out. "No more, please." The dealer put the deck in the shoe, killed the first card, and called for bets. I laid my chips out on the cards painted on the green baize and waited. Salter did the same, and alternated between drinking his whisky and smoking his thin cigar.

"I've never seen a woman so single-minded on gambling."

"Have you not?" The dealer paid out on my seven and dealt the next two cards. I kept my eyes on the board but leaned closer to Salter and whispered, "This may surprise you, but men always think women are easy to cheat. I have to be vigilant."

"Oh, I doubt anyone would put you down as an easy mark."

I glanced sharply at Salter, who grinned at me as he drank. From the corner of my eye, I saw the dealer take my money from the seven. I swore under my breath, computed what cards had been shown, and put a copper down on a three.

I lost track of time but was aware enough of my surroundings to know that people were taking notice of me, and Salter had decamped to the arms of the redheaded whore. When my current game ended I tipped the dealer, took my winnings, and left the table. I counted my chips. Sixty dollars. A good showing considering I'd started with five, but nowhere close to two hundred. I needed a higher-stakes game.

Remembering Kindle's advice on the *Grand Republic*, I secreted twenty dollars' worth of chips in the hidden pockets Rosemond had sewn into her gown. I would at least leave this den with money for food, a room for another night or two, and Dunk's burial.

Mr. Neck Whiskers materialized at the bar next to me. He motioned to the bartender, who poured a drink automatically. "Are you new in town?" the man asked.

"Passing through."

"Going where?"

I smiled thinly. "Depends on how much money I win."

The man's watery blue eyes settled on my breasts. "There's an easier, more pleasant way to earn money."

"I can't imagine anything more pleasant than gambling."

"You seem like the kind of woman who can."

If I were Rosemond, or Camille, my madam friend in New York City, I could charm and manipulate this man out of money without having to spread my legs. I would confess to manipulating my fair share of people in my life, but this type of game was beyond me, and I knew it. I'd delved into many facets of my personality in the past year, brought parts of me to the forefront to play different parts when necessary so that I wasn't sure who or what I was. I might gamble with my life, but I couldn't gamble with sex. A man laughed behind me, and my palms went slick with threat, memories I thought I'd banished creeping back into my mind.

I called for a whisky, hoping it would numb my mind and drown out the images trying to flicker back to life. Mr. Neck Whiskers watched me, waiting for an answer to a question I'd forgotten.

"Good luck with your game," I said, grasping my whisky.

"There you are," Salter said, putting his arm around my waist. Mr. Neck Whiskers took his drink and scurried off.

"Please take your hand off of my waist."

Salter did so and motioned to the bartender. "Beer."

"Why is everyone frightened of you, Mr. Salter?"

"Are they? I hadn't noticed. Are you frightened of me, Mrs. Graham?"

"No."

He grinned and sipped his beer.

A man lost everything and vacated a chair at the blackjack table.

"Excuse me," I said, and moved away.

I sat down, hoped the chair wasn't cursed, and anted up, relieved no one would dare talk to me during a game.

I was almost broken twice but managed to play my way back in as I became more familiar with my opponents' tells. Between hands I would catch sight of Salter sitting across the room at a poker table, the prostitute draped over his shoulder like a poncho. It seemed no matter when I glanced in his direction, he was staring at me. The whore noticed, and her eyes shot daggers at me. My stomach growled loudly, as good a signal to end the night as any.

I cashed out and tried not to look too pleased at the one hundred seventy-one dollars the bank counted out.

"You lied to me, Mrs. Graham."

I turned to find Salter standing behind me, a thin cigar in the corner of his mouth.

"What about?"

"Faro isn't your game. Blackjack is."

"I am surprised as you, I assure you."

"Can I buy you dinner?"

Of course my stomach growled again, but I ignored it and hoped the noise in the room covered my body's betrayal. I couldn't imagine any situation where I would agree to dine with this man.

"Thank you, but my sister is expecting me. Good night."

I turned, but Salter grasped my hand and threaded it through his crooked arm. "I'll see you to your room."

"Thank you, but I know the way."

His grasp on my hand tightened. "I turned Ruby's proposition down because I knew I had a commitment from you."

"You really shouldn't have. I gave you no commitment."

"You took my help to enter the room easy enough. Who did you think paid for your drinks all night? What, did you think it was free?"

Salter put his arm around my waist and pinned me close to him. Panic flooded my chest and paralyzed me. My body trembled. Salter steered me across the lobby toward the stairs. The knife in my boot was out of reach. I feared that causing a scene would only bring attention and not the aid I required. There were few men in the lobby this late at night, and they all glanced at us and looked away, giving the discretion to Salter they would expect if escorting a whore to their room.

With a shaky voice I said, "I am not a whore, Mr. Salter."

Salter assessed me and lingered for an uncomfortably long time on my décolletage. I determined not to quell under his gaze and hoped the flush from earlier wouldn't show my confidence as a lie.

"Your sister is."

"My sister is an artist."

Salter laughed. "No, she ain't. This dress hers? What are you playing at, *Mrs. Graham*?"

Salter stopped us at the bottom of the stairs and released me.

His dark eyes were knowing, as if puzzling out liars were second nature. He suspected I wasn't who I said I was, but did he suspect I was Catherine Bennett?

"Nothing, I assure you. I'm here to help my sister get established, and I will return east."

Salter chewed his cigar and nodded slowly. He removed the cigar and released a cloud of smoke in my face. He leaned forward and whispered in my ear. "You're hiding something."

I leaned away but met his eyes. I gave him a brittle smile. "Isn't everyone?"

He was studying my features again when I heard a train whistle sound. If I hadn't already planned to sneak away, I would have to now. If Salter suspected who I was, it would be best for me, and Rosemond, to leave immediately. My plan hadn't changed; I only needed to get rid of Salter to execute it.

"Thank you, Mr. Salter, for your assistance. Good night." I lifted my skirt and walked up the stairs. I rounded the corner out of sight from the lobby and went into the bathroom and locked the door. Though my breaths came in shallow bursts, I couldn't breathe. I clutched at the bodice of my dress, but it buttoned up the back. Panic flooded me. I cupped my hands over my mouth and nose and thought only of breathing in and out. Eventually, my breathing slowed, and my lungs stopped burning. I grasped the edge of the vanity and forced my mind to settle. I heard another train whistle and knew my time was running short. I hurried back downstairs and went to the desk and rang the bell.

A different clerk came from the back room. "May I help you?"

"Yes, could I buy an envelope and paper from you?"

"Are you a guest at the hotel?"

"Yes."

"No need to purchase." I took the paper and pencil he gave me and walked to a secluded alcove to scribble a note to Rosemond. I enclosed the money and note in the paper, wrote *Eliza Ryan* on it, and asked the clerk to see that she received it. "You're holding a bag for me."

"Do you have your ticket?"

"Yes." I pulled the ticket from my pocket when I heard Rosemond call to me. I turned and hid the ticket behind my back.

Rosemond stood at the top of the stairs. "Helen." Her voice was tender.

"Ros—Eliza, what are you doing awake?" I asked. "It's the middle of the night."

She came down the stairs. "It's morning. I waited up for you." Her gaze fell to the paper she held in her hands. She looked up at me, her face full of compassion. "I left the bridge game and went to the telegraph office last night." She held the open telegram out to me.

Now that the moment was here, I didn't want to know. I wanted to live in ignorance a while longer, the place where Kindle was alive and well, was on his way to find me, the place where we lived a long and happy life together. The paper trembled in Rosemond's hand, but I couldn't reach out for it. Tears pooled in her eyes and she said, almost inaudibly, "My condolences."

My body went numb. I took the telegram and walked away. When I was far enough away, I unfolded the paper.

Capt. WK convicted of desertion and disobeying a direct order. Stop. Executed by firing squad...

The words swam off the paper. Far away, I heard a woman scream.

PART TWO

CALICO ROW

CHAPTER 13

Dear Cousin,

If you're reading this, it means you've forgiven me for not making our ship in New Orleans. We were betrayed on the Mississippi. Kindle was taken into custody by the Army and I was whisked off to safety in Cheyenne, Wyoming, by a whore who said she was working on Kindle's orders. I suspect she was lying to gain my trust, or my acquiescence.

Word to the wise, Charlotte: don't trust whores.

It doesn't matter what I do, a swath of death and destruction follows me. By my count, eighteen deaths have resulted from my choosing Texas over staying and facing my accusers.

Eight of those deaths I regret.

One will be the death of me.

The door to the room struck the wall with a resounding thud.

I turned over onto my back, holding my hand up against the light emitting from the lamp Rosemond held in her hand. Two more people with more offending lamps entered behind her. "Oh, dear."

I turned away and closed my eyes. "Go away, Rosemond." The words were barely discernible, my throat dry from disuse.

You will want me to come to you, I have no doubt. Even if I had the money, which I do not, I couldn't bear the journey. Thousands of miles across land and sea. Even the comfort of your embrace cannot entice me for the journey.

I am so very tired, Charlotte.

"My God, the smell." A cough, and a gag. "Her chamber pot is almost overflowing."

"How much laudanum did you give her?" a third voice accused. Portia Bright.

"Enough to calm her down," Rosemond said. "She was hysterical."

"This bottle is empty."

"Do you blame her? Her husband is dead."

"You shouldn't have left her alone so long."

"Stop being judgmental and help me."

Someone shook my shoulder. "Laura, open your eyes."

Rosemond crouched in the tiny space between the bed and the wall.

"Go away."

"You're coming home with me."

"I don't have a home."

"Yes, you do. We do. I'm sorry I left you so long, but I wanted to make sure everything was ready." Rosemond brushed my hair from my face. Her gaze landed on the paper I clutched to my chest. She placed her hand on mine. The telegram. "Give it to me."

"No. Get away from me. You did this. You're to blame."

It's not her fault, Charlotte, not really, though it makes me feel better to say it. The eighteen deaths are on me, a direct result of the impulsive decision I made to leave New York City instead of staying and facing the baseless charges.

"Let me try," Portia said.

Rosemond stood and made way for the preacher's wife. "Laura." Her voice was soothing and gentle. "Let us take you out of this dungeon and to Rosemond's house. Your room has two windows and has the nicest little breeze flowing through in the middle of the day. You can go right back to bed, if you want."

"Not before she takes a bath," the third woman said. Her voice was muffled by a handkerchief covering her mouth.

I shook my head. "This is what I deserve. For all of them. Maureen, Cora, Dunk, Will—" My voice caught on Kindle's name. I'd come to think of my room as my own grave, much like the one Kindle was in, his body rotting, worms crawling through his eyes, nose, and mouth. I started to sob.

"You don't deserve this."

I tried to move away. "Please leave me alone."

"Move." A male voice broke through and I was being lifted and taken from the room. I tried to resist but was so weak from lack of food, water, and movement I could barely lift my head from the man's shoulder. I opened my eyes and saw the pale countenance of Reverend Bright. I closed my eyes and cried softly as he carried me out of my grave and into the light.

CHAPTER
14

Reverend Bright sat in a chair next to my bed, reading the Bible. He was a trim man with long legs and small hands. His smooth face suggested a youthfulness his receding hairline and weak chin contradicted. His thin lips moved as he read but his eyes remained stationary, leading me to believe he recited the passages from memory.

He glanced up and a smile broke across his face. "You're awake."

"What are you reading?"

"Job."

"Well, at least you're not reading Psalm Twenty-Three over me."

Reverend Bright smiled. "You aren't that far gone, I hope."

I didn't answer but took in my surroundings. The room was sparsely furnished, as I suppose all new houses are. There were signs of hasty construction here and there: a crooked, jutting nail, a divot in the wood from a missed hammer hit, a gap between the glass and windowsill. It smelled refreshingly of new lumber, a scent I'd come to associate with the West almost as much as body odor, blood, horse sweat, and manure. I thought of the freshly hewn boards in Kindle's officer's quarters at Fort Richardson and turned my head from the Reverend.

"How long have I been here?"

"Two days."

"And before?"

"Three."

"Where's the telegram?"

"Your sister took it."

I turned away and, for the hundredth time, saw Kindle tied to a post in the middle of a parade ground, staring down the firing squad with his one good eye, the flash of light and smoke from the guns' muzzles and Kindle slumping against his restraints.

"And the letter?"

"What letter?"

"To my cousin, Charlotte?"

"There was no letter."

I threw my arm over my eyes against the light. Hadn't I written a letter? Or merely composed one in my mind?

The legs of Reverend Bright's chair scraped across the floor. He touched my shoulder. "Helen, your husband—"

"Don't tell me he's in a better place."

"But he is. He's with our Lord."

I rose from the bed and walked on weak legs to the nearest window. Behind a line of tents, a vast, featureless plain stretched out to infinity. Of course. "How far west do I need to travel to see a goddamn tree?"

The Reverend chuckled. "You're almost there."

"Whose house is this?"

"Eliza's. The prefabricated house arrived by train the day..."

"I found out my husband was dead."

I opened the armoire and found two skirts, shirts, a navy brocade vest, a thick brown leather belt, a pair of sensible boots, and a straw hat. A chemise, corset, and petticoat were folded on the bottom shelf. A hairbrush and mirror lay next to a pitcher, bowl, and fresh bar of soap on a nearby table. "It seems my sister has thought of everything."

The Reverend cleared his throat and stood. "She is concerned about you."

I laughed. "Don't let her manipulate you, Reverend. She is only concerned with herself." I placed the telegram on the table. *Capt. WK convicted…*

"Did you read the telegram?"

"Yes. Your sister told me your story."

"My story. You'll have to specify which story so I'll know which lies to stick with. There are so many I can hardly keep track myself."

"You have been through more tribulations than any woman should have to, Catherine."

"Ah." I nodded. "She told you everything."

The Reverend nodded.

"With Rosemond as my savior."

The Reverend paused, brows furrowed. "She helped you escape Saint Louis."

"She did. Did she tell you about her life there?"

"No."

"Cora Bayle?"

"Who?"

"No. I didn't think so. Does your wife know who I am?"

The Reverend shook his head. "Eliza told me in the confidence of a minister and my parishioner."

I laughed heartily at this. "*Eliza* a Christian? Don't believe it for a second, Reverend."

"It isn't my place to judge one's sincerity of belief but to offer counsel when needed and asked for." He studied me. "All you have to do is ask."

"You want me to confess my sins?"

"If that's what you feel you need to do."

"I'm sorry to disappoint you, but my sins and guilt are my own."

"Are they? Would Duncan agree with that statement? Or your husband?"

His voice was temperate but his eyes told of judgment, his thin mouth of disapproval. When I didn't reply, he continued. "God is punishing you, Catherine."

I found my voice, but it was raspy and low, full of a myriad of emotions. "Don't call me Catherine."

"Isn't that your name?"

"I haven't been Catherine Bennett in a long time. Here, my name is Helen."

The Reverend nodded. "You've spent so many years violating God's natural order of things that you've lost sight of yourself. Your trials are God's punishment for the sin of pride."

"God has made his point." I held my arms out in front of me, presenting my wrists for the shackles. "Are you going to turn me in?"

"Of course not."

"A thousand dollars is a lot of money for a poor preacher. Imagine the number of Bibles you could purchase with it."

"I would never profit off another's misfortune."

I laughed again. "If you get desperate enough, you will." I moved close enough to see the tiny creases on his lips. I raised my eyes and met his. "What is religion if not profiting off the misfortunes of others? If it weren't for sinners you wouldn't have a congregation, or a living."

He swallowed. "I know of no preacher who is called to the ministry for riches. We struggle with our own demons, and want only to offer comfort in the word of the Lord to those who suffer."

"Who offers you succor?" I whispered. "Your wife?"

The Reverend dropped his eyes to his Bible. "Of course. And God, his forgiveness."

I wondered what sins the good Reverend had to confess, and if they were significant enough to make mine look small. "Did you wonder if the rumors about me are true? Is that why you were waiting patiently by my bedside? To ask for comfort in exchange for your silence? What do you want from me?"

The Reverend blushed and opened his mouth to reply when Rosemond interrupted.

"Alleluia, she's out of bed." She stood in the door, wearing a white smock dotted with paint over men's trousers tucked into riding boots, a knowing smirk on her face as she glanced between the two of us. She was cleaning a paintbrush with a cloth. "You are a miracle worker, Reverend. Are you hungry, Helen? I have some stew on the stove."

I was hungry but didn't want to admit it. "Working already?" I said.

Rosemond smiled and looked genuinely happy for the first time since I'd known her. I could almost forget she was a manipulative bitch. "Yes. A sign for the new apothecary."

"I've been meaning to ask you if you would paint a portrait of Portia," Reverend Bright asked.

Rosemond stopped twisting the paintbrush in the cloth. "Of course. Does your wife want to sit for it?"

"She doesn't know yet."

Rosemond's face brightened mischievously. "If she resists, tell her I promise to make her as comfortable as possible."

"I will." He walked to the door. "How much?"

Rosemond looked up at him with a flirtatious little grin. "For you, free. As long as I can use it as my calling card for future portraits."

"Of course!"

"If anyone asks, tell them I am charging you ten dollars."

The Reverend laughed. "Now, Eliza, I cannot lie."

"It's a little white one."

He shook his head in amusement. "I'll talk to Portia right away."

"I'm available at her convenience."

The Reverend turned to me. "You asked me earlier what I wanted from you. I would like your help. My wife and I are trying to help the prostitutes on Calico Row leave that life."

I laughed. "You want me to help you preach to whores?" Camille King had asked me if I was a missionary when she met me, a starving and desperate doctor begging for clients, even whores on Twenty-Seventh Street. Now, it seemed as if her initial impression would turn out to be true, though I was shocked Reverend Bright wanted me as a missionary after our earlier discussion.

Rosemond moved forward. Without her eyes leaving the Reverend's face, I could tell she was sizing him up from head to toe and finding him lacking. "Indeed? What a noble cause."

"Thank you."

"What life are they saved into?" Rosemond asked.

"Marriage," the Reverend replied.

Rosemond lifted her chin and nodded slowly. "Yes, there does seem to be a demand for wives in the West, almost as high as the demand for whores."

"What do you need me for?" I asked.

"There is a doctor in town, Hankins is his name, that treats the whores. But he demands payment in kind from them, as well as money. We, Portia and I, thought it would be a nice change for the women to receive care from a professional who is only interested in their health and well-being."

"As you and your wife are only interested in their souls?" Rosemond asked.

The preacher's shoulders lifted and his face flushed, but his eyes didn't meet either of ours. "Yes. Precisely."

"Of course I'll help you," I said. "I have nothing better to do with my time."

The preacher dipped his head. "Thank you. We will come by in the morning to take you to Calico Row, introduce you to the women."

Rosemond let the Reverend out and returned, her expression one of amusement. "Were you trying to seduce the preacher?"

"I wouldn't know how."

"Don't sell yourself short." She looked back toward the front door. "Though I can tell you from experience he wouldn't need much seducing."

"Do any men?"

She laughed. "No. No, they don't. Enough about that boring little man. How are you feeling?"

"Tired."

She nodded. "You need to move around, shake off the malaise. Let me finish my sign and we'll go for a walk. I'll show you the town. There's water in the pitcher and soap and a washcloth in the drawer." She turned to leave.

"How was Dunk's funeral?"

Rosemond's shoulders straightened. She turned to face me. "Nice. Portia sang 'Amazing Grace.' Dunk loved that hymn."

I nodded. "It was sung at my father's funeral." I poured a glass of water and drank deeply. I closed my eyes as the water flowed down my throat, slaking my thirst and cooling my body, warm and languid from inactivity. "Rosemond, if I could change the past...I know I'm responsible—"

Rosemond put her hand on my shoulder. "Laura, stop. I know you like to think the entire world revolves around you, and that every decision a person makes is somehow related to you, but it's not."

"Why did you tell Bright who I was?"

"He read the telegram before I could burn it."

"You burned it?"

"Of course I did. Bright is proof that even an idiot could put together the initials *WK* with the Murderess and the Major."

"He's not the only threat. Everyone is talking about it. I see the man from the train everywhere I go. I should leave."

"Yes, I got your good-bye note from the hotel clerk, and the money, obviously. Where were you going?"

"Away." *Where I can't hurt anyone.* "I don't know."

"Laura, you saw the man from the train in a busy railroad hotel. He's probably passing through. And hotels are hubs for gossip. It's been two weeks. Interest in the story is already waning, and soon enough there will be another story to take its place. Stay here, cement yourself in everyone's mind as Helen Graham."

"Kindle's dead. You're freed from any obligation you thought you were under."

"I wasn't helping you out of obligation."

"Then why?"

"Isn't it enough that I am?"

"Kindle warned me about you."

"Did he? What did he say?"

"That you aren't a charitable woman."

"I'm not." Rosemond moved closer to me. "What else?"

I held her gaze steadily but didn't reply. Kindle hadn't been forthcoming on Rosemond or their relationship.

"Nothing? Do you really think Kindle *knew* me? He saw what I wanted him to see. What he wanted to see. You and I both know men don't want to see the real woman beneath the silks and perfume and powder. How many men of your acquaintance knew you as you truly are?"

"Kindle, in the end."

"I know you, and like you. I want to help you, to be your friend. It's really as simple as that."

Could it be that simple? I wanted it to be, but didn't trust it, the purity of the reason. I wasn't the type of person who engendered uncomplicated feelings, and looking into her eyes, I realized she wasn't the type of person to have them.

In an effort to focus on anything else but myself or Rosemond, or whatever it was she wanted from me, I turned her head to the side and looked at the sutured gash on her temple. "You've kept it clean. Good. Have you been having headaches?"

"I'm fine." She pulled her chin from my grasp. "I'm offering you a home, Laura. Stay or leave, it's your choice. But your best chance to have a life is here, with me, and you know it."

I found her in the front room. She took stock of me in my new clothes and smiled. "I wasn't sure of your style. I, for one, am sick of wearing dresses. With skirts and shirts, we can share clothes. Once you gain a bit of weight, our size won't be so different."

I ran my hand down the navy brocade tailored vest buttoned over a white shirt and lifted my khaki skirt. "The clothes are fine, thank you."

"Are you hungry?"

"Yes."

Rosemond set her brush down. "What do you think?"

She had turned the front room into a studio. Light flooded in through the bay window on the front wall and filtered in through a gauzy curtain covering the side window. Paints, brushes, empty cans, scissors, knives, a handsaw, tools, and a partially framed piece of canvas sat on a table that butted up flush with the interior wall. Long, one-inch pieces of squared wood and a roll of thick canvas leaned against the wall. A drop cloth was thrown haphazardly over a trunk in the corner. Two easels sat in the middle of the room, one holding a framed canvas with broad black brushstrokes, the beginning of a painting; the other, sturdier easel held a large wooden sign, painted white with precise lettering.

"Did you spend every dime I earned?"

"Almost. Come. I've got stew in the kitchen."

She led me down the dogtrot hall in the middle of the house—a room-for-room replica of the one in Jacksboro where I'd recuperated from my ordeal with the Comanche—and to the kitchen in the back of the house. The cast-iron pot sitting on the wood-burning stove gave off an amazing aroma. My stomach growled.

Rosemond ladled soup into a bowl and handed it to me. Besides the stove, a small worktable, and two chairs, the room was bare. We made space on the worktable and sat down to eat.

I spooned the stew and blew on it. My hand trembled, slightly, but the worst of my withdrawal had happened when I was in bed. I was exhausted from tossing and turning with insomnia and weak from refusing to eat the food that had appeared periodically on my dresser. My stomach had revolted at the idea, but my refusal had been fueled mostly by belligerence, as if rejecting Rosemond's food would hurt her instead of me.

A thick roux coated the meat and carrot cradled in my spoon.

The aroma of garlic and thyme wafted into my nostrils as I brought the morsel to my mouth. I chewed slowly, remembering sitting across a table from Maureen in my New York house, sopping up the last of the stew with a piece of thick bread. I'd never appreciated the touchstones of memory—smell, sound, touch—until I'd lost everything. Home. Profession. Love.

"Did you make this?" I asked, hoping Rosemond would attribute my thick voice to the stew instead of heightened emotion.

"I wish. Lily Diamond brought it. Do you know how to cook?"

I shook my head in the negative, since my mouth was full of stew. "Maureen taught me a little on the wagon train. Biscuits and beans. I learned how to skin and cook a rattlesnake in Indian Territory."

Rosemond raised her eyebrows. "You're hired. I'll take care of the laundry."

I abandoned my spoon in the bowl and held it in my lap. "We're splitting up housekeeping duties?"

"It's hardly fair for one or the other of us to do all the housework, don't you think?"

"Rosemond, I'm not staying."

She nodded. "I understand why you want to leave. You've had a shock. But it's never a good idea to make an impulsive decision after your world's been upended."

"Do you speak from experience?"

"Hard-earned experience." She stared off into the distance, her expression clouded with regret. When she focused on me again, her eyes were clear. "I'll make a deal with you. Stay here with me for three months. It will give you time to grieve, and give the story of Catherine Bennett time to die down again. If you still want to move on after that, I'll buy your ticket."

The thin silver ring on my left hand clinked against the mug handle. The image of Kindle holding the ring with a bruised and bloody hand swam before my eyes. I would never touch those hands again. My recurring dream of Kindle playing the piano and our child running up to hug me would never come true. Every decision I'd made since the Salt Creek Massacre led to me sitting in this kitchen, and to Kindle being tied to a post and executed. Arguing with Rosemond wouldn't change the past.

I nodded in agreement, too exhausted to care. I finished my stew while Rosemond sat quietly, her hands folded in her lap, apparently lost in thought. I rinsed the bowl in the tub of water on the worktable, dried it, and returned it to its correct place.

Rosemond shook herself from her reverie, smiled, and stood. She placed her chair back against the wall and I did the same with mine. "Your cloak is in your chest. Grab it and I'll show you the town."

CHAPTER

15

What day is it?"

"Friday."

"No, what date?"

"April fifth."

Two weeks since Kindle was taken from me. It seemed a short amount of time for a trial, judgment, and execution.

I pulled my cloak on but wondered at the need. The air was fresh, clear, and warm. The shadows were lengthening as the sun set over the horizon to our right.

"The temperature drops quickly, I've found," Rosemond said, as if reading my mind.

Rosemond's was the only house amid a line of tents stretched out along the northern edge of town. On the other side of the street were more tents and a couple of houses in various stages of completion. Behind the houses the desert stretched out to infinity. In the distance, I saw a butte, much like the one I saw in my sweat lodge vision.

We walked south toward the main part of town and the railroad tracks. A train whistle sounded and a black plume of smoke shot into the air and curved to the left as the train pulled out of the station heading toward California.

"Do you remember Amalia Post? From the bridge game?" Rosemond said.

"Of course."

Rosemond found my arm beneath my cloak and intertwined hers in mine. "Turns out, she's as good at business as her husband, or better. She keeps her own money and is buying up real estate across town. She owns the lot the house is on and gave me a reasonable rate and payment plan."

We turned onto a wide street and Rosemond regaled me with details about Cheyenne: where the legislature met and when it was in session, the creation of a library, which businesses were soon to be rebuilt into stone structures, Amalia's help in getting her sign business going and her promise to introduce Rosemond to the powerful men of the territory to paint their portraits. She mentioned Reverend Bright's church and waved in its general direction. She made note of businesses whose signs she believed she could improve on.

She prattled on when we walked past the gallows, as if it wasn't there, though I heard a slight hitch in her voice. Deputy Webster tipped his hat as we walked by. "Ladies."

"Deputy," she said with a coy smile that dropped from her face when we were past.

"You've learned quite a lot about Cheyenne in a short amount of time."

"One of the more surprising talents I cultivated from whoring was to ask questions and listen. People love to talk about themselves, especially men. Sometimes, I was lucky enough they forgot about the sex part. Not often, though. There's the apothecary." She pointed to a false-front building across the street. "I'm repainting his sign. I think I'm going to turn the *Y* into scales. What do you think?"

"Clever."

She grinned. "I hope Amalia comes through on the introductions. Signs are fine, but there's a limit to my creative ability with letters. We're here." Rosemond opened the door to WC Post's General Store and let me enter. Amalia greeted us from behind a glass counter topped with jars of brightly colored hard candies.

"Well, look who's here."

"Hello, Amalia," Rosemond said.

"Eliza. Helen, good to see you up and about."

"Thank you," I said.

"Sorry to hear about your husband. But if there's an ideal place for a woman alone to start over, it's Cheyenne."

"She's not alone," Rosemond interjected.

"Of course not. But you aren't married, either," Amalia said. "Don't need to be, as far as I can tell. Not here, if you've got a mind for business. And I think you do." She nodded at Rosemond, who looked pleased at the compliment. "I've got a couple more orders for you." While Rosemond and Amalia put their heads together over the new orders, I wandered around the well-stocked general store.

The store burst at the seams with all types of goods: food staples such as flour, sugar, and salt; hardware and building supplies; cloth, patterns, and ready-made clothes (which were strikingly similar to what I wore); tents, kitchen utensils, plates, and cups. I walked behind the counter and inspected the small shelf of medicines with dubious claims to effectiveness: Hostetter's Bitters, Mrs. Winslow's Soothing Syrup, Dr. Morse's Indian Root Pills, Mrs. Moffat's Shoo-Fly Powders for Drunkenness. I'd had to counsel more than one patient against using these cures, which were mostly nothing more than opium, cocaine, or alcohol mixed with dangerous ingredients, and had treated a fair few who were made more ill by their use. I turned away and stopped completely at the sight of a Colt revolver lying on a shelf beneath the front counter. I picked it up and opened it. Five chambers, five rounds.

I missed my gun. The last I saw it was at the bottom of my and Kindle's trunk on the Mississippi stern-wheeler. I was certain everything we owned had been dispersed among the cabin boys or officers, not that any of it was worth much. I grieved for the loss of my wedding dress, but the pang of loss was brief. I'd left New York City with little to my name. Everything I acquired since had been lost, looted, stolen, or unintentionally abandoned. Now I stood in a general store bursting with many of the items I'd gained and lost over the last months, wearing clothes purchased for me by a woman I despised but relied on for survival. I stared at the guns displayed and wondered if I'd finally plumbed the depths of despair, or if I had further to go.

"May I help you?"

I pulled the gun beneath my cloak and behind my back. A gray-haired man with unlined skin stood on the other side of the counter with a pleasant smile on his face. Mr. Neck Whiskers from the gambling den stood next to him. The man visibly started.

I moved out from behind the counter. "I was looking at your medicines."

"Can I get something for you?"

"No, thank you. I'm waiting for..." How to describe Rosemond? The word *sister* stuck in my throat.

"Me." Rosemond sailed up, a broad smile on her face that froze when she saw Mr. Neck Whiskers.

"Well, I'll be damned," he said.

"Hello, Miss Ryan," the clerk said to Rosemond.

"Mr. Post. Good to see you."

"Amalia get you squared away?"

"Of course I did. Harry, how do you know Eliza?" Amalia asked. I wondered the same thing myself, but if Mr. Neck Whiskers' expression was any indication, I thought I knew.

I moved back a step and hoped to escape Amalia's close scrutiny. She was too perceptive by half.

Mr. Neck Whiskers glanced around, wondering who Eliza was, no doubt, but Rosemond came to his rescue. "I don't think I've had the pleasure," she said, holding out her hand. "Eliza Ryan. This is my sister, Helen Graham."

"Harry Diamond."

"Lily's husband!" Rosemond said with forced cheer. "How nice to meet you. Your wife is quite the cutthroat bridge player."

"Ah, yes. She mentioned you and your...sister." Harry Diamond looked me up and down.

"Eliza is a painter," Amalia put in. "Signs, mostly. If you know anyone who needs a sign, come to me. I take the orders for her."

Harry Diamond nodded appreciatively. "Leave it to you, Amalia, to already have your finger in a new endeavor."

"I'm invested in this one; sold her a lot over on Mill Street. She had her house up and move-in ready in four days. Helen, this is my husband, Mr. Post."

The gray-haired man nodded to me. "Pleasure to meet you."

"Likewise," I said.

"Helen and I must be going," Rosemond said. "I want to show her as much of the town as possible before sunset. Amalia, have your boy bring the blank signs along tomorrow."

"Will do."

When we were down the street Rosemond's tight smile faded

to a scowl. "I played poker with Harry Diamond. He propositioned me," I said.

"He would."

"A former customer?" I asked.

"Yes." Her step was determined.

"You had to know this would happen."

She sighed. "Yes, but I hoped it wouldn't happen so soon."
She stepped off the sidewalk to cross the street. I followed,
enjoying the weight of the gun I held behind my back.

Unlike the town, the Cheyenne rail yard wasn't winding down
for the night. Freight trains shunted off onto side tracks were
being unloaded, uncoupled, and reorganized for diversion to
Denver. Ash and bits of coal from the plumes of smoke emit-
ted by the locomotives floated through the air, coating everything in a gray dust. Rail workers yelled instructions, rail cars
clanged into one another, brakes screeched before emitting an
exhausted hiss, locomotives rotated in the stone roundhouse
for their return journey. The yard was ten tracks wide, and a
train in various states of readiness waited on every one.

Across the tracks was a second city, this one less prosperous
than the one behind us. A street ran next to the far track, and
a line of wooden buildings fronted it. The land rose slightly
behind the buildings and there I saw the familiar sight of a tent
city, glowing with lamplight.

"Calico Row."

"The Brights' cause."

"It's mostly two-bit whores. Some Negroes and a couple of
Chinese," Rosemond said.

"Where are the nicer houses?"

"Around Nineteenth Street."

"I wonder if the Brights visit them as well?"

A stream of men walked in the direction of Calico Row. They dipped their heads to us, touching the brims of their hats respectfully. We turned and started walking back to Rosemond's house.

"I doubt it," Rosemond said. "It's not a terrible life, if you're in the right house. I've heard of some whores marrying newly rich miners and becoming prominent citizens in their own right."

We walked in silence for a while. "Why didn't you ever go that route? Surely you were asked."

"I've never met a man I wanted to be beholden to. And no matter how much money or influence they have, they'll always be known as former whores."

"Are you going to help the Brights in their reform efforts?"

Rosemond laughed. "No. I have enough to be going on with reforming myself. I'm sure you will do fine without me." Rosemond opened the front door to her house and let me enter. "I've been telling people you're a midwife, were a nurse in the war. That your father was a doctor."

"No lies so far."

"You can't hang your shingle as a doctor." Rosemond removed her coat and walked into her studio. I noticed a cot folded up in the corner for the first time. "But you can do the next best thing. Treat the people the doctor doesn't want to."

"As a midwife."

"Or nurse. It's not the perfect solution, I grant you, and you'll have to be careful not to be too terribly good at your job. You should probably stay away from the hospital if you want to be able to quietly ply your trade. The two-bit whores will complain at first, but they'll be so happy someone competent is helping them they'll keep their mouths shut, especially if you keep the cost down and buy their loyalty."

My gaze fell on an unfinished painting facing away from the door. I expected the early stages of the sheriff's portrait and was surprised to see the outlines of a portrait of a woman, sitting on a bench, gazing out a window. I recognized it as a replica of the sketch from her notebook I flipped through on the train.

"It's me."

"Gazing longingly east toward the man you love. At least, you will be gazing longingly."

Bile rose in my throat at my remembrance of Kindle's fate. How could I consider settling in with Rosemond, creating a life in Cheyenne, when Kindle's had been cut short? Why did I deserve to live when he did not?

"Why are you painting me?"

"I need to practice before I paint Portia—the Reverend Mrs. Bright. And the good sheriff. You are, unfortunately, the most familiar face of the past few weeks."

Rosemond pulled the drop cloth off a standing trunk, flipped open the latches, and, with a jingle of glass hitting glass, pulled out my medical bag. "You were clutching the ticket when you fainted." She kept her hands on the top of the bag. "You were planning to leave before you left the room that night, weren't you?"

I nodded.

She shook her head, opened the bag, and pulled out a small wooden box. "The apothecary said this is a good start."

Rows of medicine bottles and rolled bandages fit snugly together inside the box. So familiar was the gun I'd been hiding behind my back I almost reached out with it. I caught myself in time, and lifted a bottle with my free hand. *Laudanum.* My mouth watered.

"Can I trust you?" Rosemond asked.

I removed the bottle from the box and gave it to Rosemond. "Why are you helping me?"

She placed the laudanum on her worktable and laughed. I stuck the gun in the back of my skirt. "You don't get it, do you? You've made it. Oh, it's not Timberline, Colorado—that's where you were heading originally, wasn't it?"

I nodded.

"But it's probably better. Women can own property in Wyoming, vote even. You've been trying to start over for a year. Here you are. Your new life."

Without Kindle.

"This is your opportunity, Laura. You can take it or you can go back East where you'll surely be caught and hanged. Give it three months." She pushed the box toward me. I grabbed it with both hands and held it to me. "Please?"

I nodded slowly. "Three months."

It was easier than arguing.

The polished wooden gun handle was smooth and unblemished, and fit comfortably in my hand.

I broke the barrel, checked the bullets, and clicked it back together.

The house was dark and quiet. The smell of paint and the occasional bump from the other room told me Rosemond was awake but engrossed in her work. Unconcerned about me.

Ignorant of the gun I held in my hand.

I broke the barrel, checked the bullets, and clicked it back together.

No more killing, I'd resolved after the sweat lodge cleansing ceremony. I closed my eyes and inhaled, trying and failing to recapture the place of solace I found in Indian Territory. I'd put the events of the Canadian behind me, mostly, and moved on with Kindle. We had been given a glimpse of what life together would be like, only to have it snatched out from under us because of who I was.

I took a shuddering breath, felt the tears stream down my cheeks, broke the barrel, checked the bullets, and clicked it back together.

And lifted it to my temple.

There would be no reprieve this time. Rosemond would find me, brains sprayed across the bed and onto the wall. I would finally be with Kindle, forever, no more worry about being pulled apart.

No more deaths in my name.

My hand trembled.

No more being used by others for their own ends.

I put my thumb on the hammer.

No more cravings.

Through the tears pooled in my eyes, I saw myself in the small dresser mirror. Who was that woman with the gun to her head?

I pulled the gun down.

Sobs shuddered through me. I covered my mouth to keep Rosemond from hearing and coming to me.

I didn't want to die, and I didn't want to live.

I heard a knock at the front door and stilled, listening for Rosemond. Who would call so late? A rustling, another knock, and Rosemond's voice. "Who's there?"

An indistinct male voice replied. A long moment passed; the male spoke again. Finally, Rosemond opened the door.

I crept over to my bedroom door, cracked it, and peeked into the hall.

"Harry. Why am I not surprised?"

"Let me in."

"No. Go home to your wife."

"I will, after we catch up." The door opened a bit, but Rosemond forced it back.

"I'm not in that business anymore."

Harry Diamond laughed. "You're a painter now?"

"Yes."

"Once a whore, always a whore."

"If that's your idea of talking your way inside—"

Rosemond lost control of the door and it slammed against the wall. "I don't need to talk my way in." I stepped back and pulled my door almost shut. "Where's your *sister*? I knew she was a whore when I first saw her."

"Helen's asleep."

"Hmm. I seem to remember a rather raucous story you told about your sister once. Her name was Cordelia."

"You're mistaken."

"Who is she, Rosemond?"

"She's my sister."

"You're sticking to the lie. I'd expect nothing less. Regardless, wake your sister up. The three of us can have a good time."

"No. You need to leave."

Diamond looked into Rosemond's studio. "You really *are* painting."

"Did you think it was a front for a whorehouse?"

"It's not a bad idea. Cheyenne's the capital. Lots of important men would pay a premium to fuck Rosemond Barclay, the most exclusive madam in Saint Louis."

"I'm retired."

Diamond laughed. "As I said before..." He encroached on Rosemond. "I know you could use the coin. Lily told me that Negro lost your money."

"We're fine. I appreciate you stopping by..." She moved toward the door, but Diamond put his arm around Rosemond's waist.

"You want to be selective in your customers. I understand." His hand moved down to Rosemond's ass and he pulled her toward him.

She turned her head. "If I were being selective, you would be the last man I would fuck."

Diamond reared back and struck Rosemond across the face. I was across the hall before Diamond could pull his hand back again. I pressed the barrel of the gun against his head, right behind his ear.

"Let her go."

Diamond stilled but didn't release Rosemond. The *click* of the hammer being pulled back was loud in the hall. "Let her go, or Rosemond will have to scrape your brains from her freshly lumbered walls."

Rosemond pushed away from Diamond, who remained motionless. I pressed the gun against his head, pushing his chin down into his neck. Diamond held his hands out. "I don't take kindly to men beating on women, whore or no."

"I—I—"

"You probably don't think I would do it, don't you? Turn around."

Diamond did, and I pressed the gun to the middle of his forehead. "My sister's done with that life. If you, or anyone like you, shows back up here, I won't hesitate to put a bullet in their head." I took the gun from his head and shoved it in his groin. "Or somewhere else."

Diamond tripped over his feet in his haste to leave. Once outside, he regained his confidence, even if his dignity was nowhere in sight. "You'll regret this."

Rosemond closed the door and leaned against it; her eyes lingered on the gun I held by my side until they finally rose to meet mine. The humor in her eyes finally made it to her lips.

"And you wonder why I like you?"

CHAPTER

16

We pulled the worktable to the middle of the kitchen and drank our whisky out of tin coffee mugs. The gun lay on the table in front of me.

"Where'd you get the gun?"

"I stole it from Amalia's store."

Rosemond nodded. She refilled her mug, then mine, and drank. "Were you thinking of using it on me? Or yourself?"

I drank my whisky and stared at the mug, remembering choking on my first drink of whisky months ago. "I hadn't decided."

Rosemond laughed. "I do like your honesty. Why do you want to kill yourself?"

I held out my hand. "Can we not talk about me? I'm so tired of myself I could..."

"Kill yourself?"

I finished the whisky in my mug and held it out for Rosemond to refill. "Where's Lyman?"

"What?"

"Lyman. The man who sold out Kindle and wanted to turn me in. Why didn't he follow us?"

"Lyman wouldn't want to get too far away from civilization.

He likes the finer things. He's probably waiting for Kindle to lead him to you."

"What will he do now?"

Rosemond furrowed her eyebrows. "Now?" Her expression cleared. "That Kindle's dead, you mean?" Rosemond shrugged.

"He told me you two had a history."

"Did he?" Rosemond sloshed whisky onto the table with the next pour. "Oops."

The silence between us was uneasy, neither of us sure where this conversation was going or how much of each other we wanted to reveal. My strength came from hating Rosemond, not what she was, but that she had meant something to my husband in the past, and maybe the not-too-distant past. I didn't trust her in the least, but my options were thin and she seemed eager to pursue a friendship with me. What else explained the clothes, the medicine, and the idea for my nursing practice? What else explained that she hadn't turned me in for the new one-thousand-dollar reward?

Rosemond isn't a charitable woman.

I couldn't let myself become complacent and forget Kindle's words. She wasn't trying to help me, she wanted something from me. Legitimacy, she claimed, but there was more to it. She would never tell me willingly, probably afraid I wouldn't go along with whatever it was. I had to keep my guard up but manipulate her to let hers down.

Rosemond's gaze kept settling on the gun in front of me. I turned it so the barrel pointed away from her. Her mouth quirked up into a half smile. "I wasn't concerned."

I chuckled. "How did you become a prostitute?"

She raised her eyebrows and waited to answer, holding my gaze while she did. "I spread my legs for the wrong man."

"Lyman?"

"Why would you assume that?"

"Kindle said—what were his words? 'She has no respect for John Lyman.' It's not unreasonable to assume it's a long-standing animosity."

"You don't go through what Lyman and I have and call it animosity."

"What would you call it?"

She pursed her lips and lifted her eyes to the ceiling. "Mutual admiration, with a healthy dose of suspicion."

"Admiration?"

"Lyman taught me a lot about myself, and other people. Specifically, how to manipulate them so I get what I want."

"What a lovely characteristic to hone."

"Don't act as if you haven't done the same thing to get where you are."

I drank my whisky. She was right, to a point. I preferred to forge headfirst into conflict, but there were times when I took a more prudent approach to getting what I wanted. What had the last year been but a tactical approach to staying free? I'd lied, cheated, and killed to survive. I rolled my shoulders to banish the weight of familiarity that had settled there.

"Lyman was the man you spread your legs for?"

She finished her whisky and poured more. "He was a Union officer occupying Nashville. He took my virginity, probably took bets on how long it would take him to deflower me."

"Surely you didn't have to become a prostitute."

She smiled, and I knew there was much more to the story. "Why did you want to be a doctor?"

"To prove everyone wrong."

Rosemond's mug stopped halfway to her mouth. "Truly?"

"I wanted to help people, too. But mostly I wanted to be better than the men." I chuckled. "Maureen called me out on it in

Galveston. Said I..." I stopped, refilled our mugs. "We're not talking about me."

"Are you trying to get me drunk?"

"No, I'm trying to get *me* drunk."

"Would you like the bottle of laudanum?" Rosemond smirked.

I shook my head. "Why do I feel like you're leaving something out of your story?"

"Because I am. I know what you're doing." She pointed at me and squinted out of one eye. Her speech was noticeably slurred. Part of me wondered if this was an act. I'd drunk as much as she and was pleasantly numb around the edges but far from drunk. I'd assumed Rosemond would be an experienced drinker, enough so a few glasses of whisky wouldn't affect her like this.

"What am I doing?"

"Besides trying to get me drunk, you're pretending to care about me so I'll tell you my secrets."

"Sisters tell each other everything, don't they?"

Rosemond's head jerked back. "They do. Yes, they do. Do you have a sister?"

"If I had anyone at all I wouldn't have left New York."

"Of course. I had a sister. Cordelia. She was the favorite, naturally. Beautiful. Sweet. Innocent. Trusting. Everything I wasn't."

"You resented her."

"No. I loved her. I would have done anything for her." Rosemond poured more whisky. "And did." She shook out the last drop into her cup. "Don't worry. There's more. Somewhere."

"I think you've had enough."

Rosemond shook her head. "Now I've started, I don't want to stop."

"What happened to your sister?" I asked.

"Nothing. Not a Goddamn thing. She's married to a Tennessee politician and is having babies with alarming regularity."

I waited while Rosemond laughed manically at her joke. When her laughter died down, her expression slowly faded to thoughtfulness. "I chose the winning side, but Cordelia won anyway."

Rosemond drank her whisky in one swallow, rose unsteadily, and walked out of the kitchen. Curious, I picked up my gun and followed.

I found her in the studio, rummaging in her trunk. She straightened and held up a full bottle of bourbon. "It's time for the good stuff. I'm surprised Dunk didn't drink it."

"Rosemond, you've had enough."

"You're taking this sister act too seriously," she said.

"Am I?"

While Rosemond struggled with opening the new bottle, I returned to the kitchen and retrieved a bowl.

"What's that for?" she asked.

"When you get sick in the night." I placed the bowl on the floor next to her cot.

Rosemond twirled around, bottle high in the air. "I don't have a Goddamn sofa to sit on." She stumbled over to the cot and landed heavily on it, sloshing bourbon on herself in the process.

I set the gun down on the worktable. "I'll confess; I'm surprised you're such an easy drunk." I sat on the cot next to her and pried the bottle gently from her hand.

Rosemond shrugged and exhaled dramatically. "I gave up drinking whisky a couple of years ago."

"You're temperance?"

"God, no. Selling cheap whisky at exorbitant prices was

almost as lucrative as whoring. Until I became the most expensive madam in Saint Louis." She said the last with a healthy dose of derision. She smacked her lips. "I'm out of practice, drinking whisky. Wine isn't the same. I see you're one to be reckoned with." She nodded to my empty tin mug. "Drink. There's nothing worse than a lone drunk."

I let her splash bourbon in my mug but didn't drink it. "Why did you stop drinking?"

Rosemond leaned her elbows on her knees and stared off into the distance. "A lover."

"What?"

"I stopped drinking because my lover didn't like it."

"A lover?"

She turned her head and glared at me. "I had lovers who didn't pay." She stared back into the middle distance. "Not many, but a few."

My stomach clenched as I realized who she was talking about. Kindle had started as a client and morphed into more. "Kindle asked you to quit?"

Her glare was more brutal the second time. I defiantly held her gaze, and she exploded in laughter. "My God, you're one of the most egotistical people I've ever known, including myself. Move." She pushed against my shoulder. I stood and she lay down on her cot and closed her eyes. "Don't forget your gun when you leave."

I placed the bourbon on the table and picked up the Colt.

"If you decide to kill yourself, have the courtesy to do it outside so I won't have to clean it up," Rosemond said.

"And if I use it on you?"

Rosemond opened her eyes and grinned. "I'll be beyond caring, now, won't I? You won't do it, though."

"Why not?"

"You like me, though you don't want to admit it. We're alike, you and I. Survivors."

I laughed. "What have you survived? You choose to be a whore."

She closed her eyes. "Don't kill me, and maybe one day I'll tell you."

CHAPTER

17

I can't decide if that smells delicious or if it makes me want to vomit."

Rosemond was a mess. Her dark, tangled hair stuck up in every direction, framing her wan face. Her normally rosy lips were pale and cracked, and dark circles underlined eyes squinting at the harsh morning light.

"I made biscuits and coffee." Rosemond clutched her stomach. I motioned to the chair. "Sit."

"Don't yell at me."

I twisted my mouth to keep from laughing. I poured a cup of coffee in my mug from the night before.

"What's that?"

I placed the coffee in front of Rosemond, who was staring at the paper and pen on the other side of the table. "A letter to Mary."

"The pious Sister Magdalena? Do you think that's a good idea?"

"Why not?"

"She probably blames you for Kindle's death. And chances are the Pinkertons are watching her like a hawk, hoping you'll do just that." She motioned to the letter.

I knew she was correct but didn't want to admit it. Instead, I grasped her chin and lifted her face to the light. "Your face is red from where Diamond hit you."

She moved her head away. "It's nothing I haven't covered up before. How long have you been awake?"

"A while." I continued to pay the price for the relief laudanum gave me for my menses. I was nervous and irritable and couldn't sleep. I kept my cravings at bay by staying busy, keeping my mind occupied, and eventually I knew I would feel myself. Then the next monthly cycle would start. The time between the former and the latter was getting shorter and it was getting more and more difficult to resist the release of one tiny draught. Whisky helped, but I knew it was merely another vice that would be difficult to resist.

Rosemond clutched her stomach again. "I have to go clean your mess up today."

"What mess?"

"Well, there's the small problem of you threatening to shoot Diamond's cock off with a stolen gun. You can't threaten a man like that."

"I won't help you next time."

"Brooding men are dangerous, and a thousand dollars is a lot of money. He knows you're not my sister. Be careful of Diamond."

"I will, but he won't tell that story. He'll look the fool at the hands of a woman."

She seemed to consider. I placed a plate with a biscuit in front of her. She grimaced again. I served myself and sat across from her.

"We need sorghum," I said.

"What?"

"Sorghum syrup. I have an affinity for it."

"I'm sure Amalia has some at the store. They're going to miss their gun, if they haven't already, and Amalia'll figure it was you soon enough. I need to take it back."

Rosemond picked at her biscuit and tentatively took a bite. She swallowed with difficulty and pushed the plate away. "What brought on your bout of biscuit making? Are you done wallowing?"

"Yes."

I'd had plenty of time to think during my sleepless night. I'd cried until tears wouldn't come, then spent hours staring mindlessly at a large knot in the wooden ceiling, going over the events of my life since leaving New York—the peaks and valleys, the deaths, the terror, the moments of happiness and joy—until I saw myself as the eye on the ceiling did: an addict wallowing in grief and self-pity, hoping for a death that would not come, but not brave enough to make it happen. The eye judged me and found me lacking. There was nothing I hated more than weak, helpless women, and I had become one quicker than I ever imagined possible. Grieving wouldn't kill me, but betraying who I was would. I rose determined to survive my loss despite myself.

"Good. Kindle would want you to move on."

"I can't promise to not burst into tears at inopportune times."

"And I can't promise to hold your hand every time you do."

"Trust me, I know." I sat back and studied Rosemond. "I can't decide if you are as cold as you pretend to be, or if it's a carefully crafted facade."

Rosemond picked her biscuit to shreds. "Emotions have always betrayed me."

"How?"

She lifted her eyes to meet mine. "By not being returned."

With those four simple words, Rosemond's character became

clear. She wasn't unfeeling in the least; she felt too much, and worked assiduously to mask it, lest she be hurt. Again.

"Cordelia?"

Her brows furrowed.

"Your sister."

"I know who Cordelia is."

"You told me about her last night."

"I did?" She stood. "You'll have to get me drunk again to get anything else out of me."

"If your appearance is any indication, that might take months."

"You might be right."

We chuckled together, and I immediately felt shy. Sometime in the night, our relationship had changed from antagonistic to something like an uneasy truce. Rosemond must have sensed it, too, because she joked, "Are we becoming friends?"

"We aren't enemies, at least."

A heavy knock at the door broke up our conversation, a relief to us both, I thought.

"Should I get my gun?" I asked.

"It's probably Amalia's boy delivering the blank signs. You get it. I'm hardly presentable."

I opened the door to Reverend Bright, who wore an open, happy expression, and his wife, Portia, who gripped her hands together so tightly her knuckles were white. "Good morning!" Reverend Bright said. He and Portia caught sight of Rosemond over my shoulder. When I followed their gaze and saw her through their eyes, I was embarrassed for Rosemond. She looked like a hard-used woman. Portia's mouth bent further into a frown, but the Reverend merely looked chagrined. "Are we too early?"

"For what?" I said.

"To visit Calico Row. Have you forgotten?"

"Yes, actually." I touched my forehead with my hand.

"Oh, well. Is it a bad time?" the Reverend asked.

Portia reached out with her hand. "Of course it is. You've been through a lot. We'll come back another day."

"No, it's fine. I need to get out and about. Let me clean up breakfast, and I'll be ready. Would you two like a biscuit? We have extra."

"A biscuit would be delicious!" The Reverend stepped through the door.

"Oliver, I fed you breakfast."

"Yes," he said with a chuckle, "but you and I both know your biscuits aren't very good."

Rosemond glared at the man and was readying to speak when Portia moved forward and reached out to Rosemond. "What's wrong with your face?" She remembered herself and pulled back before touching her.

"I don't know what you mean," Rosemond said, trying for dignity.

"It's red. Did someone hit you?" Portia's accusing gaze landed on me.

I laughed heartily. "You think *I* hit her?"

"It's nothing. Excuse me while I get dressed for the day," Rosemond said.

The Reverend had been looking in the studio. "Is that your work?" He stepped inside and went to the easel without asking leave to do so. We followed.

"Yes," Rosemond replied. "It's Helen, gazing out the train window."

The Reverend's expression was all appreciation. "How wonderful. Look, Portia."

"Yes," his wife said. "It's very nice."

"Maybe while Helen and I go see the girls, you and Portia

can talk about your portrait. Won't you do some sketches or something first?"

"Yes, I—"

"I'd rather go with you," Portia said.

An uncomfortable silence followed. "How nice," Rosemond finally said. She addressed the Reverend. "I have one order to finish and two others to start. We'll have to start the portrait another day."

"I didn't mean..." Portia began.

"I know exactly what you meant. If you'll excuse me."

We filed out of the room and Portia turned toward Rosemond as if to apologize again, but Rosemond walked to her room and shut the door with a solid thump. Portia blushed but regained her composure quickly.

"This way," I said.

I served the Reverend a biscuit. Portia demurred.

"How long have you been involved in your mission?"

"It's how we met. Would you like to tell the story, Portia?"

"You're a much better storyteller than I am, Oliver."

He smiled fondly at Portia. "A good thing for a minister, don't you think?"

"Indeed." Portia returned her husband's smile.

"I left Missouri back in sixty-seven to minister to the railroad workers. Let me tell you, everything you've read about the hell-on-wheels towns was true. When the final stake was driven, I kept going up and down. I liked the itinerant life, you see. But to be that kind of preacher you have to be inspiring and"—he chuckled self-deprecatingly—"I've never been called inspiring."

"Oliver," Portia chided.

"No, no. It's okay. If I hadn't taken a hard look at my life and my ineffectiveness, I would have never met you." He took her hand and squeezed it. He kept his eyes on his wife as he continued. "We met at church, of course. I was visiting a friend, seeking his counsel, when his wife introduced us. It took no time at all for us to discover we suited very well." He patted Portia's hand and looked up at me expectantly.

"We bring people to the Lord by setting an example," Portia said. "Our behavior is our witness. If someone asks, we will surely tell them about the Lord. But we do not preach to the sinners."

"It's a novel approach," I said.

"Portia suggested it, and I have to say, it's been more effective than I would have ever imagined. I've tried evangelizing and got run out of more than one Western town."

"What precisely do you do?"

"Befriend them. Talk to them about cleanliness, nurse those who need care, help those who want to leave the life however we can," Portia said.

"The biggest problem we see is their alcohol and opiate addiction," the Reverend said. "They need money to support it, and the easiest way is to sell their body."

I nodded in agreement. It was the same problem I'd seen in less reputable houses in New York City. Typically, the madam encouraged the addiction, all the better to keep her girls under her power. My face flamed as I realized that Rosemond's giving me laudanum on the train, in Grand Island and after the Kindle telegram, fell into the same vein.

"Helen, are you feeling quite well?" the Reverend said.

"What?"

"You went pale all of a sudden," Portia said.

I shook my head as if to clear it and smiled. "You're a nurse, Portia?" I asked.

"No more than any other woman. My knowledge is basic."

"She makes up for it in the care she gives," the Reverend said, adoration clear in his expression and voice.

"Shall we go?" Portia said, rising from the table.

"Yes," I said. "Should I get my gun?"

"You have a gun?" Reverend Bright said.

"Doesn't everyone west of the Mississippi?" I said.

"I don't," he said, scandalized, but Portia didn't seem surprised in the least.

"You're a man. I'm sure you can defend yourself."

"It's not that, it's that I couldn't imagine taking another man's life."

I smiled wanly at him. "You've never been pushed to the point, Reverend."

I wedged the gun in my belt as much to keep Rosemond from returning it to the Posts as to see the expression on the good Reverend's face when I walked out with it. He didn't disappoint. I think Portia smiled, slightly. As satisfying and surprising as their reactions were, I couldn't deny the underlying truth of my small rebellion.

The soiled doves of Calico Row congregated in small groups outside their tents, slatternly and exhausted after a busy Friday night. Their jokes and conversations were loud and boisterous, as if they were trying to convince themselves their lives were normal and they weren't doomed to die an early death from disease, addiction, or violence.

A large woman noticed us first and separated herself from the throng. "Well, well, who do we have here? A female gunslinger?" The women laughed, as they were required to do.

"Stella, this is Helen Graham," Reverend Bright said. "She's a nurse."

"That gun says different," Stella said.

"Yeah, I ain't never seen no nurse carry a gun," another woman said. "You ain't that female bandit everyone's talkin' about, are you?"

Bright laughed too loudly. "Don't be silly, Clara."

"You think you need protection from us?" Stella said, moving closer to me. She was a few inches taller than me but easily a hundred pounds heavier. Her skin was pale and soft, her waist cinched tight to highlight her expansive bosom. Stella's face might have once been pretty, but it was marred with the broken blood vessels and red eyes of a woman who liked her drink.

"From your customers," I said.

"Afraid they might mistake you for a Calico queen, are you?"

"It's not outside the realm of possibility. Drunk men do stupid things."

"Oh, listen to the fancy talk," Stella said. She looked me up and down. "So, what are you doing here, Slim?"

My breath caught, as a pang of grief shot through me hearing Kindle's endearment in the mouth of this whore. I lifted my chin. Tears would signal weakness to this woman, and I was determined to fight them. "I'm here to offer my services."

The whore Bright called Clara sidled up to me. Her eyes were watery and red. She sniffed and tried to give me a seductive smile. "We don't get many of your kind here," she said, caressing my arm. "It's my specialty."

"My *nursing* services."

Clara's eyes lingered on my bosom. "Too bad." She leaned forward and whispered, "I've been longing for the soft touch of a woman. Come see me if you change your mind." Clara moved away and winked at the Reverend and Portia.

"Clara, show some respect," the Reverend snapped. He shot

a nervous glance at his wife, who remained stoic, with nary a blush touching her cheeks. She was obviously inured to the prostitute's teasing. A good and necessary defense with this crowd.

"We've already got medical services, courtesy of the good Dr. Hankins," Stella said.

"We thought you might like to be treated by someone who wouldn't expect carnal payment," the Reverend said.

The woman laughed again. "Hell, Reverend, polishing that old cooter's knob don't cost us a dime," Stella said.

I was suddenly exhausted, tired of pushing my way into where I wasn't wanted, and for what? A few dollars from hardened women who wouldn't listen to me? These whores were a different breed from the laundresses of Fort Richardson and Camille King's women on Twenty-Seventh Street. An aura of helplessness and hopelessness hung around their bravado that I was afraid I would never be able to crack. For the first time in my practice, I didn't want to try. Whores might be the most numerous women in Cheyenne, but they weren't the only ones.

"I apologize. I was told you weren't being cared for. If any of you would like to use my services, the Reverend knows where to find me."

I turned and walked off. Portia caught up with me and stopped me with a hand on my arm. "That was uncharitable."

"Yes, they were. But they have a doctor."

"I meant you."

"I'm uncharitable because I don't want to poach another physician's patients?" I crossed my arms over my chest. "Enough of this. Why don't you like me?"

"I don't know what you mean."

"I'll grant you there are plenty of people in the world who loathe me, but at least I've given them a valid reason for their antipathy. What is your reason?"

Portia's face reddened from what I assumed was embarrassment at being confronted. "I do not loathe you."

"But you do not like me."

"I don't know you."

"Precisely. To be frank, whether you like me is the least of my worries right now, and you've done nothing to endear yourself to me. I will at least endeavor to hold judgment on you until I get to know you better. I would appreciate it if you would do the same for me." I held out my hand. "Agreed?"

She shook it with a surprisingly firm grip. "Agreed."

"Thank you." I continued walking. "As to the soiled doves, they don't want my services, so I left."

"You don't understand their ways. Their hard exterior is their armor."

"I understand whores better than you think." I stopped and appraised Portia. Now that her expression had relaxed out of a constant state of puckered disapproval at the sight of me, I saw a different woman. She wasn't beautiful by conventional standards due to the freckles dotting her face and the halo of frizzy hair that always seemed to escape her best attempts to tame her curls. But her mesmerizing eyes and the general pleasantness of her features made her a truly striking woman. "How do you know so much about them?"

"I've worked with soiled doves for years."

"Trying to make them see the error in their ways?"

"At first."

"Until you discovered their profession was rarely a choice they made freely, but something they came to for survival?"

"Yes." Portia studied me with genuine curiosity for the first time. "You sound like you've had a similar revelation."

From her innocent expression, I knew her husband hadn't told her of my past, and I was relieved. I didn't need to worry that another person was befriending me to further their own good fortune.

"I worked with similar women in New York. With my father."

Not precisely a lie. My heart sank a bit. Would I ever again be able to share the unvarnished truth of my past without worry?

I continued. "These women have little control over their life. They pretend they do, but we know the truth. If rejecting my services gives them a feeling of power and confidence, who am I to push them to do otherwise? They know I'm here, and willing to help. They'll come to me eventually."

Portia nodded. "When Stella called you Slim…"

"It was my husband's nickname for me," I said quickly, hoping to stave off tears.

"My condolences."

A purple caravan pulled by two stout brown horses jingled its way down the street, interrupting us. A portly man drove the wagon, resplendent in lavender pants and purple coat that perfectly matched the wagon. He lifted his black derby from his head as he passed and said, "Ladies." The painting of a nearly naked woman feeding a snake graced the side of the caravan, advertising Mugwump Specific, "For the Cure and Prevention of All Diseases of the Flesh."

"Is he selling a chastity belt?" I asked. "Otherwise, that's a tall order."

Portia smiled wryly. "If he sold those he wouldn't have any business, would he?"

The man put the brake on his wagon and disembarked. He clutched at his backside and grimaced before grinning hugely at the gathered crowd. "Ladies, did you miss me?"

"Well, if it isn't Dr. Drummond," Stella sneered. "There's no takers here for your snake oil. It don't cure nothing, unless

179

giving my girls the shits counts. No one wants to poke a girl who's got the trots."

"That can happen if you take too much of it. Lucky for you, the formula has been changed such that it not only decreases that unfortunate side effect, but has been proven to cure the pox within days."

"It's a waste of our money," Stella said.

"You'd be better off buying sheaths," I said, stepping forward. "Stopping the infection before it starts, as well as stopping the spread to your johns."

The snake-oil salesman's expression changed so subtly I doubted anyone but me noticed it. Beneath his bonhomie exterior lived a calculating, manipulative man. He took me in from head to toe, his gaze lingering on the gun in my belt.

His smile widened and he stepped forward. "I don't think we've had the pleasure."

"That's our very own gunslinger," Stella said. "If your new stuff don't work, we'll send her after you."

"I'm a nurse," I said.

He held out his hand. "Theodore Drummond."

"Helen Graham." His grip was strong, and I winced.

"I'm sorry," Drummond said, not sorry at all. "Did I hurt you?"

I gripped and released my hand a few times. Since leaving the Mississippi and falling under sway of the opiate, I'd fallen out of the habit of massaging my hand, and it was stiff as a result. My mouth watered at the thought of laudanum. I felt my skin go clammy, and I swallowed. "No. It's an old injury. I'm fine."

"Pain? Stiffness? I have something for that," he said, motioning to his caravan.

"I'm sure you do, *Doctor* Drummond," I said, looking at the side of his caravan.

He leaned forward and whispered, "Only in the very loosest sense of the word."

Drummond noticed Portia. "Mrs. Bright, how lovely to see you. I see you aren't using the hair tonic I gave you."

"The ineffective tonic and draught you sold me at an exorbitant price, you mean?" Portia said.

"The very one. Some hair is too much for even the best treatment. I can mix a stronger potion, if you like."

"I wouldn't buy anything from you even if it promised to be from the fountain of youth."

Drummond raised his eyebrows, and I knew she had given him an idea for another ineffective, but profitable, potion.

"I'll be in town for a couple of days. Come see me if you change your mind." He lifted his hat from his head and ducked into Stella's tent.

"I can't believe I fell for it," Portia said in a harsh voice.

"Sometimes we believe what we want to believe, all evidence to the contrary." I forced myself to not look at Portia's hair, furrows of waves pulled tightly against her scalp. Her eyes met mine, and I was struck again by their singular beauty and uniqueness. Now that they had lost their animosity toward me, I was enchanted by the depth of intelligence I saw there.

"Miss?"

Startled, I turned from Portia toward the voice. A plump, dark-complexioned Negress stood a few feet away, hands held in front of her, eyes downcast.

"Yes?"

"I heard you talkin' to Stella before, and wondered if your offer extended to us."

"You were there? I didn't see you."

Her eyes met mine. "No, ma'am. I expect not."

"Of course the offer is for any woman who wants my help. Do you need my help?"

"No, ma'am. But my friend does."

"Lead the way."

The woman turned, but I put a hand out to stop her. "What is your name?"

"Monique."

"Monique. A lovely name." She nodded and walked away. "Portia, are you coming?"

"Yes."

"Where's your husband?"

She shrugged one shoulder. "He'll be along shortly, I'm sure."

Monique led us back toward Calico Row, but instead of walking in front of Stella and her girls' tents, she turned right and walked behind the tents opposite for a hundred yards, and moved back to the main row. We walked down a small incline and across wooden planks laid across the bottom of a dry wash in readiness of the rare occasions of high-desert rain. The tents and buildings on the other side were identical to Calico Row, except the women and men standing in groups and walking to and from were Negroes.

"That there's our shebang," Monique said, pointing to a small wooden building with a corral attached. Inside the corral three pigs attacked the slop a large man threw over the side.

"Morning, Monique."

"Jesper."

The man nodded to us and went inside his store. Monique stopped in front of a tent on the opposite side of the street. "The doctor don't come see us," Monique said. "I guess he don't want our payment, though we willing to pay money instead."

"Your money is good with me."

She held open the tent flap and Portia and I walked inside.

It was large, and neat as a pin. At the back of the tent, three cribs were cordoned off by sheets. A quick glance inside one showed pallets on the floor instead of cots, but the bedding seemed clean from my vantage point. The front of the tent was used as a waiting room, with a small table and four chairs, a deck of cards on one side, a sheet down the middle, and an identical setup on the other side, along with a small stove where a pot of coffee warmed.

"Would you like a cup?" Monique offered.

"Oh, no," Portia said.

"Yes, thank you," I replied. When Monique went to make me a cup I motioned to Portia to accept.

"On second thought, I'd love a cup."

Monique served us and motioned for us to sit down. We did and I sipped the coffee. "Oh my word, Monique. That is the best coffee I've had in months." Portia concurred.

When Monique smiled, she kept her mouth closed, I suspected to hide a jumble of crooked teeth. "You'll have to do some mighty fancy nursing to get the secret out of me."

"Oh, a challenge." I smiled at Monique and placed my mug on the table. "Are the separate rooms for whites and blacks?"

Monique nodded and glared at Portia when she stiffened. "You don't like the idea of your men laying with us?"

"No, it's that..." She trailed off.

"They been doin' it since they brought us over. Least now they're havin' to pay for it. And pay they do. Though some try to get it for free."

"How do you make them pay?" I asked. Duncan had proved that no black man in the country would be allowed to beat a white man for nonpayment and live, let alone do it repeatedly.

"I got a white boy who watches over us at night. We give

him a portion of every white man's payment, and he gets some snatch for free every night. He just have to beat a couple men and the rest learn. They pay pretty easy now, though there's always some railroader who comes off for a quickie during the red light who don't know what's what."

"And the Negro men don't mind you servicing white men?" Portia asked.

"Nope. We charge our men less. They visit Stella's, pay a premium for white snatch. 'Course, they have to poke them in the alley so the white men don't know. The crackers don't mind fucking a black woman, but God forbid sticking their pecker in a white woman who's opened her legs for a nigger. 'Course, we have to do the Chinamen standing up out behind the tent, too. No one, white or black, wants to dip it where a Chinaman's been. There ain't many of them, so's it don't matter overmuch."

Portia made a valiant attempt to take this information in with equanimity, but I could see the strain around her mouth and eyes. An interesting reaction for someone who said she'd worked with prostitutes for years. "Who is it you want me to see?" I asked Monique.

"Lavina. This way."

Monique led the way to the crib on the far side of the tent, off the whites' waiting room. "Do these women only see white men?" I asked.

"Uh-huh," she said, but I could tell she was lying. "Lavina, a nurse is here to see you."

The woman lay on her side, facing away from the crib opening, a large soft lump beneath the blanket. She turned over and looked at us through opiate-hooded eyes. "What?"

"A nurse is here to see you."

"What for?"

"What do you mean, what for? To take care of it."

I moved inside and to the bottom of Lavina's pallet and rolled up my sleeves. "She's pregnant?"

"Yes."

I knelt down. "Hello, Lavina. I'm Helen. Would you lie on your back for me?"

With a sigh, the woman rolled over, pulled her legs up, and opened them in the practiced manner of a woman who'd done it a thousand times and the resignation of a woman who knew she would do it a thousand more.

"I think I'll wait outside," Portia said in a faint voice, and left the crib.

I watched Portia leave, then turned back to Lavina. I closed the whore's legs and pressed them gently down. "I want to feel your stomach first."

I pulled her dress up and revealed a soft, expansive stomach, one that would easily hide a pregnancy for weeks. "When did you feel the quickening?" It was impossible to tell how far along she was by sight. When I pressed against her abdomen and measured the head I estimated thirty weeks.

"Couple of weeks ago."

Monique couldn't see the expression of disbelief I gave Lavina, who looked away. I pressed on her stomach this way and that, trying to get the baby to respond. I pulled her dress down to cover her nakedness.

"When was the last time the baby moved?"

"I don't know. I try to forget it's there."

"What are you high on? Opium? Laudanum? Morphine?" She looked away.

"Can you get rid of it?" Monique asked.

"No. She's thirty weeks along, at least. Maybe more. Why didn't you try to get rid of it earlier?"

"We did," Monique said.

185

"When?"

"A month, or little more. It didn't take," Monique said. "Got the herbs from that huckster, Drummond. It was Stella's doin', I know. She know Lavina my best girl. She'll do anything she can to ruin our business, and she got Drummond by the cock. Little do she know that Drummond dipped hisself into Lavina, too. Part of his payment, he say."

"I imagine there's plenty of men to go around."

"Yes, well, we get the rich men from across the tracks who wanna relive the old days with a little nigger snatch. Rubs Stella raw she's stuck sucking off miners and railroad men and won't ever be welcome in the saloons on Nineteenth Street."

I stood. "You're going to have to bring it to term."

"I don't want no white man's baby."

I thought of the girl at Mary's orphanage, Sophia. No matter how intelligent she was, or how good at midwifing, or possibly surgery, she would be, she would always struggle because of her mixed parentage. A mulatto child born to a whore in the West would have an even more difficult time of it, especially if the baby was a girl.

I thought of another pregnant whore I'd tried to help a year earlier at Fort Richardson. She and her baby had both died. At the hands of Cotter Black, because of me.

I rubbed my forehead. So many lives lost in my name. But, I was still bound by my oath, *believed* in it. My goal—my purpose—as a physician would always be to save everyone I could. This child would be no different.

"Between the herbs you took and the opium you're eating, the baby might be stillborn. If not, I know of an orphanage in Saint Louis that will take your baby."

Lavina propped herself up on her elbows. "You do?"

"I do. You'll have to pay for my train passage east, but I will take the baby there for you."

"That's mighty nice of you," Monique said. "Why would you do that? You gonna sell it?"

"What? God, no. It's a Catholic orphanage run by my husband's sister."

I'd promised Rosemond three months, and if Lavina brought her child to term, I would almost make it. She'd promised to pay for my train ticket, but there was no guarantee she would keep her word. In ten weeks the newspapers and gossips would have moved on from Catherine Bennett, and traveling with a baby would give me an invaluable disguise. I would give Mary the baby and cable my cousin, Charlotte, to book passage for England, finishing the trip Kindle and I had started.

"I'd like to visit my sister-in-law, and taking Lavina's baby will give me the opportunity," I explained.

"Where's your husband?"

My throat thickened, but I managed to get one word out. "Dead."

Monique looked down her nose and studied me, as if trying to figure out where the lie was and how much she could trust me.

I shrugged as if it meant nothing to me, and realized it didn't. Going to Charlotte held no appeal, and neither did staying in Cheyenne. "The offer is there. Do you have a midwife who delivers your babies?"

Monique scoffed. "We delivered plenty of babies on the plantation. I expect this one won't be no different."

"You're probably correct. If you run into trouble, send for me. I'm glad to help."

"Even a nigger whore?"

"I'm taking her baby to Saint Louis, aren't I?"

"What's it gonna cost?"

"My passage. One way."

"Don't like Cheyenne?"

"It's not home."

"Where is home?"

"I wish I knew."

Portia waited for me outside the tent. "Would you like to explain why you ran out of the tent? I thought you were a nurse," I said, as we walked back the way we came.

Portia blushed again. "I didn't imagine she wanted me watching the examination."

I laughed at the obvious prevarication. "She's beyond caring who sees her pudenda."

"I didn't want to see it."

"It's no different than a white woman's, I assure you."

Her face reddened further. "Why would you think—"

Drummond interrupted us. "Mrs. Graham?"

"Mr. Drummond."

"I hoped I might have a word with you in private."

"Of course."

"You can find your way home, I assume," Portia said, stiffly.

"Yes."

She nodded and walked off, back straight and stiff. I supposed all the good feeling we had managed to cultivate in our morning together had been lost, though I wasn't sure why. "What can I do for you, Mr. Drummond?"

"Theodore. I, um…" He cleared his throat. "I have a boil that needs to be lanced."

I remembered his grimace when he got down from his wagon

and had an inkling where his boil might be located. I knew as a physician I shouldn't shirk my responsibilities to heal, but I was exhausted from my sleepless night, and my cravings for laudanum were returning. The thought of lancing a boil on Theodore Drummond's backside held no appeal at that moment.

"Wouldn't a doctor be better suited for such a procedure?"

"Yes, well, Dr. Hankins and I had what you might call a run-in on my last swing through town. I wouldn't want him holding a knife over me in such a vulnerable situation."

Though the sun was bright in the cloudless sky, chills rushed across my body. Though the worst had passed, the mere mention of laudanum was enough to awaken my craving. Soon I knew I would be a pale, shivering, and trembling mess. Drummond watched me with a discerning eye. "Are you ill?"

"Recovering."

"We can help each other. Payment in kind. Whatever I have on my shelf." He lowered his voice, though there was no one around to hear. "Or under the counter, if you wish."

I swallowed and pushed away the urge to take him up on his offer. "Coin is fine." I considered asking him to meet me at my house in an hour but decided I didn't want this man to know where I lived.

"Do you suppose Stella would let us use a cot?"

Drummond raised his eyebrows, and I realized how the suggestion sounded. "Don't insult me, Mr. Drummond, or you won't want me to have a knife near your nether regions, either."

He held up his hands in surrender, though his amusement didn't abate. When we arrived at Stella's tent, Drummond went inside as if he owned the place. "Stella, my dear. We need to use your facilities." Stella's response was muffled. Drummond stuck his head outside the tent. "Well, come on, then."

The bright sun struggled to permeate the dirty canvas tent,

throwing the inside into a perpetual gloom. The detritus of a busy night littered the floor at the edges of the room—whisky bottles, cigar butts, a leather belt with a broken buckle, a neck cloth stiff with dried blood, a used sheath. Stella sat at the table in the main area, drinking a beer with a thick head of foam, while a young whore picked up a deck of cards scattered on the floor. Drummond went to the keg in the corner of the room and drew himself a beer. "Want one, Mrs. Graham?"

"I would, as a matter of fact."

"Help yourself," Stella said sarcastically, waving her hand.

"I'll give you a free bottle of Mugwhumps," Drummond said.

"I don't want no free bottle of that snake oil."

Drummond handed me the beer. He removed a small pouch from his inside pocket and tossed it on the table in front of Stella. "Cannabis. You roll it like a cigarette."

"I know what it is," Stella said. "You've cut it with oregano, most like."

Drummond clutched at his heart. "That cuts to my very core, Stella dear."

The beer was lukewarm and tasted like piss. I forced it down and tried not to grimace or cough from disgust.

"You're right," Stella said. "Oregano would cost you money. Prairie grass is free." Stella evaluated me. "Do what you need and get on, Slim. I wanna sleep." Drummond bent down and spoke into Stella's ear.

I set my medical bag down and set to work, and was immediately sidetracked by an empty water bucket. "There's no water."

"Pump's across the street," Stella said.

I looked to Drummond, expecting him to be a gentleman and offer to fetch it, but he and Stella continued with their low-voiced conversation. I picked up the bucket and went to find the pump.

With the whores sleeping off their busy night, Calico Row had gone quiet, the only evidence of life the stray dogs sniffing for food in the alleys, feral cats darting between the shadows, and a plume of black smoke floating behind the tents across the street. I walked between the tents, disturbing a pair of copulating cats and getting a terrifying hiss in return. The female didn't move but stared into the distance, an expression of resignation on her little feline face. With my back to the wall of a tent, I inched past, hoping the tom wouldn't launch himself at me.

The water pump was in the middle of a large U-shaped area bordered by outhouses on one side, a washhouse on the other, and a large fire pit at the top of the "U." A Negro woman with turbaned hair and her sleeves rolled up past her elbows washed clothes in a large wooden tub. Next to the fire pit, Jesper leaned on a two-by-four scorched on one end, watching the flames. He nodded at me and poked at the fire with his board. The woman ignored me. I hooked the bucket over the nozzle and pumped water into the bucket. I removed the bucket with my right hand and dropped it, spilling the water all over my skirt.

I rubbed my right hand with my left, silently cursing myself. Even after almost a year, my instinct was to use my right hand, which would never be as strong as the other. It didn't help when I used it to punch a man in the nose. A pain shot from my middle knuckle up through the finger. I grimaced and flexed my hand and was relieved that it trembled only slightly. I was lucky Drummond would be turned away, and unable to be discomforted by my shaking hand.

I filled the bucket halfway, hooked it on my left arm, and returned to the tent. Stella sat at the table as before, and

Drummond stood across from her, near where my medical bag sat, top unbuckled. I met Drummond's shrewd eyes with a pang of fear. Was there anything in my medical bag that would connect me to the Murderess and the Major?

I set the bucket on the worktable. "Did you find what you were looking for?" I asked.

"You don't have any laudanum."

"I suspect you have something in your caravan that will help with the pain. More cannabis, maybe?"

"That I do. Just odd for a nurse to have everything but an opiate. Not to mention a surgeon's kit."

"It was my father's," I said. I stepped close to Drummond, keeping my eyes on his, and hoped I was brazening his questioning out, though my insides had turned to jelly. I opened my bag and looked inside. It was a jumble, but nothing seemed to be missing.

"And you know how to use it?"

"Well enough to lance a boil on your ass, yes. Do you want my help or not?"

"Hush your yapping and get on with it," Stella said. She motioned to the corner crib. "Use Clara's crib. She's off with that preacher, sweet-talking him into giving her something for nothing." She rose unsteadily and disappeared behind a sheet. I heard a rustling, the creak of a straining cot, and a groan of exhaustion. Almost immediately, she began to snore.

"Bring the basin of water," I ordered Drummond.

A gingham dress draped over the back of a chair. An empty beer stein sitting next to an oil lamp on a small table. An 1868 calendar with a drawing of a bird's-eye view of Chicago nailed to the corner post. A cot, low to the ground and covered with a cloth, stained with the fluids of dozens of men and Clara's blood. The sum total of this woman's possessions. I covered my mouth as the true depth of hopelessness and despair of these women's lives hit me.

Drummond tossed the stein into the corner and placed the basin on the table. I sprinkled carbolic in the water and dropped my instruments and a couple of squares of cloth in. When I turned around, Drummond stood before me, pants around his ankles, his penis hanging well past the tail of his shirt. I sighed, fully aware he was trying to intimidate me. Or frighten me. Or test me. I glared at him. "I'm a married woman. I've seen it before. Turn around and lie down."

With a smirk, he did as told, but not before removing his coat and draping it over the chair. I pulled the chair near the bed, set the basin on it, and lifted the back of his shirt. A boil the size of a walnut jutted out from the top of the crack in his buttocks. I placed a carbolic-soaked cloth over it and put two more into the water. Drummond hissed.

"If that hurts I can't imagine how you drove a wagon."

"It wasn't easy."

"Tell me about your route." I held the lamp near the boil and dabbed gently around it to sterilize it. It was red and tender around the base, and the bulb of the boil was filled with pus. It was a difficult location, with a high chance of infection once I lanced it. But there was no other remedy, to my knowledge.

"I stay near the railroad, from Grand Island on, and down to Denver."

"Wouldn't taking the train be safer?" I set the lamp down and picked up my scalpel.

"I started on the train. Lugging a box of medicine from town to town."

"The caravan is a step up, then?"

"Indeed."

I held a carbolic-soaked cloth next to the boil and hovered my scalpel above it. "Are you ready?"

Drummond inhaled, nodded, and buried his head in the pillow. I pressed the scalpel into the boil and just managed to dodge the stream of pus that shot out of it like a geyser. Drummond's scream drowned out my yelp of disgust. I cut through the boil as Drummond sobbed quietly into his pillow. "It's almost over," I said, mopping up the seeping pus with one of the cloths, tossing it onto the floor, and grabbing another. By the time all of the fluid had drained, I'd used every piece of cloth that had cushioned my bottles of medicine, save one, which I wanted to use for a bandage.

"Mr. Drummond, I need to bandage your wound, but I need long strips of cloth. There is nothing here that is clean enough, and I don't have a bandage that long. Do you have a clean sheet in your caravan?"

He nodded. I patted him on the shoulder. "Don't move. I'll be right back."

"Key's in my jacket pocket," he said.

The inside of Drummond's caravan was neat as a pin, much to my relief. I stripped a sheet from the bed built into the inside front and searched through his drawers for scissors. I found them in the third drawer, next to a brass-and-glass syringe. Why would a snake-oil salesman need a syringe? I opened the upper cabinets and found all manner of ineffective patent medicines, mostly the purple bottles of Mugwhumps Specific. In the bottom cabinets I found what I suspected was his true line of goods: cannabis, opium, laudanum, and vials of morphine. No wonder the whores didn't run him away from Calico Row for his medicines' ineffectiveness.

Someone pounded on the caravan door, and I almost dropped

the vial of morphine I held. I replaced it, closed the cabinet, and picked up the sheet and scissors. I opened the caravan door to see Reverend Bright, red-faced and lifting his arm to pound on the door again.

"Helen!" His brows furrowed in confusion, and he tried to look around me. "What are you doing in there?" His voice was harsh and accusatory.

I closed the door behind me and padlocked it. "Not what you think. I treated Drummond for a minor complaint, and I need a bandage. I might ask what are you doing, banging on his door?"

"I wanted to talk to him about the dope he's selling these women."

"Talk? You looked like you wanted to fight."

"We have no chance to save these girls if he keeps returning to sell them opium."

I stopped in the middle of the street. "How many women have you and Portia saved?"

He jerked his head back. "Why?"

"I'm curious. How many?"

"Two."

"And where are they now?"

"Both married good Christian men."

"Farmers?"

"Miners."

"They went from spreading their legs for money to spreading them for free and having to do chores sunup to sundown?"

"It's a more respectable life than prostitution."

"Only a man would think so."

"You can't mean to say you think prostitution is a good life for a woman."

"Of course not, but we object to different things. You object to what they do. I object to how they are forced to live. Have you seen inside Stella's tent?"

"Yes."

"It's deplorable. Why are they forced to live that way? Because they have no other options, no other way to earn money. Society only values women's bodies and what they can do for men. Take care of them, make their children, or give them pleasure."

Flushed and angry, I walked off. The Reverend followed. "What would your husband think, you talking about marriage in this way?"

I stopped abruptly and stuck my finger in Reverend Bright's chest. "Don't you dare talk to me about my husband as if you know him. We had a marriage of equals in every way."

"That is a blasphemy in the eyes of God."

"It's a good thing I don't care much for what God thinks, then, isn't it?"

By the expression on the Reverend's face, his opinion of me hit rock bottom. In for a penny, in for a pound. "If you want to save whores, you should educate them so they can stand on their own two feet, not have to rely on a man."

I entered Stella's tent, leaving the Reverend red-faced and gaping at me. Wonderful. I'd managed to befriend and alienate Portia and her husband before lunchtime. I pulled back the curtain dividing Clara's crib and found her on her knees in front of the cot, fellating Drummond. I dropped the curtain closed and turned away.

"Be done in a moment, Mrs. Graham," Drummond said, slightly breathless but without a bit of shame. I would have left except my medical bag was in the crib and, though I found him absolutely reprehensible, I couldn't leave Drummond's wound untreated. I sat at the table, cut the sheet into strips, and was starting to tie four strips into one long bandage when I heard Drummond's completion.

"Now will you give me it?" Clara said.

"That was hardly long enough for a full dose."

Hardly long enough? "From this side of the curtain it was an eternity."

Drummond opened the curtain, the bottom half of his body naked. "I feel a new man," he said. "Would you like to finish me off?"

I stood. "You see this gun, Mr. Drummond? I know how to use it. If you ever speak to me that way again, or even speak to me with a passing hello, I will pull this gun and blow your brains out." His grin slipped. "Clara?" The whore came around the divider. "Come here."

She shuffled over to me, all of her coyness from earlier gone. In front of me was a young woman who might have been pretty at one time but was now a whore desperate for escape into an opium-induced stupor. Drummond watched us. I waved at him in dismissal. "Leave us be."

Clara nibbled on the side of her thumb.

"What is he giving you?"

"I don't know, something new. He said I'd like it better than the opium."

I sighed. *Morphine, most like.* "Clara, do you want to die in this crib?"

She dropped her hand. "You sound like Ollie. I don't need no preaching. I just want to relax a little before the johns come tonight. It's Saturday, and we'll be on our backs all night."

"How many men do you service?"

She shrugged one shoulder. "Thirty on a good night."

I rubbed my temple. Thirty men a night, and Cheyenne was

growing exponentially. With that kind of use, and the dope, she would be dead in a couple of years. "How old are you?"

"Don't rightly know. Twenty, or thereabouts."

Drummond came out of the crib, fully clothed, smug and sure of himself. I looked toward the outside at where I'd left the Reverend, and back to Clara in the middle, trapped.

I can't save everyone. But shouldn't I at least try?

Yes.

CHAPTER
18

∽◦⚬◦∽

Dear Mary,

I've been starting and stopping this letter for weeks. The urge to speak to you overshadowed every time by the knowledge that my letter will not be received with joy or equanimity. I understand if you blame me for your brother's death. I will never forgive myself for being the cause of his downfall. If I had kept my distance from him, as I knew I should, he would be alive today. The knowledge is almost too much to bear. A pall has fallen over my existence, and I'm not sure it will ever lift, nor do I want it to. I don't want to move on and be happy if Kindle isn't with me.

I wish I could find comfort in your God. I have tried, but there is no solace, no voice speaking to me. I don't blame Him. I've ignored Him for years, to only call out when I'm in pain. He is rightly angry with me and, truth be told, I'm angry with Him.

I am sure you visited with Kindle before the trial, and he possibly told you the story of his capture. Rosemond Barclay helped me escape, at Kindle's request, she says. I still don't believe her, but, both being orphans with no friends, we have come to the conclusion that having each other is better than no one. At least, that is the conclusion I have come to. I suspect Rosemond genuinely likes me. I cannot fully trust her yet. Maybe in time.

We have settled in Cheyenne. We get along tolerably well. She seems to have found a genuine happiness, and has lost the hard edge of her personality I've known from the beginning. She and Cheyenne are kindred spirits, both working hard to polish off their rough edges into some semblance of civility. Rosemond is a painter and has opened a sign business, and is doing well, well enough that she has obtained the respectability she craved in a short time. I am nursing the portion of the population the doctor refuses to care for, and working toward saving enough money so I can return east to see you, pay my respects to Kindle's grave, and continue on to my family in England as originally planned.

My days have fallen into a rhythm. Waking, making breakfast, cleaning up, going across the tracks to visit patients, stopping by the Posts' general store on the way home to pay down on the gun they sold to me at a high interest rate after I confessed to stealing it (I do not feel safe without one now), picking up orders for Rosemond and whatever supplies she needs, returning home to fix a late lunch. The afternoons are filled with suture practice—I have transitioned from needlepoint to working on a dead piglet to more closely mimic human flesh—and walks around town. Occasionally, I will stretch canvas on frames for Rosemond, or do other odd jobs to help her stay on top of her thriving sign business and fledgling portrait business.

Kindle is never far from my mind. When I am alone, tears prickle my eyes and flow freely down my cheeks during whatever task I perform. I fall asleep crying, and wake crying. If

Rosemond sees my red eyes each morning, she doesn't mention it, a small gesture of grace I appreciate.

Every day as I walk through this new life, as I talk and smile and cook and sew and visit my patients, I think: this is the life I should have had with Kindle, then realize it was the life I argued with him about, that I pushed back against. At this moment, I would gladly give up my profession for a routine day with Kindle.

I finally had the courage to write because I need a favor. Do not be indignant; the favors aren't for me. A woman named Portia Bright and I have started teaching women to read. Prostitutes, specifically. These are women who have no hope of any life but servicing men and dying in a filthy crib, either from being beaten by a john or by an overdose of opium. It's our hope that a little bit of education will allow them to leave the life and stand on their own. Most of these women just want to feel valued, and have someone see them as something other than a body to be used. Teaching them to read and write is a small step on a long road. Will we be successful? I do not know. But I am convinced that I need to try. I have seen so much death, been responsible for too much, that I want to be responsible, if even in a small way, for bringing hope into someone's life.

We are in the process of raising money for a library in Cheyenne, and the committee chair has promised that a portion of the money will be spent on readers. Until then, we are reading out of the Bible and using the few books we can borrow from other women in town. If you have any books from your library to spare, it would be greatly appreciated.

There is a woman here, a Negro prostitute, who is pregnant (most likely with a white man's child, though it could be a Chinaman or Negro's child, as well) and does not want to keep the baby. For the cost of a one-way ticket, I have offered to bring the baby to you and your orphanage. I can't think of a safer place for a child such as this. She should have the child in a couple of months, and I will leave as soon as possible. Cheyenne is pleasant enough, as frontier towns go, but I cannot seem to feel settled here, no matter how routine my days are. My body hums with a nervous energy, a need to move, to escape.

Please telegram if I and the baby are not welcome so I can make other arrangements for the child.

With Warmest Regards,
Laura

"What's this I hear about you amputating a man's foot?"

"Good morning to you, too, Amalia," I said. I noticed Lily Diamond across the large, open-sided tent, bustling over to us.

The sun was rising in a burst of orange and pink on the eastern horizon as the town readied for a spring festival to benefit the future library. Instead of a staid fund-raiser in the confines of one of the numerous Cheyenne hotels, the committee had planned it as an outdoor spring festival, celebrating the end of a long, cold winter. It was a brilliant move, as almost every resident of Cheyenne, regardless of class, occupation, or color, had been buzzing about the fair for weeks. Amalia Post, as chairwoman of the library committee, was everywhere at once but made time to quiz me about an event I had hoped to keep secret for a while longer.

Three weeks after visiting Calico Row the first time, I'd returned one early evening, dispensing mercury to the afflicted whores and talking about the importance of using sheaths consistently for protection against venereal disease and pregnancy, and offering to teach the women to read. The latter suggestion received as much teasing and scorn as the suggestion of using sheaths, but I saw cautious interest beneath their brittle, suspicious exterior and suspected that in time they would come around.

I was in Monique's crib, checking on Lavina and assuring the women there was no ulterior motive with my offer to teach them to read, when we heard a commotion outside and went to see what was happening. Two young men were carrying another between them, entreating Jesper to help. A thick trail of blood followed them.

"In here," I said. They looked at me in shock for a moment, a white woman in their neighborhood ordering them around, until Monique gave the same order and they obeyed without question.

The man's foot hung to his leg by a thin strip of muscle and his dark complexion was turning gray from loss of blood. I quickly fashioned a tourniquet to stop the bleeding and save his life, and stared at the injury. I'd seen enough amputations in the war I could've done my own even without years of training. But I also knew if I healed this man, I would bring unwanted attention to myself, in the form of Dr. Hankins, who thought so little of the white widow ministering to the denizens of Calico Row he hadn't bothered to meet me. I agreed to help and exacted a promise of secrecy from the people assembled around the boy's bed, a promise that hadn't lasted a day.

"Yes, yes, it's a fine day," Amalia said. "Is the rumor true?"

"Are you asking her about the Negro?" Lily said.

"Yes."

I sighed. "To be honest, it was hardly an amputation. The foot was held on by merely a thin piece of muscle. More a snip and a suturing."

Lily Diamond gasped. "Helen, why would you do such a thing?"

"He would have died if I didn't."

"Why didn't you call Dr. Hankins?" she asked.

"There wasn't time."

"I doubt Roger Hankins would have hurried over to help a Negro. He's a Rebel," Amalia said.

Lily blanched. "I'm a Southerner, too."

"As am I," Rosemond said, sidling up to the group with Portia in tow. This morning Rosemond had diligently scrubbed dried paint from her cuticles, and didn't reach for her paint-splattered work clothes. Instead she wore a dress with large, bright green flowers on a buff background. She was turning heads, men and women alike, and I appreciated for the first time the beauty and charisma that had made her so successful as a madam in Saint Louis. Portia seemed dazzled, and though she tried to show interest in the conversation, her gaze kept sliding to Rosemond.

"And I don't hold it against either of you," Amalia said. "Will the boy survive?"

"Of course he will. My sister is a brilliant nurse," Rosemond said, showering me with a fond smile. It was a far cry from the reaction she had when I arrived home, bloodstains streaked across my shirt and skirt.

Godammit, Laura! Do you want to get found out?

He would have died, Rosemond.

Better him than you.

"He's young and strong," I said to Amalia. "As long as infection doesn't set in, he should recover. Monique and Jesper are caring for him, and doing an excellent job following my instructions on keeping his wound and bandage clean. I'm going by later to check on him."

"I feel I should warn you," Lily said, leaning forward and

dropping her voice. "You've raised some eyebrows, Helen, showing up Dr. Hankins like that. I assured Mr. Diamond you didn't mean anything by it, but he wasn't moved. He doesn't like you for some reason," Lily said, puzzled.

Rosemond and I glanced at each other, knowing full well why Harry Diamond didn't like me. "I have that effect on men," I said.

"Enough chitchat. Let's get to work," Amalia said. "Do I need to go through your job here, Helen?"

I looked at the table full of jars of candy from Amalia's general store. "No. I imagine I can muddle through selling penny candy."

Amalia nodded curtly and walked off, Lily in tow. "Are you sure you can handle this grave responsibility on your own?" Rosemond teased.

"It will be a struggle, I'm sure."

Rosemond waved at a new arrival who entered the tent. "There's the governor's wife. I am determined to get her commission today. Excuse me."

Rosemond sashayed away, leaving the faint scent of lavender in her wake. Portia and I watched her go, both more than a little awestruck.

Rosemond had thrown herself into earning respectability with an enthusiasm I frankly didn't expect. Gone was the cagey, calculating whore. In her place was a woman who fit so easily into Cheyenne society no one challenged her right to be there, or her new identity. It was the territory capital, after all, and Rosemond had been a favorite of many of the politicians and businessmen for years. Rather than expect to continue their commercial relationship, the men were eager to pretend the history didn't exist, especially if their wives were Cheyenne residents. Rosemond's civic participation gave many a married man heart palpitations until they realized she had no intention of revealing her previous occupation or their support of it. Portrait business started to flow toward Rosemond, so much so that she was in a near way to be out of the sign business altogether. A small voice in my head said there was a connection between her willing silence on her clients' pasts and the blooming portrait business. I was torn between admiration and judgment, with admiration winning more often than not.

I had been enveloped into society by way of her dragging me along to every bridge game, church service, women's committee meeting, and philanthropy effort Cheyenne had to offer, and they were innumerable. The men wanted to capitalize on the West; the women wanted to civilize it. A theater, symphony, and opera were all on the drawing board, though years away from fruition. Modernizing the hospital—which I'd avoided; I knew myself well enough that I could not walk into a hospital without giving away who I was—and starting a library were more immediately attainable and easier to sell to the philanthropic public.

I'd gone with Rosemond willingly—it was my job to help her settle in, after all, and I had my own project I wanted to see to fruition: teaching prostitutes and Negroes to read. It soon became apparent that Rosemond got along with the society matrons of Cheyenne very well without me, and that no one was terribly interested in educating whores and former slaves. Though I found all of the causes worthy, I could barely stand most of the women involved in the various committees. I'd never been able to stomach the obsequiousness of society women and their good deeds, suspecting that many of them cared not a whit for the deed but only how managing it or participating in it made them, and by extension, their husbands, appear to the world. Which, I came to realize, fully explained why none of these women were interested in my cause. Since no one would help me publicly, I decided to throw myself into the one committee that I could possibly manipulate to achieve my goal: the Cheyenne Public Library. Which explained why I was selling penny candy at a fund-raiser barely four weeks after arriving in Cheyenne.

"Where is the Reverend?" I asked Portia.

"Saturday morning is his devotional time, when he readies his sermon. He will come later."

"Has he come around on our project?"

Portia looked across the tent and shook her head.

When I finished bandaging Drummond's boil, I'd gone to make amends with Portia and the Reverend. On the walk to their house, I'd kicked myself for arguing with the one other person, besides Rosemond, in Cheyenne who knew my identity. My mouth had always gotten me in trouble. I had to pray this time it would get me out. The Reverend had been easy to coerce back into my good graces. I spoke of having time to see the error of my ways, and of course the natural course of things was for the man to be the dominant mate. I'd almost choked on the words, and when I glanced at Portia, I could tell she saw right through my lies. I'd thought she would once again look upon me with puckered disapproval but was gratified when her face relaxed into a smile so faint, her husband was too obtuse to see it.

I mentioned my idea about teaching the soiled doves to read and write and almost lost all of the Reverend's goodwill. He launched into a diatribe about how Wyoming territory made a colossal mistake giving women the right to vote and own property. Five minutes later, when he transitioned into the four horsemen of the apocalypse and Revelation, I'd had enough. I started to rise, but Portia put her hand on my arm and shook her head, her eyes never leaving her husband, who'd long since stopped seeing us and instead saw the world burning down around him.

When he at last ran out of steam, Portia spoke. "Of course you're right, Oliver. But think of how a literate wife might be able to aid her husband. Many miners and farmers aren't, and would find a literate woman, who had the appropriate deference for the man's superiority, a great solace. We wouldn't teach them to read so they get ideas above their lot, but so they may be of greater use to their husbands. Isn't that right, Helen?"

In that moment Portia and I became, if not friends, at least comrades. I swallowed my retorts and agreed. Portia, being a former schoolteacher, took the lead on teaching the women to read. I focused on their physical well-being and the Reverend focused on their souls.

I turned to Portia. "Did you educate the prostitutes back East? Oh, I've been meaning to ask: where are you from? I've never known."

"No. The madams were protective of their charges, and many of them knew how to read. Excuse me."

She made her way quickly across the tent and was soon lost in the crowd.

I set about straightening the candy jars, and opening the lids and smelling the candy, wondering who in the world I was going to sell hard candy to, and why Portia had avoided telling me where she was from. I looked around the tent: Amalia and Lily Diamond manned the booth with the auction items, explaining and talking up all the good the money would do for the community; Rosemond seemed to be trying to shake hands with every prominent citizen Cheyenne had to offer. I snatched a lemon drop from a jar, turned my back to the crowd, and popped it in my mouth. When I turned around, a swarm of wide-eyed chattering children descended on my booth, eager to spend their pennies on the brightly colored confections.

I spent a solid fifteen minutes trying to calm the rambunctious children, excited and indecisive with so many options to choose from. They asked questions of me and one another, discussed the options, argued about which flavor was the best. They all decided at once, and changed their mind two or three times. I would serve one, and two would take his place. It was like chopping off Hydra's head. At the height of it, I spotted Amalia across the room, watching me with a small smile on her face. I pushed an errant strand of hair from my eyes and continued serving the never-ending stream of children.

Finally, after what felt like hours, the children had disappeared, and I was left looking out at a sea of adults—politicians, farmers, miners, prostitutes, and wives. If I didn't have the half-full jar of pennies and the half-empty jar of candy as proof, I would wonder if the last few hours had been a nightmare.

"Why do you look so dour?" Rosemond sidled up to my booth, a large, teasing smile on her face.

"I'm eating a lemon drop. Don't tell Amalia I'm sampling the goods."

"Your secret is safe with me. I've come to help you."

"Now that the rush is over? I didn't know there were so many children in Cheyenne."

Rosemond laughed.

"I suspect Amalia gave a penny to every one. I think she still holds the gun against me."

"You *did* steal it."

"I'm paying her for it, at an exorbitant rate, I might add."

"Oh, stop griping. It's for a good cause."

"Amalia better make good on purchasing the first readers for the collection, and a Brontë or two."

A little boy came up to the booth with a penny. His hair was parted in the middle and slicked down with a shocking amount of oil. His clothes were clean but worn at the edges, and his hands had the look of being freshly and savagely scrubbed. He took his time choosing, not out of excitement but with the mien of a child who wasn't about to waste this unforeseen opportunity to treat himself.

"How did you manage to finagle your way out of any responsibilities?" I asked Rosemond.

"It's a gift."

"You're insufferable."

"You love me."

"I do not."

"Can I have a stick of peppermint, miss?" The little boy placed the penny on the counter and looked up at me with soulful brown eyes framed by long eyelashes.

My heart clutched, and a wave of crushing grief and guilt at forgetting Kindle overcame me. Though I managed brief moments of forgetfulness, the loss of Kindle was always with me, brought forward in dozens of little ways, even in the eyes of a child buying candy.

I forced a smile. "Excellent choice."

He clutched the thick stick of peppermint in a hand that would soon be red and sticky. He smiled and could hardly get his thanks out of his mouth before licking the peppermint. I dropped the penny in the glass jar that served as a bank.

"Thanks for the penny, miss." He touched his flat hat at Rosemond.

"You're welcome," Rosemond said. She watched the boy walk off and turned a playful smile toward me. "What? Children deserve a treat every now and then."

"You're the devil."

"I'm a Good Samaritan. Treating children"—she squeezed my arm—"and keeping you busy."

Warmth spread throughout my body. I felt stupid, and a little ashamed. I'd assumed Rosemond's insistence that I attend every social activity had been to help her get a toehold in society. I was sure that was part of it, but another part had been motivated by her desire to distract me from my grief. If I was honest with myself, my desire to help the prostitutes was as much to keep my mind off Kindle as it was to balance out the scales of the lives I'd ruined in the last year. I wondered how much of Rosemond's manic energy these past few weeks was her attempt to keep her mind off Dunk's death. We never spoke of him, but his ghost was there.

"Thank you," I said. I kept my eyes on the crowd in front of me, lest I start crying.

Rosemond sold a rope of licorice and dropped the penny into the jar.

"What have you been doing?" I asked Rosemond.

"Convincing men to bid on my services so I can paint their lovely wives."

"Are any of them afraid of the secrets you might tell?"

"They should only be nervous if my donation isn't the highest seller." She smiled, and I knew she was teasing. "Honestly, your portrait is doing my job for me."

Across the way, people crowded around the sample of her work: me staring out a train window. As good as her word, Rosemond had managed to capture my expression of longing, as well as my grief. I could hardly look at it, no matter that it was brilliant.

"Why don't you take a break? Walk about a bit," Rosemond said.

"I shouldn't leave my post."

"It's not sentry duty. Here." She pulled a nickel from her pocket. "They're selling iced tea across the way. It's so strong and sweet a spoon will stand up in it. Get us both a glass. Later, if you play your cards right, I'll buy you some of Gustav's sausages."

"You're feeling flush," I said.

"I have a feeling I'm going to have at least four commissions after today."

"Did you get the governor's wife?"

"I did, and I have you to thank for it." She kissed me on the cheek. "So go on, while I'm feeling generous." She waved at someone and I followed her gaze to Portia, who looked disapproving.

"She puzzles me," I said.

"Who?"

"Portia. There are times when I think she likes me, but she always seems to look disapproving around me."

"You have that effect on people."

"I do not."

Rosemond held her thumb and forefinger close together. "Maybe a little."

"And here I felt I was being conventional. For the first time in my life, I might add."

"Convention fits you like a glove."

I glared at Rosemond, though I couldn't argue with her point. I'd been doing my best to stay beneath the town's notice—helping the boy with the amputated foot was the exception—and had discovered how easy, and almost pleasant, an ordinary life could be. In my optimistic moments, I felt like a phoenix readying to rise from its ashes. Other times, I was put in mind of a snake shedding its skin.

I waited in line for the tea and let the energy of the crowd infuse me with strength. Gustav was selling his sausages two booths down, but the amazing aroma of roasted meat was everywhere. My mouth watered and I smiled, looking forward to eating something I hadn't cooked for the first time in weeks.

"Helen Graham?"

Whenever I met a stranger, my instinct was to determine whether he was a Pinkerton or a bounty hunter. The man who stood next to me was too respectable-looking to be a bounty hunter, and his face was too soft and open to be a Pinkerton. The cuff of his right sleeve was stained with a drop of blood and he held a well-worn satchel in the same hand. "You must be Dr. Hankins."

"How did you know?"

"I figured you would come find me eventually."

"Yes, you can't amputate a man's foot without someone taking notice. It was a fine piece of work."

"You've seen Thomas?"

"I did. The prettiest bit of suturing I've ever seen."

"Well, I am a woman. Sewing always has been a talent of mine. I'm going to check on him after the benefit ends. You are welcome to come along and take over his care."

I stepped up to the counter and ordered the two teas.

"Have anything stronger?" Hankins asked the man, who nodded and drew Hankins a beer from a keg.

"Stop being cagey, Mrs. Graham. Tell me how you knew to amputate his foot, and how you keep infection from setting in."

"I was a nurse during the war and saw my fair share of amputations. My father was a doctor, and I nursed for him after the war ended. He took me under his wing, so to speak. He knew I could never be a real doctor, but he thought it would serve me well to be able to do basic medical procedures when he was gone."

"I hardly call amputation a basic medical procedure," Hankins said.

"The amount of times it was performed in the war made it routine, don't you think?" I continued. "Before my father died, he became obsessed with Joseph Lister's work." Hankins scoffed. "I thought Lister's theories were logical and decided there could be no harm in using his guidelines if I was ever in the position to need them. I've made sure I have carbolic in my medical kit since."

Two iced teas and a glass of beer with a thick head were placed on the counter. Hankins put his hand out, said, "Allow me," and paid for my tea. The ice clinked against the glass. Hankins started walking behind the booth, expecting me to follow.

"I need to take this to Eliza."

"It won't take but a moment."

I sighed and followed, determined to get the scene over with.

"It's a good story, as far as it goes." Hankins took a long pull of his beer and wiped the thick foam from his mustache.

"I don't know what you mean."

"I've never known a nurse to perform an amputation when a doctor is easily called and there is a hospital available."

"I was under the impression neither treated Negroes."

"Of course I would have treated such a grave injury if they had come to me. But they do not."

"Maybe you should ask yourself why."

Hankins lifted the glass to his mouth but stopped before he drank. He lowered the glass with deliberate slowness. "I know who you are, Miss Bennett."

I kept my face passive but internally kicked myself for baiting the man. "Who?"

He set his bag on the ground and reached into his inside

pocket. He removed a folded piece of paper and tried to give it to me. I lifted the sweating glasses of tea.

"Aren't you curious?" he asked.

"I know what it is. What do you want, Hankins?" I said with a weary sigh.

He tucked the Wanted poster in the top of my vest to mock me, but his expression regained its friendliness. "Now, Miss Bennett, don't sound so dejected. Did you honestly think you could hide in the West? With the rapid communication we have now through the telegraph and the railroad? We get news from New York within the week, and your story has dominated the papers at different moments since last February. Everyone west of Saint Louis is on the lookout for a woman with unnatural medical skills. A thousand dollars is a fortune."

"I only intended to be a nurse."

"But you couldn't let that boy die. Like a good doctor. You risked your safety to save him."

There was no point in trying to placate the man. He knew who I was. I was at his mercy and the worst he could do to me was to turn me over to the sheriff. The more people threatened me with it, the less I cared.

Hankins leaned forward, met my eyes, and said with feeling, "I admire that. I saw the work you did on that boy and, as much as I don't want to admit it, you did a fine job."

"I've done better. I'm out of practice."

Hankins smiled. "The papers said you were arrogant, but you sound almost humble. You're quite skilled."

No surgeon worth his salt would have said my work on Thomas was "skilled." Serviceable, yes, but well below my usual standards. Standing over Thomas's severed foot, fumbling with the thread and needle, my hands awkward and stiff as I sutured his wound, I told myself it was because I hadn't worked on flesh in so long, that needlepoint was a poor substitute. My heart raced with nerves and my hands shook, and I'd realized I hadn't taken up the needle for surgery since General Sherman held a lantern for me in Fort Richardson's hospital. The procedure took twice as long as it should have, and my fumbling and incompetence, while appropriate for a nurse out of her depth, haunted me still, and had planted an idea in my mind that was growing stronger, and more alarming, by the day.

Hankins drank his beer and said, "I'm want to offer you the best of both worlds. You keep your assumed name; Graham is it now?"

I nodded.

"How many have you had since you left New York?"

"Too many."

"You keep your name, and you become my nurse. You'll attend me on calls on this side of the tracks, to establish that you are extraordinarily skilled, and to establish my mentorship. You'll be a quick learner, obviously, and, will soon take patients of your own. You'll continue on with your practice on the other side of the tracks. If there's another case like the amputated foot, you will call me, so as to not raise suspicion. I'll let you assist as much as necessary. You are better at sutures than I am."

"What will you pay me?"

"Pay you? You'll pay *me* half of whatever you get from your patients."

"My patients are able to pay little. It would take months to earn what you could get immediately from handing me over to the sheriff. Wouldn't that be the smarter play?"

"Heavens, no. I know myself well enough to know I'd drink through that one thousand dollars in record time. Taking half of your earnings in perpetuity will be much more lucrative."

"I could leave town."

"If you do, I'll send Sheriff Hall after you. And we won't bother with bringing you back alive. I told him who you are, by the way. He gave me the poster. He gets a cut of what you give me. Everyone benefits."

"Someone paid me last week with a kitchen table. What then?" I didn't bother to inform him of my favorite in-kind payment: a small leather scabbard fashioned inside the top of my boot to secret the knife, newly sharpened, I had stolen at the Nebraska whistle stop.

"I guess it'll depend on if I need one or not."

"What exactly will my tasks be?"

"Typical nursing tasks, as well as some doctoring over across the tracks."

"I'm not going to wait on you, wash bandages, or clean up vomit or diarrhea."

"Those are nursing duties."

"I'm not a nurse."

Hankins furrowed his brows and with a puzzled smile said, "You aren't in the position to make demands."

"Am I not? You forget, I can ride into the next town and turn myself in."

"You'll be taken back to New York and hanged."

I evaluated Hankins. Despite the fact that he was blackmailing me with the option of servitude or death, I didn't think he was entirely bad. Most doctors of my acquaintance would have found some fault, no matter how small, with my work, not praised it. It told me more about him than he intended. I believed that with time, and my ability to charm when I wanted to, I could win him over.

Then again, killing him would be easier.

"What exactly have you heard about me?"

"Excuse me?"

"It's a simple question, but I'll be plainer. What have the newspapers written about me?"

"You don't know?"

"I've been told generalities, but I've never read an article. I take it back. I read one that was full of lies." I thought of Pope and wondered how the penny dreadful of my adventures was selling.

"You killed your lover in New York…"

I chuckled and shook my head.

"…And ran to Texas. You survived one massacre, to be captured by Indians when you were almost to Fort Sill." Hankins blushed and wouldn't meet my eye.

"Go on."

"You were rescued by an Army major, another lover, and you two were on the run across Indian Territory when a Pinkerton caught up with you. Obviously, the article about you dying was a total fabrication."

"Obviously."

"The Major was caught on a riverboat about a month ago, and they suspected you were with him. That you got away. Which you did. How accurate is it?"

"Not too far off the mark, to be honest. What else?"

"Your major killed a lot of men to keep you safe. Some say he killed his brother, but no one believes it."

My throat thickened, and I stared off into space. "The things I've seen, and done, this past year…I thought the war…" I met Hankins's eyes. "I never really understood what men, and women, were capable of. Kindle paid a high price for loving me. I'm sure I will eventually be held to account, too."

"Paid a high price? What do you mean?"

"Haven't you heard? He was executed a few weeks ago."

Hankins jerked his head back. "He was?"

218

"Yes. We got a telegram."

"Last I read, he was convicted of disobeying an order and sentenced to three months."

My heartbeat throbbed in my chest, my head, in every part of my body. I couldn't hear, and could barely think. I focused on the man standing next to me—what was his name?—and said, "What did you say?" in a voice so low and strangled I barely heard the words myself.

The man finished his beer. I drank from one of the glasses in my hand, wanting whisky, and revolted when the cloyingly sweet tea slid thickly down my throat. It was cool, and allowed me to speak clearly and see Hankins with focused eyes. "What did you say?"

"Your major is alive and serving time at Jefferson Barracks."

I stared past Hankins at the edge of town. In the short weeks we had been there, the tents beside us had been pulled up, sold to a new settler, and moved to a new street farther out on the desert. The smell of fresh lumber would dominate until the dirt and grime traveled from the older streets to this one as it aged. Things moved fast in the West and could change in an instant.

I faced Hankins. "When can I start?"

"Tomorrow."

"Perfect." I turned away from him and stopped. Harry Diamond and Salter were in a deep discussion on the edge of the crowd. Salter had his head bent down so Diamond could speak in his ear, but Salter's eyes were on me. Salter nodded and Diamond looked in my direction. I inhaled and turned back to Hankins.

"Who is the man Harry Diamond is talking to?"

"Salter's his name. He's a Pinkerton." Hankins leaned close. "Better stay clear of him." He laughed and walked off.

My breath came in short bursts. Salter a Pinkerton? Were

he and Diamond speaking of me, or was I merely in their sight line? Or was this just another instance of me thinking the world revolved around me, as Rosemond said? Regardless, I couldn't risk facing them, of Diamond and Salter seeing the fear I knew covered me like a second skin. I walked outside the tent and made my way to the candy booth from behind.

Rosemond and Portia were laughing and talking as if they didn't have a care in the world. They were a study in contrasts: effortlessly beautiful versus quietly handsome; vivacious versus demure; manipulative and soulless versus steadfast and principled.

"What are you singing tomorrow?" Rosemond asked.

"'For the Beauty of the Earth.'"

"To celebrate spring?"

"Yes. I thought I would continue the theme."

"And will your husband's sermon do the same?"

"We haven't talked about it. He has been distracted of late." She paused, and continued. "Your dress is lovely. You put all the other women here to shame."

Rosemond leaned close to Portia. "Not a terribly difficult task, present company excluded."

Portia dipped her head. "Rosemond," she whispered.

I shoved the glass at Rosemond and she jumped. She pressed her hand against her heart and smiled, a slight blush creeping over her pockmarked face. "Helen! Where did you come from?"

The edges of my vision darkened. Portia's smile dipped slightly at the sight of me.

"I saw you taking to Dr. Hankins," Portia said.

I somehow found my voice. "Yes."

"I suppose it was only a matter of time." Rosemond drank deeply from her glass. Her eyes lit up. "That is wonderful. Do you like it?" She nodded to my own.

I breathed deeply, the urge to run as far from Cheyenne as

possible battling with the urge to retrieve my gun from the house and make good on my threat to kill her for lying to me. With hundreds of witnesses there would be no doubt to my guilt and conviction if I did, and with law-and-order citizens like Amalia Post on the jury, I'd surely hang. "She lied to me" would be a weak defense. No, Rosemond's punishment needed to be a living hell instead of fire and brimstone.

"Helen, are you feeling well?" Portia asked.

I stared at the preacher's wife. "No."

"Did Hankins upset you?" Rosemond said. "What did he want?"

Hatred bubbled up, threatened to consume me. I inhaled a long, shaky breath. "For me to work as his nurse."

"What did you say?"

"I had little choice. He knows—" I looked at Portia. "Do you mind? I need to speak to my sister alone."

Though taken aback, Portia agreed and left.

When she was well out of earshot I moved close to Rosemond. "Salter is a Pinkerton."

"Who?"

My brows furrowed. "Salter. From Grand Island?" Rosemond shook her head. "The man who threatened me at the hotel."

Her eyebrows rose in understanding. "How do you know he's a Pinkerton?" I could see the flecks of gold in her worried brown eyes. I resisted the urge to gouge them out.

"Hankins told me. Hankins knows who I am, by the way."

"What?"

"He thought my work was quite good, too good for a nurse. It took little effort to put two and two together."

"I told you you should have let that boy die," Rosemond said.

"No. No more people will die to save my skin."

"What does Hankins want?"

221

"I'll work for him and he will take most of my earnings."

"Instead of turning you in?"

"He doesn't trust himself with such a windfall."

"That's good."

"How is indentured servitude good?"

"It keeps the noose from around your neck." Rosemond's brow furrowed and I knew her mind was working, calculating how to manipulate this best to her advantage.

"Worried I won't get to fulfill my end of our deal?" I said, the rage at learning about her deception too fresh and strong to mask. I shall never forget the expression of shock and dismay on her face.

She hid it quickly, but her voice held the remnants. "I was trying to think of a way to convince you to stay. I assume leaving is your priority now?"

I thought of the weeks I'd spent grieving for Kindle, her willful deceit. She'd been manipulating me from the beginning. It was time she learned what it felt like. I would stay, take my revenge on Rosemond, until Kindle was set free. Pretend I was still the grieving widow, deepen our bond, make her rely on me, love me like the sister I pretended to be, and abandon her without a word.

I smiled. "I have nowhere to go, no one to go to. You're stuck with me."

She pulled me into a strong embrace. With a relieved sigh she said, "I'm so glad."

I returned her hug, my gaze falling on Portia and Salter across the way, near each other but not together, both watching us.

CHAPTER
19

Biding time wasn't as difficult as I thought it would be. If I could have paid to leave immediately, which I could not, being in Saint Louis wouldn't help Kindle. I wouldn't be able to see him and though I assumed I would be welcomed back to Mary's orphanage, there was no guarantee it would be a safe place for me to hide. Now that Kindle was caught, and the world knew I was alive, the orphanage might be watched for my arrival. When I mulled the question "stay or go?" I discovered not only was the safest decision to stay, but that I wanted to stay. The draw of practicing medicine again, even in Hankins's twisted version, was too strong.

May arrived on a wave of thunderstorms and train upon train of people seeking their fortune through legitimate and illegitimate means. Cheyenne's population ebbed and flowed as passengers disembarked and moved on south to Boulder and Denver, and headed north and west to the mines. Enough were intrigued by Cheyenne's potential that the town grew inexorably northward. Streets surveyed in March were dotted with tents in April and lined with wooden buildings in May. Fifteenth and Sixteenth Streets were slowly transforming from small false-fronted wooden buildings to more majestic brick and stone. Rosemond's portrait business was growing, and her sign business was booming, as was Dr. Hankins's practice, though Dr. Hankins's workload was not.

Hankins's plan for me to aid him and apprentice lasted a week, the amount of time for him to realize I could do all the work and he could get most of the remuneration. There was little objection to me taking over Hankins's practice: the women in town preferred a female treating them, even if it was a nurse, and the men who urgently needed Hankins's services were rarely in a condition to object, bloody and in pain as they were from knife attacks and gunshot wounds. When I tied the final suture off, they were impressed with my work and, feeling magnanimous and light-headed with loss of blood, most like, occasionally gave me extra coin on top of the standard fee. It was in this way I was able to slowly secret a personal stash of money unbeknownst to Hankins, who took his portion off the top, and Rosemond, whom I combined my earnings with for household expenses and was slowly paying back for the clothes she'd bought me. Though she insisted payment wasn't necessary, I didn't want to be beholden to her in any way.

With a few discreet inquiries on my and Rosemond's parts, we discovered Salter was contracted with the railroad, investigating crimes that happened up and down the line or on the trains themselves. Salter disappeared from town without a word to me, and Rosemond convinced me I was seeing a threat where there wasn't one. As the days wore on and Salter didn't return, and Harry Diamond continued to pretend I'd never threatened to shoot his cock off, I began to feel safe again, if not entirely easy.

Rosemond and I were so busy we rarely saw each other, nor did we have time to perform our respective household duties. On Amalia's recommendation, Rosemond hired a stout, whiskery

Swedish woman to come in twice a week and cook and clean for us. Ingrid spoke little English and took no interest in us other than our ability to pay her for a day's work. She arrived, donned an apron, performed her duties, and left, with nary a word passing her lips.

One morning, a little after dawn, I walked into the kitchen and discovered Rosemond sketching on a pad of paper, a steaming cup of coffee on the table in front of her. She looked up from her sketch pad and smiled. "Hello, stranger."

"Please tell me there's more coffee." I placed Cora Bayle's carpetbag on the table.

"An entire pot."

I poured a mug and sat across from her.

"What are you sketching?"

"Portia. She's coming today so we can get started."

I blew on my coffee and watched Rosemond work. Her hand was light on the pencil, her strokes long and sure. She tilted her head to and fro, pursing her lips and furrowing her brows as she worked. There were times I looked at Rosemond and didn't recognize her from the woman I'd met on a Mississippi riverboat. Besides the obvious differences in dress—she wore men's trousers more often than not, for climbing up and down ladders to paint signs on buildings—and the lack of paint on her face, her entire mien had softened into a sort of glow. Her eyes seemed less calculating, her smile more genuine.

"What?" Rosemond looked up from her work.

"I'm sorry?"

"You're staring."

"Watching you work. Too tired to talk."

"Busy night?"

"Lavina went into labor." I warmed my hands on my coffee mug and tried to banish the memory of the woman's screams.

"What happened?"

I looked up at the softness in Rosemond's voice. "Some women handle pain better than others."

Rosemond nodded. "What did she have?"

"A girl. Stillborn. Deformed." My throat thickened and I couldn't continue. For all of Lavina's apparent disinterest in the baby, she'd looked down her body at me with expectation and hope when the baby delivered. Monique's exclamation of disgust at the sight of the baby's slanted eyes and deformed lip deflated Lavina and she lay back, turned her head away. I knew immediately the baby was dead but tried to spur it to cry anyway.

Rosemond touched my hand and I opened my eyes, tears trickling from their corners. Rosemond didn't say anything, only kept her warm hand over mine, ice-cold despite holding the hot tin mug. I felt monstrous, crying for the loss of the train passage to Saint Louis more than the death of an unwanted baby.

"Have you ever been pregnant?" I asked her, desperate to reject her undeserved compassion in the cruelest way possible.

Rosemond's hand stiffened on mine. She sat back and took her pencil back up. "Of course. Few whores haven't. I've never taken a pregnancy to term, if that's what you're asking. Have you? Been pregnant?" She said it mocking, sure she knew the answer.

"Yes." I enjoyed her surprise for a beat and continued. "The doctor in Jacksboro took care of it. I was unconscious, high on laudanum and wanting to sleep forever, to forget what I'd been through." I closed my eyes and felt myself floating above the feather bed, warm, safe, and senseless of everything, wishing it could have lasted forever. "He didn't know it could have been Kindle's."

"But it could have been an Indian's?"

"One of seven, yes." Rosemond grimaced but didn't drop her eyes from mine. I liked her for that. "It was as horrible as you can imagine. I don't know if my cramps are from their abuse, or from scar tissue in my uterus from the procedure."

"You didn't have them before?"

"Never." I drank the rest of my cold coffee, rose, and poured more. Out the kitchen window, the town was waking. A thin layer of fog skimmed along the ground. "I'm fairly certain I won't be able to get pregnant. If I didn't while Kindle and I were in Saint Louis, there isn't much hope."

"I'm sure with time you can."

I leaned against the worktable. "My husband is dead, remember?"

Rosemond opened her mouth as if to speak but closed it. I waited, wondering if she would tell me the truth about Kindle, hoping she would. Instead, she dropped her eyes and continued sketching. "Did the delivery take all night?"

I sighed. Since Hankins's revelation about Kindle I'd discovered two things, one surprising, the other gratifying: stoking hatred took great emotional, almost physical, effort, and it wasn't in my nature. I knew I should hate Rosemond for what she'd done, and antipathy flared within me at the most unexpected times. But there were long stretches when I forgot about her duplicity, her manipulation, and felt something close to affection for her. I would never trust her, but I couldn't hate her outright. The realization filled me with hope that my morality hadn't been completely lost after everything I'd been through.

"No. A supply train leaves this morning for Sweetwater, and every miner and teamster was determined to make the most of their last night in town. Three fights, two brawls, a bullet-grazed ear, and a dead whore."

Rosemond glanced up, her eyes landing on the carpetbag.

"Why do you carry that thing?"

"There's room for the medicines you gave me. Plus, it helps me remember."

"Remember what?"

"My guilt."

Rosemond's hand stopped, but she didn't take her eyes from her sketch pad. The corners of her mouth tightened and her eyes bored into the sketch as if searching for answers or inspiration or strength. I thought she would speak, mention Dunk to put me in my place, but her face cleared of all guilt and uneasiness and she resumed sketching without a word.

Rosemond's solution to addressing her past actions was to pretend they never happened, that her life began when she got off the train in Cheyenne. When anyone asked her about her history—our history—she was vague, and turned the conversation to them. People knew more of me than of Rosemond, which was ironic considering I was the one who *needed* my past to remain secret; Rosemond merely wanted hers hidden. Considering her severance of her past, I assumed she would take a hard stance against the evils of prostitution. Much to my surprise, Rosemond had taken up visiting Calico Row with me and Portia whenever she could. To Stella and her girls, and Monique and hers, Rosemond was a lady. They gave no hint of suspicion of Rosemond's previous life. Though we didn't talk about it, I could tell the first time we went that the possibility had been on Rosemond's mind. It wasn't until we'd finished our visits that Rosemond's expression cleared. She'd been giddy with relief, intertwining her arms with mine and Portia's and offering to buy us a slice of pie at the Rollins House Hotel.

"I would love a piece of pie, but Hankins is expecting me. Bring one home for me?"

"I will. I guess it's you and me, Portia."

I thought Portia would refuse but she smiled and said, "I suppose it is."

Whatever tension had been between the two of them from Portia's initial refusal to sit for a portrait had dissipated. More than once, I'd found Portia keeping Rosemond company while she painted, or sitting with her at the kitchen table over coffee.

"I assumed you had already started Portia's portrait, with the amount of time she's spent here."

"She isn't here as often as you think."

"Only during the irregular times I come and go."

She shrugged a shoulder. "She's here to see you, to talk about the education of our fallen women. How is that going, by the way?"

"Portia has taken on most of it. Hankins is keeping me too busy. Clara has been sneaking away from Stella and going to the Brights for reading lessons."

Rosemond stopped sketching. "Has she?"

"I think Clara has even been off the dope for a few weeks. She may be their first true success story. From the conversations I've had with Portia, she is encouraged by Clara's enthusiasm."

"Which one is Clara?"

"She's a small, dark-haired woman. Twenty, if she's a day." I chuckled. "She propositioned me on my first trip to Calico Row. She's a big one for teasing."

Rosemond closed her sketchbook with a thump. "I doubt she was teasing."

"What? No." I paused. "They do that?"

Rosemond stood and looked at me pityingly. "A whore will do anything if you pay her enough."

A knock at the back and front doors at almost the same time interrupted us.

"Ingrid."

"Portia."

"I'll let Ingrid in, then I'm going to catch some shut-eye before Hankins and I go see Lily." I stood and clutched at the dull pain in my stomach.

"Is it your time again?"

"Yes."

She placed a hand on my back. "What can I do for you?"

It was a simple question, one to be expected between people living together and familiar with the ebb and flow of life together, a question between friends. Moments such as these had been happening more frequently over the past few weeks as Rosemond and I got to know each other and settled into a daily routine. Whether from her history as an older sister, or as a madam for a house full of prostitutes, Rosemond had a protective streak in her. The part of me that saw everything Rosemond did as a grand manipulation wondered what her angle was. That she had a long-term plan I had no doubt, but for the life of me, I couldn't figure what it was. She seemed genuinely concerned for me and actively cultivated our uneasy friendship.

"Keep the laudanum out of sight," I said.

She sighed and smiled. "I'm so glad to hear you say that. I've seen what it can do to women who use it habitually. I don't want to watch you waste away. I've gotten used to you being around." She squeezed my shoulder in acknowledgment, and went to let Portia in.

It didn't take me long working with Dr. Hankins to suspect that my original plan for settling in the West and being a physician had been a good one. He was a decent doctor with a pleasing bedside manner. When he was sober enough to listen to his patients' complaints, his diagnoses were usually correct, and his treatment plans were almost always precisely what I would prescribe. But he liked his drink too well, and with Cheyenne's growth having the same effect on Hankins's practice, he decided to focus his attention on the important men of Cheyenne—the politicians and businessmen and their families—and leave the rest for me. Which was why it was somewhat surprising that he asked me to accompany him to his appointment with Lily Diamond, the wife of one of the richest men in town.

The Diamonds lived in a two-story stone house on Ferguson Street with a large cupola and a curved porch. Workers were planting tree saplings in the narrow yard fenced in from the wooden sidewalk with an iron fence. The front door was opened by a Negro maid in a dove-gray uniform. Without a word of greeting to the woman, Dr. Hankins gave her his hat and headed up the stairs. I smiled and said hello to the maid and followed through the dark-paneled entry hall and up the stairs, the thick carpet runner muting my steps. Hankins went to the second door on the left, gave a cursory knock, and let himself in.

There was an oppressiveness, a heaviness, to the room, which seemed to be at odds with the sweet woman I'd come to know during my weeks in town. The walls were paneled in dark wood, like the entry hall and stairs. Heavy brocade curtains covered the windows. The velvet curtains hanging from the canopy bed, the heavy carpet on the floor, and the cloth-covered walls absorbed almost all sound. Lily sat in the middle of the bed with her knees drawn up. She wore a nightdress and a lace cap tied with a large bow beneath her chin. Her eyes were bloodshot, as if she hadn't slept in days.

"Hello, Lily," Dr. Hankins said.

"Oh, Dr. Hankins, I'm so glad you've come."

"Of course I've come." Hankins set his bag on the bedside table and sat on the edge of the bed. He patted Lily's knee. "And I've brought Mrs. Graham along as well."

Lily smiled wanly at me.

"Good to see you, Lily," I said.

"How are you feeling?" Hankins said.

"Terrible, same as always. Shortness of breath, headache, and my stomach is constantly bloated."

I watched Hankins carefully. He nodded and smiled but his eyes were unfocused, as if his mind were on something else. "And is there pain in your stomach?"

"No. But it's bigger than it was last time."

Hankins's smile turned condescending. "Cutting back on the sweets will take care of it."

Lily looked abashed. "You're probably right."

"Of course I'm right." He patted her knee and stood. As if it were a cue, Lily lay down flat on the bed and pulled her knees up. She clutched her hands across her chest and stared at the canopy above her bed. "Lily."

The woman turned her head in question.

"Mrs. Graham is going to do your treatment today."

"What?" Lily said, astonishment clear in her voice and expression. "But she isn't a...doctor."

"She might as well be," Hankins said.

"Has she done this before?"

Hankins turned to me. "I'm not sure. Have you treated hysteria before?"

"Is that your diagnosis?" I asked.

"Yes. Lily has suffered from it ever since they moved to Cheyenne. A not uncommon complaint for women in the West. It's a hard life and some are fitted for it better than others."

I glanced at Lily and saw the shame on her face at the rebuke.

Hankins continued. "She's responded well to treatment, much to her husband's relief. We must continue it, but with the number of patients I have lately…"

"May I speak to you for a moment, Doctor?" I asked.

He nodded and walked to the door.

I smiled at Lily. "Relax. I'll be right back."

I met Hankins at the door and crossed my arms over my chest. "You didn't examine her."

"I don't need to. I've been seeing her for nearly two years. It's a clear case of hysteria, and the success of the genital massage treatments has proven my diagnosis every two weeks since."

I stared up at Hankins in wonderment, though as he stared back at me with complete innocent ignorance, I didn't know why I was surprised. Almost from the moment I graduated medical school, I fought against hysteria as a diagnosis, not because I didn't think a few women truly suffered from emotional complaints, but because it was routinely asserted as the cause of *every* woman's medical complaint.

"What about her abdominal complaint?"

"It is all tied to the hysteria. When Lily gets upset, she eats sweets. She's gained forty pounds since they moved to Cheyenne."

"In my dealings with her, she has always struck me as very levelheaded."

"In private she is not. Harry speaks of her emotional volatility often." His tone turned placating. "Listen, Helen. I brought you here because I want you to take over her care completely."

"Why?"

"Frankly, her treatment makes my rheumatism flare up. When we first started, it took five minutes, maybe ten. As time's worn on, it's become an hour-long ordeal. My right hand is useless for hours."

I bowed my head and covered my mouth, trying not to laugh. I cleared my throat, arranged my expression into a serious one, and said, "I can imagine."

He patted me on the shoulder. "Wonderful. Because you are helping me out so much, you may keep the fee for yourself. Five dollars. Women pay a premium for genital massage."

"Yes, I know."

It had been a significant part of my New York practice, mostly because my patients wished to continue the treatment begun by my male predecessors. They paid dearly for it, and I was only too eager to take their money to fill my barren bank account.

Now, I knew different. My time with Kindle opened my eyes to the true nature of the hysterical paroxysm: sought after and reached clinically, it could be achieved between a man and woman who understood how to give and receive pleasure. How many cases of hysteria would disappear if this were more widely understood? Instead, women were expected to be willing vessels for a man's seed, to view sexual relations as a means to an end: procreation. I smiled at the thought of the uproar it would cause in the medical establishment, and the world in general, if it were ever implied a man should do more than penetrate his wife and spill his seed, but also give his wife pleasure. I knew well enough it wouldn't be only men who would be outraged. To the women who received the hysteria treatment it was medical, not sexual. The idea that they could or should enjoy sex would be appalling.

If they only knew what they were missing.

"I thank you for the patient. Will she allow me to treat her?"

"I'll settle that right now." Hankins walked to Lily and spoke to her in a low tone. She seemed to want to argue but not have the courage. Hankins patted her shoulder, picked up his bag, and came to me. "She is fine. Where are you going after this?"

"Home, I should think. After last night."

"Oh, no. That man Drummond is back in town selling his medicines."

"He's a huckster."

"Well, of course he is. But his customers have legitimate physical complaints. You will hover around, listen to their complaints, see who buys, and give them a card offering your services when, or if, the snake oil doesn't work."

"I most certainly will not. I have not sunk so low that I will chase after sick people and foist my services upon them."

"You have no say in it, Miss Bennett. Unless you want a visit from the sheriff."

I clenched my jaw to keep from telling Dr. Roger Hankins precisely where he could shove his threat. "I don't have a card," I said through clenched teeth.

"I took the liberty of ordering some for you. They're at the newspaper office. They cost five dollars. You can pay with Lily's fee today."

"I suppose if I need you I'll find you at the bar in the Rollins House Hotel?"

"Most like." He closed the door with a snap.

I inhaled four or five times to regain my equilibrium and turned to face my patient.

I set my bag on the bedside table next to a framed picture of two soldiers.

"Going somewhere?"

I followed Lily's gaze to the table and Cora Bayle's carpetbag. I pulled out my stethoscope. "Not today." I helped Lily sit up.

"What are you doing?"

"Examining you."

"But Dr. Hankins's treatment...?"

"We'll get to that. First, I want to see if you're as healthy as I think you are." I helped Lily sit up and listened to her lungs. "Swing your legs around here," I said, motioning for her to sit on the edge of the bed. I placed the stethoscope on her heart. "Strong and steady." I smiled at Lily, who looked relieved. "Have you been having heart pain? Or palpitations?"

"No. Why do you ask?"

"You looked surprised."

"Oh, well. It's just I'm so nervous all the time."

"Hmm." I untied her lace cap, put it aside, and felt her lymph nodes. "Tell me about your weight gain."

Lily blushed. "I'm sure it's because of the sweets, like Dr. Hankins said."

"I'm not."

Lily's eyes widened as if from shock at being listened to.

"How old are you, Lily?"

"Forty-seven."

I lifted the lamp from the table and shined it in one eye, then the other. "Do you still have your menses?"

"No."

"When did it stop?"

"A couple of years ago."

"When you moved to Cheyenne?"

"Around that time, yes."

I nodded. "Lie down for me."

I pulled her nightdress up to reveal a soft, thick stomach covered in stretch marks. "Are those your sons?" I nodded toward the framed photograph.

"Yes." She gazed at the photo. The sadness and longing in Lily's eyes, as well as the full mourning she always wore, told me their fate.

"Which battle?"

"Troy was lost at the First Manassas. Benjamin at Sharpsburg."

Tears leaked from her eyes. I kept my focus on listening to her stomach with my stethoscope to give her time to compose herself. I draped the stethoscope around my neck, pressed on her stomach, and knew immediately her weight gain wasn't from sweets.

"When did you start gaining weight?"

Lily inhaled. "Oh, November, maybe. Yes, I think that's when I noticed it first."

"What did you notice?"

"Well, honestly, I thought I was pregnant. It felt like a little bottom, you know? But it had been over a year since my last menses."

"Did you mention it to Dr. Hankins?"

"Not until last month. I haven't been eating much, no appetite to speak of."

I pressed around on her stomach and closed my eyes, envisioning her organs. The mass wasn't hard, but squishy like a balloon of water. It seemed to be settled on the left side of her abdomen, below her ovary. I opened my eyes and pulled her nightdress down. "How are your breasts?"

"I'm sorry?"

I lifted her left arm and pressed around her lymph nodes. "Do they look normal? Are there any hard areas? Do they hurt?" I put her arm down and moved to the other side of the bed.

"No. Is everything all right?"

"Why do you ask?"

"Dr. Hankins has never examined me like this."

"Has he not?" I lifted her right arm.

"I've never had a nurse be so thorough."

I smiled and put her arm back down by her side. "Does your stomach hurt?"

"No."

"Have you had any abdominal pain since you started gaining weight?"

"No."

"Backache? Trouble with urination or defecating?"

"My back aches, some. But no trouble with the other." She looked away.

I walked to the end of the bed.

"Is it time?" The hopefulness and anticipation in her voice embarrassed me.

"Not yet. I need to examine you first."

Lily scooted down to the end of the bed, bent her knees, and opened her legs. Though she was covered modestly by a sheet, I could not help but be reminded of the same resigned motions from Lavina a few weeks earlier. I walked to the dresser and washed my hands in the basin. When I returned, I reached beneath the sheet and internally examined Lily, while pressing down on her stomach with my other hand, confirming my suspicion of a large ovarian tumor. I removed my hand and returned to the dresser to wash my hands.

"What about my treatment?"

I sat on the edge of the bed and was silent for a moment, trying to decide what to tell her, or if I should tell her at all. On the one hand, Dr. Hankins had handed her treatment over to me. She was my patient and I should tell her my suspicions. On the other hand, to her and everyone in town I was a nurse, a midwife. A nurse might be able to diagnose a tumor, but it would draw suspicions. If I suggested operating, my ruse would be up. The safest course would be to tell Dr. Hankins my suspicions and convince him to operate, though I wasn't sure he had the skills to perform it. I knew he didn't follow Lister's guidelines, so putting Lily Diamond into Hankins's unsanitary hands would be risking her life. She wasn't in pain and the tumor wasn't hard—both good signs. Her lymph nodes felt normal as well. There was no indication from an external examination that the tumor was cancerous, which meant I had time to consider the options before making a decision.

But that was only half of my problem.

"Please, Helen. I beg you," Lily said. Her eyes were red with threatening tears. "This is the only thing that gives me relief."

"Temporarily."

"Yes, but I receive the treatment regularly."

"And pay dearly for it."

"Harry doesn't mind the expense if it keeps our house peaceful."

I placed my hand over Lily's. Poor woman. Grieving for two lost sons, uprooted from her home and moved to a rough frontier town with few women to befriend, her legitimate physical complaints dismissed by her doctor, and married to a man who frequented whores. Was it any wonder she was emotionally distraught? How could I possibly refuse to give her the one thing that helped her?

"Of course I'll do the treatment."

She sighed. "Oh, thank you."

"But I'm going to teach you how to bring yourself to crisis so you don't have to...pay." My mouth twitched when I realized that the treatments male doctors were giving and receiving money for were akin to the services and charges of a soiled dove.

Lily gasped. "I can't do that!"

"Why not?"

"I can't touch myself down there."

"It's a medical treatment I'm prescribing, like prescribing laudanum for pains."

"But if people found out!"

"Who will tell them? I surely won't. Will you?"

"Good heavens, Helen. What a question."

"Then no one need know."

Lily fidgeted with the edge of the sheet covering her. I waited, suspecting there was more she wanted to say. The silence finally did its work. "But it goes against Christ's teachings."

"This isn't a sexual act," I lied. "This is a medical procedure."

"It can't be done without a doctor."

"Yes, it can."

"Why isn't it?"

"Because women, and their husbands, pay handsomely for it." I leaned forward and whispered, "And doctors are greedy."

"I don't know."

I sighed. "How about this: I'll explain to you what I'm doing. If, before our next appointment, you feel a spell coming on, you can try the treatment yourself. If it doesn't work, we'll have the upcoming appointment on schedule."

Lily smiled and said, "That will be fine," with such relief I knew she had no intention of trying to help herself to crisis. I stood and turned away, steeling myself to do a task I had no urge to perform.

CHAPTER
20

Irritated, exhausted, and feeling rebellious, I returned home, went to bed, and fell into a deep sleep almost as soon as my head hit the pillow. When I woke the frenetic noise outside had transformed from daily activity to the winding-down music of twilight. A dog nearby barked and was answered by a deeper bark farther away and another farther away still, as if relaying messages or gossip. A horse or mule clomped by in rhythm to the creaking wheels of the wagon it pulled. A shout and men's laughter. The snort of a pig. I turned over and pulled the pillow over my head, trying to return to the dream I'd woken from.

Kindle.

Less a dream than the certainty of his presence, the sense of calm and safety that surrounded him and enveloped me like a knight's armor. I reached across the bed, deluding myself that he was next to me, that it was the morning before our departure from Saint Louis. He would turn on his side and curve his body into mine, whisper, "Good morning, Slim," in my ear as his hand stroked my hip with the promise of slow, almost lazy lovemaking, the desire for connection greater than the need for release.

My hand fell on cold cotton sheets. I sighed and pulled

the pillow away from my head but couldn't ignore the physical response the memory gave me. I rose from the bed quickly, went to the dresser, and splashed cold water from the basin onto my face. I scrubbed my face dry with a coarse towel and stared at myself in the mirror. I refused to satiate myself without Kindle. Let my physical need for him be motivation for leaving Cheyenne. As if I needed more.

I folded the towel and placed it on the dresser next to the pile of five silver dollars Lily had given me. I closed my eyes against the sight of them. It was a medical procedure, nothing more. I derived no pleasure from it, and wasn't that necessary for it to be something different? I thought of the whores I'd known and how little pleasure they received from their daily tasks. The difference, I supposed, was intent and understanding. Society understood that the purpose of transactions between whores and their johns was the man's sexual release. Whereas society deluded itself that the treatment for hysteria was medical in nature. After all, women weren't supposed to want or need pleasure the way men did. Responsibility for maintaining society's moral and spiritual laws rested squarely on women's shoulders. Pleasure or release did not figure into it.

I put the filled basin on the floor and undressed, trying and failing to banish the memory of my and Kindle's first nights as husband and wife. Passion and tenderness, exploration and experimentation, taking as much satisfaction in giving as receiving pleasure. Of course I'd known on some level how unique Kindle was, that his willingness to let me take the lead, to teach and be taught, would be considered weak by society's standards. But we'd been so thoroughly cocooned that I'd forgotten about the outside world, and took for granted what a treasure it was to have a man like him.

Until I was reminded of it today.

I was one woman in a sea of ignorance, ignorance ground into society's morals and opinions by generations, nay centuries, of faulty diagnoses and logic. It would take many generations more for a change to come about, many voices built one upon the other until these ridiculous opinions were seen for what they were. As it was, Dr. Catherine Bennett's voice would not be one of them. Nor would Laura Elliston's.

I lathered soap on a cloth, stepped into the basin, and washed myself.

Helen Graham had no voice, no name, no true profession.

I lifted the pitcher of water from the dresser and poured it over my body. I cringed at the shock of cold. Goose bumps prickled my skin. My nipples tightened and stood erect.

No freedom.

I toweled off.

This was the life I chose when I left New York City instead of facing the charges against me. I'd been deluded to think my new life could be a semblance of my old. With Kindle beside me I had the opportunity for normalcy, a different life from the one I knew, sure, but one that promised to be better in many ways. I was trapped by my lies. No power. No voice. A dreary future of being used and manipulated by others to further their own goals.

I stepped into my bloomers and laced my corset.

A pawn.

I jerked the laces tight, enjoying the pain, the loss of breath.

I buttoned my dark blue shirt and thought of the man who attacked me on the street in New York City on that fateful night. That was the moment that changed me. Faced with death for the first time in my life, I'd lost the characteristic that had defined me, that had driven me to cut my hair and put on boys' clothes to serve in the war, that had pushed me until I'd been accepted into medical school, that had prompted me to stand erect, head held high when derided by teachers and fellow students, that had led me to graduate at the top of my class, that encouraged me to walk to Twenty-Seventh Street and start treating whores to survive: fearlessness. Since being held against the stone wall at knifepoint, every decision and action of mine had been geared to survive. I didn't realize until now that surviving wasn't the same as living.

Kindle wasn't there to help me. I was on my own.

I knew what I needed to do, had known for weeks. Months, maybe.

I donned my skirt and boots with the secreted knife, threaded my arms through my vest, and buttoned it. I buckled the holster Rosemond had given me, checked the ammunition in my gun, and drove it home. I jerked the front of my vest down, stared into a pair of determined eyes, and smiled.

Lily Diamond's parlor resembled the rest of the house but little. It was light and airy, the walls painted a soft blue, the furniture traditional but unvarnished and upholstered with a light floral pattern. The lilies on the sideboard waved gently in the breeze blowing through the floor-to-ceiling windows. The room was full of light and smelled refreshingly of wood polish and flowers. Despite the pleasant surroundings, the ticking clock in Lily's parlor turned deafening in the prolonged silence.

I poured her a finger of whisky from the decanter on the sideboard. She stared into the middle distance still, as if she hadn't heard me. I held the glass out to her, and she looked up at me with unfocused eyes.

"I don't believe it." She took the glass and drank absent-mindedly. She choked and coughed in surprise. I caught the glass before she dropped it and spilled it on herself. The whisky had the desired effect; her eyes focused. She woke up.

"Which part?"

"You're Catherine Bennett?"

"I am."

"But you're wanted for murder."

"I am."

"Did you do it?"

"No. I plan on returning to New York City soon and clearing my name." I sat on the edge of the chair adjacent to Lily's. "I told you who I am so you will have confidence in my diagnosis."

"A tumor?"

"Yes. But I believe the prognosis is good." I explained my diagnosis to her again.

"Would you do the surgery?"

I pressed my lips together. "No."

"Aren't you a—"

"A surgeon? Yes. I don't have the tools or the sterilization ingredients necessary to perform surgery." I lifted my oft-injured right hand and rubbed it with my left. "My skills have eroded since I left New York City." I swallowed and continued with the knowledge I'd been struggling against admitting since I amputated Thomas's foot. "I couldn't in good conscience perform a surgery not up to my standards."

"Would Roger perform it?"

"No," I said quickly. "He isn't a surgeon. Dr. Hankins mentioned a surgeon in Denver, but I know nothing of his skills."

"Whom do you recommend?"

"Unfortunately, I only know New York surgeons, though I can write and get recommendations for Saint Louis or Chicago doctors, so you won't have to travel as far."

"Wouldn't that reveal who and where you are?"

"As I said, I plan on leaving soon anyway."

"But you'll return."

"I'm not sure."

"Oh, please do. I—I would hate to lose the best doctor I've ever had after one examination."

I flushed with pleasure, though I tried to hide it. "Thank you, Lily. It means more than you will ever know to hear you say that. It felt good, taking care of you. It's been too long. It was taking care of you that made me realize I have to return to clear my name."

"Oh, don't say that! What if you hang? I'll never forgive myself."

I clasped Lily's hand. I was so accustomed to people using me, betraying me, and threatening me that genuine care and concern caught me off guard. My eyes stung with unshed tears.

Lily, apparently sensing my emotional state, patted my hand roughly and turned businesslike. "I suppose you've told Harry and Oliver. What did they say?"

"Indeed I have not. I believe you should hear it first."

"How refreshing."

"I'm going to tell them when I leave you."

Lily nodded. "Good luck. I can imagine how the conversation will go."

"So can I." I picked up my bag and rose to leave.

"Does Dr. Hankins know who you are?"

"He does."

"He's making you work for him instead of turning you in?"

I nodded.

Lily rose. "Sounds like something Roger Hankins would do. Who else knows?"

"Eliza, Reverend Bright."

"Portia?"

"I don't think so, though she might."

"Does Amalia know?"

"No."

Something like triumph crossed Lily's expression. "Good. She'd turn you in before you got the confession out."

"Do you not like Amalia?"

"Of course I do. She's done a lot for women in the territory. But she's a bit of a dragon when it comes to law and order. It never crossed your mind I might turn you in?"

I shrugged. "I can't imagine anyone I'd rather have receive the reward."

"You are a strange creature, Helen."

"People have been telling me the same thing, in one way or another, my entire life."

True to form, Hankins was at the Rollins House Hotel drinking with Harry Diamond. I smiled widely at the men as I glided across the floor. Hankins looked overly pleased to see me, no doubt due to his level of intoxication, if his ruddy complexion was any indication. It had been six hours since he left Lily's, after all. Harry Diamond's face clouded at the sight of me. He pressed his shoulders back in a show of arrogance.

"Oh, perfect. Just the men I need to see."

"Helen!" Hankins waved at me and pushed a chair out with his foot. "How did Lily's treatment go?"

"What?" Harry Diamond snapped.

"I've given Lily's treatment over to Helen."

"I didn't agree to that."

Hankins looked puzzled. "Is there a problem?"

I sat and placed my bag on the floor. "None whatsoever," I

said, giving Diamond a meaningful look. He sat back in his chair, unconvinced. I continued, "Lily's treatment went fine."

Hankins flexed his hand. "Is your hand sore?" He laughed heartily at his predictable and unimaginative joke.

"No, actually. She reached her crisis in under ten minutes."

Hankins's laugh died slowly. Harry Diamond harrumphed. "I'm not paying five dollars for ten minutes' work."

I met Diamond's gaze steadily. "It does seem a high price when you look at it through that lens. But are you paying for my time, or the act?"

Diamond narrowed his eyes. "The act?"

I smiled. "The treatment. If you're unhappy, you are welcome to perform the treatment yourself, Mr. Diamond. Some husbands enjoy it as much as the wife."

"Mrs. Graham!" Hankins said. "That is wholly inappropriate."

"Of course Dr. Hankins isn't going to tell you it's something you can do. He would be ten dollars the worse off every month. But I assure you, you can be as effective treating your wife's hysteria as I, or Dr. Hankins. As I said, some men even enjoy it."

"Mrs. Graham!"

I reached out and touched Harry Diamond's arm. "I was sorry to learn of your sons. My condolences."

My compassion arrested Diamond's anger. His expression went through a series of emotions, before finally settling on a determined strength.

"I think your wife's hysteria can be directly linked to the loss of her sons and the move west."

"It's been seven years," Diamond said. "She has to get over it."

"She will never get over it," I said. "Perpetual mourning for the dead has become commonplace, almost expected of mothers. Imagine what others would say if she removed her weeds." Diamond opened his mouth to speak, but I continued. "There is no cure for grief. But I didn't come to talk about your wife's hysteria." I hated using the term, but I knew it was the only way to frame Lily's state of mind in a way they would understand. "When I examined her—"

"You examined her?" Hankins said.

"Of course. She's my patient."

"That was completely unnecessary."

I ignored him. "I found what I believe to be a tumor attached to her left ovary."

"What?" Hankins said.

"It isn't hard, which is most likely why you didn't notice it, Dr. Hankins. It feels like a balloon filled with water."

"A tumor?" Diamond stared at me in disbelief. "Is it cancer?"

Hankins stood. "I'll go over right now to examine her and prove Mrs. Graham is mistaken."

I stayed focused on Harry Diamond. "No, I don't think so. Her lymph nodes are normal and she's in no pain. I suspect it's benign, but there's no way to know with an external examination. I recommend—"

"That is enough, Helen." Hankins grasped my arm, pulling me from the chair and away from the table. "What exactly do you think you're doing talking about this in front of Harry?"

"Husbands were routinely consulted on their wives' treatments in New York City. Is it different in the West? If so, I apologize. I didn't know."

"You made me look the fool in front of my client."

"I apologize, Dr. Hankins, that was not my intention. Would you please release my arm?"

Hankins started, as if unaware he held my upper arm in a vise grip, and released me.

"Thank you. I welcome your examination of Mrs. Diamond. A second opinion on such an important diagnosis is always a good idea."

Hankins's indignation returned. "Second opinion?"

"You forget, Dr. Hankins, I'm a skilled physician. I graduated at the top of my class full of men, and have been working in surgery for five years. I'm well able to diagnose a tumor, but by all means, satisfy your curiosity, or save your face, however you prefer to think of it. As a courtesy to you, since you were her doctor, we can confer on the best treatment plan after you've made your determination."

"You are very full of yourself."

"I've had to be."

"Don't forget who's beholden to whom in this relationship."

"Oh, never."

"Did you go by the printers?"

"I'm on my way there now."

Harry Diamond joined us. "You started to say what you recommended."

"No need to talk about that yet," Hankins said. "I'm going to examine your wife right now. Come with me." He stalked off.

Harry Diamond stared at me through narrowed eyes. "Did you tell my wife?"

"No. I like her too much to cause her pain."

"You aren't a nurse, are you?"

"I want what's best for your wife, as I'm sure you do."

Roger Hankins returned. "Harry, do you want my expert opinion or not?"

Harry Diamond hesitated, but nodded and followed.

CHAPTER
21

It was dusk when I exited the Rollins House Hotel to mostly empty streets. Smoke billowed periodically from the trains resting on the tracks a few streets over. A whistle sounded. One would be leaving soon.

A teamster touched his hat to me while I waited for his wagon to pass. I stepped off the wooden sidewalk and headed to the newspaper office. The door was locked but I could see the printer inside. I knocked on the glass and waved at the printer when he looked up. Sydney Cotton wiped his hands on a rag as he crossed the room to open up. "Mrs. Graham. You here to pick up the business cards?"

I stepped through the door and was assaulted with the noise of the printing press and the sweet smell of ink and paper. "Yes, I am."

Cotton stepped behind the counter and pulled out a stack of business cards wrapped in brown paper and tied with string. "Would you like to review them?"

"I'm sure they're perfect."

"Did you read today's paper?" Cotton asked.

"Not yet." I didn't want to tell the newspaperman that I rarely read the newspapers. After being in the West for a year, and knowing Henry Pope, I knew newspapers for what they were: purveyors of entertainment, not news. Mr. Cotton might not believe my disinterest in any case. After learning of Kindle's fate from Hankins, I'd gone to the newspaper office immediately and, telling one more lie with an eye to survival, asked to see news of my husband's former regiment officer, William Kindle.

He slid the day's paper across the counter to me. "Page four. A new story about your husband's commander."

My head jerked up. "Captain Kindle?"

"Yes." I opened the newspaper but Cotton kept talking, more interested in telling me the news than my reading it. "His sentence was commuted by Uncle Billy himself. Got out with time served. A dishonorable discharge, mind you."

I gasped as my eyes skimmed over the very words Cotton said. Kindle was free. I scanned the article for a date and, when I didn't find one, looked up at Cotton.

"When?"

He pulled his head back and his brows furrowed. "You okay there, Mrs. Graham?"

I forced my expression to relax, and I smiled. "Yes, of course. I'm pleased for him. Do you know when he was released?"

"I got it out of a two-day-old Saint Louis paper, but it didn't say whether he'd been released or not. Just that the sentence had been commuted. You know how slow the Army works."

"They convicted him quick enough. Thank you." I picked the cards up and turned to leave.

"Dr. Hankins said you were going to pay for those."

I unlocked the door and was halfway through when I said, "Bill him."

I hurried down the street toward the depot, throwing the business cards in the trash as I went, while mentally calculating how much money I had: fifteen dollars spirited away in the false bottom of my medical bag, including the five from Lily Diamond. I didn't think it would be enough. A train whistled three times, signaling its departure from the station.

The station clock read 8:35 as I watched the caboose of an eastbound train click-clack its way out of the station.

"Damn."

The platform was dotted with stragglers who'd disembarked from the latest train. I stood in front of the darkened ticket window and studied the timetable and fee schedule. Twenty dollars for the emigrant train that had just departed, twenty-four for the next train leaving, the first-class limited departing tomorrow at one thirty. Seventeen hours. I had seventeen hours to beg, borrow, steal, or earn nine dollars, or more if I wanted to eat on the way.

My heart soared. In seventeen hours I would be on my way to Kindle.

"Going somewhere?"

I jumped and turned at the deep voice. A tall, dark figure in a low-brimmed hat leaned against the metal column topped by the station clock. The hands on the clock clicked forward. The end of the man's cigar glowed brightly, and dimmed.

"Mr. Salter."

"Mrs. Graham." He pushed off from the clock and moved toward me. I stood my ground, though my instinct was to shrink back. "Are you leaving?"

"Eventually."

"Your sister will be unhappy."

"She's settling in nicely."

"Returning to your husband?"

"He died. Or didn't you hear?"

"I didn't. I've been in and out of town. Condolences."

"Thank you." I glanced around the now-deserted platform. The ticket master closed his window with a snap, and I was alone with Salter. I opened and closed my right hand and rubbed it against my hip to rid my palm of the sweat that had popped up on it.

Salter nodded at my hand. "Why do you do that?"

"Do what?"

He mimicked my stretches. "Getting ready to break my nose?"

My laugh sounded forced. "No. I'm stretching it. It's been broken a couple of times."

"From punching men in the nose?"

"No." I turned slightly away. "I have an appointment I must keep. Good evening, Mr. Salter."

"Would you like me to walk you home? Offer my protection?" Though his hat was pulled low, I could see the mocking expression in his eyes.

"No, thank you." I touched the gun holstered on my waist. "I can protect myself."

He stepped closer and loomed over me. "Can you?"

I met his challenging gaze with my own. "I won't hesitate to kill who needs killing."

He raised his eyebrows and let his eyes roam over me. "Maybe you should offer your protection to me."

"I would, but I have an appointment to keep." I turned and walked away.

"Do you remember Martha Mason?"

I stopped, and my stomach fell through the floor. I swallowed my terror, arranged my face in a benign expression, and turned to face my nemesis. "Who?"

"Martha Mason. Wife of the hotelier in Grand Island."

"Oh, right. Martha. I didn't know her last name. What of her?"

Salter moved toward me, taking a long drag on his cigarette. "She took a beating in Omaha. Almost died."

"That's awful," I said, voice faint. I wanted to know more, was desperate for information, but knew appearing too interested would increase Salter's already heightened suspicions. "I hope she will recover."

"Better hope she doesn't. Mason won't take her back. She'll probably have to earn her living on her back. She wasn't attractive before the beating; now only a blind man would fuck her." Salter's eyes didn't leave mine. "Don't you care why she was beaten? Or how I know?"

"You're a Pinkerton," I said.

He pulled out his badge and showed it to me. "The railroad pays me to keep an eye on crime up and down the tracks."

"Isn't that a sheriff's job?"

"They want to protect their investment. So many sheriffs are incompetent. How'd you know I was a Pinkerton? You've been asking around about me."

"No."

"I've been asking around about you."

"I can't imagine why."

"You and your sister were the last two people to speak with a woman who ended up dead, and another who might as well be."

"You think we are somehow responsible?"

"The thought had crossed my mind."

"We barely knew them."

"On its face it seems a stretch, I admit. But Martha left town without a word to her husband, and no warning, the same morning you did. She was the only witness to a Mr. Bullock sending a note to Cora Bayle, the dead woman. Now, I find that compelling, don't you?"

255

"It's interesting, at least."

"Couldn't figure why she wanted to kill Cora Bayle, but it seemed like the logical answer. 'Til I heard about her being robbed and beaten."

"Robbed?"

"A necklace she said she got from your sister."

Here it was: my opportunity to get my revenge on Rosemond. Salter suspected that one or the other of us killed Cora Bayle, but he had no proof. Not that proof would matter much with the kangaroo courts of the West. I could give Rosemond to Salter and tell him a version of the truth, keeping my true identity out of the story. Or I could save Rosemond, turn myself in, and hope Salter preferred the "alive" version of "dead or alive" so I might see Kindle before I died.

I shook my head. I didn't want to die, and I didn't want Rosemond to die, either.

"She implied Rosemond gave her the necklace?" I laughed. "She stole it. We didn't realize it was missing until we arrived Cheyenne."

"She said Rosemond gave it to her."

"Of course she won't admit she stole it." I shook my head. "I horribly misjudged Martha. I thought she was a sweet woman." I sighed. "I suppose it's my lot in life to be perpetually disappointed in people. Now, I really must go and check on my patient. Good evening."

I walked across the platform, down the steps, and started across the tracks to Calico Row. Once I was clear of the rail yard, I glanced over my shoulder and saw Salter following me at a distance. I picked up my pace and when I passed an alley bisecting the main street I was on, I ducked into it, taking a shortcut to Monique's I'd learned over the last few weeks. I immediately realized my mistake: I'd never taken the shortcut in the dark, or alone.

The light from the glowing tents lit the alleys, but barely. I stumbled on the uneven ground and reached out for the guy rope holding up a tent. Back the way I came, I saw the shadow of Salter walk past the mouth of the alley. I took a few deep breaths to settle my trembling body. I supposed regaining my fearlessness would take more than a steely determination.

When steady, I released the rope holding me up and headed toward Monique's, my hand on the handle of my gun and my mind on Salter. Did he believe my lies, or would he continue on with his investigation? If Martha lived, it would become her word against Rosemond's. I knew Rosemond well enough to be confident she would be the more believable liar. Still, Cheyenne wasn't safe for her anymore. I had to warn her before I left.

The alleys behind and between the tents were full of trash and human waste. A small goat tied to a stake in the ground bleated as I walked by. I saw the lights of Calico Row one section over as I passed the last alley perpendicular to it. A woman was pushed up against a stack of crates behind one of the few wooden buildings. Her legs were wrapped around the man's waist, his pants around his ankles, his white rear glowing in the moonlight as he pumped his seed into her. Instinctively, I stopped and the man groaned his release.

"That was mighty nice, Reverend," the woman said, her voice calm and unmoved. The man pulled away and revealed Clara. "Hello, Slim. Care to join us?"

The man's head jerked up in the process of pulling up his pants. Reverend Bright's eyes met mine. I turned and walked away and was soon lost in the crowd on Calico Row. I doubted Reverend Bright would follow me and try to explain himself. What was there to explain? He was a man being serviced by a prostitute. It didn't matter he was a man of God. They were as prone to sins of the flesh as others, maybe more so.

257

I'd suspected Bright was partaking in the services of the women on the row, but Clara? Of all the soiled doves to poke, he'd chosen the one he and Portia had taken a special interest in. The one they were working so tirelessly to save. Was the Reverend's true purpose to receive carnal thanks for his efforts? Had he done the same with the other prostitutes? It was an almost unfathomable betrayal of his wife and her mission.

I'd known my fair share of hypocrites, and too often they used the word of God as their protection and forgiveness. The more I thought of Reverend Bright's actions, the more I realized I wasn't surprised by what I'd seen. His marriage with Portia seemed more based on mutual respect than love. I doubted their private life was satisfying for either. I thought of the day they brought me to Calico Row, how they had barely interacted, though it was supposed to be their joint mission, how the Reverend had disappeared and how Portia seemed completely unconcerned about it.

I stopped in the road. Portia knew and didn't care.

No doubt when Portia met the Reverend she saw someone who would save her from a lonely life as a schoolteacher, from constantly moving between the settlers' houses of the children she taught; from being one bad harvest away from the pioneers not being able to pay her salary or to board her, one drought from losing her job. Portia might not have answered an ad for a wife, but she came west with the same goal as other women like her, the same goal as the single men had: to start a new life and better their lot.

Calico Row teemed with these very men, rambunctious and eager to spend their money. Women called out to tempt it away from them. Fiddle music floated from one tent, harmonica from the other. Down the street, in one of the few wooden buildings, a piano could be heard. Laughter, the clink of glasses, the smell of cigar smoke and the mouthwatering aroma of meat roasting over an open fire, it all mixed together to create an atmosphere charged with anticipation and possibility.

A volley of gunshots startled me out of my reverie. The crowd in the road moved to the edges, taking cover and looking for the culprits. Was it another running gunfight over a card game or a prostitute? A cowboy rode down the center of Calico Row, whooping and hollering, firing his pistol into the air. Salter stepped out from the shadows in front of the galloping horse and raised his hands. The horse reared, throwing the cowboy. The riderless horse ran off down the street.

"Far be it from me to interrupt your revels," Salter said in a level voice, "but there's one thing I can't abide and it's the wanton discharge of a pistol." He stalked toward the man on the ground, who was groaning and holding his arm. Salter stood over the squirming man. "You ask me, it's a waste of a good bullet. You never know when you might need it."

"You broke my arm, you crazy son of a bitch," the cowboy said.

Salter squatted down. "You're drunk, so I'll forget you called me that." He gestured in my direction. "There's a lady right there who can fix your arm." Salter stood and waved me forward.

I hesitated, my eyes drawn to a man standing near Stella and her girls. Dr. Drummond smiled at me and tipped his hat. Most everyone on the street had stopped to stare at what was going on. More to end the spectacle than anything, I moved forward and helped the man up. Salter had turned and walked away. "Let's get out of the road."

I sat the man down on a bench outside Stella's tent and asked her for a lantern. The shirtsleeve on the cowboy's lower right arm bulged, and blood bloomed on the material.

I ripped his shirtsleeve. "What's your name?"

"Zeke." His face was pale and sweaty. He swallowed with difficulty, as if swallowing bile. "God, this hurts." He wiped his watering eyes roughly but kept them turned away from his arm. He knew as well as I did that the bone was sticking out of the skin.

I grasped my stomach at the familiar stabbing pain of my menses.

"I can help you with the pain." Drummond was beside us, pulling a small case from his inside coat pocket. He was looking to Zeke, but I suspected the offer encompassed me, as well.

"What's that?" Zeke asked.

Drummond held up the vial. "Morphine. It'll ease your pain while Mrs. Graham here works on you."

"I cannot pay you for it," I said. I gritted my teeth against my own pain, trying to mask my weakness from Drummond and my patient.

"From one professional to another," Drummond said with a sly smile. He held up the syringe. The young cowboy's eyes widened in alarm at the needle.

"I don't think so," Zeke said.

I couldn't tear my gaze from the brown liquid in the syringe. I imagined it flowing through my veins, releasing the ever-present tension in my muscles, dulling the pain I knew would lay me out for days, would keep me from going to Kindle. One dose would make travel on the emigrant train more bearable but would make a woman traveling alone vulnerable.

"Maybe you need this more than the cowboy," Drummond said with a knowing smile.

"Give it to him."

"You sure?"

I ignored him and said to the cowboy, "I can't treat you here.

We're going to have to go to Dr. Hankins's office." Drummond pushed up the cowboy's sleeve, hit his arm to raise the vein, and pushed the needle home. The cowboy cried out and turned green.

Salter walked up with the man's horse. Drummond removed the needle and returned the syringe to his case.

With more gentleness than I expected, Salter helped Zeke stand. Before helping him onto his horse, Salter said, "I'm sorry about your arm, son. I'll pay your bill."

Zeke's legs buckled beneath him. "What about my lost wages?" he slurred.

Salter boosted Zeke onto the horse and patted him on the leg. "If you lose your job, come find me at the Union Pacific Hotel." He handed the reins to me. "I'll leave your payment at the front desk. Unless you want me to pay Hankins? Five dollars?"

"No," I said. "The front desk is fine."

"If you need another dose, you know where to find me," Drummond said.

Salter and I watched the huckster return to the whores he'd been with when the commotion began. Clara took him inside.

"He gives the whores a free taste to hook them, then sells it to them at a premium," Salter said.

"I know."

Salter looked down on me and studied my face. Did he see tension there from holding back the pain increasing in my abdomen? "Stay out of the alleys, Doc. Nothing good happens in the shadows."

I clicked to the horse and led him away. I went by Monique's and told her I would return to check on Lavina and Thomas as soon as I could. We were crossing through the rail yard when a shadow stepped in front of us. "Mrs. Graham. How do you feel?"

It was too dark to see his face clearly, but I recognized the voice. "I'm fine, Mr. Drummond."

He reached into his coat. "I thought you might rather get your dose away from prying eyes. Doesn't look good for a doctor to be partaking, does it?"

"I do not need your morphine, Mr. Drummond."

"Don't you? I knew who you were the first time I met you." Drummond's eyes gleamed with anticipation.

Fear and pain mingled in my stomach and I clutched at it instinctively. "Who am I?"

"An addict."

Relief almost overshadowed the stabbing pain in my lower abdomen. He didn't know me as Catherine Bennett. "I'm going to have to ask you let me pass. I need to help my patient."

Drummond laughed. "The cowboy can wait. He doesn't feel any pain. Unlike you. I can help. I *want* to help."

I couldn't help myself; I laughed. The thought that this man had my best interests at heart was too much. "You are reprehensible, preying on whores who have no hope."

"I help make their lives more bearable."

"Oh, you're doing it out of the goodness of your heart?" I scoffed. "I'd be surprised if you had a heart."

Drummond's expression changed in a flash. He drew his arm across his body and backhanded me across the face. The force of the blow spun me around and I fell heavily on my hands and knees. Zeke's horse reared and bolted, jerking me forward by the hand still holding the rein. The leather strip whipped out of my hand and I fell forward onto my chest, which knocked the wind out of me.

I lifted my head to gasp for breath and saw the horse trip on the railroad tracks, regain its footing, and continue on. Zeke tumbled over the side of the horse and hit the ground. Drummond turned me onto my back, pulled my gun, and tossed it aside. It hit the tracks with a metal clang. "The problem with women like you is you don't know when to keep your mouth shut."

I tried to scramble back on my elbows, but my chest felt as if it were in a vise. I couldn't breathe, my tight corset working against me. My vision swam as I clutched at my chest, ineffectively trying to loosen the corset beneath my shirt. Drummond knelt down and straddled me. I bucked against him, trying to dislodge him, while my hand reached down toward my leg, bent so I could access my knife. Drummond took my arm clutching at my corset, shoved my shirtsleeve up, and hit my arm a couple of times, while I continued to squirm beneath him. "You're feisty, but you'll be compliant soon enough."

I could barely hear through the pounding in my ears and my gasps for breath, but I felt his erection and knew what he intended for me.

I saw the needle at the same moment I grasped the handle of my knife. "You'll be begging to suck my dick for another dose," he said. Drummond stuck the needle in my arm and pushed the plunger a moment before I stabbed him in the back of his shoulder. I bucked against him with as much power as I could muster. He screamed, reached for the knife, and flew backward off me as if plucked by the hand of God.

I pulled the syringe from my arm and rolled over onto my hands and knees. I crawled away still clutching the syringe, the edges of the world dark from lack of oxygen. With a final, unsuccessful heave, I collapsed on my chest. I saw nothing but the hard metal of the railroad track, heard my heartbeat slow, the sound of fighting, the *oof* of a man being punched in the stomach, and finally the crunch of gravel beneath running feet. I closed my eyes and relaxed, exhausted. A sublime feeling of well-being flowed through me.

I'm sorry, Kindle.

Strong hands turned me over and fumbled with my clothes—the buttons of my vest, my shirt, and finally, the laces of my corset. I knew I should fight but didn't have the strength. The man pulled the corset open and said, "Take a deep breath, Helen."

I did so and air, glorious air, filled my lungs. I tried to rise, but the man placed a hand on my shoulder. "Catch your breath first." He held my hand and when my vision came into focus I saw who my savior was.

"Reverend." One side of his red face was dirty and he rubbed his abdomen.

He helped me sit. "Better?"

I nodded as the morphine seeped into the far reaches of my body. *God, why have I avoided this for so long?*

"Can you stand?"

"Not yet, I don't think." I lifted the syringe. It was three-quarters full. Drummond only managed a small dose. I pushed the plunger and the liquid shot out of the needle onto the ground. No need to tempt myself. I had a patient to take care of and it would be hard enough with the dose I'd received.

"What is that?" the Reverend said.

"Morphine. It's Drummond's new line. He tried to make me a customer by force."

The Reverend's face darkened in anger, and he looked back toward Calico Row, his forehead creased in thoughtful concern. He turned back to me.

"Did he violate you?"

"No."

The Reverend sighed and shook his head in relief. "I'm glad I wasn't too late."

I took a few deep breaths and stood with the Reverend's help. I turned my back to button my shirt and found that they had been ripped off. The Reverend had managed to save my vest, so I pulled my shirt together as best I could and closed my vest.

"I apologize for your shirt," the Reverend said. "You were turning purple."

"Buttons can be replaced." I looked around the dark train yard. "I don't suppose you have a lantern."

"No."

"Drummond threw my gun." I turned around. "I'm not sure which way."

Reverend Bright picked up my carpetbag and handed it to me. The sound of broken glass explained the blots of wetness on the side of the bag that had been lying on the ground. I opened it and saw my small bottle of alcohol destroyed, and my carbolic powder gumming up in the liquid.

A man groaned.

"Zeke," I said, pointing to a lump on the ground a little distance off. I hurried to my patient, trying to walk in a straight line, the Reverend on my heels. Zeke's head was pillowed awkwardly on a railroad track. I slid my hand beneath his head and probed the base of his skull, relieved to find a large bump instead of the soft, pebbly sign of a crushed skull. "I fear his horse is gone for good. Can you help me with him?" I asked the Reverend, my words slurring together.

"Can you?" the Reverend asked.

"Yes. I'm fine."

He took Zeke's good arm and pulled him upright. Zeke's legs gave way, but Reverend Bright wrapped the cowboy's arm around his neck and supported him. I gently took Zeke's broken arm and dipped below it to help the Reverend as much as possible. It had the added benefit of supporting my numb legs. Zeke's head lolled around on his neck, finally settling back so if conscious, he would be staring at the stars. We continued on.

"Where are we going?"

"My house."

"Dr. Hankins's is closer."

"Yes, but it's more important I get his wound disinfected first. I have more carbolic at my house."

We labored on for a while in silence. My chest burned with the effort of helping hold Zeke up. The man was dead weight. "Let me," the Reverend said, taking Zeke from me. It wasn't until we were in sight of my house that the Reverend spoke on what I had little doubt had been plaguing his mind for a while.

"Mrs. Graham, about what you saw…"

"Reverend—"

"It is something I've struggled against—"

"Really, Reverend, I do not care about your struggles. I am not the one you should be discussing this with."

"My wife and I rarely—"

"Oliver," I snapped. "I do not want to know of something so personal. There is nothing special or unique about a man fucking a whore. Spare me your excuses and justifications. If you want to ask for forgiveness, talk to your wife."

I led him between the houses to the kitchen door at the back of Rosemond's house. I hurried on to open the door and light the lantern.

A pot of coffee was warm on the stove. One mug with dregs sat on the table across from an empty glass and a bottle of whisky. Rosemond had company and hadn't cleaned up after herself. Typical.

I cleared the table and moved the chairs out of the way and directed the Reverend to lay Zeke out on it.

"Thank you," I said. "Now, I must ask another favor."

Reverend Bright put his hands on his knees to catch his breath. "Of course."

"Find Hankins. You can try his office, but you might want to go by the Rollins House first. Tell him I'm treating a compound fracture and need some plaster of Paris."

The Reverend nodded.

"First, sit for a moment," I said, moving a chair toward him. I poured a cup of coffee from the pot and handed it to the Reverend. "Rest for a minute while I get the carbolic."

He nodded and drank. I took the lantern and left the room.

CHAPTER
22

I grasped the top of the dresser to steady myself and took a few deep breaths. The morphine had dulled the pain in my stomach but dulled my senses as well. My eyelids were heavy and the sight of the bed in the mirror was almost too enticing to ignore. I closed my eyes against it and shook my head. I needed to eat something, drink a cup of coffee, and regain my focus. The clock ticked ever closer to my time of departure, and I had many tasks to complete before I left.

I lifted my extra bottle of carbolic from the box of medicines Rosemond had given me and was returning to the kitchen when I heard a thump and scrape from Rosemond's studio. She was awake. Best to tell her about the cowboy in the kitchen.

Lamplight glowed through the crack in the door. I reached out to push the door open when I heard a moan of pleasure. I pulled my hand back as if burned. I couldn't imagine who she would be entertaining in such a way. She spent her time painting and working on the sheriff's portrait and now Portia's. Surely she wasn't servicing the sheriff. I recoiled in disgust and turned to leave. The sound of a woman's voice stopped me.

"Rosie, what are you doing to me?"

My heart hammered in my chest. Not the sheriff, but Portia

Bright. Was Rosemond seducing her against her will? I moved forward and opened the door wider, not sure what I expected to see. It took a moment to understand there was no undue coercion on the part of either woman. Portia was against the wall, her face tilted to the ceiling, eyes closed. Her wild hair was unbound from its bun, framing her glowing face. Her shirt gaped open, baring one naked breast. Portia held Rosemond's head against the other one.

Rosemond released Portia's breast and said, "Loving you. The true you. Not the prim preacher's wife you pretend to be."

"I'm not pretending."

"Not now, you're not."

"No."

Rosemond kissed Portia deeply. Portia returned the kiss and let her hands move tentatively down to Rosemond's hips.

I turned my head away, ashamed at my voyeurism, ashamed at the longing it ignited in me, but didn't move away.

"I love you, Portia. I came all this way for you." They kissed again, frantically, as if afraid their time was limited and they wanted to taste and feel as much as possible. Portia's hands went to Rosemond's shirt and worked at the buttons. Rosemond pulled Portia's skirt up and pushed her hand between her legs.

Portia groaned and said, "Yes," in a breathless whisper. Her mouth turned up into a smile of happiness and contentment, like returning home after a long time away. She opened her eyes and caught sight of me over Rosemond's shoulder. Incomprehension morphed into horror. "Oliver!"

Rosemond followed Portia's gaze, as did I. Oliver Bright stood behind me, staring wide-eyed at the sight of his wife in the throes of passion with another woman. For the first time since I'd known her, Rosemond looked terrified. Portia removed Rosemond's hand from between her legs with one hand while the other tried to close her shirt.

"Oliver, this isn't—"

The Reverend looked at me with dead eyes and said, "I'm going to find Hankins." He walked out the front door without closing it and turned in the opposite direction of Hankins's house and the Rollins House Hotel.

Quiet sobs turned my attention back to the studio. Portia'd covered her face with her hands. Rosemond reached out for her and pulled her into her arms. "Shh, don't cry. It's okay." She rubbed Portia's back. "We can be together sooner than we thought."

Portia pulled away. Her striking eyes stared at Rosemond with incomprehension. "Be together?"

"Of course. That's why I came west. Gave up everything. To be with you." Rosemond caressed Portia's face. "I love you, Portia. I've loved you since the first moment I met you. You love me, too."

"It doesn't matter," Portia said, voice rising. "We're deviants. Unnatural."

"No. Stop it."

"Did you think I would leave my husband for you? If I wanted a Boston marriage I wouldn't have left Saint Louis."

"He doesn't love you. He's a Calico Row john."

"Of course he is. That's why we suit. He has his whores, and so do I."

Rosemond stepped back. "What?"

Portia turned away from Rosemond and buttoned her shirt. Portia's face was in profile, but I could see her pained expression clear enough. It didn't match the cold timbre of her voice. "You weren't the first, or the last. But you were the best." Portia grimaced with the last verbal dart; Rosemond's expression behind her was one of astonishment and deep, deep pain.

"You're lying."

Portia faced Rosemond with a stony expression. "Good-bye, Rosemond." She walked toward me, head held high. Her eyes met mine and, try as she might, she couldn't hide her devastation. "Helen." Her voice broke ever so slightly as she glided past and out the front door. Once on the street, Portia covered her mouth and ran.

I stared at the empty street, too stunned to move. I knew Rosemond had been lying, been keeping something from me, but this? The strange caresses and comments Rosemond had made in front of Portia took on a new light. Portia would have known immediately I wasn't Rosemond's sister. Knowing where Rosemond's predilections lay, of course she would think I was her new lover. Rosemond had killed Cora Bayle not to protect me at Kindle's behest but because she needed me to make Portia jealous, to win back the woman she loved.

Incredulous and disgusted, I turned in time to see Rosemond charging me. She wrapped her hands around my throat. The surprise of her attack and her forward momentum thrust me backward off my feet. I fell on my back and Rosemond's full weight slammed into me. The breath I'd struggled for so recently was, again, pushed out of me. Rosemond squeezed my neck, her thumbs pressing into the hollow of my throat. Her face was red with the effort of strangling me. Weak from the morphine, I ineffectively clawed at her hands.

"You did this on purpose," she said through gritted teeth.

I tried to shake my head, to say no, but could do nothing but slap at her hands and try to buck her off me. Panic welled inside me, but my energy ebbed. My hands were clumsy and heavy.

A thump and crash from the kitchen distracted Rosemond enough that my increasingly ineffective bucks threw her off balance and loosened her grip. She fell forward and I hit her in the nose. My punch was weak but it surprised her, and that was all I needed. I grasped her neck and rolled her off me and beneath me. I didn't bother choking her. I pulled my fist back and punched her in the face one, two, three times, and would have kept going until her lying, manipulative, pockmarked face was a bloody pulp if the groaning from the kitchen hadn't reminded me of Zeke. I sat back, shaking my rebroken right hand, the hand I'd worked so hard to rehabilitate over the last year. I looked at the knuckles, which were a bloody, pulpy mess. "Son of a bitch," I said, knowing finally that surgery as a profession was lost to me. I lifted Rosemond by the shirt and punched her in the face again as I hard as I could. I had the satisfaction of hearing her nose break. "That's for lying to me about Kindle." I dropped her back down to the floor and stood on legs as weak as a newborn calf's. I kicked her in the side. "That's for Cora Bayle."

I picked up the bottle of carbolic I'd dropped and went into the kitchen. Zeke was facedown on the ground, his broken arm beneath him. I rolled him over with difficulty. His compound fracture was bleeding freely now. I fashioned a tourniquet from a nearby dish towel, screaming in pain with my own injury. With his upper arm tied off, I felt for a pulse in Zeke's neck and was relieved to find it strong. The trembling that had originated in my legs overtook my entire body. I staggered to the nearest chair and fell heavily into it.

I closed my eyes and inhaled deeply, vowing to never take breathing for granted again and to never, ever touch morphine or laudanum for the remaining days of my life. I touched my throat, confirming that Rosemond's hands weren't around it, though it felt like they were, still. A sharp pain shot through my broken right hand, too much for the morphine to mask. I stared at my hand, deformed once again, and chastised myself and my temper. The burst of satisfaction I'd received for punching Rosemond was dissipating with each stab of pain in my hand. Though I was hours from leaving Cheyenne and putting this behind me, Rosemond's memory would haunt me every time I looked at my ruined hand—and I was afraid it was damaged beyond repair—every time the longing to be a surgeon returned. Nor would I ever forget the rage in her eyes as she strangled me and blamed me for Portia's betrayal.

I tried to recapture the anger at Rosemond I'd nurtured since finding out she'd lied to me about Kindle's death. I wanted to hate her, and a small part of me did. But the rage in her eyes... I understood it. I understood the tremble of emotion in Rosemond's voice when she told Portia she loved her, the elation when she thought their path had been cleared, the devastation when Portia left. In the space of minutes, Rosemond had journeyed the emotional gamut that I'd traveled over the past year. I couldn't condemn her reaction. Hadn't my plan in staying in Cheyenne been to earn money? Yes. But to find a way to ruin Rosemond's life? Now I had the perfect opportunity to tell the world about Rosemond's Sapphic tendencies, and all I could think of was how alike we were. Could I ruin someone's chance at happiness for my own revenge? What kind of person would that make me?

I love you. I came all this way for you.

I closed my eyes and turned my head away, ashamed at myself for spying on a private moment between two people who obviously loved each other, for not being disgusted by watching them.

Zeke groaned and shivered in the cold. I rose and left the

kitchen. The entry hall was empty, save a puddle of blood where I'd left Rosemond. I went to my room, pulled the blanket from my bed, tucked my pillow under my arm, and returned to Zeke. Breathing through my teeth against the pain in my hand, I tucked the pillow beneath his head and laid the quilt over him. I needed to clean his wound and splint the arm, at a minimum, but I couldn't do it alone.

I found Rosemond standing at her dresser, holding a wet cloth against her bleeding nose. She glared at me in the mirror, her left eye puffy and bruising. "You broke my nose."

I moved through the studio, catching a quick glimpse of the beginning of Portia's portrait and the finished painting of me on the train leaning against the wall nearby. I turned Rosemond to face me and tried to pull the cloth away. "Let me see."

"No."

"Don't be belligerent."

"Don't try to be nice to me now."

"You tried to strangle me, or have you forgotten?" Rosemond removed the cloth. I felt the sides of her nose with my thumb and forefinger of my left hand. "Hmm. I thought I did a better job than this."

"Stop being glib, Laura. It hurts."

I pulled my hands away. "Do you want me to help you or not?"

"Will my nose look like it did before?"

"That depends."

"On?"

"If you can set your own nose."

"What?"

I held up my ruined right hand.

"Serves you right," Rosemond said, but her heart wasn't in it. She sighed. "This is going to hurt, isn't it?"

I nodded. "Are you honestly telling me you never had your nose broken while whoring?"

"There are whores and there are *whores*. I was the first kind. I need whisky."

"Don't be a baby."

"Have you ever had your nose set?"

"Not while conscious, no."

"When?"

"After Kindle rescued me from his brother."

Rosemond studied me for a long moment. "What do I need to do?"

"Blow the blood out of your nose."

"I just stopped the bleeding."

"It shouldn't bleed again."

Rosemond didn't look convinced, but she obeyed, ending the blowing session with a coughing fit. She held out the bloody cloth to me. "I don't want it. Put it there." I motioned to the dresser.

"Now what?"

I stood behind her, reached around, and felt her nose with my left hand.

"What happened to your arm?"

There was a large blot of blood on the inside of my shirtsleeve from where Drummond dosed me. "It's nothing." I found the break. "Put your left thumb where my thumb is, and your right thumb where my finger is. Do you feel the break?"

She nodded.

I placed my hand on her shoulder. "When I count to three, push your thumbs against your nose. You ready?"

Rosemond nodded again.

"Are you sure your fingers are in the right place? Do you feel the break?"

"Yes, Goddamn it. Stop prolonging it."

"One...two...three..."

After a loud pop, Rosemond screamed. "Son of a bitch!"

I laughed, turned her toward me, and gently pinched the bridge of her nose. "Straight as an arrow."

"Stop laughing," Rosemond said.

"You're going to have black eyes for a while."

"I've seen broken noses before."

"Now you know how to fix one."

"Let me see your arm." She grabbed my arm and shoved my sleeve up. The puncture was large and jagged. "Good Lord, Laura. What happened?"

"Drummond dosed me with morphine."

"What? Why?"

I focused on remembering what Drummond had said to me while I struggled for air. I pulled my arm away and rolled down my sleeve and told her the story of Drummond's attack, omitting the part where I insulted the man.

"Are you in pain now?" Rosemond asked.

"Thanks to the morphine, no. I need you to help me fix a compound fracture. I have a cowboy in the kitchen who needs his arm fixed, and I need another hand."

"Why should I help you?"

"Because I've decided to let you live."

Rosemond's head jerked back, and she laughed.

"I *know*, Rosemond. I know you've been lying to me about Kindle from the beginning, that he's alive. What kind of person does that?"

Her mirth died and was replaced by something like fear. She opened her mouth as if to argue but apparently thought better of it. Her shoulders straightened, and her expression turned defiant. "You would do the same thing to be with who you loved."

"Of course I would. That's why I'm letting you live. We're both reprehensible people. Happy? Are you going to help me or not?"

"I need to go to Portia."

"She'll be there in the morning."

"How do you know?"

"Because I saw the expression on her face when she left."

The hope in Rosemond's expression nearly broke my heart. It switched to skepticism in a flash. "Are you lying to me?" she asked.

"I'll lie about a lot of things, but I wouldn't lie about that. Will you help me?"

She smiled in relief and nodded. "First, I'm going to bandage your arm and broken hand."

"It's fine."

"You don't like being taken care of, do you?"

"Not particularly."

"Too bad." She grabbed my good hand and pulled me into the kitchen.

CHAPTER
23

After Rosemond bandaged my injuries and, following my directions to the letter, washed, set, and splinted Zeke's arm, we sat at the kitchen table. Rosemond drank whisky, still grimacing slightly from the sound and feel of setting a compound fracture. I drank coffee in the hopes it would counteract the morphine. The small circle of lamplight from the lantern on the table faded into darkness where our hands held our glasses, shadowing our faces enough to give Rosemond the safety to confide in me.

"It started with Lyman. In the war," Rosemond began. "He was part of the occupying Army. A quartermaster. He never saw a battle, as far as I know. Unsurprising, if you know him. My father, Edgar March, was a well-known Confederate sympathizer. When the Union came into town, he tried to change his allegiance, for survival as well as to spy for the Confederacy. He pinpointed Lyman as the easiest officer to con." Rosemond laughed. "God, my father was an idiot. But he was smart enough to know the Army would never trust him, one of the biggest slave owners in the state. But a silly girl enamored with a dashing officer? No one would ever suspect her. Unfortunately, I wasn't silly or enamored with officers." She twirled her glass on the table. "Yes, even then my preferences tended the other way. It made it easier, to be honest. Lyman would have been easy to fall in love with. He can be devastatingly charming." She drank her whisky and poured more. "My brother was killed in nothing more than a skirmish. Not only did my father lose his only son, but he was robbed of being able to claim his death had been in glorious battle. I could have told him Ned would die ignominiously. I would have made a better soldier. My father didn't come out and tell me to become Lyman's mistress, but he made it quite clear my virtue was a small price to pay to avenge my brother's death by destroying the Yankees from the inside."

"You were your father's favorite, I gather."

Rosemond laughed long and hard. "I fell somewhere above the slaves, but it was a near deal sometimes. I was too outspoken, too assertive. Didn't know my place. Truthfully, Father knew I would have been a better heir to his fortune than Ned, and he hated me for it." She drank. "I think I believed if I did what my father wanted, if I struck a blow for the Confederacy, he would take me into his business. God, I was naive."

She took a long drink. "When Lyman took me to bed the first time, I expected to hate it. But Lyman is a skilled lover. There were times I thought I might come to enjoy being with a man. I was smart enough to fake it."

"Does Lyman know about...?"

"My Sapphic tendencies?" She nodded. "I thought I was doing a rather good job of pleasing Lyman, but as I said, he was experienced. He saw right through me. One night, he came to my room—he'd set me up in a hotel when my parents kicked me out, as they had to do to keep up the ruse—with another woman. A prostitute. He said he wanted to watch. I refused because I knew I was supposed to, but I didn't want to. The woman was beautiful. A beauty mark right here"—she pointed to the right corner of her mouth—"above her plump, red lips. She read me immediately but told Lyman I wasn't interested and started to leave. I stopped her, of course." She lifted her finger and wiggled it in the air. "Right there. That's where Lyman had me. I ended up spying for the Union. Giving my father enough correct information that he didn't suspect I was taking back everything he told me to Lyman. Lyman rewarded me with women.

"We went on like this for a while. Lyman taught me how to please a man, and Danielle taught me how to please a woman. Ménage à trois were my favorite. Occasionally Lyman would bring in a fourth. A man." I held her gaze, though I felt my face flush with mortification.

Rosemond smiled, slightly, and I knew she was trying to shock me. "I had no idea what Lyman was grooming me for. I thought we were partners, you see. I thought after the war he might marry me. I would never love him, not like I loved women, but he knew about that side of me and didn't care. Lyman was always looking for an angle, and he saw in me a present for fellow officers, or businessmen he wanted to con. I refused, at first. It only took a veiled threat of exposing my tendencies to make me spread my legs for the first client. After that, it became easier. And I was good at it."

"Rosemond…"

"After the war, my family forgave me for being Lyman's mistress. My father practically ordered it, after all. For a short period, I was a heroine, a true daughter of the South who gave her innocence for the cause. Since Lyman's clients had unique tastes, my whoring wasn't widely known. Those who did kept quiet. Self-preservation is the greatest motivator."

"And the family business?"

Rosemond chuckled. "I'd almost convinced my father.

Then they learned I'd been spying for the Union and Lyman's whore."

"Lyman told them?"

"He was long gone by this time. I betrayed myself. I came down with smallpox and in one of my deliriums told much more about my time with Lyman than my sister, who sat at my beside, wanted to hear. Especially as it related to her fiancé, who was one of my more regular clients. When I was well, my parents gave me a hundred dollars, told me to change my name and never return."

"Saint Louis?"

Rosemond nodded. "I rented a room and got in touch with the Army officers I'd known in the war. Within three months, I'd bought a house and had four girls working for me. Within a year I was the highest-paid madam in town. About a year later I met Kindle."

I reached for the whisky and poured some into my cooling coffee.

"Don't bristle so," Rosemond said. "I didn't like Kindle any more than the other men I lay with. He was one of the nicer ones, so I taught him everything I knew. Naturally, I was an expert in teaching men how to please women. Feel free to thank me."

"I will not."

Rosemond laughed. "Laura, I'd much rather fuck you than Kindle. But don't worry. I'm a one-woman woman."

"Did you fuck him that night on the riverboat?"

She stared at me while twirling her whisky glass and didn't answer, which was answer enough.

I stood, went to the sink, stared out the window, and remembered Salter and the threat he was to Rosemond's safety and future happiness. Was I jealous enough of her past with Kindle to turn her in? To tell the world about her and Portia? I closed my eyes and searched deep within myself to find the source of my anger. It wasn't Rosemond. Had it ever been Rosemond?

"The good Reverend isn't returning with your plaster," she said. "No."

I turned and leaned against the sink and opened my mouth to tell her about Salter when she spoke. "I'm sorry I told you Kindle was dead. I didn't want you to leave."

"Because you still needed to make Portia jealous."

"Partially. How long have you known?"

"Hankins told me the day I met him."

Rosemond's face relaxed. "You didn't leave."

"I needed to earn money, and I wanted to find a way to hurt you."

She nodded slowly. "I would have done the same."

"Kindle didn't ask you to help me, did he?"

Rosemond shook her head. "I saw an opportunity to leave and took it."

"Sherman commuted Kindle's sentence. He's free."

Surprise, followed by satisfaction. "That's good news." Her smile drifted into a frown. "Then you're leaving." I detected a slight tremor in her voice.

I nodded. "The one-thirty train."

"What about the cowboy?"

"I'll send Hankins a note after I get on the train."

Rosemond rose and placed her glass in the sink. I crossed my arms. She noted the movement and smiled slightly. "I don't blame you for hating me. But I think you understand why I've done the things I've done." I stared at her and didn't answer. "Admit it, you like me a little bit."

"I don't hate you. Anymore."

"Good enough." Rosemond took my arm and pulled the sleeve up. She ran her hand over the burn scars she must have noticed bandaging my arm but didn't mention at the time. "What happened?"

"I fell off my horse and into a prairie fire."

She lifted my injured hand. "And this?"

"The first time the Indians broke it when they beat me."

"Can it be fixed?"

"I don't know."

She lifted my hand to her lips and brushed them against my fingers. "I'm sorry."

I tried to pull my hand away but she held fast. She looked into my eyes and smiled teasingly, testing me. Rosemond knew I'd watched her and Portia and hadn't been disgusted, or rejected her after. "Are you afraid I'm going to try to seduce you?"

"No."

"Good, because I'm not."

"I'm almost insulted."

"Oh, I've considered it. More than once. You would be easy to conquer."

"I would not."

Rosemond released my hand and laughed. "I almost always get what I want, Laura."

"Now I *am* insulted."

"Oh, it's been a struggle. But I'd much rather have you as a friend than a lover. But if you ever think you want to dabble, let me know."

"What would Portia say?"

Rosemond's expression darkened. "It hardly matters now."

I grasped Rosemond's hand and held fast. "Portia loves you. I saw it in her expression as she left."

Rosemond's eyes met mine. "If you're lying to me, I'll kill you." Her stern expression broke into a grin.

I grinned back. "I'd be disappointed if you didn't try."

CHAPTER
24

I left Rosemond watching over Zeke while I went to fetch the plaster from Hankins and to discuss Lily Diamond's treatment. In the chaos of the last few hours I'd forgotten about Lily's plight and felt guilty for it. So much had changed since I diagnosed her and told Hankins and Harry of her tumor. Kindle was free and I needed to go to him, and now there was the issue of my broken hand. How Hankins reacted to the latter would depend on whether he agreed with my diagnosis. I wouldn't put it past him to agree with me and recommend surgery as soon as possible to soak Harry Diamond for the fee. I needed to coerce him into believing the break was but a blip and I would be cutting people open for profit in no time.

The town was waking up slowly, it being Sunday. A few men straggled down the street, no doubt from a whorehouse or saloon, and toward home or their room. Businesses would remain shuttered, and the pious and the guilty would make their way to church in a few hours. What would be the inspiration for Reverend Bright's sermon? Sins of the flesh? Whose sin would receive the most indignation, I wondered. Bright's meaningless encounter with a whore, or Portia's with a woman she loved?

Hankins's street was a quiet residential street much like Lily Diamond's on a more modest scale. The houses were smaller, but neat for all that, with rows of new trees planted that would make a majestic tunnel when mature in fifty years. Nineteen twenty-two. We'd all be dead by then, most like. How different would Cheyenne look? Would it have left its rough-and-tumble past behind and moved fully into the world of respectability it clearly strove for? I was surprised to realize I wanted to be here to find out.

The sight of Hankins on his front porch with Portia Bright arrested my musings of the future. What was she doing there? And was that blood on her dress?

I stopped at the end of the sidewalk. "Portia?"

The two noticed me for the first time. "Mrs. Graham," Hankins said, "I'm glad you're here. Can you take Mrs. Bright home?"

I stepped through the gate and up the sidewalk. "Of course. But what's going on? Why are you covered in blood, Portia?" She stared at me with an uncomprehending expression.

Hankins came to me and pulled me to the side. "Reverend Bright is dead."

"What? But I just saw him. I sent him here to get plaster of Paris."

"Why am I not surprised your fingers are all over this?" He noticed my bandaged hand. "What's wrong with your hand?"

"I broke it. What do you mean, my fingers are all over this? What happened to Oliver Bright?"

"Drummond, your snake-oil salesman, showed up here with a knife in his back. Thanks to you, he said. Is that true?"

"He attacked me, tried to shoot me full of morphine. I defended myself. Oliver came to my rescue before Drummond could do more, thank heavens."

"When the Reverend arrived and saw Drummond, he flew into a rage."

"Over me?" I said, with disbelief.

"From what I could gather with all the yelling, yes." He glanced at Portia and leaned forward to whisper, "And a whore named Clara. I've treated her before. She's been a doper as long as I've known her. Bright realized, from rescuing you I guess, that Drummond was switching to morphine, more powerful, as you know, and went after him. Horribly outmatched. Drummond stabbed Bright in the scuffle. With your knife, as a matter of fact. Bled out on my floor. There was nothing I could do." When Hankins saw my disbelieving expression, he said, his tone defensive, "Drummond knew what he was doing with a knife, no doubt about it."

"Where is Drummond now?"

"In jail or soon to be. Sheriff is watching the trains. I imagine Drummond'll hang. Can't go around killing preachers."

"But doping up whores and getting them hooked on morphine is perfectly fine."

Hankins's expression darkened. "Drug-addled whores should be the least of your worries. When will you be able to operate on Lily Diamond's tumor?"

I kept one eye on Portia, who hadn't moved. She stared into the middle distance as if it held the answers to the questions of the world. "You agree with my diagnosis?"

"No, but the only way I could keep Harry from asking questions about you and how you were possibly qualified to diagnose a tumor was to say it was obvious to an idiot. He doesn't like you in the least, you know. I'm sure he'd love the reward."

I couldn't bring myself to thank Hankins for keeping Diamond in the dark by calling me an idiot. "I don't think we should wait until my hand is healed," I said. "There's a surgeon in Denver?"

"Not him. You said the tumor is harmless. We'll wait. Now, take Mrs. Bright home. I have to deal with the Reverend's body."

"I need plaster."

"I'll be right back."

I stepped forward and touched Portia's arm. "Portia?" Her red eyes accentuated her pale, tear-stained cheeks.

She looked at me with the same uncomprehending expression. Slowly, her eyes focused and recognition dawned. Her cheeks flamed and she turned her head away, wiping roughly at her cheeks. She stepped away from me, her body trembling from delayed shock at her husband's death.

"Dr. Hankins has asked me to take you home," I said, quietly.

"Thank you, but I can manage." She walked down the porch steps.

"Portia, wait," I said, following. I grasped her arm to arrest her progress. She kept her face averted from me. "You have no need to be embarrassed with me," I said. Portia met my gaze—questioning, hopeful—before glancing over my shoulder and looking away again.

Hankins clomped across the porch and down the steps, a bag of plaster in his hand. "I assume you have strips of cloth."

"I'll manage, thank you."

"Come back when you've delivered her home and seen to the cowboy. We have a lot to discuss."

"Such as?"

"Your ability to keep our bargain with a deformed hand, for one."

I smiled. "It will be no problem, I assure you. I'll return at say, two o'clock?"

He shrugged. "The sooner the better. It will take you hours to clean all the blood off my exam room floor."

I narrowed my eyes and he stared back at me, challenging. He was punishing me for Lily Diamond and lording his power over me. Why were some men so pathetically insecure and predictable?

I smiled sweetly. "Of course. I'll get back as soon as I can. I need to check on Thomas over on Calico Row, and Lavina. She had her baby."

Hankins turned and waved over his shoulder. "Don't forget the money you owe me."

My smile dropped like a bag of rocks and I turned to Portia, who'd been watching me. "Come," I said. "Let's get you home."

I sent Portia into her bedroom to change out of her bloody clothes and went to the kitchen to put on a pot of coffee.

Portia's house was plain—as befitted a man of God and his wife—clean and completely without personality. The kitchen, which would have naturally been Portia's domain, was simple to the point of sparse. I thought of my house in New York: Maureen's kitchen, warm, inviting, always smelling of fresh-baked bread or Irish stew; the small pots of herbs on the windowsill; the scarred wooden table where I ate at one end while Maureen kneaded bread or diced vegetables at the other; the homemade curtains hanging on the windows; the brick oven blackened from years of fires and smoke. I loved my father's library, spent countless hours there as a child, then later as a medical student, but more than any other room, the kitchen was home. Portia's kitchen spoke of a woman who cooked because it was expected of her; she took no pleasure in it, nor did she want to linger there. I wondered how different a kitchen shared with Rosemond would feel to a visitor.

Portia returned, her full mourning dress and severe hairstyle shocking, though I should have expected it. Her expression spoke of a woman in torment, though I wasn't sure what tormented her the most. I poured us a cup of coffee, set hers on the table, and sat down with my own, letting her know I had no intention of leaving without a conversation. Portia sat and we drank in silence.

"The grieving vultures will descend soon. Say your piece and leave," she said.

"Do you think I'm here to judge you?"

Portia dug her fingernail into a scratch on the table and wouldn't look at me. "I'm an abomination."

"Don't be ridiculous. You're nothing of the sort."

Portia was quiet for a while. "It started as a game with her, you know. Rosemond. A challenge to deflower the pious missionary. I resisted her for months, ignored the flirting, the touches, while inside I was singing *yes, yes*." Her voice was soft, melodic, a small smile playing on her lips at the memory. She swallowed, and her voice hardened. "I could have stopped visiting, but I told myself it was my mission to save as many women from the life as I could. When, of course, returning week after week only fed my desire." Portia met my gaze for the first time since outside Hankins's house. I was arrested by the fierceness, the fear, in her mesmerizing, uniquely colored eyes. "How am I to know *this* isn't a game with her, still? I left her in Saint Louis, and Rosemond doesn't like to lose."

"No, she doesn't. I—" Would Rosemond kidnap me, kill an innocent woman, and let Dunk hang in an elaborate scheme to win a seduction game? I could have easily believed it a week ago, but now? I knew too much about Rosemond, had heard the pain in her voice when she told of her family, her past, had seen the expression on her face when I told her Portia loved

289

her. I had to believe Rosemond's motives were true. Otherwise, she was a monster of unimaginable proportions. "If she merely wanted to win, having Oliver see you two together would have sufficed. She wouldn't have tried to strangle me after you left."

Portia closed her eyes and grimaced. I reached out and placed my hand over hers. "I am sorry. I didn't know you were there. And I never would have imagined..."

"I was sure you knew."

"It isn't where the mind naturally goes."

"I thought you were in on it with her."

"I was an unwitting partner in winning you back, it would seem. She hoped my presence would make you jealous."

Portia shook her head. "How can I trust someone who is that manipulative?"

"It's a good question, and one you could easily answer if you were in love."

Portia's head jerked up. "I am." Her eyes widened at the instinctual admission, and she started to cry. She pulled a handkerchief from her sleeve and dabbed at her eyes. I stared at the royal blue monogram in the corner. Portia followed my gaze and gripped the cloth protectively. She stood and turned away. "I'm sitting at my kitchen table, talking of loving a woman, clinging to a small scrap of her, when my husband has been killed." She sobbed. I went to her, pulled her into my arms, and let her cry. That was how Lily Diamond and Amalia Post found us.

"Oh, dear, you poor thing," Lily said, placing a dish of food on the table. Amalia did the same. It was as if the floodgates opened. A steady stream of women came into the house and took over, talking in quiet voices and searching in vain for something to clean or organize. Portia accepted the condolences with brief words of thanks, her expression appropriately grief-stricken. I stood with her for a while, my arm around her waist, holding her up. I leaned in and told Portia I needed to leave. She nodded and smiled grimly. "Rosemond will want to come when she finds out. Should I tell her she's welcome?"

Portia squeezed my hand. "Tell her to hurry. Please."

I smiled, nodded, and squeezed her hand in good-bye. I was at the kitchen door when I realized this was a final good-bye. When I turned back, Portia had been waylaid by Amalia Post and I couldn't catch her eye. Lily Diamond came to me instead. "Let me walk you out, dear."

At the front door she said, "What is wrong with your hand?"

"I broke it last night."

Lily began to shake. "What about my surgery?"

I took Lily's hand in mine. "Lily, do you trust me?"

"Yes, of course I do."

"I want you to promise me, no matter what you hear, you believe I will take care of you."

"What do you mean?"

"I can't explain right now. Promise me."

"I promise."

"Good. Now I have to get home and cast a cowboy's broken arm and send Eliza over. I'll be in touch soon."

I hurried off before Lily could think too much on my choice of words and what they could possibly mean.

Finding my gun was next to impossible. Freight trains had arrived in the night, as well as east- and westbound passenger trains, clogging the rail yard and making the area where Drummond attacked me difficult to locate. I was on my hands and knees, searching beneath a freight car, when a train whistle blew and was followed by the church bell chiming the hour in the distance.

One o'clock.

When I'd returned to Rosemond's and told her about Oliver Bright's death and Portia's plea to come to her, I had to physically restrain her from running out the door.

"You have to help me with Zeke and cast my hand." Rosemond didn't get the chance to argue. "You owe me at least thirty minutes."

She pointed to her face. "You do remember you broke my nose. We're even."

"Not by a long shot."

Rosemond acquiesced with as much bad humor as only a woman eager to be with her lover could. A combination of her ineptitude, my frustration with not being able to do it myself, dammit, Zeke's writhing and begging for morphine, and my anxiety hearing the clock ticking away, telling me time was moving quickly toward missing my train, resulted in Zeke's cast being the worst effort I'd ever been involved in, including during the war when cannons were booming in the distance and bloody and maimed soldiers continued to stream into the barn on Antietam Creek. Rosemond held her plaster-covered hands in the air and waited to do my cast, trembling with impatience.

"Go. I don't need a cast," I lied.

She rinsed her hands in the sink while I poured the last of my laudanum into a glass of whisky for Zeke. He drank it down in one gulp. "Better?" I asked.

He nodded, and I gave him instructions for what would happen next. An argument broke out when I told Zeke he needed to stay in Cheyenne for a few weeks so Hankins could check on his wound, now covered with plaster, to make sure it wasn't infected. By the time it was over, Rosemond had left.

Without saying good-bye.

I sat back on my knees and sighed. Finding my gun had been a long shot, but I felt naked without it strapped to my waist. If I wanted to get the five dollars Salter had left at the Union Pacific Hotel and make my train, I had to give it up. I stood and dusted dirt off my skirt and made my way to the hotel. The lobby was full and the line to the front desk was ten people deep. I stepped in line and kept my eye on the clock on the wall. Five minutes and the line hadn't moved, thanks to the couple at the front arguing with the clerk about a bigger room. I gritted my teeth, tapped my foot, watched the clock, and tried to ignore the pain in my hand. I hadn't taken laudanum, knowing I needed to have my wits about me on the journey and not wanting to test my newfound opiate sobriety.

One ten. I needed Salter's five dollars to buy my fare. I walked up to the front of the line and interrupted the argument. "Excuse me, Charlie," I said to the clerk. "I'm trying to make the one-thirty train and I need to pick up something that was left for me."

"You'll have to wait in line, miss."

"And I have been. Patiently. But I am going to miss my train. It won't take but a second. Helen Graham."

Charlie shrugged. "If I did it for you, everyone else would expect special treatment and the whole system would break down."

"Yeah, why do you think you're special?" the man behind the arguing couple said.

"I don't. I only need my package. Please." My eyes burned with impending tears as my opportunity to get to Kindle slipped away. "I'm trying to be reunited with my husband, you see. And I need this package to do so."

Charlie the clerk was unmoved, but the woman standing next to me wasn't. "Oh, give her the package, for heaven's sakes."

Charlie, though, wasn't about to bend. He pointed to the back of the line. I returned and waited. It was one twenty-five when I got to the front of the line. Charlie wrote in his book for an interminable time. I gritted my teeth and said, "Hello. I'm here to pick up a package."

The clerk looked up, feigning innocence. "Name?"

"Helen Graham."

"One moment."

He removed an envelope from the mail slots behind the desk and placed it on the counter. "Have a nice trip."

I took it without a word of thanks.

I ran to the depot and pushed my way through the disembarking crowd to the ticket window that, shockingly, didn't have a line. "One ticket for the one thirty." I pushed the envelope through the window and was about to rifle in my bag for the rest of my money. Two short whistles and the hiss of brakes being released told me I was too late a split second before the ticket master did.

"Would you like a ticket for tomorrow's train?"

My head fell forward onto the glass separating us. I nodded. "Thank you."

I paid for the ticket and put it in my bag. I sat down on the nearest bench and plopped my bag on my lap. One more day. I'd survived this long. I could survive one more day. I had no intention of returning to Hankins's house to clean up a floor covered with blood and hear his chastisement for my many transgressions. I couldn't go back to Rosemond's; Hankins would find me there. I closed my eyes and leaned my head back against the wall, wondering where I could hide safely for the next twenty-four hours. I rubbed my aching stomach. The morphine was wearing off, which meant the sharp pains would return soon. I considered breaking into Drummond's caravan and hiding out there. If I knew Sheriff Hall, the purple wagon had already been looted by him and his men.

I'd gone through everyone I knew and dismissed each one again when someone sat down next to me. I would need to get up soon, but my two sleepless nights were catching up to me. Now that I was sitting quietly, I could feel the slight jangling of my nerves beneath my skin, a physical craving for laudanum or morphine. If I concentrated, maybe I could recapture the sensation of floating the morphine gave me. A few minutes more and maybe I could fool my body into believing I didn't need it, and fool my mind into believing I didn't want it.

The person next to me shifted on the bench.

"Waiting for someone?"

My heart stopped, but I kept my eyes closed. It wouldn't have been the first time exhaustion played tricks on my mind. I'd fallen asleep on the bench. It was a dream.

The man placed his hand over mine, lightly, like the touch of a feather, before intertwining his fingers through mine like so many times before. I kept my eyes closed, determined to make the dream last.

"Laura."

A sob broke through me and my head fell forward. He wrapped his arm around my shoulder. My body trembled from happiness and relief. He guided my head to his shoulder and the familiar scent of horse, leather, and sweat hit me. I inhaled deeply, imbued anew with a sense of safety and security missing since being separated from Kindle. I laughed between my sobs, lifted my head from his shoulder, opened my eyes, and found myself holding hands with a one-eyed priest.

CHAPTER 25

"When you sat down on the bench, I was trying to decide how to spend the next twenty-four hours until my train." I rested my chin on Kindle's bare chest. "Unsurprisingly, spending it in bed with a priest never occurred to me."

Kindle had long since lost the cassock and collar, so there was only a slight sense of sinfulness being in bed with him.

He ran his hand up and down my arm. "What were your choices?"

"I didn't have any. With the exception of Rosemond, no one knows I'm leaving. And almost everyone would be angry if I did. A couple will try to kill me."

"You do have a way of making friends, Slim."

"Hmm. Tell me everything that's happened to you since you walked out of our cabin on the riverboat."

I'd taken Kindle to a new hotel on the edge of the business district where I would be less likely to be recognized. Despite the cassock, with his erect military carriage, eye patch, and beard, Kindle turned heads. Which, now that he'd been in so many papers with this visage, meant he would be recognized as William Kindle, accomplice to the at-large Murderess.

"Lyman turned me in, the bastard. The Army took me to

Jefferson Barracks and threw me into the brig. The officers'
brig, so it was nicer than the three-by-six cell I had at Fort
Richardson. And I waited. They let me stew for a couple of days
before questioning me. It started off with questions about Fort
Richardson, my orders, going after Cotter Black, the escape."

"You didn't tell them Harriet helped."

"Of course not. I told them Little Stick did it. He's dead, and
beyond their jurisdiction."

"What about the bounty hunters?"

"They asked about a few men who disappeared after going
in search of us. But the Army didn't seem too interested in
them. What they were interested in was you."

"Me? The Army?"

"That's what I thought. It took them a few days, hours and
hours of interrogation, before they finally got around to you. I
told them you were dead. Had died in Indian Territory."

"They didn't believe you?"

"No."

"You didn't cry, did you?"

"No," Kindle said, as if it were a ridiculous question.

"A little emotion and they might have believed you."

"I'll save my emotion for private." He grasped my chin and
kissed me in that slow, deep way that made my body burn with
desire from head to toe. "I've missed you."

"I suppose I am preferable company to being alone in a jail
cell."

He lifted my bandaged hand gently, but I hissed against the
pain. "Can it be fixed?"

"I don't think it matters." I told him of my subpar work on
Thomas's amputated foot and about my fear of working on Lily
Diamond. "I can practice as a physician, but surgery is lost to me."

"I doubt it."

I looked at my hand. "Even *I* have limitations, William. I suppose I will have to make peace with teaching others to be brilliant doctors instead of being one myself."

"Nonsense. You're one of the most tenacious people I've ever known."

"Is that a compliment?"

He kissed my hand gently. "Do you have some laudanum in that carpetbag?"

"No, I used it on my last patient, thank God. I've come to crave it, like my father did before he died. I don't trust myself."

"How are you feeling?"

There had been only the barest of hesitations on either of our parts when I told him my dark days had begun. I didn't know what to expect, but I had never imagined intercourse would lessen my pain. "I'll be fine," I said. I didn't know if either of us would be eager to use intercourse as a monthly remedy, though the thought of suffering through the pain every month for the next twenty years was enough to make me take a knife to my stomach.

"I can't believe you broke Rosemond's nose."

"Do you blame me?"

"No."

I'd couched the story of Rosemond's broken nose as my reaction to finding out she'd lied to me, which was true. Rosemond's romantic preferences, and her relationship with Portia, were not my secret, or news, to tell.

I straddled him and ran my good hand through his chest hair, proving to myself this wasn't a dream. I traced the scar on his cheek, hidden partially by his graying stubble, rubbed my thumb on the cleft in his chin, bent down to kiss him. "I cannot believe you are real."

"Do I need to prove it to you again?"

"Cheeky man." I ran my hand lightly over his eye patch but didn't lift it. Kindle rarely let me see him without it. It didn't matter that I was a doctor. I was his wife first, and I suspected he was vain about the gaping black hole on the left side of his face. I hadn't fallen in love with his eyes, and I thought he was as handsome and appealing now as when we met. But a part of me grieved for the unscarred face he had when we fell in love. His deformity was a constant reminder of my culpability in everything that had happened for the last year.

"I'm glad you've resolved everything with the Army. Being on my own for the last weeks has made me realize as long as the bounty is on my head, people are going to either turn me in for the money or try to use me for their own ends. I'm never going to be free of it. No matter where we go."

"That's not true."

"It is true, and you know it. With your eye patch and scar, there's no possibility we can blend in."

Kindle studied me for a while. He sighed. "I hoped we could have more time to ignore the rest of the world."

"I can't, Kindle. I have to confront this."

He disentangled himself from me, rose from the bed, and walked across the room to where his coat had been hastily discarded. I bit my bottom lip as I drank the sight of him in. The dark hair on his pale legs. The scar on his left shoulder from the surgery I performed at Fort Richardson. The scar on his right thigh from the surgery I performed amid the smoldering wreckage of my wagon train. The slender fingers I longed to watch dance across piano keys. My eyes slowly made their way to his sensual mouth, which was turned up into the same self-satisfied smirk I saw on his face after the first time we made love. "Can I walk back to the bed or would you like for me to stand here a little longer?"

I nodded to the paper he held in his hand. "If you're going to read to me, you can do it from there just as well."

He raised his eyebrows and shook his head.

"Stop pretending you don't love when I ogle you," I said.

He unfolded the paper. "It's a letter from Pope."

"That's one way to douse my desire."

"Poor Henry would be crushed to hear you say it."

"Don't be silly. I love Henry. But I don't want to think about him while I'm staring at you."

"You'll feel guilty soon. Turns out Henry decided to put a portion of his royalties for *Sawbones* into hiring someone to investigate your case."

"What?" I jumped from the bed and snatched the letter from Kindle and read it aloud.

" 'Major,

" 'I should have known you'd go and get yourself caught as soon as you emerged from your hidey-hole. There aren't enough' "—my mouth twisted in the effort to not laugh— " 'one-eyed pirates in the world for you to be able to blend in successfully, for long. Your grave and taciturn demeanor probably doesn't help, though those of us who know you well know you're a cuddly little kitten deep down.' "

A laugh burst from me. Happiness, relief, and hope all rolled into one. "Henry would never have the courage to say that to you in person."

"I know."

" 'From the accounts I've read in the papers here—and we know how accurate papers can be—Laura is in the wind somewhere. I'll confess to be more worried about her fate than yours. With the reward at $1,000, the clamor to find her will be even higher than in Indian Territory. Of course, this is Laura we're talking about; a more capable, intelligent woman I've never met. But we know it's only a matter of time before she is apprehended. When you rejoin her with your dark looks and eye patch, her capture will be more imminent still. So it falls on me to clear her name in New York City so you two can have some semblance of a life.

"'After the publication of *Sawbones* I was feted by every literary society in town. I came across dozens of people who knew Catherine Bennett, and they were only too willing to give their accounts of her, good and bad. There isn't enough space in this letter to detail them all, but I knew enough of Laura from my own experience to gauge that at least half were outright lies. But dispersed in the chaff were dribs and drabs of insight into the story surrounding George Langton's murder and Laura's flight. The short version: few people believe Laura murdered Langton, and no one wants her to hang. No one felt the need to come forward since Laura was gone, safe from the noose. They think a life of adventure in the West is preferable to life in the city. I'll confess *Sawbones* probably cemented the idea of a grand adventure. We know better.

"'I've lost access to the people most concerned with the case. Turns out, fame is a fickle friend. The next installment of Laura's adventures should open some more doors. In the meantime, I've engaged the services of a quite unique investigator. We are determined to clear Catherine Bennett's name, so you and Laura can live in peace.'"

I looked up at Kindle. "We need to go back."

He nodded slowly. "Not until we hear from Pope."

"I can't stay here."

"I know." Kindle opened his leather satchel and pulled out a plain gray robe with one hand and a rosary with the other.

I shook my head and chuckled at the ridiculous turns my life had taken. "You *do* know there's a good chance God will strike me dead when I put that thing on."

Kindle tossed the robe onto a chair and hung the rosary on the dresser mirror. "If I didn't get struck down for pretending to be a priest, you won't for pretending to be a nun." He reached back into his bag and removed a small holstered derringer.

"My, my. You've thought of everything." I pulled the pearl-handled gun out.

"Careful. It's loaded." I shot him a withering look. The holster strap was thick and short. "For your leg. Your calf. Here." He knelt down and put my boot on. He ran his finger along the top of the knife scabbard and looked at me with a raised eyebrow.

"Men aren't the only ones who can hide knives in their boots."

"Where is your knife?"

"In Drummond's back, last I saw."

Kindle chuckled and shook his head. He buckled the holster around my calf.

"How does that feel?"

The holster rested on the top of my boot and was snug enough on my leg that I could pull the gun quickly, but not so tight as to be distracting. "Like a second skin."

He ran his hands up the length of my legs, peppering my lower abdomen with kisses. When he stood, his eye wasn't the only part of his body filled with desire.

I took him in my hand. "Is this from me wearing a gun or the idea of me in a nun's habit?"

Kindle's hands stroked my hips and he pulled me against him. "It's from being away from you for too long. Once we put our disguises on I won't be able to look at you like this. Or touch you like this."

"Then we shall put off the ruse for as long as possible."

CHAPTER
26

Entering the hotel as a woman and leaving as a nun meant I had to sneak down the back stairs and around the hotel to meet Kindle on the street. A man carrying a sack of feed on his shoulder looked askance at me. I smiled, nodded, and blessed him. I was trying to fix my face into a serious expression when I rounded the corner and saw Kindle standing on the front porch of the hotel, talking to someone. When the man came into view, my smile had no trouble disappearing.

"Lyman."

John Lyman hadn't bothered trying to blend in to the rough-and-tumble West. The riverboat gambler wore a navy coat over tan breeches and waistcoat with a faint navy pinstripe running through. His fawn-colored, flat-brimmed felt hat sat at a jaunty angle and the thin mustache on his upper lip quivered in amusement. He laughed. "Well, I'll be Goddamned."

I glanced around the street, hoping no one heard the profanity. Across the street, a woman's step faltered. I smiled and nodded to her. "Keep your voice down," I said.

"Look at her, taking to the disguise like a duck to water." Lyman scrutinized me in such a way I knew his thoughts would get him struck down if I were a real nun. The inappropriate proposition he'd made to me on the Mississippi came rushing back to my mind. My face burned with embarrassment. He raised his eyebrows and licked his lips. Satisfied we'd been thinking of the same thing, he moved his assessment to Kindle. "You, on the other hand, are much too stern. Even for a priest. You look like you could murder someone."

"Just you."

Lyman grinned. "I always liked you, Kindle."

Lyman held a small gun to Kindle's side and for a moment, I thought it was mine. But no; my gun was snugly strapped to my lower left leg.

With his free hand, Lyman patted Kindle's chest and beneath his arm. He smiled, reached inside Kindle's coat, and removed his gun. Kindle glared at Lyman but didn't move.

"Why don't we have breakfast? I worked up quite the appetite listening to you two fuck all night," Lyman said. My head jerked around. "I took the room next door. Frightfully thin walls."

"You're disgusting."

Lyman shrugged, took me by the elbow, and shoved Kindle's gun in my side. "The hotel clerk recommended a place where we could have some privacy. Down the alley there. Kindle, lead the way. We'll be right behind you."

"We'll be recognized. I'm well known in town," I said.

"Your disguise is better than you think."

Lyman directed Kindle down an alley to where the new wooden buildings switched to tents and pointed out one of the dirtier ones, and we entered. A swarthy man with a greasy apron tied around his waist said, *"Bienvenidos, amigos. ¿Comida? ¿Café?"*

"Yes, *gracias*," Lyman said. He leaned toward me and whispered, "That's the only Spanish I know."

We sat on camp chairs around a rickety table in the back

corner of the tent. Through the open flap at the rear of the tent a short, fat woman with two thick braids of hair hanging down her chest cooked over an open fire. The man brought a pot of coffee and three tin mugs. *"¿Desayuno por tres?"* the man asked.

"Yes," Lyman said. *"Gracias."*

The Mexican woman cracked eggs into a skillet, stirred them around expertly, and left them to cook. She removed a ball of dough from a cloth-covered pan and tossed it back and forth between her hands until it became a flat circle, which she tossed on the grate covering the fire.

Lyman poured our coffee, sat back, and sipped his. He grimaced and set the mug on the table. He nodded and smiled at us. "It really is good to see you both."

"What do you want, Lyman?" Kindle said.

"Always in a hurry, Kindle."

"I don't like listening to hucksters."

"I haven't said anything yet."

"I know it's coming."

"We have a lot of miles to talk."

"You're taking me back," I said.

Lyman nodded. "Obviously."

"I asked Rosemond why you didn't follow."

Lyman's face lit up. "How *is* Rosemond? I should thank her for stealing you out from under me. A thousand dollars sounds much better than five hundred. How did she ever get you to come out here with her?"

"She told me Kindle asked her to help me. To get me away from you."

Lyman nodded as if impressed. "I always knew Rosemond was a master manipulator, but I didn't think you would be so easily taken in. It's a shame she didn't want to marry me. We would have been a formidable couple."

"Didn't want to marry you? That wasn't the story I heard."

"She told you her story?"

"Yes."

Lyman narrowed his eyes at me. "And you weren't repulsed?"

"By which part? You pimping her out to officers during the war? Or abandoning her after?"

Lyman laughed. "That's what she told you? Well, I suppose looking at it a certain way you could get that out of it. You should know by now Rosemond has a talent of twisting things to her advantage. She didn't seduce you?" Kindle's head jerked around. Lyman laughed at his expression. If we weren't in the straits we were in, I might have laughed, too. "You didn't know Rosemond has a taste for snatch?"

"No," Kindle said.

"I always thought the right man would set her straight," Lyman said. "I tried, and had a good time doing it, but her eyes never lit up with me like they did with the women I brought her."

The Mexican brought three tin plates loaded with eggs, refried beans, and a tortilla and placed them in front of us. The scent of wonderfully foreign spices made my stomach growl loudly. I tried to remember the last time I'd eaten and couldn't. The woman placed a small bowl of green sauce on the table between us. She motioned between the sauce and our plates, said *"Huevos,"* and left.

I picked up my fork with my left hand, and Lyman pointed his fork at my injured hand. "What happened?"

"I broke someone's nose."

Kindle spooned the sauce on his eggs and took a big bite. His eye widened, and he swallowed and coughed. He turned to the waiter. "Milk?"

The man was on his way with a glass. Kindle drank the milk

and nodded his thanks. "I'd forgotten how hot chile sauce can be." It didn't stop him from continuing to eat his eggs and beans.

Lyman watched him with fascination. "Hungry?"

"I figure this might be my last meal, so I better enjoy it."

"That was the original plan."

I scoffed. "Do you honestly think—"

Kindle placed his hand on my arm to quiet me. "What changed?"

"Thin walls, remember? I didn't just hear you rekindling your love affair. Henry Pope is looking into your charges?"

"So it would seem."

"Perfect. This is working out much better than I anticipated. I'll admit, Rosemond stealing you out from under me wasn't part of the plan. But it actually made things easier. I was able to stay in Saint Louis, gamble a little, and wait for Kindle to lead me to you."

"What if Kindle'd been executed?" I asked.

"That would've depended on how large the new reward was and how much I needed the money."

"Gambling wasn't good in Saint Louis?" Kindle asked.

"It was. I don't need the money, but a thousand dollars is a thousand dollars. Plus, stealing Laura back from Rosemond would have been satisfying. Too bad she isn't around to see my triumph."

"There is no triumph. She knew I was leaving."

"She let you go?" His brows furrowed. "I was sure she wanted you as a lover."

"No."

"When Rosemond becomes obsessed with someone..." Lyman's frown broke into a knowing grin. "The missionary."

"What?" Kindle said.

"What was her name? Something from Shakespeare."

"Portia."

Lyman snapped his fingers. "That's it." He wiped up his beans with his tortilla and took a bite. "I wondered if there was more to that one than Rosemond toying with her. She did that with women, you know. Led them down the garden path, made them fall in love with her, and broke their hearts by blackmailing them."

"Blackmail?" My heart sank. I didn't realize until that moment how much I wanted to believe in the best version of Rosemond. I scooted my chair back, leaned over, and dropped my head. Lyman glanced up at me. "You look disappointed. Did you actually start to trust Rosemond?"

"Yes." I kept my head bowed and eyes closed while I pulled the hem of my skirt up, thankful Lyman was more watchful of Kindle than me.

"Big mistake," Lyman said. "I've never met anyone more self-centered than Rosemond March."

"Have you looked in the mirror lately?" Kindle said.

Lyman shrugged and pushed his empty plate away. "Be careful, Kindle, or I'll change my mind about taking you back with us."

I straightened in my chair and rubbed my forehead, as if coming to terms with the news about Rosemond. Knowing what I was doing, Kindle kept up the conversation, and Lyman's focus on him.

"Don't try to act altruistic," Kindle said. "If you hadn't overheard our conversation I'd probably have a bullet in my gut right now."

"But you don't, so stop dwelling on what might have been. We go back East together, I get the one-thousand-dollar reward, and you end up going free. You two can live happily ever after. Everyone wins."

"Or, we kill you here and go back East by ourselves," I said. Lyman chuckled. "You're unarmed."

"Am I?" I pulled my gun and pointed it at Lyman.

Kindle stood and punched Lyman in the nose, knocking the table over in the process. I saw my plate overturn onto the dirt floor with some regret. I was hungry and it was the best meal I'd had in weeks. Kindle was over Lyman, a priest punching the gambler into unconsciousness, blood splattering on the ground and on Lyman's buff waistcoat. The Mexican couple stood back, the man holding a rifle on us. I lifted my hands to signal I was no threat to them. "Kindle."

Kindle stood, holding a wallet in one hand and Lyman's gun in the other. Kindle placed the gun in his pocket.

"Usted no es un padre."

"*Sí, sí.* I'm a priest. Her brother wanted her to marry a bad man. She chose God. We're going across the ocean to do God's work." The man adjusted his hold on his rifle but didn't lower it. His eyes flickered between Kindle and Lyman.

Kindle pulled money from Lyman's wallet and counted out one hundred dollars. He held it out to the man. "Take him outside of town and leave him. Help us get away to do God's work."

The woman stepped forward, took the money, and waved us away. *"Abandonar."*

We grabbed our bags and left before they changed their minds.

"Think they'll do it?" I asked.

"Yes. Did you see the cross around her neck?"

"No."

"She'll make sure Lyman doesn't follow us."

We slowed to a determined but unremarkable pace as we made our way to the business district. I kept my eyes downcast in what I hoped was an appropriately demure pose for a nun. Kindle was greeted often, with deference. One man said, "Devil get the best of you, Padre?"

"You should see him," Kindle returned, to general laughter. Though we weren't touching, I could feel the tension emanating from him, hear it in his voice.

He bought his ticket with Lyman's money and ushered me into the train carriage. We found an empty compartment, pulled down the window shades, and fell into opposite seats. After a moment, we laughed. "It's never easy, is it?"

"No," Kindle said. He picked up my bag and put it on the shelf overhead, along with his. He sat back down and pulled at his collar.

"Tight?"

"A little."

"It looks good on you."

"Don't start."

The compartment door slid open with a bang. A woman dressed in men's work clothes, her hair in a long braid down her shoulder, studied us, astonishment clear on her bruised face. "God Almighty." Rosemond closed the door behind her. "I thought I was seeing things." She sat down next to me and looked me up and down. "I wouldn't have recognized you if not for Blackbeard over there. I thought you were gone."

"I missed my train."

She grasped my hand. "I forgot to say good-bye."

"I know."

Rosemond turned her attention to Kindle. "I'm glad they didn't shoot you."

Kindle glared at her. "Not only are you a whore, but a liar, a killer, and a deviant."

Rosemond straightened as if struck. The portion of her face not bruised from the beating I gave her paled and she looked at me as if she didn't know who I was. "You told him?" Rosemond's chest rose and fell as if she were struggling for air.

"No. Lyman told him. You were right. Lyman followed him from Saint Louis. William, you need to apologize."

"For what? You've called her a whore and told of her lies and Cora Bayle."

"You know very well what you need to apologize for, William."

Rosemond turned to face Kindle, her expression defiant and proud. "I knew I made the right choice helping Laura instead of you."

Kindle stood, and I moved between the two of them. "Helping?" Kindle said. "You kidnap her, lie to her, kill a woman and use *me* as the reason, tell Laura I'm dead, and for what? So you can tempt her to play the game of flats with you?"

"Kindle, that is enough," I said.

"Why are you defending her?"

"Because I've lied and killed to be with you. And I would do it again if I had to."

"I suppose you don't want this *deviant* to save you, which is what I came here to do," Rosemond said.

"What?"

"Hankins and the sheriff are furious at you, and they know you didn't make yesterday's train. The ticket master knew you, told them you missed your train when they asked. They're checking every train before it departs. You need to get off. Now."

"We shouldn't trust her, Laura," Kindle said. "Think of how many times she's lied to you."

I looked between the two of them. I had no doubt Hankins and the sheriff were out for my blood. But Kindle's suspicions of Rosemond were warranted, too. Rosemond saw my indecision. Her shoulders slumped and she shook her head.

There was a commotion of activity outside. Raised voices,

one of which was clearly the sheriff's. I peeked out of the blinds. Hankins scanned the train. I pulled back and dropped the blind just in time.

"Now do you believe me?"

"What do we do?"

"Leave separately. Kindle, you come with me. I'll say you're a priest from Denver come to pay your respects to Oliver. The eye patch will turn heads, but no one's looking for Captain Kindle. Hankins and the sheriff will look right past you in a nun's habit. Go to Jesper's. We'll meet you there."

I reached up for my bag. Kindle grabbed my arm. "Laura, this is a bad idea."

"Do you have a better one? Hankins and the sheriff aren't going to turn me in. They're going to kill me. They've said as much. If Rosemond wanted the reward, she could have turned me in anytime."

"I don't trust her."

I thought of these last weeks, how my relationship with Rosemond had gone from antagonistic, to suspicious, to distrustful, to something resembling a friendship. I knew, suddenly, that if Kindle had been executed I would have stayed in Cheyenne, built a practice under Hankins's thumb, and settled into a life here with the friends I'd made, and Rosemond was a big part of the reason why. Had Rosemond played with and manipulated me like Lyman accused her of doing with others? Or was what passed between us two nights ago genuine? Rosemond's history was full of betrayal and abandonment—her family, Lyman, Portia, Dunk—and her actions, her life path, was a result. I hadn't betrayed or abandoned Rosemond, though I'd had plenty of opportunity and more than enough motivation for it. Whatever Rosemond felt for me, love or friendship, I believed it was genuine.

I pulled my bag from the shelf. "I do." I left the compartment and, feeling more terrified than bold, walked out of the train on the side Hankins and the sheriff were on. I stopped and pretended to look up at the train schedule. I glanced down the platform and saw Kindle and Rosemond get off the train and walk toward Calico Row. I turned the opposite direction and ran right into Sheriff Hall. He looked straight into my face. "Excuse me, Sister."

I dropped my eyes. "Go with God, my child," I said, and walked around him and slowly away, expecting his meaty hand to land on my shoulder at any moment. Hankins hurried past me toward the sheriff, barely glancing at me. I continued on, down the steps and onto the street, where I finally chanced a glance behind me. The two men were talking and gesturing wildly, Hankins at the train, the sheriff at the road beyond the depot. I continued on, turned toward Calico Row, and released a long-held breath. Too soon, as it turned out.

A man fell into step beside me. "I see you're still in town."

I flinched in surprise. Salter stared down at me with an amused smile. I looked ahead and kept walking. "I see you have an uncanny ability to show up when least expected."

"Nice disguise, Miss Bennett. Or should I call you Dr. Bennett?"

I stopped. "How long have you known?"

"Grand Island. You called me Kindle."

I closed my eyes and sighed. "Why haven't you turned me in?"

He shrugged. "Not my case."

I stopped again. "But the reward?" I couldn't believe I was arguing with a man who didn't want to turn me in, but the idea that someone like Salter—a Pinkerton—would forgo such a windfall was surprising.

313

"Doesn't seem right taking the reward by turning in an innocent woman."

"How do you know I'm innocent?"

Salter pulled out a silver cigarette case and removed a thin cigar from it. He took his time replacing the case, lighting his cigar, and taking a drag. He picked a piece of tobacco from his tongue and wiped it on his pants. "Rumor has it, Reed wasn't only working for the agency. Someone wanted him to make sure you didn't make it back to New York City."

"Yes, he alluded to that." I shook my head. "I don't know why Beatrice Langton would want me dead."

"A dead woman can't prove her innocence, can she?" Salter took a long drag on his cigar. He nodded toward my hand. "Though a dead woman's bag might prove someone's guilt."

I swallowed. I remembered Salter watching me and Rosemond talk to Cora on the street in Grand Island, the carpetbag in her hand. He also saw me with it on the train. Was this the only physical piece of evidence connecting us to Cora Bayle? My guilty conscience might hang my friend.

What had Rosemond said? Tell a lie with enough conviction and the listener will doubt themselves.

"It has sentimental value."

"Does it?"

"It was my father's."

"Your father."

"Yes. He left me little else. Now, I really must be going. I have an appointment."

"Got a telegram yesterday," Salter said.

I stopped again and closed my eyes. He was toying with me. Gravel crunched under his boots as he walked around me. I gathered myself and met his gaze steadily.

"Martha Mason died of her injuries. I'll be sending a report to Chicago explaining she killed Cora Bayle for the necklace. Case closed. Tell your *sister* I might need a favor one day." He held my gaze. He knew Rosemond killed Cora, and there would be a price for his silence. My stomach lurched with fear for my friend.

"Take care, Dr. Bennett." He turned and walked off.

Rosemond and Kindle waited for me in Jesper's store. Kindle came to me immediately. "Where were you?"

"I ran into Salter," I said to Rosemond.

"What did he want?"

I told them about my conversation with the Pinkerton and him laying Cora Bayle's death at Martha Mason's feet.

"Why would he do that?" Rosemond asked.

"He said he may need a favor from you one day."

Rosemond's eyebrows raised, and she smirked.

I reached out and grasped Rosemond's arm. "Don't underestimate him, Rosemond. Salter is dangerous."

"Are you worried for me?"

"Of course I am," I snapped.

Rosemond's grin faded into a pleased smile and her hand covered mine. "Thank you, Laura. I can take care of myself. I'm a survivor."

Kindle harrumphed.

"I thought you would be more open-minded, Kindle," Rosemond said. "Or is your pride wounded?"

"Because you prefer my wife to me? Hardly."

Rosemond nodded with a knowing smirk. I glared at Kindle and pulled Rosemond to the side. "What happened with Portia?" I asked in a low voice. "Did you work things out?"

"Nothing can be settled until Oliver is buried and Portia's

had time to grieve. But if her anger at you for breaking my nose is any indication, she's head over heels in love with me."

Jesper and Monique walked in. "Wagon's ready," Monique said.

"Thank you," Rosemond said.

"I need to check on Lavina," I said, trying to pull away from Rosemond.

"No, you don't," Rosemond said. She pulled me close. "These two don't know who you are, but I guaran-damn-tee if they did, they'd turn you in. I'll make sure Lavina's okay. You need to get out of town before everyone knows who you are. Jesper's going to drive you to Archer, eight miles away. You should easily make the emigrant train at six o'clock." I groaned. "You can switch to a better train further on," Rosemond said.

"We need to go, Laura," Kindle said from the door.

"He's right. Hankins and the sheriff will come looking here soon enough."

I grasped Rosemond's hands. "Good luck, with everything."

"Thank you." Her eyes darted in Kindle's direction and back. "I would say come back when your name is cleared, but I don't think that's likely."

"I've learned to not plan too far in advance. It never works out for me somehow." We laughed.

"Good advice."

I squeezed Rosemond's hands and tried to release them. She held fast. "I'm sorry for lying to you. At first I thought it was about Dunk, making you suffer a loss like I did. I considered telling you the truth more than once, but I didn't want you to leave. I still don't. I don't make friends easily and, well, I suppose I didn't know how to go about it. We made it in the end, though, didn't we?" My heart broke with the hope and vulnerability in her voice and her expression.

I pulled her to me. Rosemond March was the most complicated and contradictory person I'd ever met. She wasn't perfect,
nor did she pretend to be, but she was fully human in a way
so many people were not. I'd hated her at times but I couldn't
deny the deep well of affection I had for her. Wasn't that true
friendship? Loving someone, flaws and all?

"Yes, we made it in the end." I pulled away. "Tell Portia
good-bye for me."

Rosemond nodded. I released her and left quickly, before
either of us would be embarrassed by the tears flowing down
our cheeks.

PART THREE

WASHINGTON SQUARE

CHAPTER
27

We stepped off the train in Grand Central Depot to a cacophony of noise and activity. Porters hurried along the platform, removing baggage and loading it on wheeled carts. Newspaper boys shouted the latest news. A stationmaster called, "All aboard" for the next train. Laughter, voices raised in exuberant greetings, tearful good-byes, the faint scent of brewed coffee, light streaming through the windows set high in the cavernous main room: it washed over me, surrounded me, closed in on me, discombobulated me. It was familiar and foreign all at once. I needed to get outside, fresh air. Space.

Kindle grasped my elbow and propelled me through the mass of people. After a week of pretending to be clergy, we'd become used to the greetings and stares our disguises elicited. Kindle got more double takes than I did. Children stared at him wide-eyed; women would quickly avert their eyes but continued to sneak glances. Men nodded at him and some shook his hand, assuming he'd been injured in the war. I could tell the attention irritated him.

We stepped out of the station and queued up for a taxi. It was midafternoon, but the tall buildings blocked the sun, turning the city to an early twilight. I covered my mouth and coughed against the smell of trash and human waste. People jostled against one another with nary an apology or acknowledgment, too intent on hurrying to their destination. We waited in line in silence and within ten minutes were loaded into a hansom cab.

The driver opened the trapdoor on the roof and said, "Where to?"

I gave him an address before Kindle could speak. The driver closed the trap and flicked his whip against the palomino's rear. It jostled forward and set off at a brisk trot.

"I want to see my house," I said, by way of explanation.

Kindle nodded and took my hand, hiding our affection beneath my skirt. For more than a week, we'd played the role of a priest and nun to the hilt, never touching, rarely looking each other in the eye, blessing people who asked for it. Kindle'd had to think fast when a man asked him to hear a confession in Chicago. As we drew nearer New York, my anxiety and my doubts increased. I longed for Kindle's comforting embrace, but the most I could wish for was a meaningful glance and the brush of his fingers against mine during the rare moments we were alone. I pressed my shoulder against his, using the small bench in the hansom cab as an excuse to feel his warmth. He leaned against me and squeezed my hand.

"Where are we going to stay?" I asked.

"Pope recommended a small hotel west of Central Park."

"I cannot wait to shed these clothes."

"I can't wait for you to shed them, either. You look more and more like my sister."

We'd avoided Saint Louis in case the Pinkertons were watching the orphanage, but I longed to see Mary and Sophia. Especially Sophia. According to Kindle, she was thriving as a junior teacher at the school, teaching the younger girls the midwifing and medical skills I had taught her.

322

The hansom cab wove through the traffic. "There are so many people. And so much noise." I looked up. "And no sky to speak of."

"Once we get your name cleared, we can go wherever you like," Kindle said.

"Where do you want to go?"

Kindle's expression softened and he squeezed my hand. "Wherever you are."

I didn't care who saw, or what the cabdriver would think if he saw; I reached up and touched Kindle's beard. "When this is over, will you shave your beard for good?"

"I thought you liked it."

"I waver. Today, I want to see your whole face."

His grin faded. "The face of the man you fell in love with is gone."

I shook my head and touched his eye patch gently. "No, it's not."

The cab turned and slowed down. I dropped my hand and stared at the street where I grew up, played with friends, walked a thousand times with my father. We passed the Smiths', Reynoldses', Jenningses', and Williamsons' brownstones, each unchanged. My eyes were riveted to Number 17, the eight steps to the green front door, the window where I would read Gothic novels in my youth and medical tomes in my young adulthood. The house was dark, the windows grimy. A poster was glued to the bay window, announcing an auction of the house and its contents in a week's time. I gripped Kindle's hand tightly as the cab continued to the end of the street and stopped.

"Will you pull over here and wait for us?" I asked, motioning to a spot around the corner.

He turned the cab and parked. Kindle helped me out. "We're leaving our bags," he said. "I've taken down your number and will find you if you leave."

"It's your dime, Father."

Kindle looked taken aback. "Of course. Right."

I led Kindle down the alley behind my house. "You forgot you're wearing the collar, didn't you?"

Kindle nodded. "The one benefit to being a priest is no one is brave enough to cheat you."

I stopped at the sight of the rear of the house. Boards covered the kitchen windows. We descended stairs covered in broken glass to the back entrance. The door was surprisingly whole.

"Why worry with the door when you can break a window?" Kindle said.

Beneath the window I jiggled a loose stone until it came free, reached into the void, removed a skeleton key, and replaced the stone. "My father was forever losing his key. After he died, we left it in case we ever lost ours." The lock resisted at the quarter turn, as it had done for thirty years, before releasing. Emotion at the familiarity of it welled in my throat. I opened the door and walked in.

The kitchen was in ruins. Broken crockery littered the floor. Maureen's worktable had been overturned, kitchen chairs broken and splintered. The icebox door stood open. The whole room was covered in what I thought was dust but realized was flour. A rat scurried past, creating a new trail amid the dozens of older, uneven trails woven in, around, and over the trash. I walked through the butler's pantry, saw the open tin that had held the extra household money Maureen squirreled away in case of emergency, the money she'd taken and hidden at the bottom of a basket of produce when she left the house the last time.

There had been little of value in Maureen's room, but what there had been was gone. The quilt she hand-sewed. The crucifix hanging on the wall above her bed. A small sewing kit my father gave her one Christmas. Clothes hung haphazardly from hangers, not nice enough to be stolen. I ran my finger through the thick layer of dust and rubbed it against the pad of my thumb. Kindle watched me from the doorway. "Maureen would be horrified."

He stepped aside to let me by and followed me up the stairs to the main hall, which looked undisturbed. The furniture was too heavy to be portable. I pushed open the door of the library with trepidation. I gasped at the sight of the empty shelves and books scattered all over the floor. A few were stacked around the room and on top of the desk as if someone had tried to clean up, a tiny bit of order in the chaos left from the looters. The curtains covering the bay window had been pulled down and the paisley cushion I'd curled up on to read was faded with dust. The medical tome I'd left open and facedown on the window seat was tented on the floor, the pages bent and deformed. I picked it up, closed it, and placed it on the seat. A shaft of weak light filtered through the dirty windows, illuminating the cloud of dust floating around us. I ran my fingers over the threadbare cushion corner I'd absently fiddled with through the years and wondered at how something so comfortable and consistent in my life, a touchstone even, now looked forlorn and shabby. I turned from the room and walked upstairs.

The bedrooms on the third floor hadn't been disturbed. Maybe the looters had been run off before making it this far. Maybe they'd been discouraged by the lack of valuables in the other parts of the house.

"Genteel poverty has its benefits," I said.

Kindle squeezed my shoulder. "The cab is waiting."

I shrugged his hand away and stepped into my room. "I'll be there in a minute."

The landing creaked with Kindle's retreating tread.

I opened my wardrobe. There, undisturbed and covered with

dust, were the clothes I'd left behind. I lifted out a deep purple dress and swallowed the sudden lump in my throat. I was at the dressmaker's, full of excitement, the promise of a successful future spread before me like a feast. I was graduating from medical school and wanted a dress to mark the occasion. Deep purple to honor the mourning the country was still in, thin ruffles framing the buttons down the front and on the cuffs to make it feminine enough to satisfy society but tailored in a way to project my professionalism. It was the dress I wore underneath my robe when I received my diploma. The dress I wore when I stumbled down Twenty-Seventh Street, starving and begging for patients, and met Camille King. The dress I wore on the visit to my first Washington Square patient, Beatrice Langton.

I buried my face in the fabric, inhaled its musty, unused scent, and struggled not to cry. For the last year with everything I'd been through, everything I'd done, this dress hung in my wardrobe, forgotten and useless, full of lost possibilities, waiting for my return. I held the dress against me and stood in front of the mirror. The light was poor, but the image reflected back at me wasn't the woman returned, but the woman I had been. The woman full of hope and possibility. The woman determined to take on the world. The woman I hoped I still was. I would find out soon.

If Catherine Bennett had a good-luck charm, this dress was it. I took it from the hanger and removed my headscarf.

Ten minutes later I exited the back door, clutching my folded nun disguise. I pushed the skeleton key up the sleeve of my dress and walked down the alley toward Kindle and the waiting cab. Peg McCord, one of Maureen's closest friends and the Reynoldses' cook, stepped out the back door of the house. I looked at her square on, forgetting I wasn't in the nun's habit that had protected me for so long.

"Peg," I said.

She nodded back distractedly, then did a double take, her eyes widening. I continued on, my stomach dropping in realization of my error.

"Katie Girl?"

I walked on as if I hadn't heard her and turned the corner at a trot. Kindle leaned against the cab, smoking a thin cigar he'd apparently bummed from the cabdriver, who was smoking his own. He straightened at the sight of me. "Get in, get in," I said.

He threw the cigar aside and followed me into the cab. The driver, understanding the urgency, cracked the whip and the horse took off like a shot past the alley where Peg McCord stood, eyes wide, hand raised, calling out my name.

"Godammit, Laura. What were you thinking?" Kindle threw his hat across the room.

Kindle waited until we were alone to explode, which was impressive considering how long it took. Not knowing I was going to discard the disguise, Kindle had told the driver the address for the hotel Pope had suggested. The driver dropped us off and we walked in as if checking in. Instead, we walked straight through the lobby and out the back service entrance. We barely hid in time to avoid our driver catching sight of us as he made the block with a new fare. Kindle ripped off his priest's collar and threw it onto the trash-strewn ground. He waved down another hansom and gave an address for a different hotel in a seedier part of town.

"I don't know. I wanted to feel like myself again. Catherine Bennett." I ran my hand over the front of the dress. It was looser than when I'd last worn it and would need to be taken in to look like anything other than a hand-me-down dress. I turned and looked at myself in the mirror. I'd pulled my hair back into a messy twist, held with a comb I'd found in my dresser drawer. It was looser and more feminine than the tight bun I'd worn for years—again, to denote a level of seriousness to my male counterparts. My cheekbones were more pronounced and there was a slight bump in my nose from its being broken by Cotter Black. I closed my eyes, dizzy from trying to square the woman who stared back at me with the woman I wanted to be.

"And do you? Feel like Catherine Bennett?"

I turned to Kindle, marveling once again how he always seemed to be able to read my thoughts.

"I don't know who I am."

Kindle stepped forward and took me in his arms, his anger from before gone. "I do. I know precisely who you are."

I sobbed into his shoulder and immediately felt ridiculous. Where was the strength I was so proud of? Why had returning to New York turned me into a blubbering mess?

"Did we make a mistake coming back?"

"Say the word and we'll leave."

I gritted my teeth and shook my head. "No. I can't." I pushed away from Kindle and paced the room. "When we were at the orphanage we had a good life, didn't we?"

"Yes."

"That's what I want. I want that life with you. We will have no life at all if I don't get out from under this...this...sword of Damocles. Rosemond used it to convince me you sent me away. Cora Bayle was killed because of it. Hankins used it to take advantage of my skills, to line his pockets. Every person I meet, I wonder if they recognize me, if they're going to use me or turn me in. You're too easily recognizable now. There is nowhere we can run." I sighed. "You know it's true."

"Who was the woman?"

"A friend of Maureen's."

"Will she talk?"

I shrugged. "I honestly don't know. She and Maureen were close, but she didn't approve of my profession. Though it didn't bother her overmuch when she was sick." I rubbed my forehead. "When do we meet Henry?"

"First thing tomorrow morning in Central Park."

I unpacked, hanging the clothes Rosemond bought for me in the wardrobe. I ran my hand along the navy vest's lapel and wondered what the future held for Portia and Rosemond. They were embarking on a future much like the one I was trying to shed. Their public life would be based on lies, and the threat of exposure and loss of everything they held dear would hang over their heads for the rest of their lives. Their only solace would be when they were alone together. I'd decided that wouldn't be enough for me. Would it be enough for them?

"Laura?"

I turned to find Kindle watching me with a strange expression. "Yes?"

"I like that. It looked good on you."

"Rosemond bought them for me. As an appeasement for her lie about your execution, I suppose." I chuckled and shook my head. "It was a despicable thing to do."

"Yet you forgave her. You seem to like her."

"I understand her."

Kindle laughed. "You understand the motivations of a Sapphic whore? No, you don't."

"I understand the lengths she went to, to be with the woman she loves." Kindle scoffed. "Think of the things you've done for me. What's the difference? That she did it for a woman and you think it's unnatural?"

"It is."

"Or is it your pride is wounded that she would rather lie, kill, and cheat to be with a woman instead of a man?"

"My pride? What about yours? I saw how she looked at you on the train. Did she seduce you?"

Kindle's gaze was challenging, ready to switch to confrontational if I gave the wrong answer. "No." The muscle in his jaw pulsed. "Then again, I'm not as easily seduced as you are."

Kindle tried to look defiant but failed. Guilt was written plainly on his face.

I turned and started to undress. "Thank you for confirming it for me. She wouldn't." When he was silent, I continued. "You aren't going to try to deny it? To blame Rosemond? Or me?" I stepped out of my dress and draped it on a hanger. I went to the dresser, removed my comb, and brushed my hair. I saw Kindle in the mirror, rooted to the floor by anguish. "You wondered in Cheyenne how I could trust Rosemond. There are a half dozen reasons, but the root of my trust, I think, was her refusal to confirm your betrayal. One word would have devastated me, and she knew it. She remained silent, which was confirmation in its way, because she respected me? Loved me?" I shrugged. "It doesn't matter." I placed my brush on the dresser and faced my husband. "I have to face the accusations against me or we will be forced to make other decisions that go against our better judgment, our morals. I can't do it anymore. I won't."

"What if Henry's investigator hasn't found the evidence we need?"

I didn't answer, which was confirmation enough.

I made love to Kindle that night as an act of absolution and was almost moved to true forgiveness by his murmurs of affection, pleas for forgiveness, and promises for eternal loyalty. I finished him quickly so I didn't have to hear another word; his incessant talking made it real, turned an encounter I had been able to push from my mind, to think of as fiction, into the realm of reality. When done, I rolled over onto my side and faced away from him. He curved his body into mine and rested his hand on my bare hip, everything I'd dreamt of in Cheyenne when I thought I'd lost him forever. This ache was different, sharper, harder. Not grief at all, but anger.

I rolled over. Kindle's one good eye reflected the moonlight shining through the window. His empty eye socket was partially hidden in the pillow. I stroked his beard. "William, I love you."

"I love you."

I ran my hand down his chest and over his flaccid cock, sticky from our lovemaking, and cupped his testicles. His eyebrows rose, as if surprised, but hoping I was instigating another, better, encounter. I squeezed his testicles and he flinched and grabbed my wrist. "But if you ever betray me like that again, I'll cut your balls off and shove them down your throat."

Kindle stilled in astonishment. He released my wrist and I released him. His smile unfurled slowly, like a flag in a tepid wind. "I'll sharpen the knife for you."

I kissed him briskly. "Shave your beard tomorrow. No more disguises. We meet Henry as ourselves or not at all."

CHAPTER 28

He's late."

After a quick breakfast of boiled eggs, toast, and coffee in the shabby but clean dining room of our hotel, Kindle and I walked to Central Park to meet Henry. With no mention of me or Kindle in the papers, we walked down Seventy-Seventh Street toward the park with a cautious confidence. We garnered nary a glance from passersby, and the ones who did notice us took Kindle's eye patch and serious mien as acceptable and expected eccentricity for the theater district.

"I thought ten o'clock in the morning was too early for Pope," Kindle said. He threw a rock side-armed into the lake and counted the number of skips. "Five. Pathetic."

"He chose the time," I said.

Kindle positioned another flat rock in his hand and threw it.

I was bored and fidgety. I needed to walk off the nervous energy that had been building since we woke. Instead, we'd been waiting next to the lake staring at a well-dressed woman down the bank feeding bread crumbs to ducks from a paper sack for twenty minutes. "How deep is that sack?" I asked Kindle. He followed my gaze. "I've never seen anyone so intent on feeding ducks in my life." I took a rock from Kindle's hand and threw it into the lake. It skipped twice and fell into the water with a plop. "I wish *I* had a sack of bread crumbs."

Kindle turned to me with a wry expression. "Would you like for me to teach you how to skip rocks?"

I lifted my injured hand. "I am an expert rock skipper, thank you very much. When my hand heals, I'll show *you* how to skip a rock."

"Oh, you think so?" Kindle took my hand. "You implied in Cheyenne there was someone east of the Mississippi who could fix your hand. Are they in New York?"

"Yes. But I cannot think of that until after my name is cleared."

"You don't trust he will not turn you in?"

"There was a bit of competition between us. He probably reveled in my downfall."

"How is the pain?" Kindle asked.

"Better," I lied. My hand ached incessantly, with occasional stabs of excruciating pain. The fear that my hand was beyond repair was real and grew every day my pain didn't dissipate.

"Let's walk around," I said. "We won't leave sight of Hernshead in case Henry decides to show, but I cannot stand still another moment."

Kindle pulled my hand through his arm and led me down the path. The duck lover upended her sack to dislodge any errant bread crumbs and folded the sack carefully. We met where her path intersected with ours. Kindle stopped and motioned for the woman to pass in front of us. I smiled and nodded politely, expecting her to pass along. Instead she stopped and studied first Kindle, then me. There was no shock of sudden recognition on her face, rather an expression of confirmation and pleasure. "Dr. Bennett, so good to see you again."

I pulled closer to Kindle, who tensed. The woman smiled and held out her hand in a placating gesture. "I mean you no harm."

Kindle moved to go around the woman, but I held him fast and studied the woman's face. Her clear, kind eyes were set in a pleasant face devoid of wrinkles, save the fine lines around her eyes, no doubt from laughing. Streaks of premature gray hair framed her face and escaped the loose, high-bun hairstyle she wore beneath a large straw hat. The hat was a masterpiece of eccentrics: white flowers pinned with brightly marked butterflies and a large, curved, iridescent peacock feather sticking out from the left side of the hat.

"You don't remember me? How extraordinary. I've been told I'm quite unforgettable, though it's never been in a complimentary way. No matter. It will not set me low. Hazel Dockery."

"Yes," I said. How could I have forgotten Hazel Dockery? When my reputation as a doctor for the women and children of New York society had taken off, Hazel Dockery had sent for me. After an examination where I discovered she was as healthy as a horse, she'd offered me coffee in a library full of an odd and interesting collection of items from Africa and South America acquired by her bedridden father. When I realized Hazel was Gerald Dockery's daughter, I hoped the interview would lead to an opportunity to examine him. Rumor was Dockery had been bedridden for years with a vague, general, incurable complaint. Every doctor in town was sure they could solve the riddle of Dockery's sickness if they only had the chance. His care was closely guarded by his elderly doctor and his last living relative, his daughter. My hopes were dashed when Hazel quizzed me on the effectiveness of the latest snake-oil cure being peddled by mountebanks. When I clearly and concisely repudiated their effectiveness, she looked extremely disappointed and dismissed me after a polite amount of time passed. I'd never heard from her again, which, considering her good health, wasn't a surprise.

"Good to see you again, Miss Dockery," I said uncertainly.

"Call me Hazel, please." She appraised Kindle, waiting for an introduction.

I stumbled over what to say next. Instinct was to lie about Kindle, but to what purpose? Hazel knew who I was and surely knew the one-eyed man next to me was Captain William Kindle.

"And this is the Major, I assume," Hazel said, not waiting for me to decide what to do.

"I was a captain," Kindle said with a slight bow. "William Kindle, a pleasure to meet you."

"Forgive me for staring," Hazel said. "With the war cripples crowding the streets of New York City you'd think I'd meet you with some degree of complacency, but indeed I find you absolutely fascinating."

"Thank you," Kindle said politely enough, though I could tell Hazel Dockery was getting off on the wrong foot by likening Kindle to war cripples.

Hazel turned her attention to me. "I wouldn't have recognized you. You've aged ten years. Five at least, since I last saw you."

"You haven't changed a bit," I said.

"Yes, I know. I say the most inappropriate things. I blame Mr. Pope. He spoke of you as still in fine looks. I should have known. He's an inveterate liar. It's one of his charms."

"You know Henry?" I said. Kindle's head was on a swivel, checking the park around us for people who looked out of place.

"Yes. I'm his benefactress. He asked me to come meet you. He thinks a Pinkerton has been shadowing him since your arrest, Major. I think it's Mr. Pope's active imagination, but he seems quite sure. When he told me you two were in town... well, I would have found a way to come with him to see you in any case."

"It seems Pope has told you quite a lot about our movements. He must have great faith in your loyalty," Kindle said. "You'll forgive me if I do not."

"Oh, but you should," Hazel said.

The park was filling with people: nannies pushing prams, women strolling together deep in conversation, men exercising their horses. Hazel noticed the growing crowd. She reached into her purse, pulled out a pair of dark-lensed spectacles, and held them out to Kindle. "Put these on. You're going to draw attention with the eye patch."

"I thought you said I blended in with the cripples."

Hazel tilted her head. "Did I say that? Well, it's ridiculous. You're much too handsome to be overlooked and your eye patch only makes you more intriguing."

Kindle took the glasses with great skepticism. "These won't draw attention?"

"Of course they will. But William Kindle wears an eye patch, not dark glasses. No one will recognize her," she said with a dismissive wave in my direction. I bristled. Hazel really was the most inappropriate person I'd ever met. I suppose being rich and beholden to no one gave her that kind of freedom.

Kindle turned away, removed his eye patch, and hooked the glasses around his ears. He turned around, shoving the eye patch in his front pocket.

"My God," Hazel said, breathlessly.

"I look ridiculous, don't I?" Kindle asked me.

No, he looked more appealing than ever, but I didn't want to stoke his ego. Hazel's schoolgirl eyes would do the job well enough. "You look like a scar-faced blind man." Kindle's mouth quirked up. He knew I was lying.

"Come, my carriage is waiting on Seventy-Seventh Street,"

Hazel said. She walked off without a backward glance, assuming we would follow.

"What is Henry thinking?" I said.

"I like her."

"Only because she thinks you're handsome and intriguing."

"Obviously she is a woman with a keen sense of discernment."

"You're incorrigible." Hazel had stopped at a curve in the path that would have taken her out of sight. She motioned to us, and with no better option, we followed.

Hazel's coachman pulled the carriage into the mews behind Hazel's Washington Square town house. An elderly, slightly stooped butler opened the carriage door for us to alight. "Thank you, Graves," Hazel said. "Is Mr. Pope here?"

"In the library, Miss Hazel."

"Very good. Coffee and such at Mrs. Graves's convenience."

The man bowed, closed the carriage door, and followed us inside. Servants scurried to stand when they saw Hazel, but she waved and said, "Passing through. Carry on."

We walked up the servants' stairs and went through a green baize door into the entry hall, Hazel shedding her gloves and coat as she went and leaving them wherever was most convenient. The hall was heavy and dark, with walls of deep mahogany and dark green carpets on the floor and running up the stairs. Hazel unpinned her hat from her hair, deposited it on a round table set in the middle of the hall, and picked up the mail from a silver tray. She flipped through it as she walked straight toward closed double doors. A footman materialized and opened the door a split second before Hazel would've run into it. She entered and, without looking up, navigated the most cluttered library I'd ever seen. The bookshelves were overflowing with books, newspapers were stacked in columns around the floor, and the desk was covered with towers of papers, on top of which Hazel threw the day's mail. I automatically reached out for the mail out of fear it would get lost in the chaos of the desk.

"Mr. Pope, I have retrieved your packages," Hazel said, her eyes dancing and landing on Kindle.

Henry Pope stood from a leather wing chair and held out his arms as if to embrace us. Kindle held back, but I enveloped Henry in a strong hug. I held him at arm's length. "You're looking well, Henry." I patted his stomach, which was rounder and firmer than it had been eight months earlier.

"As are you, Laura. Marriage agrees with you. I suppose this old grump has been taking good care of you." Henry realized his mistake as soon as he said it.

Kindle shook Henry's hand. "Thanks for bringing up my failures, Pope."

"Not what I meant, Major. I'm glad they didn't execute you."

"So am I."

"Let's get down to business, shall we?" Hazel said. "Henry, grab that chair over there. Yes, that one. Put that stack of papers…" She surveyed the office and pointed. "Over there. Yes, by the ashtray. No, the elephant-foot ashtray. Perfect. But wait. Turn them to the side, crossways, so they will stay organized."

Kindle and I looked at each other in amusement. I mouthed, *Organized?* Kindle shrugged one shoulder and waited for me to sit in one of the wing chairs. Henry placed his chair to the side of Hazel's desk near me, apparently unperturbed by being ordered around in such a haphazard fashion.

"Down to business," I said. "Henry, when Kindle told me

you'd engaged an investigator"—I grasped Henry's hand and almost choked on the words—"I always knew I could trust you."

"An investigator? Is that what you called me, Henry? How fantastic!" Hazel pursed her lips and her eyes searched the ceiling, as if imagining herself a modern-day, female Maupin. "Yes, I like that idea very much. One day. We should probably start at the beginning. Henry." She waved her hand for him to start.

"Yes," Henry said, scooting to the edge of his tall straight-back chair. "When I arrived in New York last fall there was a certain amount of…celebrity with my arrival." Henry blushed and hurried on. "The article I wrote about you, you see, caused quite a stir."

"I'd say so," Hazel interjected.

"*Sawbones* was picked up immediately and published to even more fanfare, as I'm sure you know."

"We avoided the world for months, Henry," Kindle said. "We know nothing of this."

"Right. Where were you anyway?"

"My sister's orphanage."

Henry nodded and I could tell he was filing that little nugget of information away for future fictional use. "Of course, I changed your names, but everyone automatically assumed the characters were based on you two."

"What names did you give us, by the way?" I asked.

"Delilah Gascoyne and Wyatt Steele."

"Those are two of the most absurd names I've ever heard," I said, laughing.

Henry looked hurt. "I quite liked them."

"Oh, yes," Hazel said. "I know of a fair few babies named Delilah in her honor. Everyone loves her pluck."

"Pluck?" I knew without looking that Kindle was smirking.

"Bravery," Henry clarified. "We're rambling off subject."

"Yes, I'll take over," Hazel said. "As soon as *Sawbones* started making its way from drawing room to drawing room—on the sly, of course; no one would actually admit to reading a penny dreadful—Dr. Catherine Bennett became a renewed topic of conversation. And the conversation was quite different than what it had been seven months prior. To hear talk, no one ever believed you'd killed George Langton. I think *Sawbones*, along with the previous news that you had been brutally murdered by a Pinkerton, made you much more sympathetic and allowed your former enemies to look on you with more compliance and approval." Hazel's expression turned serious. "You were no longer a threat to their way of life, you see."

"And now I'm back from the dead?"

"Society had seven months to mourn you, to burnish your reputation if not to a golden shine, at least to a dull, brassy one. It had become such a generally held opinion that you were railroaded for poor George's death they could hardly call you a killer anew. Though some have, of course."

" 'Poor George'? Did you know him?"

"Of course. All old money knows each other. George was a curious man, open-minded. He and I shared an interest in the supernatural."

"Ghosts?" Kindle said.

"Spirits. I'd always viewed the claims against you with a skeptical eye, Dr. Bennett. Based on our brief acquaintance, you didn't seem to be the type of woman to be carried away with her emotions. Too uptight and professional. No imagination whatsoever."

"Excuse me?"

Hazel continued on as if she hadn't offended me. "If you were having an affair with George, which I doubted. He wasn't the type of man to whip any woman into a frenzy of passion great enough to result in murder by fireplace poker. I had resolved to visit Sister Sophia to make contact with George when my father had a flare-up. I was at his bedside for weeks."

"How is your father?" I asked, eager to diagnose his mystery malady after all these years.

"He died."

"Oh. I'm so sorry."

"He was old and had been sick for years. By the time I was able to continue with my own interests, the reports of your deaths had surfaced. Fate interjecting. I determined to contact you and George in the beyond, get to the bottom of his death and maybe hear firsthand details from you about your own."

I caught Henry's eye. *Honestly?* He shrugged and looked abashed at Hazel's far-fetched beliefs. He wasn't about to contradict his benefactress.

"It won't be a surprise to you what I found out," Hazel continued.

"On the contrary," Kindle said. "It will be a surprise to me you found out anything."

"You don't believe in the afterlife?" Hazel asked.

"I do, but I don't believe you can contact spirits and have detailed conversations with them."

"They're rarely detailed conversations. More likely have to parse what is said to make sense of it. But if you know the spirit, it's easily done."

I sighed. "What did you find out, Hazel?"

"George assured me you didn't kill him, and he told me you weren't in the beyond. I contacted Mr. Pope immediately. It took some doing, but I was finally able to get him to confess to his ruse."

"Henry!" I said. "You promised."

"Don't blame Henry," Hazel said, looking at Pope with affection. "Very few artists can resist the steady income promised by a benefactor. And I agreed to do spying on your behalf."

"Let me make sure I understand," Kindle said. "You knew Laura was alive from talking to George Langton from the beyond, contacted Henry and bribed him to tell you everything, and offered to spy on the Langtons to prove Laura's innocence."

"That's about the sum of it, yes."

"I don't suppose George told you who did kill him, did he?" I asked.

"Unfortunately, no. His spirit was weak."

"Of course it was," I said. "What have you learned?"

"Not as much as I would like," Hazel admitted. "I spent years spurning society; I find the women vacuous and boring as watching paint dry, but the Dockery name will always get me entrance when I want it. I've been attending more and more social engagements, and receiving more calls than I care to return." She lifted the calling cards in the day's mail. "But I have diligently done it in service to your freedom."

"Thank you."

"I hear lots of gossip; the trick is picking the truth out of the chaff. There is so much chaff. But that's not the biggest problem. You know as well as I do, Dr. Bennett—"

"Please, call me Laura."

"Laura?" Hazel raised her eyebrows. "Indeed?" She shrugged. "Laura, you know women's society is limited. We don't have access to the men's world, and business and politics are beyond so many women's interests or concerns. Either they don't care, or their husbands think them too stupid to understand if they were to have a conversation about it. It's patently ridiculous, which is why I never intend to marry, but there you are. George wasn't known to diddle with the servants, and if you weren't having an affair then your motivation for killing him vanishes. If it's not a crime of passion, then it had to be business, and that is information I cannot easily find out."

"Then we are no closer to clearing my name than before."

"Not what I said."

Hazel looked to Henry, who sat forward. "We have an idea."

He opened his mouth to continue, but Hazel interrupted. "Since your escape from the *Big Republic*—"

"*Grand Republic*," Henry said.

"*Grand Republic*—and since Henry's article was found to be a lie, he's been persona non grata everywhere he goes."

"*Blood Oath* will change that, mark my words," Henry said. When he saw my confused expression, he said, "The sequel to *Sawbones*. At first, people were eager to tell me what they knew of you. They were less forthcoming about the Langtons, but then I met Miss Dockery here."

"I've known the Langtons my entire life. Living across the square from them, it would be difficult not to. Our families aren't close; we are much too interesting and the Langtons are much too boring for us to mix well. But George and I were always friends and I was able to fill in some blanks for Henry."

"I'd like you to fill in the blanks for me," Kindle said. "I know nothing about Langton, other than Laura is accused of being his lover and killing him."

Hazel looked at me in puzzlement. "You didn't tell him about George?"

"I didn't know George that well. We spoke rarely, and when we did it was almost exclusively about medicine."

Hazel nodded. "Doesn't surprise me. George wanted to be a doctor."

"Yes, I knew that," I said.

"If his brother Bertie hadn't died in the war, he might have been able to do that. But when Bertie was killed, their father transferred his plans for the older son to George. He paid an Irishman to take George's place in the Army and sent George to Harvard."

Kindle shifted in his chair, his mouth set in a thin line.

"Everyone with means did it, Major," Hazel said, "especially when the losses piled up and they saw that the war was going to drag on. George wanted to serve, avenge his brother—as if he could—but he would have been a rubbish officer. He was not a natural leader like Bertie. George worshipped him, followed him like a puppy. He was willing to step into his brother's shoes. Including marriage to Beatrice Sheridan. Have you heard of Judge Stuyvesant Sheridan?" Hazel asked Kindle.

"I've heard of the Stuyvesant family."

"The Sheridans married into the Stuyvesant family a few generations ago, and they're sure to remind everyone every chance they get. Judge Sheridan is on the state supreme court."

Kindle reached for my hand. "No wonder you ran." I nodded and squeezed his hand.

"With powerful men like that as your father and father-in-law, is it any wonder George gave up his dream of being a doctor? He went to law school instead. The next step was politics. There were powerful Republicans at the dinner party where Langton was killed, there to size George up to see if they should back him or the incumbent in the next election."

I stared at the nearest stack of papers, remembering my last conversation with George Langton.

"What is it, Laura?" Kindle said.

"Something Langton said in our last conversation. I was telling him of the difficulties I was having getting time at the local medical schools, for dissections."

"Why were you having difficulties?"

"Because I'm a woman. I hoped to get him on my side so maybe he could use his influence on my behalf." I stood and tried to pace but was thwarted at every turn by stacks of newspapers. "That was when he told me he still dreamt of going to medical school. I made some comment about how it wasn't too late. That as hard as it was at times, I'd never regretted going after what I wanted, that I would have thought myself a failure if I didn't at least try. George seemed struck by the comment and said, 'Precisely the way I feel.'" I crossed my arms over my chest. "Judge Sheridan came in and looked none too pleased to see George being kept from the cigars and port by his daughter's female physician. I suppose if I'd been a captain of industry, Sheridan would have reacted differently. His greeting to me was perfectly cordial, but cold as ice as well. So, I left."

"And went to the resurrection man?"

"Yes."

"You didn't see anyone else?"

"No. Only the resurrection man until James found me the next morning."

"James?" Hazel said, straightening.

"James Kline. My oldest friend. He helped me leave New York."

"Did he?"

"Do you know him?" I asked.

Hazel shook her head, but her brows were furrowed. "I haven't had the pleasure."

"I should contact him," I said. "See if he can help. Maybe he's heard something that will aid in my defense since I left."

Hazel shook her head. "I've read everything written about you since you left. Mr. Kline is rarely mentioned, and when he is, it's as a spokesman for the Langtons."

My breath rushed out of me. I didn't expect James to offer a full-throated defense of me—he had his career to consider—but to completely disavow knowing me? "He was at the Langtons' that night," I said, almost to myself.

I stared at Henry uncomprehendingly. "What?"

"Why was Kline there?" Kindle asked.

"I don't know. I suppose he was invited, though he is only a junior partner at George's firm."

Hazel narrowed her eyes and drummed her fingers on the arms of her chair.

"Thank you for filling me in on Langton, but you haven't told us what your plan is," Kindle said.

Hazel shook herself out of her thoughts. "Right. Your story has waned again in my neighbors' parlors. There was a flurry of gossip when the Langtons upped the reward and changed the terms, but when no word was heard of you...well, they moved on to the latest gossip, more interesting and less lethal. What we need to do is to put you back on the tip of the gossips' tongues."

"How?"

"An extra in the afternoon paper."

Henry held his hands out like he was holding a poster. *"The Murderess and the Major sighted in New York City."*

"That is a terrible idea," Kindle said.

"I agree with William. What exactly would that do for us?" I asked. "You wouldn't hear anything new."

"No, but you will."

"Me?" I laughed. "If you tell the world I'm in New York City I won't be able to leave our hotel room."

"Oh, you won't be staying in a hotel. Too dangerous. You will stay with me."

"Here? Within sight of the Langtons' town house? I'm sorry, Hazel, but you are being quite ridiculous." I turned to Henry. "I thought you wanted to help me, but you've brought us back to New York to an eccentric spinster who knows no more new information about my case than I did! Really, Henry. Do you *want* to see me hang? Is the grand finale for your series of books me swinging from the gallows?" I turned away and straight into a stack of papers. I pushed the stack over and kicked at the papers as they fell onto the floor.

Silence followed my outburst. I walked to the far end of the library and kept my back to the three of them. I wanted to wallow in my anger for a few minutes more, and I knew if I saw hurt on Hazel's face I would apologize.

Finally, Hazel spoke. "You and William will be safe here precisely because no one would expect you to lodge so close to the Langtons."

"What about your servants?" Kindle said. "A thousand dollars is a lot of money for the servant class."

"They are paid well and their loyalty is complete."

"Forgive me if I am skeptical," I said over my shoulder. "I've met few people in the past year who aren't willing to use me or turn me in."

"Which is why you have to trust us," Henry said. "We have your best interests at heart."

I scoffed, crossed my arms over my chest, and faced the room. "If we are hiding in your house, how exactly am I going to hear new gossip?"

Hazel and Henry exchanged a significant look. Hazel nodded to Henry, who stood and walked to me.

"We need a man we can trust to attend the Langtons' dinner party Thursday night with Hazel and get access to the men's conversation. I've been shunned and Kindle is too recognizable."

"The only men I trust are in this room. Who do you have…" The question died on my lips. I knew the answer before Henry said it.

"You."

CHAPTER
29

Glowing lights from the town house next door to the Langtons were visible across Washington Square. Carriages pulled up, deposited their passengers, and pulled around the square to park on side streets or in the rear alleys. Music drifted faintly on the cool nighttime air. The front door to Hazel Dockery's house opened and closed. I leaned forward to look down the front of the mansion but needn't have bothered. Hazel marched smartly down the stairs, across the street, and through the park to the town house opposite. A footman followed at a discreet distance, no doubt on Graves's orders. Hazel would scoff at the need of an escort across the well-lit park between the houses.

I turned from the window and surveyed the newspapers strewn around the room. I sighed and picked them up, folding them neatly and making sure to organize them by date, newest on top, as per Hazel's orders. Her library, which seemed so disorganized and chaotic at first blush, was indeed an elaborate filing system known and understood only by her.

After Henry's announcement of their grand plan, Graves had rolled the coffee cart into the office. Hazel took up the newspaper Graves handed her and spent the next five minutes with her head between the pages while Graves served the coffee. Henry filled the conversation void by talking of a Jewish deli he'd discovered with the most delicious pastries and sandwiches we could imagine. "I'll take you there," he promised.

When Graves left, Hazel handed the paper to me, picked up her coffee cup, and watched me over the rim as she sipped. The front page headline couldn't be missed:

GEORGE LANGTON'S KILLER SIGHTED IN NEW YORK CITY

I handed the paper to Kindle. "Peg McCord told. The newspapers have already convicted me, I see."

"The newspapers convicted you months ago," Hazel replied. "You visited your old house?"

I nodded.

"One half of our plan has been set in motion for us," Hazel said. "What of the second part?"

"Absolutely not," I said.

"You have experience masquerading as a man," Henry said.

"I was only able to pull off my orderly disguise in the war because everyone was distracted by death and dying."

"It was ten years ago," Kindle said. "A woman pretending to be a teenager is easier to pull off than a woman trying to be an adult."

"There are plenty of men with fine features," Hazel said. "And we would glue a beard on you."

"Oh, of course." I threw my hands up. "Why didn't I think of that?"

"I told you earlier, dear, no imagination," Hazel said. She raised an eyebrow and I knew she'd sent the verbal dart in retaliation for the "eccentric spinster" comment. She continued. "Graves's grandson, Richard, is in the theater and will help us kit you out."

"One more person who could potentially betray us," Kindle said.

"Oh, Richard won't betray you. I endow his little theater. He would starve if not for me."

I paced. "I cannot. If I'm caught they will arrest me. It will be more ammunition to use against me."

"Let's say for a moment Laura does this," Kindle said.

"William!"

He held up his hand in a placating gesture. "What then? No one is going to confess to her."

"Well, of course not," Hazel said. "But Laura might overhear something that will give us a new direction to investigate. The goal is to find information to take to the police, so they can investigate more fully."

I laughed. "The police are in the Langtons' pockets. That's why I left, remember?" I shook my head. "It's too risky."

"Is that your final word?" Hazel asked.

"Yes."

She slapped her hands on the desk. "Then I'm afraid there's little else I can do to help you. You're welcome to stay here until you decide where to go next. In fact, I recommend it. You're much too recognizable, Major." Hazel rose from behind the desk and picked up a stack of newspapers from its corner. She walked around and handed them to me. "In case you're interested in what's been said about you in your absence."

Kindle left to retrieve our belongings, and Mrs. Graves, the housekeeper, led me upstairs to the room we would be using. I spent the time alone reading.

I wish I hadn't.

I was the worst kind of harlot; men to whom I'd barely spoken now told of unwanted advances on my part. Fellow doctors fabricated stories about misdiagnoses and subsequent patient deaths and implied I'd achieved my high graduation rank from medical school by seducing the professors. Jonasz Golik, the resurrection man whose basement lab I'd frequently used, was quick to tell the world—anonymously, of course—that I paid double what other doctors did, and conveniently forgot to mention I'd been dissecting a cadaver the night George Langton had a fireplace poker embedded in his head. When Golik had been arrested months later for grave robbing, my name had been dragged back into the spotlight as one of his best customers.

Depressed and angry, I'd skipped to the bottom of the pile of papers, hoping my reputation had been redeemed somewhat with Henry's bogus story of my death. The same lies were rehashed, though with less relish, and much was made about the trials I had endured in Texas, and I'd been praised for saving Kindle under dire circumstances, and for my role in managing the dysentery outbreak at Fort Richardson. But there were too many strikes against me—my initial flight, my alleged coercion of a gentleman officer to help me escape, being a woman in a man's profession, my association with Golik, treating whores on Twenty-Seventh Street—to forgive me completely. Once it became known I was alive again, all benefit of the doubt was at an end. I was a liar and a killer and deserved to swing.

I was working myself into a fine lather when Kindle walked into the room with our baggage.

"I feel like I've been hoodwinked," I said.

Kindle paused, one bag under his arm. He closed the door and set the bags on the floor. He took off his dark spectacles and replaced them with the eye patch. He squeezed his eye shut and looked around like a newborn calf. "God, those glasses are strange."

"Did you hear what I said?"

"Yes. How have you been hoodwinked?"

I motioned to the newspapers, which I'd gone through again and discarded willy-nilly, stoking my anger at Henry and Hazel. "Hazel gave these to me on purpose. She knew how I would react."

"Like a Brontë heroine?" Kindle sat on the bed and removed his boots.

I ignored the comment. "Have you read any of this? No, don't. If you read it enough you start to believe it. I did! I found myself thinking, 'Who is this woman? She's a despicable human being!' Hazel was right. James never once came to my defense. He stood by and let them lie about me." I held back a sob.

"I never liked him," Kindle said.

"You don't know him," I snapped. I walked to the window and rubbed my arms against the chill that had overtaken me.

"If what they're saying is all lies, what do you care?" He dropped a boot to the floor.

"*If* it's all lies? What is that supposed to mean?"

"Of course it's lies, Laura. But again, what do you care?"

"Because they're dragging my name through the mud!"

"You aren't Catherine Bennett any longer. You're Laura Kindle. Or have you forgotten?" He dropped the second boot next to its mate.

"It doesn't mean I want Catherine Bennett to be remembered as a harlot and a murderer."

"Precisely." Kindle stood and loosened his tie. "Which is why we're here. To clear Catherine Bennett's name, so Laura Kindle can have a life."

I gasped. "You want me to go along with their plan."

He shrugged out of his coat, folded it, and laid it on the bed. "I've been trying to think of a better plan to and from the hotel."

"You realize if they find me out they will arrest me, convict me quickly, and hang me. Judge Sheridan and the newspapers will make sure of it. They need the scandal to sell newspapers, and I've walked right into their hands."

"How many times have you mentioned the charades you and your cousin played at?"

"We were children. It was just that: playing. This is my life, William."

He put his hands on my shoulders and massaged them. "It's my life, too."

I looked away. "Of course it is, but..."

"There is one other option."

"What?"

"Sail for Australia."

"Australia? But it's full of criminals and murderers and... Oh. Right."

There was a knock on the door. "Come in," Kindle called.

Graves opened the door. "Your bath is ready, sir."

"I'll be right there."

Graves left silently.

"I don't like the idea of you going into the Langtons' with no support other than Hazel. But I'm sure of two things: one, you're the only person who knows what questions to ask to get to the truth. Two, you're a good enough liar to pull it off."

"That is the worst compliment I've ever heard."

"Tell one last enormous lie, and you'll never have to lie again."

CHAPTER
30

"Cigar, Glover?"

"Yes, thank you."

I selected a cigar from the box James Kline held out to me and nodded my thanks. I snipped off the end as Kindle had taught me and leaned forward for the light James offered, puffing a few times until the tip was lit, inhaling deeply and exhaling. "Excellent," I said, amazed I'd managed not to cough. A warm sense of well-being flowed through me, and I puffed again. I was growing to like the taste and feel of smoking cigars. Besides the feeling of complacency, practicing smoking for almost two days had transformed my voice from a deep alto to a rough tenor perfect for my disguise.

The role of Samuel Glover had been surprisingly easy to slip into. He was a doctor from upstate, a friend of a friend of the Dockerys, who was appealing to Hazel to fund a hospital for indigents in Buffalo. It had the dual benefits of being an easy subject for me to converse on, and also being a subject my fellow diners would care little about and know less about. As such, I was able to give short, succinct answers and spend more time asking questions. No one looked twice at the little man with a full beard and spectacles. Meeting James in the parlor before dinner went off without a hitch, though I had an almost uncontrollable urge to slap him across his hirsute face. James shook Samuel Glover's hand, spoke politely, and let his eyes wander off. I followed his gaze to Beatrice Langton.

I'd survived dinner without raising suspicions and was now smoking cigars and drinking brandy with the men in the billiards room. It was the part of the night I'd most looked forward to. It offered me the best chance to learn something new about the Langtons, as well as giving me access to a sanctum I'd always longed to join. Now that I was here, I realized it was as shallow as the women's conversation in the drawing room, only the subjects were different.

"Why are you smiling, Glover?" James asked. "You must tell me the joke."

"Oh." I chuckled. "I was thinking of something Hazel— Miss Dockery—said today. She didn't mean it as a joke, but I can't help but find it humorous. If she is to endow my hospital she insists it should offer privileges to female physicians."

"Miss Dockery is known for her eccentricities."

"Indeed she is. I was warned as such, but never expected such a demand."

"Did she say why?"

"Apparently she's been inspired by Catherine Bennett's case. She's quite on her side in the whole matter."

James's head jerked back. "Did she know Catherine?"

"Only slightly. Dr. Bennett examined her once. She, Miss Dockery, wasn't impressed with Bennett's lack of enthusiasm for Hamlin's Wizard Oil."

James laughed. "I would imagine not."

"Did you know Dr. Bennett?"

James paused. "We were childhood friends but had grown apart over the years."

I stared at the tip of my cigar. I'd expected the lie, but to hear it stung. "Indeed?"

"Yes. I couldn't agree with her decision to pursue a man's profession instead of something more suitable."

"Such as marriage?"

James scoffed. "I doubt there are many men who would put up with her independent streak."

I drank deeply from my brandy snifter. "I read in the *Times* she's back in town."

"It would seem so. Idiotic thing to do. They'll find her and hang her."

"Do you think she did it?"

"Of course. Who else?"

I chuckled, when really I wanted to gouge James's eyes out. "I wouldn't know. I'm from Buffalo, remember? How is Mrs. Langton holding up?"

"Beatrice?"

"Yes. I would imagine it would be a tax on her nerves that this Bennett woman has returned."

"Beatrice is made from stronger stuff than that. She's confident the police will find Catherine and arrest her. She didn't have many friends to begin with. She has fewer now."

"So it would seem," I murmured. James didn't seem to hear.

I studied James. He looked extremely well and prosperous. His clothes were of a finer cut than they had been a year earlier and he now had long, bushy sideburns that made him look older than his thirty-two years. "What is it you do for a living, Mr. Kline?"

"I'm a lawyer. I've recently been made partner."

I hid my shock behind exclamations of congratulations.

James had always been a middling lawyer. How had he gone from delivering papers to George Langton at almost midnight to partner in a little more than a year?

"I heard Langton was going into politics before he died."

James looked at me full on for the first time. "Why are you so interested in the Langtons?"

I held James's gaze steadily as I puffed on my cigar. "One of us has to keep the conversation going, and since you don't seem too interested in me, why should I feign interest in you?" I blew smoke in James's face. "Excuse me while I search for someone more interesting to converse with."

I watched the billiard game and answered when spoken to and asked a few inane questions, but James's question had spooked me. I needed to deflect attention from Samuel Glover, and became more of an observer than participant. No one seemed to mind. They were likely afraid I had wangled the invitation with Hazel to ask for money.

Bored with billiards and wondering when we would be released to return to the women, I sat down in a wing chair and hid behind a newspaper. I was reading about Boss Tweed and Tammany Hall when I heard James's name. I turned my head slightly to the side and saw Judge Sheridan standing near my chair talking with another man I couldn't see.

"I don't like him, and I know George didn't. Didn't trust him a lick. A fawning climber, and you've helped him get there."

"But his kind is the easiest to control, Bertram. As long as we have someone in the state house who will do what we ask, it doesn't matter who it is," Sheridan said.

"That's all George was to you, wasn't he? Someone you could control."

"He was a beloved son-in-law. You know I was devastated when he was murdered by that woman. As was Beatrice."

Bertram Langton scoffed. "She seems to be over it now."

"It's been over a year. She's a young woman who is very much in love."

"George is rolling over in his grave."

"George would want Beatrice to be happy."

Bertram Langton walked away without answering. "Let's rejoin the ladies, shall we?" Langton said to the room at large.

I folded my paper, placed it on the table, and rose as Judge Sheridan walked past, his narrowed eyes never leaving Bertram Langton's back.

"Word to the wise, brandy and cigars with the men is the same as tea and cakes with the women. Its enjoyment depends on the company."

"Did you find out anything interesting?" Hazel asked.

"Yes." I watched James go straight to Beatrice Langton and her face light up when she saw him. My stomach twisted as a repulsive idea began to form in my mind.

"Well, what?" Hazel said.

"I will tell you later." I moved across the room and sidled my way into a conversation with Bertram Langton and an elderly woman. We spoke on generalities, the weather, travel, the woman's longing to travel across the country by rail.

"It is a long, arduous journey," I said.

"Oh, have you done it?"

"Once. Only to Cheyenne."

"I hear Cheyenne is perfectly heathen. Is that true?"

I smiled. "Mostly, but there are good people to be found everywhere."

Bertram Langton smiled, but it didn't reach his eyes. "It's a nice sentiment."

"You don't believe it?" the woman said.

"I used to."

The woman's face fell and she moved off rather quickly. Langton smiled and shook his head. "Never fails."

"What's that, sir?"

"Allude to George's death and they scurry away, like rats."

"George was your son?"

"Yes. You haven't heard the story? It's all over the newspapers, once again."

"I have, but I wasn't sure of the relation. Let me offer my condolences." My throat constricted. "I hear he was a good man."

"Yes, he was."

Langton's eyes were riveted to Beatrice and James.

"I suppose you are as eager as everyone else to see the Bennett woman hang for her crime," I said.

"If she did it, I am."

"You don't think she did?"

"I know he wasn't having an affair with her. If she wasn't a spurned lover, what motivation could she have possibly had to kill George?"

"Maybe it was one-sided, on her part. He refused her."

He nodded. "I believed that for a long time."

"What changed?"

A bell rang and Bertram Langton's face hardened. I followed his gaze along with everyone else's to the front of the room. James and Beatrice stood in front of the fireplace along with Judge Sheridan. "Our host, Bertram Langton, gave me permission to speak to you tonight. First, I want to thank Bertram for his hospitality and wonderful company. We, Bertram as the father-in-law, and I as the father, would like to announce our daughter's engagement to Mr. James Kline."

The reaction in the room was part gasp, part knowing

exclamation. Servants materialized with trays of champagne. Beatrice beamed up at James, who put his arm around her and looked at her with an expression I'd seen directed at me once before, long ago. "James has been a staunch friend of the family during the last year," Judge Sheridan said. "Imagine our pleasant surprise when their friendship turned to love. Bertram told me, and I agree, George would be happy for them both." Sheridan raised his glass, as did the rest of us. "To the bride and groom. May they have a long, happy, and prosperous life together."

I raised my glass, said, "Hear, hear," and drank. Bertram Langton lifted his glass to the couple, placed it on the nearest table, and walked out of the room.

CHAPTER
31

The fire in Hazel's library crackled and popped, the only sound in the room after I finished telling what I'd learned at the Langton's. The clock on the mantel chimed two a.m., but none of us were tired, or moved to retire to bed. I'd charted a path through the library and paced, trying to keep my body working at the same speed as my mind.

"Would you take off that beard?" Kindle said.

I waved my hand in dismissal. "Not yet."

"This Kline fellow was your friend?" Henry said.

"Yes. My oldest and dearest. So I thought." I didn't look at Kindle, who knew my relationship with James had at one time been intimate. "He told me about Langton's death, and the accusation against me."

"And encouraged you to leave town," Hazel said.

"Yes."

"Do you think he killed Langton?" Henry asked.

"Because he was in love with Beatrice?" I shrugged. "Maybe. But my friendship with James was known to George Langton. I would think if George knew James was having an affair with his wife, he wouldn't have conversed so complacently with me the night he died."

"You think he would have asked you about it?" Hazel said.

"No. But he didn't seem upset until the end of the conversation, when we spoke of medical school. We never spoke of Beatrice or James during the entirety of our relationship."

"Kline kills Langton and covers it up by blaming you so he can marry Beatrice Langton. Is that our working theory?" Kindle said.

I threw my hands in the air. "I cannot imagine James killing someone."

"We know everyone has it in them," Kindle said.

"But James was not in love with Beatrice."

"He wouldn't have told you if he was," Kindle said with maddening certainty.

"You don't know anything about him," I snapped.

The silence was almost complete. Kindle appraised me. "No, but I know men, and there's not a one alive who would tell a former lover he was in love with another woman."

Hazel's and Henry's eyes widened. "You and Kline?" Hazel said.

I turned and waved my hand in dismissal again. "Once, years ago. It was meaningless."

"He asked you to marry him," Kindle said.

I turned on him again. "What does this have to do with George Langton? Nothing."

Henry said, "It would explain why he framed you for the murder."

I crossed my arms over my chest. "You think James framed me for Langton's murder because I turned down his marriage proposal? Seven years ago. He's felt slighted for *seven years*? Thank you, Henry, for thinking I am so enchanting that a man will spend nearly a decade pining for me, but it's the most absurd thing I've ever heard."

"Laura," Hazel said, "what is more upsetting to you? The thought that James killed George or that he framed you for it?"

I covered my mouth, surprised to feel the fake beard, and closed my eyes. "We don't know he killed George."

"But we do know he framed you," Hazel replied. I opened my eyes to Hazel's compassion-filled face. The eccentric spinster was gone, replaced by a woman I suspected understood betrayal all too well.

"Yes," I whispered.

Kindle came to me and pulled me into his arms. I cried silently into his shoulder, trying to come to terms with the biggest betrayal of my life. How could James have done it to me? How could he have risked my life like that? His actions led to Maureen's death, my capture and abuse at the hands of the Comanche, and the deaths of all the men who had chased after us. Lorcan Reed. Cora Bayle. Dunk. The loss of Kindle's eye. For a year, I'd blamed it all on myself, my impetuous decision to leave instead of staying and fighting. Now I knew I'd been expertly manipulated by a man whom I trusted, whom I loved like a brother, and whom I thought loved me the same.

I pulled away from Kindle, looked up at him. His head jerked back. "The beard," he explained.

"If Kline killed Langton, where was the judge?" Henry asked.

"What?" Hazel, Kindle, and I said in unison.

"The judge is the one who interrupted your conversation with George the night of his murder, right?"

"Yes."

"He wanted George to return to his guests?"

"I think so."

"But he didn't."

"I don't know," I said. "I know few details of the night, other than what I experienced."

"According to the papers, he went to his library from the billiard room and never returned," Hazel said.

"I was treating George and Beatrice's daughter. She was recovering from chicken pox. I'd wanted to get to their house earlier in the day but had a childbirth that took longer than I expected. George wanted to talk to me when I was done, to see how Elizabeth fared."

"Beatrice didn't?" Hazel asked.

I shrugged. "I assumed George would tell her."

"Could Judge Sheridan have killed him?" Henry asked.

"Why?" Kindle said.

"George told him he wasn't going into politics. That he was going to medical school instead," I said.

"Seems a thin motivation," Kindle said.

"It's not," Hazel said. "You forget, Beatrice was originally engaged to George's brother, and he and George were two very different people. As fond as I was of George, I would imagine having him for a son-in-law would be a tax on a man like Stuyvesant Sheridan."

"Enough to make his daughter a widow?" Kindle said.

"If his daughter didn't love her husband? Yes," Hazel said, her eyes brightening with the possibility. "Think of it, killing George frees Beatrice of a weak husband, but she retains the money. George and Beatrice had a son, who will inherit. Bertram Senior isn't going to turn out his heir."

"Or his heir's mother," Henry said.

"The judge kills George and gets Kline to help cover it up," Kindle said.

"He tells Kline he'll further his law career," Henry said.

"Kline asks for a partnership, and Beatrice," Hazel said.

"No," I said. "James would further his career, I have no doubt. But I think his feelings for Beatrice are real." They looked at me in astonishment. "I've seen that expression on James's face before." My face flamed with embarrassment. Henry and Hazel looked away.

"We can't prove any of this," Kindle said.

"Judge Sheridan isn't going to confess," Hazel said.

"Kline has everything he's ever wanted. He's not going to turn on Sheridan," Henry said.

"You're right. All of you," I said. "But I know who will."

"That's Langton's," Hazel said to me, nodding to a carriage that had turned the corner and was pulling up alongside the Langtons' house.

"For someone who doesn't socialize with them much, you sure do know their habits and equipage."

"I've lived across the square from them for thirty-five years."

"Wish me luck," I said, and crossed the street two houses up from the Langtons'. I smoothed down my beard, adjusted my glasses, and walked with a masculine purpose toward the carriage. Langton came down the steps sooner than I anticipated, throwing off my plan to accidentally run into him. The footman opened the carriage door.

"Mr. Langton," I called. He looked the other way, then mine, startled. I raised my hand in greeting and increased my pace. "Samuel Glover," I said, when I reached him. I held out my hand.

"Of course, how do you do?" He gripped it with less strength than I expected.

"Very well, thank you. Going home today."

"Oh," Langton said. "You were visiting Hazel Dockery, correct?"

"Yes. She's funding my hospital for indigent women in Buffalo."

Langton nodded appreciatively. "Excellent. We need more of those."

"Yes, we do," I said, somewhat surprised at Langton's comment. Businessmen such as he were usually more interested in increasing profits than in helping the poor. Charity was the purview of their wives. I remembered that George's mother had died not long after his older brother had been killed in the war, presumably of grief, though I had my doubts. I'd learned first-hand that grief wasn't fatal, unless you wanted it to be.

"Would you like a lift somewhere?" Langton asked.

"Oh, I would hate to impose."

"No imposition. Please." He motioned for me to enter the carriage before him, and I did so, placing my carpetbag on the seat next to me.

"Grand Central Depot?" Langton asked.

"Yes. Thank you."

I knew I had roughly ten minutes to make my case to Langton, but now that I was in the carriage with him, the ideas I'd had on how to start the conversation escaped me. My life was trickling through my hands like grains through an hourglass. I opened my mouth to brazen it out when Langton spoke. "You travel light, I see." He nodded to my carpetbag. "I tend to do the same, much to my valet's distress."

I placed my hand on the carpetbag. "This isn't my carpet-bag." Langton nodded politely, thinking we were making boring, polite conversation. For a moment, I pitied him. "It belonged to a woman named Cora Bayle. She was killed, need-lessly. One in a long line of senseless murders."

Langton looked alarmed. "My word. I hope the police are involved."

"They were looking for the wrong person. A woman named Catherine Bennett."

Langton's expression was blank for a moment, before turning a mottled red. "What's the meaning of this? What do you mean?"

"You were on the verge of telling me something last night at the dinner party. What was it?"

"I don't know what you're talking about."

"You don't think Catherine Bennett killed your son. Why?"

"Of course she did. Who else could have done it?"

"Your son wasn't having an affair with Dr. Bennett. You and I know it."

"How could you possibly know that?"

I removed my glasses, folded them, and placed them on the carpetbag. With great care, I peeled the beard and mustache from my face. I ran my fingers through my hair to loosen it from its slicked-back style, though it was still short. Richard Graves had dismissed the possibility of me wearing a wig, which meant I was saddled with short hair for the foreseeable future.

Langton gasped. "You!"

He moved to tap on the ceiling with his cane to alert his driver. I pulled my gun from the carpetbag and aimed it at him. "Please don't. Too many people have died already. Including your son."

Langton settled back into his seat, his hands resting on the cane between his legs. "You have five minutes until we get to the depot, at which time I will call the nearest policeman and you will be arrested."

"If I thought you believed I killed your son, I would be worried."

"If not you, then who?"

"I have a theory, but it is so far-fetched I have a hard time believing it myself."

"Four minutes."

"The night George died, we were in his study talking medicine. We did that occasionally. You know he wanted to be a doctor."

Langton nodded.

"That night, I was hoping to get him to intercede on my behalf with the local medical schools. I made a comment about how I would have considered myself a failure if I didn't try to achieve my dream. It struck a chord with George. I didn't think anything of it until I learned recently why he didn't become a doctor."

Langton's lips pressed into a thin line, but he didn't interrupt.

"Judge Sheridan interrupted us and I left. I went to a resurrection man. Jonasz Golik. Have you heard of him?"

"Yes.

"I was there all night. Dissecting a fresh cadaver." Langton winced. "I'm not proud of it, but being blocked from using the labs in the medical schools pushed me to use Golik. I don't regret it in the least. Those dissections are the reason I was able to save the life of a man in Texas, whom I fell in love with and married."

"That was true?"

"Yes. I didn't know of George's death until James Kline found me early the next morning. He told me I was the suspect and he encouraged me to hide until he could figure out what was going on. I did, and he sent word about the reward and told me to run. So I did."

"Why? If you didn't kill him?"

"I knew you and Judge Sheridan had the money and power to convict me, regardless of my innocence."

Langton looked down at the floor of the carriage.

"Mr. Langton." He looked up at me. "I liked your son very much. He respected me. Treated me as someone worth admiring instead of someone worth derision. So many men hate me on sight, for what they believe I am, or out of jealousy or fear— I don't know. Your son was different." I laughed softly. "I had too few allies such as him to go around killing them."

The carriage stopped. Through the window I saw the entrance for Grand Central Depot. "There's a policeman," I said. "If you think I killed your son, call him over. Please. For the last year, I've lived in fear of being found out. I've had people use the bounty against me, manipulate me into doing their bidding under threat of arrest. Innocent people have died, as have the guilty. My husband lost an eye because someone decided blaming me for George's death was a better option than being discovered as a murderer." I took a deep breath. "I'm tired of running, of lying, of death. I want it to end. If that means I have to swing, then so be it."

Bertram Langton studied me for so long, I wondered if he'd heard me at all.

"Do you know who killed my son?"

"I have my suspicions, but I need your help to discover the truth. Will you help me?"

Langton turned his head and looked out the window at the policeman. I held my breath, sure this was the end of me. That all of this had been for naught. The policeman noticed our carriage and started walking toward us. Langton tapped on the ceiling. The driver opened the trapdoor. "Sir?"

"Drive on."

CHAPTER
32

My God. What happened to your hair?"

Camille King was beautiful. Brilliant. My relief at hearing her sarcastic comment, seeing that perfectly plucked eyebrow rise in amusement at my expense, was the closest to home I'd felt since I'd stepped off the train at Grand Central Depot. I fell into her arms and hugged her so tightly she coughed.

She returned my embrace. "I missed you, too, Katie," she whispered. "Who is *this*?"

I could tell from the timbre of her voice she'd seen Kindle. I held her at arm's length. "Behave. He's my husband." Camille looked Kindle up and down with clear appreciation, which thrilled me. I would never admit it to Kindle, but I loved to see admiration in other women's eyes when they saw him. "Stop staring or his ego will grow to alarming proportions."

Kindle's expression was stoic, but I knew he was reveling in Camille's attention. I pointed at him. "Stop it."

He raised his hands. "I'm merely standing here."

Camille put her hand through my arm and led me upstairs. She leaned in and said, "I suppose your flight wasn't all bad."

"He's the only good thing to come of it." I squeezed her arm. "I have so much to tell you."

"Yes, you do."

She led everyone into her drawing room, ordered coffee from a servant girl, and closed the door behind her. Hazel Dockery's head was on a swivel, her eyes as wide as saucers. "So this is what a brothel looks like? I've always wondered."

Who is this? Camille's expression said.

"Hazel Dockery, Camille King."

Hazel held out her hand. "Thank you so much for facilitating this."

"Are you sure this is going to work?" Camille asked me.

"It has to."

There were footsteps on the stairs and Bertram Langton walked into the room. He didn't look nearly as surprised by the inside of a brothel as Hazel had. "Camille, this is Bertram Langton. George's father."

She held out her hand. "Pleasure to meet you." The clock on the wall chimed. "This way. Kline will be here soon."

She led me and Langton out of the room. We passed Henry at the door. "Party's in there," Camille said. "Be a dear and make me a drink."

Henry ran his hat through his fingers and nodded. "Will do."

We went up two more flights of stairs until we were in the attics. She opened the door to a sloped roof room with a dormer in the middle of the back wall. Two single brass beds with white blankets were shoved against the wall, with a bedside table between them beneath the dormer. "The maids' room," Camille said. "Didn't want to give James the wrong idea." She opened the closet door and said to Kindle and Langton, "There's only room for one of you in the closet."

"Mr. Langton," I said.

Kindle looked as if he wanted to object, but he didn't. He

knew the only way for this to work was for Bertram Langton to be the witness. Kindle kissed me on the cheek, whispered, "I love you. Good luck," in my ear, and left.

When Kindle was gone, Camille said, "When this is over, we're going to have a long talk over multiple bottles of wine."

I nodded. "It's a date."

Camille glanced from me to Bertram Langton and left. Langton opened the closet door wider and placed his cane and hat inside. The room was plain, lending nothing interesting to note for polite conversation. I set my carpetbag on the bed, placed my hand over my stomach, and took a few deep breaths.

"I almost feel I should reintroduce myself," Langton said. "You look quite different as a woman."

"I'll take that as a compliment."

"As it was intended. Your indigent hospital was part of your masquerade?"

"Yes."

He studied me as if trying to make his mind up. "Maybe it doesn't have to be." He stepped forward. "I realize now that I failed George. Trying to make him into someone he wasn't." Langton inhaled. "I can't change what happened, but maybe I can do something good in his name. Something he would have done if he lived."

"I think that would be a lovely tribute to him."

Langton nodded and looked away.

There was a knock on the door and Camille's maid poked her head in and said, "He's here." She closed the door and Langton moved to the closet.

"There isn't a handle on the inside," he said, panic filling his eyes.

"We will leave it slightly ajar."

He nodded and stepped back into the shadows of the closet. I made sure the closet door didn't click and sat on one of the beds. I took my gun out of Cora Bayle's carpetbag and slid it beneath the pillow. My heart raced as I wiped my damp palms on the blanket.

The door opened, banging against the closet. Everything about James's appearance said he was a man in control—his clothes were impeccable, his shoes highly polished, not a hair out of place, his sideburns expertly groomed—except his eyes, wild with astonishment and something else. Desperation?

I stood, my legs wobbling beneath me.

"Katie?" It was the voice of my friend, the man who'd loved me, wanted to spend his life with me. The man who had my best interests at heart when he encouraged me to leave town. But his eyes gave him away.

I opened my arms. "James." My voice cracked, thick with anger. James saw in it what he wanted and rushed to me. He took me in his arms.

"Oh, Katie, I'm so glad you're safe. I've heard so many outlandish stories." He held me at arm's length. "You look...well."

"You're a terrible liar."

He touched my hair. "What's the matter with your hair?"

"I've had to dress as a man." An expression of distaste crossed James's features. "I had little choice, James. It was either that or live my life in constant fear of being found out."

"Why did you come back? It's not safe for you here."

"It's not safe for me anywhere. You must have heard what I've been through."

"The lies that hack Pope has been peddling?"

"They aren't lies, James."

James's head jerked back as if he'd been struck.

"I came back to clear my name. I need your help."

"Where is your *husband*? Was that one of Pope's fabrications or the truth?"

"I'm married."

"Where is he? Why can't he help you?"

"He's doing what he can, but we don't have access to the people involved in George's murder. You do."

"The people involved in George's...? You're the—"

"I'm the what? Killer? You know I didn't do it."

James walked around me and looked out the dormer. He placed his hat on the pillow hiding my gun. "Yes, but if not you, then who?"

"That's what I need you to help me find out. You have intimate access to the Langtons, or so I hear. Congratulations."

James turned to me, his face reddening. "Thank you." He tried to cover the stammer in his voice with a laugh. "I'm as surprised by it as you are."

"You seem to have done well for yourself since I've been gone. Partner at the firm? Engagement to Beatrice Langton. And to think, you were delivering legal papers to George in the middle of the night a mere year ago. Astonishing, really."

James's shoulders straightened and his expression hardened. "Of course you would think so. You never appreciated my talents."

"Didn't I?"

"It was hard to tell. You were so wrapped up in your own."

I walked to the window, forcing James to move out of the way. "Is that why you didn't bother to defend me to the newspapers?"

"What?"

"I've read everything written about me in the New York newspapers and you, my oldest and best friend, the one person I was sure would defend me, are only mentioned as a spokesperson for the Langtons, if you're mentioned at all."

"I couldn't very well…I identified a dead woman as you to give you the freedom you needed. Then you had to go and ruin it."

"Yes, orchestrating my wagon train massacre was a mistake, I admit."

"You didn't have to save that man, turn yourself into some sort of heroine. Of course people would find out who you are if you're performing surgery with General Sherman holding the Goddamn lantern."

"How did you know about that?"

"It was in that ridiculous book."

"So Pope isn't a hack?"

"I'm sure he is, but when I read that I knew it was outlandish enough to be true."

My shoulders slumped as the last flicker of hope that we were wrong about James's role in Langton's death dissipated. "I didn't believe them, but they were right: you really do hate me," I said, with astonishment.

"What? Why would you say that?"

"Why else would you frame me for Langton's murder? Why did you kill him, James?"

"Me? I didn't kill him."

"Were you and Beatrice having an affair and you needed to get him out of the way?"

"No! Beatrice would never do that. She has no idea—"

"You killed her husband?"

"I didn't kill him."

"I left George in the library, alive and well. Were you watching, waiting for George to be alone so you could confront him about your relationship with Beatrice?"

"No—"

"Or did Beatrice kill him? Are you covering for your lover?"

"No!" James said, panicking. "She has no idea what happened."

"But you do. And instead of telling the truth you decided to frame your oldest friend for the murder, knowing full well I would be railroaded by the system. You *wanted* me to be railroaded."

"I saved you! You ruined it all!" James moved toward me. I inched toward the bed, leaning away from him, sliding my hand beneath the pillow. "Now you're back and going to ruin everything I've worked for."

"Everything you've been given for covering up who murdered George Langton."

"Yes. And I'd do it all again."

I pulled the gun from beneath the pillow, pulled back the hammer, and placed it in the middle of James's forehead in one smooth, quick motion.

"Catherine," James choked.

I pressed the barrel of the gun hard against his head, forcing him to retreat until his legs met the other bed and he fell backward. I kept the gun firm to stabilize my trembling arm. "Do you realize what you've done, James? Maureen is dead because you convinced me to run."

"I'm sorry that happened—"

"Oh, you're *sorry*? That makes it all better." I grimaced and pushed the gun against his head again. "When you're in your marriage bed making love to the wife you were given as a reward, I want you to think about me on the banks of the Canadian River being raped for hours by seven Indians. Every time you thrust into your loving, compliant wife, think of the Indian who raped me with my own gun, cocked and loaded."

James closed his eyes, as if that would stem the tide of my words. Tears streamed out of his eyes. "No."

"No? When you're standing up in court, giving what I'm sure will be a brilliant argument, think of the frontier justice that lost my husband his eye."

"You can't blame me for that."

"I blame you for everything," I shouted. "Your decision was like a pebble being thrown in a pond; it rippled out and affected dozens and dozens of people. You ruined lives, and for what? A partnership in a law firm?"

"I had no idea."

"Who killed George Langton?"

"No..."

"Tell me who killed him or I will pull the trigger. What will I have to lose? If I let you leave, you'll turn me in and I'll swing. If I'm going to be hanged, I want it to be for a murder I committed."

James wept openly, and I saw him as he truly was for the first time: a weak, pathetic man.

"Tell me!"

"Sheridan! Sheridan killed him. I walked in and found him standing over George with the fireplace poker. It was his idea to use you as the scapegoat."

"You just went along with it," I said.

"He promised me so much."

"His daughter."

"No." James shook his head. "That happened later. It's real."

The closet door creaked open and Bertram Langton stepped forward. I pulled the gun away from James's head and his placating, begging expression morphed to one of confusion, then into anger. He turned to me. "You bitch. You set—"

I grabbed the gun by the barrel and swung the handle against his temple. James's head jerked around and slammed against the wall. He slumped onto the bed, unconscious.

"Thank you," Bertram Langton said. "I always knew Kline was a lizard but had no idea the depth of his sneakiness."

Kindle and Camille walked into the room. Camille took in James's unconscious form and her astonished gaze landed on me. "Remind me never to cross you."

I grinned.

"Goddamn, you're a fine woman, Laura Kindle," Kindle said.

"Thank you," I said, though my knees were shaking.

Langton turned to me. "Dr. Bennett." He swallowed thickly. "I don't know what to say."

"Say you'll make sure the charges will be dropped against her," Kindle said. He put his arm around my waist and I leaned into him to keep from collapsing.

"Kindle and I heard everything through the door, in case you try to change the story," Camille said.

Langton looked taken aback. "I would never. It will be in the afternoon papers."

Hazel and Henry pushed their way into the already crowded room.

"Were we right? Was it Sheridan?" Hazel said.

"Yes," I said.

Langton looked slightly alarmed at the number of people.

"Yes, Mr. Langton, we all know and we will all make sure you hold to your promise of clearing Laura's name," Hazel said.

"Who's Laura?"

I raised my hand. "Me. Laura Kindle." Kindle pulled me closer and squeezed my waist. "Clear Catherine Bennett's name so Laura Kindle can live in peace with her husband."

James groaned from the bed.

"Want my boys to take him somewhere and teach him a lesson?" Camille asked.

"No," I said. "I want him to go to the police."

"I'll take him," Langton said. "If your men can take him downstairs to my carriage, Miss King?"

"Will do." Camille left. Hazel and Henry followed.

Langton lingered for a moment, as if unsure what to do or say. Finally, he said, "When everything settles down, let's discuss your idea for an indigent hospital."

"Thank you."

Langton nodded and left. Camille's men came in, took James by the arms, and dragged him out of the room.

I collapsed into Kindle's arms, sobbing and laughing at the same time. "It's over."

"It's over." He stroked my hair. "I thought you were going to kill him."

I pointed the gun to the ceiling and pulled the trigger. Kindle flinched but was greeted with the sound of the small click of the hammer hitting an empty chamber. "No more death."

"No more death." Kindle smiled down on me. "What do we do now?"

The tension and fear I'd been living with for a year evaporated into the silent room, leaving a cautious peace in its place. I wouldn't feel truly free until the world knew the truth, but it was a start. A new world unfurled before me, full of color, life, love, and possibilities.

I laughed and threw open my arms. "Whatever we want."

ACKNOWLEDGMENTS

It's difficult to believe it's been over eight years since Laura and Kindle walked into my life. When the idea started forming, I could hardly imagine it was my first step on the path to publication. This was *the* story that wouldn't go away, that I kept putting aside and coming back to, the story I choose to finish first (I had a tendency to be distracted by new ideas), the one manuscript that I wanted to see published more than any other.

Now here we are, nearly a decade later, and my germ of an idea has evolved into a three-hundred-thousand-word trilogy, with the assistance of almost too many friends, family members, writers, and editors to name. But I'll give it a go.

I absolutely would not be writing these acknowledgments today if it weren't for my cousin and mentor, Kenneth Mark Hoover. He was the first person to tell me I had talent and potential. He held my hand and led me through all the stages of my development as a writer. He listened to all of my hare-brained story concepts, encouraged me, critiqued me, and, most importantly, believed in me when I was ready to give up. He is my first reader and his insight always, *always*, makes my stories better.

Writing a good book is only the first step in the process. Having an advocate for your work is paramount and I was lucky enough to sign with my agent, Alice Speilburg, who has never wavered in her belief in my work. I always thought I was pretty even-keeled until I met Alice and saw calm, unflappable professionalism in practice. The day I met Alice changed my life, for the better in every way.

After five years of writing, I assumed I knew my characters inside and out. That is, until Kendel Lynn read a draft and pointed out a missed opportunity so glaringly obvious, I was a little ashamed. Her suggestion elevated a critical scene from good to great, and I believe that small but consequential change is what sold the book. Becoming friends with Kendel has been the best unexpected perk of my publishing journey so far.

More than anyone, I have Susan Barnes to thank for *Sawbones* being the book that it is, and for the tone of the series as a whole. When she read *Sawbones* she didn't balk at the grit and the gore. She loved it. She understood from the beginning what I was trying to do, how I wanted to peel back the mythology and show the brutality beneath, and she never flinched. She encouraged it, and her editorial insight helped me deepen my writing, my characters, and the story.

Change is inevitable, and editors move on. I thank God every day Lindsey Hall inherited Laura and Kindle's story. I have so many feels I don't know where to start. Her brilliant editorial eye is almost overshadowed by her enthusiasm, compassion, and ability to know just the right thing to say to save me from spiraling down a well of stress. Or at least spiraling too far down. She's not Wonder Woman, but she's close. You're going to be a tough act to follow, Lindsey, and I know you have a long and glorious future ahead of you.

There are dozens of people working at Redhook who have had a hand in getting this trilogy to readers. I want to thank each and every one of you for all your hard work and dedication. Special thanks goes to my publicist, Ellen Wright; copy editor, Amy Schneider; production editors, Gleni Bartels and Andromeda Macri; and graphic artists, Crystal Ben and Wendy Chen.

Where to start with my DFW Writers' Workshop peeps? I've made so many wonderful friends and have grown not only as a writer but also as a critique partner and, I hope, as a mentor to other writers starting out. Wednesday nights are my favorite part of the week.

There are highs and lows in every journey, and the publishing journey is no different. Special thanks to Brooke Fossey, Jenny Martin, and Jennifer Mason-Black for being reliable sounding boards and shoulders to cry on, and always offering the perfect piece of advice.

Thanks to Larry Brown at the Wyoming State Archives for answering my questions about Cheyenne in the 1870s.

Finally, thanks to my friends and family for your never-ending love and support.

MEET THE AUTHOR

MELISSA LENHARDT is president of directors for the North Dallas chapter of Sisters in Crime, as well as a member of the DFW Writers' Workshop. She lives in Texas with her husband and two sons.

INTERVIEW

Have you always wanted to be a writer? When did you start writing?

I wish I'd always wanted to be a writer. I was one of those kids who had no clue what they wanted to do with their lives. As a result, I ended up in an ill-fitting, postcollege job managing restaurants. I started writing a couple of years after becoming a stay-at-home mom to stave off boredom. One of the greatest fears of being a stay-at-home mom is not being able to go back into the workforce when your kids become self-sufficient, or when they leave the nest. I'm incredibly lucky to have found a second career where age doesn't matter, and one I actually want to work at for the rest of my life.

Who are some of your biggest influences?

Every book I've ever read. I don't have one writer, or even a few writers, who have influenced me more than others. I read across genres and think that keeps me from falling into genre tropes too terribly often. Authors whose works have made me want to be a better writer, or have changed my life in some way? That's a long list: Jane Austen, Elizabeth Gaskell, Edith Wharton, Anita Shreve, Larry McMurtry, J. K. Rowling, Carlos Ruiz

INTERVIEW

Zafon, Martin Cruz Smith, Anne Brontë, Anne Perry, Sandra Dallas, Margaret Atwood, Danielle Steel, Stephen King, Eric Larson, Stephen Ambrose, Georgette Heyer, Jacqueline Winspear, Mary Doria Russell, Rainbow Rowell...I could go on and on.

How did the characters Laura and Kindle come to you?
Neither walked into my head fully formed. I wanted a strong, independent woman as my main character, and as I researched the Civil War era I came across two interesting tidbits: stories of women dressing up like men to serve in the war, and of handsome women being turned away from nursing at the beginning of the war because it was believed they would distract the wounded from healing. I knew immediately my main character would have gone to any lengths to help the Union cause, and I also knew she was arrogant enough to believe she could do a man's job as well or better. When I discovered sisters Elizabeth and Emily Blackwell, two of the first women to earn medical degrees in the United States, and other trailblazing female doctors, many of whom were inspired by their nursing work in the war, Laura waved to me and said, "Really, Melissa. What took you so long?"

With Kindle, I needed a dashing cavalry officer to come on the scene and appear to be the requisite white knight, so I could flip the script and have Laura save him. One of the greatest challenges in writing historical fiction is keeping the characters' opinions, beliefs, and actions true to the time without alienating the reader. Working within the nineteenth-century prism, I needed Kindle to have great strength, and enough humility and vulnerability to admire Laura for her intelligence, determination, and arrogance, instead of being threatened by her. Since *Sawbones* was completely from Laura's point of view, we saw Kindle as she saw him, which was a tiny bit idealized, as is wont to happen when you're in the first throes of love. So it was a great relief when I was breaking the story for *Blood Oath* that I realized Kindle had a dark side, and an interesting, complicated past. I never liked the character more than when he was making mistakes, and struggling with how his past actions adversely affected Laura. Yes, I'm a little bit in love with Kindle. Why do you ask?

Fun fact about how the characters got their names: when I started writing *Sawbones*, my favorite TV show, *Battlestar Galactica*, was in its final season. My two favorite characters were Laura Roslin and William Adama. The very, very first thought I had about this story was: "What if Roslin and Adama were dropped into the Old West?" And here we are, nearly a decade later.

This series isn't quite like anything else out there. What inspired you to write this type of book?
I read Larry McMurtry's *Lonesome Dove* and was searching for another Western to read. Everything I picked up was either a male-centric perpetuation of the Hollywood mythology of the West or a straight-up romance. The West wasn't settled only by men, and there's more to women's lives than finding a man. I set out to write a book from a woman's point of view that wasn't afraid to show the West in all its contradictions—brutal and beautiful, corrupt and honorable, built on lies by honest, hardworking dreamers—with a love story that didn't solve the characters' problems but ended up complicating and enriching their lives in equal measure.

INTERVIEW

What kind of research did you do for the series, and what is your writing process like?

Having an unlimited amount of time to write *Sawbones* meant I could read voraciously about the time period, and I did. It's still my preferred mode of research. I read books, and study their bibliographies for further reading, which I also do on Wikipedia. Wikipedia gets a bad rap, but if you go into it with a critical eye, and know how to drill down into the notes and follow the sources, it can be a good starting point. I also find the websites for state historical societies, Texas State Historical Society, Wyoming State Archives, and so on, to be a wealth of information. And now, I'm going to confess my deepest, dorkiest research dream: to research at the Library of Congress. It's so intimidating; I get sweaty palms thinking about it, but one day I'll drum up the courage. I know me; I'll have to dedicate a month to it because of the many rabbit holes I'll fall down in the LIBRARY OF CONGRESS!

I suspect that writing a series is much different from writing a stand-alone novel. How did your writing process and author experience differ from book to book?

It took me five years of fits and starts to finish *Sawbones*. I had months, years, to test out different story lines, structures, tones, and so on, until I finally found the true story. I had a six-month deadline for *Blood Oath* and a nine-month deadline for *Badlands*. I didn't have the luxury of trying different things out or even writing a terrible first draft. I had to focus my thoughts, ideas, and writing in a way I never had to before. It was the best thing that's ever happened to me, developmentally. Not only did it prove to me I can write under that kind of pressure, it proved to me my writing can be as good, maybe better, with fear of failure on a slow burn beneath my office chair.

However, now that I've proven I can write like that, I'm not eager to repeat the experience.

Did you have a plan for the series when you first set out to write *Sawbones*? If so, how did that plan change by the time you got to *Badlands*?

The idea to turn it into a series came when my agent said, "The publisher wants to know if this is a series," and I said, "Of course it's a series!" Which meant I needed a plot for two books when I hadn't considered what happened next for Laura and Kindle besides "they ride off in the sunset and have adventures." I had to decide whether to jump forward in time and write connected books but not sequels per se, or to pick their story up right after the events of *Sawbones* and make all three novels one long character arc. My writing buddy said, "The easiest thing in the world to write is a chase novel," which was better than any idea I'd come up with. Because I don't tend to plot novels but jump right in and hope for the best, I had no idea where *Blood Oath* was going, other than across Indian Territory to Independence, Missouri. When I neared the end of *Blood Oath*, I realized two chase novels in a row would be boring. For the third book, I wanted to bring Laura full circle by giving her a taste of the life she originally envisioned when she set out for Colorado at the beginning of *Sawbones*, as well as wrap up the inciting incident that kicked off the trilogy.

If you could spend an afternoon with one of your characters, which would it be and what would you do?

Just one? Tough choice. Probably Camille or Rosemond. The stories they could tell.

If you enjoyed *Badlands*,

look out for the next adventure from

Melissa Lenhardt!

The woman stood motionless on the wooden boardwalk, staring into the milliner's window at a quilted sugar-scoop bonnet. She thought it was, quite possibly, the ugliest hat she'd ever seen in her life. But sugar-scoop bonnets were made to be functional, not pretty, and this one would serve very well for the coming winter.

"Excuse me, madam."

Two businessmen skirted around her, lifting their hats as they passed, the scent of cigar smoke and hair oil wafting after them. She stepped closer to the window with a wan, polite smile at the men but kept her face mostly averted, hoping the dim silvery light from the early mountain sunset would mask her features. Her basket thumped against the window.

Her gaze roamed up and down the street, which was filling up with people closing shop for the day and returning home to a roaring hearth and warm meal, a smoke for the men, sewing for the women, children playing quietly on rag rugs. They would talk about the light snow that had started as the sun dipped below the mountains and was dusting the woman's shoulders as she stared into the reflection of the milliner's windows. A man left the building behind her. Her breath fogged the air. Her frigid gloveless fingers clutched her heavy basket. A train whistle blew in the distance.

A bell jingled and the milliner stepped out of his store. "Can I help you, madam?"

"How much for the bonnet?"

The man glanced at the item, the price clear from where he stood, and back at the woman. She knew what he saw, and was humiliated. "Five dollars."

The woman pretended to consider buying the bonnet and the man, kinder than he needed to be, went along with the ruse. "Thank you, but I'm afraid it's too dear. Good evening."

She felt his eyes on her back as she walked down the main street and turned the first corner. Mud, thick and cold, oozed through the hole in her shoe. A wagon loaded with logs lumbered down the street. Tack jingled and wheels creaked as horses strained against the load and the foot-deep mud. The teamster urged them on with gentle but firm words, and slapped their backs with the reins. The teamster caught the woman's eye and nodded an acknowledgment.

She leaned back against the wooden building and tried, for the thousandth time, to think of another option. But the hole in her stomach and the cold wind seeping through her threadbare dress and the snow melting on her bare head and dripping down her neck distracted her. She thought of her family, huddled around a cold hearth with only one Army blanket to cover three bodies, Joan whimpering with hunger, Stella impatiently shushing her, Hattie comforting them both and chafing at being left at home. All waiting for the woman to return.

A man walking down the main street saw her, looked around, and slinked into the alley. Her eyes followed him, but her head remained tilted back against the wall. He made no secret of looking up and down the length of her body. She could see his imagination blooming behind his eyes. "You lost?"

"No."

He moved close to her. He smelled of whisky, and his fingers were stained with ink. A newspaperman. She straightened, moved away, and averted her face.

"Meeting someone?"

"No. On my way to catch the train. Excuse me."

He grabbed her upper arm. "The train doesn't leave for ten minutes. Plenty of time for us to get to know each other."

"Please release me, sir. My husband is expecting me."

The man laughed. Bits of tobacco were caught in the spaces between his teeth. "Not much of a husband, letting his wife out in this weather without a coat."

She shivered, as much from the cold as from his statement. It was more true than he knew. Her eyes were drawn to the coat the newspaperman wore. Though it was fraying at the cuffs, it was obviously well made: gunmetal gray wool with a red-silk lining peeking out when the wind caught his coattail. It looked warm.

This is what she'd been reduced to: coveting the coat on a man who saw her as something to use and discard. Anger flowed through her like lava down a mountain, slowly spreading from the center of her chest out to her bloodless fingers, infusing her with a hatred she had never before known.

"What time is it?"

The man took his gold watch out of his waistcoat pocket. "Ten 'til."

She lifted her face to his, and he smiled in pleasure in what he saw there. She smiled wider. Almost laughed. "Plenty of time."

The woman turned and walked deeper into the dark alley, knowing the man would follow. The low snow clouds and the sunset threw the narrow back alley into a helpful gloom. Someone tossed water through a door a few stores down. A stray tabby cat sat on top of a stack of crates outside the milliner's back door. The cat hissed and jumped down, almost tripping the john. She set her basket on the ground.

He unbuckled his belt. "How much."

"Your coat."

He paused. Laughed. "My wife would wonder where it was."

She nodded toward his hands. "You're a newspaperman. You'll think of a story."

He held out his stained hand. "Gives me away every time." His eyes were hungry now that the meal was at hand. "My coat."

He'd moved to his pants buttons.

"Before."

The newspaperman shook his head but shrugged out of his coat, eager to get on with it. The woman donned the coat, looked up and down the alley, bent down, and opened her basket. In a fluid, silent motion, she placed the gun underneath the man's chin.

"What in tarnation…"

She pulled back the hammer. "It's a Walker. My dead husband's. All I have left of him. I'm going to use it to rob the bank across the street."

The newspaperman's eyes widened with the first trace of fear.

"But, you've ruined my plan, and why? Because you saw a vulnerable woman standing alone, minding her own business."

"I didn't mean anything by it."

The woman's expression twisted into disbelief. "Your pecker tells another story."

"Please."

"Your poor wife. She's waiting at home for you, probably has a nice supper ready. Worked hard on it, too, and how do you repay her? Trying for a poke with a stranger on the way home."

The man's voice shook. "Keep the coat."

The woman laughed. "I want your hat, too."

The man lifted his hands partway and the woman pressed the barrel of the gun harder against his neck. He pointed to the hat.

"One hand."

He removed the hat and placed it on the crate.

"Thank you. This is all going to work out just fine. Much better than my original plan, in fact."

The man's brows furrowed.

"You're gonna help me rob that bank."

"I couldn't do that."

Her expression hardened. "You'd be amazed what you can do when your life depends on it."

The man swallowed and nodded vigorously. "I'll help you."

"Oh, you don't have no choice in the matter...What's your name again?"

"Alfie Gernsback."

Laughter bubbled up and burst forth on a wave of nervous energy. "Your mother hate you or something?"

"Alfred."

She nodded. "It's some better, but not much. Okay, here's the long and short of it, Alfred." The woman glanced up and down the alley again, and leaned forward. Gernsback leaned down to listen. "Your wife? She's gonna be much happier without you. Trust me."

She reveled in his confusion, and his flash of understanding before she pulled the trigger. Alfie Gernsback's brains hadn't stopped spraying the milliner's back wall before she'd picked up her basket and the dead man's hat and was walking briskly through the alley.

She stopped and looked up and down the street. She ran to the nearest clutch of men. "I think I heard a gunshot."

"Well, this is Denver."

"Back that way somewhere." She motioned in the area of the alley.

The man patted her on the arm. "We'll look into it."

She smiled and nodded, her hand over her heart. "Oh, thank you. I would hate for someone to be hurt."

"I'm sure it's nothing."

She crossed the muddy street and arrived at the bank door just as the clerk was locking up.

"Oh, no. Am I too late?"

The clerk was a thin young man with a high forehead and a weak chin he tried to camouflage with a neckbeard that would never equal Lincoln's. "Just locking up now, ma'am."

"My husband is going to be so angry. You see, we're leaving on the five o'clock and he asked me to drop off my jewelry in the safe this morning and I plumb forgot, what with packing and giving the servants instructions for while we're gone and oh, a dozen other distractions that I have ever day." The woman inhaled, smiled, and tilted her head to the side. She touched his arm. "Would you mind terribly? It won't take but a moment, I promise. I have to catch a train, after all."

The clerk blushed, and nodded. He opened the door as a commotion started down the street. "I wonder what that's all about?"

The woman entered the bank, pulling the clerk along with her eyes and sultry voice. "Heaven knows. This is Denver, after all."

The clerk led her to his desk as the woman took everything in. "Must be lonely, being the last one out every night."

"I like it." He looked pointedly at her basket. "What did you say your husband's name was?"

"Is the safe that way?" She pointed down the hall and started walking.

"Yes. Just a moment." The clerk followed her. "You can't go down there."

"I thought it would save us time, since we're under the gun." She stepped back against the wall opposite the safe, noting the bank name stenciled across the front. Bank of the Rockies. "Would you like for me to turn around while you open it?"

"I would like for you to go back to the front."

"Of course. I'll wait at the nearest desk."

Alone in the main room, she placed the basket on the desk, lid open, and pulled out a rope. The man returned in less than a minute. "Now, if you'll just..."

She stood, hands behind her back, smiling. "The jewelry is in the basket."

The clerk moved forward and bent over to reach in the basket. The woman shoved a chair into the back of his legs, toppling him back into the seat. She looped the rope around his chest and pulled tight. The clerk, stunned, merely looked over his shoulder at the woman, giving her time to place the gun in her other hand on his shoulder. "You will want to sit still for me. I'm not very good with a gun. I'd hate to kill you on accident."

The front door opened and closed. The clerk and the woman looked up. "Oh, thank God," the clerk said. He tried to wiggle free but the woman hit him in the back of the head with the butt of her gun. The clerk grunted, and dropped his chin to his chest.

"It took you long enough."

The teamster crossed the floor in five strides. "Some man was killed back in the alley over there. There're people everywhere."

"Tie him up good while I get the money."

She took the basket to the safe and loaded it with as much cash and gold as would fit. She rifled through the personal papers, pulling out some, tossing others back into the safe. She stared at a deed for a long time before placing it in her basket and returning to the front.

She tossed the personal papers into a metal trash bin, found a match on the nearest desk, and tossed it in the can. The papers were soon engulfed.

The teamster finished tying the clerk to the chair and kicked it over. "Let's go." He took the basket from the woman. "Where'd you get the coat?"

"Stole it."

The clerk moaned around the handkerchief the teamster had stuffed in his mouth. The woman crouched down next to the young man. "I'm sorry I had to hit you. But, it's either steal from you, or lay on my back for a living. You understand?" The clerk stared at her with glassy eyes. She patted his shoulder. "You'll be fine in a day or two."

She stood, pulled the dead man's hat low over her eyes. The clerk was cognizant enough to look at the gun in her hand with fear. She put the gun in her pocket and grinned, high on the smoke from the burning documents. It wouldn't ruin him, nothing so petty as a few thousand dollars and lost documents would ruin him. But it would irritate him, and that was good enough. For now. She bent down and whispered in the clerk's ear.

"Tell Colonel Louis Connolly, Margaret Parker sends her regards."

402